Daniel's Garden

· A CIVIL WAR NOVEL ·

Also by Meg North:

NOVELS
Daniel's Garden
The Heart of a Lie
The Curtain Falls

SHORT STORIES
September Sunlight: A Civil War Short Story
The Slave Block: A Civil War Short Story

NONFICTION
The 9 Master Plots for Bestsellers & Blockbusters

Daniel's Garden

Meg North

Black Rose Press
Portland ME

Copyright © 2010 by Meg North

Cover design by Meg North
Book design by Meg North

All rights reserved.
No part of this book may be reproduced in any form or by any electronic or mechanical means including information storage and retrieval systems, without permission in writing from the author. The only exception is by a reviewer, who may quote short excerpts in a review.

Daniel's Garden, by Meg North

Printed in the U.S.A.

ISBN: 978-1450555265

For dearest friends and family,
my deepest thanks.

* * *

And to Erik, for his amazing, unearthly support,
this novel is humbly dedicated.

· Prologue: Battle! ·

SERGEANT FALLS shouted to the orderlies scattered in the pale field. We were in a low-slung valley. It was too damn early for conversation, so I heard nothing but our familiar marching sounds. Tin cups banging, brogans plodding through the grass, swishing and bumping of the bayonet holsters. Andrew stepped lively. I felt mired in fog.

"Reports of cannons in the rear!" Falls shouted. "Follow in step, boys!"

His voice was eerily high-pitched. I took one step forward and stubbed my toe hard enough for my eyes to water. I grimaced in pain. My first march out and a God damned stubbed toe.

Warrenton Junction disappeared behind us and we followed the railroad tracks. The first few steps were clumsy, but I found the rhythm and moved along. Beside me were the rail ties, half-buried in the grass like forgotten pieces of kindling.

My toe throbbed with each step. I attempted to turn my foot, then rested more weight on my heel and hobbled forward, but I only succeeded in getting out of step and nearly suffered a twisted ankle. God damn rebs. God damn war. Our first real march and all I wanted was to sit on a rail tie and take my shoe off.

What a soldier I was!

The chill vanished and dawn peeped over the land. Next to the tracks appeared the bluish outline of a squat building, and we reached it at a steady pace. An acrid scent of wet burnt wood wrapped its arms around it. Singed bridges over two runs sent billows of smoke into the blurry morning, and the building's perimeter was shrouded in a misty vapor.

"It must be Jackson." A New Hampshire volunteer, curly red hair peeking from under his cap. I didn't know the man's name. He poked Andrew in the shoulder. "He up and come through here, ye know."

"Jackson? From Bull Run?" Andrew spit a wad of tobacco juice. A fitting breakfast for him.

"This is Catlett's Station." The New Hampshire man cast a haughty glance at it. "Welcome, my friends. Ye know, I ain't been here in nigh on a year now."

"You fought at Bull Run?" Matthew's eyes bulged.

"I done my share," the recruit lobbed back at him.

We skirted the remains of the wreckage and continued, keeping those railroad ties in view when our division followed the track. Sunlight burned the remainder of the dew and we fell into a rhythm. An easy, toneless rhythm of marching. Our band began a joyful ditty, but the brassy sounds grated my ears.

"If only they'd shut up," Matthew muttered, and I liked him even more.

"Easy, boys! The enemy has been sighted!"

The column veered towards a distant grove of pretty clumped trees. We were heading into a painting, for all the danger it possessed. The railroad tracks disappeared into the gold-tipped meadow. The sun was bright, the field was bright. I winced from my throbbing foot and loped along.

We reached an orchard, the trees hung with green fruit that would be ripe within weeks. A fresh and earthy scent of ripening apples. My mouth watered, but we soon passed into a cornfield. Papery stalks brushed against the blue wool on my chest, and the Indian corn ears bumped against my rifle and my knees. We kicked through the stalks, the fallen ears, the sticky strands.

We came at last to a little brown creek, a tiny river. Nearby a bridge burned, and its smoldering wood crackled over the brown water and the green grass. It smelled good, like an autumn bonfire.

"It must be a raid," the New Hampshire man was saying. He spit in the grass. "Well, what do you think, boys? Ain't so bad, now is it?"

Fireworks exploded over his head. His cap flew by me and sailed like a wool bird into the grass. I stumbled backwards, caught David's arm, and we tumbled.

Strong arms lifted me, pulling me above the body at my feet. The fallen volunteer stared from the grass, shrapnel embedded in his jaws and cheeks. He stared, shocked by the fireworks that killed him.

"Daniel!" Andrew righted me upon my feet. David was up, too, looking shaken but not hurt. "Daniel!"

I wanted to say his name. I wanted to say something.

And the world erupted into a concert of thunder and fireworks.

· 1 ·

I didn't understand the poem and I never would, so I closed the book. Its cover was plain, a flat green. June breezes drifted through the window. Summer afternoons beckoned in all their glory. I yawned and smiled. Perhaps a holiday jaunt to Europe would cure me of too many days at a desk. All semester Matthew had helped me, so I could not wait to tell him I passed the final exam!

"Did you ever think this day would come?" I said to David when class had ended. "This term is over! I never have to read that damn poem again."

At the head of the classroom, Professor Felton was shaking each student's hand. Students smiled and thanked him for his lectures, slowly filing out. David gathered his books, wiping his slate.

"You like it when things are easy. If you had to work, you wouldn't believe that God was on your side."

"As we have read again and again, gods choose sides. Whether it is the Greeks and the Trojans, or Satan and God. I'd have preferred if the poems remained simply about their subjects, rather than teaching moral lessons."

I shook Felton's hand, surprised to find it damp in the heat. He said nothing and nodded. He was President of Harvard College the previous term. Other students put their poetry books on the teacher's table before they left. I was eager to rid my leather bag of a term's worth of classic epic poetry. No more Homer! No more Virgil! No more Milton! I could sing with elation.

David nodded to Felton, joining me at the table. "The great poets became teachers so we would know the right thing to do when moral questions presented themselves."

David was fair, with a girlish complexion and pale blond hair. He was of small stature, but he carried himself with gravity and walked slowly and deliberately. A pretty girl from Cambridge was in love with him, but he didn't know it. I glanced at the table, stacked with green covers like bricks.

"So, you have settled on the Divinity School?"

"You know it's the only choice for me."

We left the classroom, smiling at the professors in the hallway. Elocution class, Natural History class, Greek class, Latin class. Fellow students alighted cold wood within me. Friendships sprang up like blossoms amidst these halls. I'd never thought I could connect with others my age, though perhaps that was because some differences were too great. Yet, amidst the disparities, I counted comrades where before I could not. My freshman year was extraordinary.

"Hello, rich boy!"

Andrew appeared from his final Rhetoric class, and we walked down the hallway together. I met my boisterous friend several months ago, as we both stood up to do our Iliad recitations in the fall term. One of the largest young men I'd ever seen, Andrew was stocky, solid, with a large square face, choppy brown hair, and startling green eyes. He strutted and grinned with a self-assured air, accustomed to being right and liked. Many young ladies wrote to him, enough to make him think they all would."

"Where's Matthew?" I said. "I have to tell him of the final examination."

"Eh, trying to beg the professor to let him borrow the dissecting lens." He shrugged and gestured back towards a classroom. "You'd think he wouldn't fret like a nervous ninny on the last day of school. How goes the

Bible verses, Davy?"

Before David replied, fellow students surrounded us. Eager faces passed us, running towards the door like a sea of suited fish. Our final day in a long year. I hadn't crossed the Charles River in months, but my carriage waited outside. In ten minutes, I'd be on my way home to Beacon Hill.

Andrew rummaged in his pocket and pulled out a yellow piece of paper. "Never mind Matty. Look what jumped up at me today."

It was a telegram, sent from the city of Washington. The Radical Republican viewpoint was alive and well amidst our halls. How Andrew managed to procure such a thing was anybody's guess.

David sighed. "Andrew, you shouldn't keep abreast of that Greeley paper. It puts violent notions in your head."

"Read it!"

```
       300,000 NEEDED TO FIGHT!
       President Lincoln announces
    quota for Massachusetts to fill!
        Volunteer regiments need
    three-hundred thousand recruits!
        McLellan begs for troops!
       Governor Andrew must comply!
    Urge all to join! Sign and fight today!
```

I waved the telegram away. "I can't believe you read *The Liberator*. This fighting nonsense will commence by Christmas. You even said the reports from that Tennessee battle were disturbing!"

"Shiloh, Daniel. And enough about Christmas! You know, there's a recruitment rally at Faneuil Hall two weeks from Saturday. You want to come see what it's like?"

"Andrew, it is my mother's birthday gala." I was annoyed he had forgotten. "Take Matthew if you wish a companion. I have an obligation to my family."

"Sorry to see you miss out, but we are going." He wrapped an arm around David's thin shoulders. David did not look the least bit pleased he had been invited along.

I sighed. "You constantly speak of war, Andrew. Now is your opportunity."

A grateful voice drifted from up the hall. "Well, I'll be writing to you, sir, then!"

Matthew emerged from a nearby classroom and approached us. He opened a notebook to a page of scribbled motion drawings, and kept pushing up his spectacles. He greeted Andrew with a friendly jostle to the shoulder.

"He won't let me take the lens, but he says I can write to him!"

"Good grief, Matty!" Andrew rolled his eyes. "Forget about school, will you?"

I smiled. "Are you going to study even over the summer?"

"I'll bet he would," David said. "The Scientific school would accept his application based on obsession alone."

Matthew flipped a page, comparing two physics drawings. He was a thin fellow, with bulbous joints and big eyes. A rational one though, more given to reason than his pea whit brother. I reached in my bag and handed him my end-of-term marks.

"I have you to thank for the passing marks, my friend."

"He nearly failed the final exam," David said. "Even after you tried to help him."

"It's *Paradise Lost*!" Matthew spluttered in his usual way. "You should thank Felton for not teaching *Beowulf*! Milton was trying to show Satan's power. Adam and Eve getting thrown out of Eden - timeless classic poetry!"

Andrew shoved *The Liberator* telegram under Matthew's nose. He interrupted when our conversations became too complicated, which was often.

"Listen, there's a rally two Saturdays from now. You're coming with me, all right Matty?"

"Daniel, try to understand Milton's epic idea," Matthew went on in that nasal tone of his. "The poet says it is Man's fault we were expelled from Paradise. He depicts Satan as a hero. It flies in the face of conventional Biblical thought!" He turned to David with a proud smile. "I bet you did well, huh?"

"I am tired of thinking about poetry!" I made as if to grab the natural sciences book from Matthew, but he deflected my arm. He was teasing me now.

"Well, if it is Man's fault, then what is God's role in our lives? If we were going to get expelled, then why show us Paradise to begin with?"

"Because God made us in His image and wants us to be better than what we are," David said impatiently. "It appears Andrew deserted us."

Indeed, our impatient friend was striding down the hall towards the open doors. David smiled and hurried his steps to catch up. Matthew tucked the sciences book inside his bag and chuckled.

"I guess I'm going to that rally. Will you be joining us, Daniel?"

"All this talk of war. There were thirty empty seats in our classes this term. War is . . . for others. I have my duties."

War fervor escalated after the Shiloh battle. Each week, Harper's magazine splayed whiskered officers and lines of fresh troops across its cover. The Confederate army was proving to be more than a mere annoyance. Now that three hundred thousand new volunteers were needed, the frenzy would definitely increase. Yet, if the Pierce brothers joined the army and left to fight, then I had little but luck to wish them.

My carriage sat outside the school. It was a gorgeous summer day, hot and clear. I loosened my cravat. Andrew pulled out a small flask and saluted me.

"To our last day as Harvard freshmen!"

He took a nip. I chuckled at David's pursed lips when he sipped. He would take Chapel classes in the fall. Matthew would return to the dissecting-room, peering through a microscope or pursuing the intricacies of plant botany. I took a refreshing swallow and passed it back to Andrew. He gave me a hearty jab in the ribs.

"Off home, eh? You will not stay for commencement?"

"The Washburns are to dine with us tonight." I leaned in closer to them. "Catherine will be there."

David smiled. "Prettiest girl in Boston. Are you going to try for a moment alone?"

"Of course." I took a few steps towards the carriage. "But you can look for me at the tavern tomorrow night. Hope to see you there."

Andrew raised the flask. "Until we drink again, Daniel Stuart!"

I laughed and waved good-bye. They were good school-mates, and I looked forward to seeing them tomorrow. Their paths would meander towards Boston's North End tonight, crossing the river bridge on foot. Mine had a far different destination.

Mother sent the open-air brougham. I was glad for it and settled comfortably into the plush seat.

"To the house, sir?" The driver said.

I set my book bag beside me, watching my friends as we drove away. Matthew pulled out a book and was explaining something to Andrew that he clearly didn't understand. David spoke to another student from his Theology class. No matter if their homes were in a palace or a tenement, I would miss them this summer.

We drove down to the banks of the Charles River and followed it to the bridge. The water was tipped with white and small sailboats rode alongside the larger steamships. An enormous three-masted whaling vessel eased into a dock and the men began unloading huge barrels of oil and sacks of goods from foreign ports. They sang as they worked, and their voices mixed with the cry of the gulls overhead. I breathed deeply of the Atlantic air. At last, I was in Boston again.

Carriages bunched up along the streets like packed train cars, jostling for position. The squares were crowded with people protesting or supporting the war, squawking like chickens in a farmyard.

Many of the businesses, churches, and homes were decorated with colorful bunting and several men in Union blue uniforms stood near the telegraph offices, smoking cigars and greeting those who went up to speak with them.

"The 33rd marched out of here this morning," the driver said. "Can you believe that, sir? Thirty-three regiments already."

"I did not see them." I remembered Andrew's telegram. "Yet Massachusetts now has a quota to fill."

We followed the edges of the Common and headed towards Beacon Hill. There were many people out this lovely June afternoon, enjoying the leafy shade of the park. A woman dressed in black had a red, white, and blue rosette pinned to her bodice. Her head was bent, her face shadowed by her bonnet. Catherine would never have to worry about me.

Leaving the busier streets behind, we turned up Walnut Street and ascended the Hill. It was quieter here, the old brick and brownstone homes insulating us from the city. Golden light reflected off the glass windows and shapely roofs.

The Stuart house was set back from the street, three stories rising above the trim front lawn. Having not been home since Christmas, I smiled when I beheld its impressive size. It was a Federal mansion, built sixty years earlier by a former mayor. I loved the deep color of the brick, the way the lacy curtains in the upstairs windows were framed by candlelight in the evening, the classic columns in the front. It was a grand home.

The driver pulled the carriage into number eighty-five Mount Vernon Street, clip-clopping up the cobblestones. He circled the carriage around and opened the door for me. I got out, thanked him, and stepped beneath the portico.

It was still strange Father was not at the doorway to greet me. I entered past the large and impressive front door. Its heavy door handle was cold, and it made a soft swish as it closed behind me. The valet was oddly absent. I'd never entered my home alone before. The foyer was quiet, save for the large clock ticking beside the staircase and clanging pans in the back kitchen. The cook must be preparing the evening meal. I heard footsteps upstairs, padding across the carpet. Then Mother appeared at the top of the staircase, wearing a knitted bed-jacket over a simple housedress.

"Daniel?"

Her voice was softer than I remembered, her frame slighter beneath the large, plain skirts. She hadn't readied herself for my arrival. Had she forgotten today was the final day of classes? I shifted my bookbag under my arm and began climbing the stairs.

"I am home, Mother," I said. "Forgive me for implying, but are you well?"

She tucked several hair strands under her lacy cap, more gray than brown now. She aged, and I felt older, too. I reached her and kissed her cheek. She smelled of firewood, though the house was warm.

"I received your letter," I continued. "We are having the Washburns over tonight?"

"Mmm," she said, then leaned past me and called down the stairs: "Mary!"

"Who is Mary?"

"Maybe I had not written. I have a new maid. Mary!"

A girl poked her head out from the master bedchamber, a bowl of water balanced on her hip. When I met her gaze, her dark eyes widened. Her apron was starched white and her dress clean. She was new.

"Yes, mum?" Her voice was clear and strong. She shut the door behind her and came out into the hall.

"My son needs his room aired. Oh, and unlock the garden for him, won't you?"

"Mother, I can do it." I turned to the new maid. "Pay no heed to my room or the garden, please. See that dinner is served at eight. We have company this evening."

"Aye, Daniel, I will." She stopped, put a hand to her mouth. "Sir. I mean, sir. I am sorry, sir."

I smiled. "You are forgiven."

"Aye, thank you sir."

Mother shooed the girl away. "Go to it, Mary. I need fresh water."

She passed by us and started down the main staircase, but Mother's sharp eye was on her and she understood. She lowered her eyes, turned and went down the back stairs.

"I cannot believe you hired another Irish maid, Mother," I said. "We never had good luck with them."

"You mean you had too much good luck." She didn't smile. "In any case, it was Erik's suggestion. He should have been home by now."

I patted her on the shoulder. "Let Mary help you into your dinner dress. I will see you at eight o'clock."

She pulled at my sleeve, questioning. I thought she wouldn't need me now. I wanted to see the roses and have a few moments alone before supper.

"Join me in the parlor. Please."

She began downstairs, moving slower than I remembered. The parlor was dark and strangely unused. A fire had not been lit for several days. Heavy drapes remained on the windows, odd this late in the season. Mother settled into the sofa near the fireplace. I leaned upon the mantel. Father's portrait still hung above, though it was more than a year since his bright, cold funeral.

"Tell me of your spring term, Daniel. Did you choose which path you wish to take?"

I played with the base of a candlestick. "My friends have. David will go to the Divinity School, and Matthew tends towards the sciences."

"That leaves the law school. Well, you certainly have experience in the field. The bar is suitable to your temperament."

"I don't think Erik wishes me to follow him around the rest of his life." The light was fading and I felt hungry.

"Did I ever mention what your Father wanted for you in his will?"

She stood and went over to the little desk in the corner, a place where she often wrote letters and tallied household accounts. She opened the desktop and took out an envelope. Inside was my Father's will. I remembered the day we all gathered at his office in town to read it. A brisk spring day, late April. Newspapers in the office shouted headlines of war. A fort in South Carolina was attacked. God, I wanted it to be over.

Mother looked down at the envelope, not at me. "Edward wanted you to be a lawyer, Daniel. He expressed his clearest wish for you to attend the law school and become a partner in the firm of Stuart, Washburn, and Gage."

"You would have both sons follow him?"

She thrust it at me. "One moment you speak of running off West, the next that you do not wish to be like your brother? I would not have my son be so aimless."

I was confused by her sudden anger. I could read the will tomorrow. Why was she insistent on showing it to me? Before I could imagine an answer, the front door closed with a bang.

"Hurrah to all!"

Erik entered the parlor. He tossed his coat and hat to the valet. He looked well, had become a man of solid and good reputation. Erik carried himself with the same air of command as Father, but his eyes were merry. He came over and kissed Mother on the cheek.

"Good evening, Mother. And Daniel, my little brother! How goes the university?"

"Quite well." I returned his vigorous handshake and clapped his back in an embrace. "You seem the accomplished fellow these days."

"Ah, yes. Drinks in the library with me? We shall talk of gentleman pursuits!"

I turned to Mother. "Have Mary help you ready for supper."

She folded up the will and placed it back in the desk. "It is good to see my boys at home. These old walls have missed you."

We both smiled at her and she retreated upstairs. Erik snapped his fingers for the valet, and our servant knew us well. Not two minutes elapsed between us receiving our twin glasses of sherry and relaxing in the library. Erik lit a lamp and set his glass on the side table, running a hand through his thick hair. I settled into the deep leather chair.

"Was that Father's will?" Erik asked.

"Yes." I took a hearty swallow. "God, I feel better now than I have in an hour."

"Don't get too comfortable. The Washburns will be here soon." He gulped his drink. "I presume Mother gave you the 'Father's last wishes' talk."

I laughed. "To remind me of my true duties, of course. You would not have me working alongside you at the firm, would you?"

"The profession never suited you. Now that you have remained in school, I assume you will choose businesses or medicine. Something with less personal politics."

"Yes, you do know me. I am going to be a professor, Erik. I have not only done well in school, I have excelled. It is a natural fit."

"A good thing you stayed." He knocked back the rest of the sherry. "Well, it is not as lucrative as the bar. Perhaps not enough to persuade Catherine, either."

I poked him in the shoulder. "She knows that my intentions, no matter what they may be, aim for the good. If she is the girl for me, and how could she not be, then she will come to accept all of my choices."

"Daniel, I think she should accept them already."

I stared into the sherry. "She does."

"Then, you have nothing but happiness ahead of you."

"Of course."

We sat in silence. I looked across the room at the rows of books behind glass cases. Many were Father's law books. I stood and went over to read some titles. This was how I remembered Father, my memories so clear in this room. He sat in the library reading, several books opened at once, spectacles balanced on his nose, his quill pen dashing lines across the pages. Maybe I could be a lawyer. I liked reading well enough.

A carriage slowed outside and horses clipped on the cobblestones. Erik stood and straightened his waistcoat.

"The Washburns are here. I shall fetch Mother."

He left the library. Somebody, probably the new maid, scrambled up the back stairs. I hoped Mother was ready to receive our guests. Hopefully, they wouldn't mention Harvard. Yes, I stayed in school and did not run off West. Yet, didn't all young men feel the hot blood call of adventure, of a world beyond square desks and moral poetry? I must purchase more dime novels before my days were wholly consumed by obligations.

Tucked beside one of the law volumes was a slim little book. I opened the glass door and took it out. A plain green cover. I immediately knew what it was and wanted to shove it back into the bookshelf and never think of it again. I tried for three months to understand the damn thing and nearly failed the exam.

The front door opened and the Washburns' voices conversed in the foyer. I tucked *Paradise Lost* inside my jacket and strolled out to meet them.

· 2 ·

"Daniel!" Mr. Washburn shook my hand. "Good evening! How was your first year at university? Mrs. Stuart, your son has settled into being a scholar, I hear."

I smiled at him. Catherine was dressed finely tonight, her face luminous. Beauty the likes of which no poet could capture. A delightful air to her being instantly cheered me. Her smile, a kind look. Complexion as white as my roses, eyes like twilight.

"It has been a good year," I said.

"Come in to the dining room," Mother said. "We have a wonderful supper prepared."

Erik placed Mother's arm in his own and escorted her down the hall. A servant took Mr. Washburn's hat and coat, and he followed them. I lingered and stepped over to Catherine.

"How are you this evening, Miss Washburn?"

"I am well, Daniel. Thank you."

She did not take my arm, so I walked into the dining room behind her. She knew that I hadn't left school and, in fact, completed my first year. Was she still angry about my letter from February? It was nearly four months ago.

Mother looked splendid in her burgundy eveningwear, and Erik ordered two more glasses of sherry for us. No matter. I was here to relax. I forgot how much I missed my family, how much I loved our dinners together.

We stood at our places and Mother said a short grace. Then the servants tucked in our chairs and dished out the first course. Mother sat at the head of the table and I sat beside Erik on one side, with Mr. Washburn and Catherine facing us. She met my eyes once and then began enjoying the meal. I wanted to speak to Catherine alone. I decided I would after dinner.

We were all the way into dessert and I was feeling relieved at the polite, but dull choices in conversation, when Mother finished her peach iced cream and said, "Mr. Washburn, can you take Daniel tomorrow to the office? He is interested in learning the business."

Catherine looked at me with a wondrous hopefulness in her eyes. I hadn't told her I did not want to go to law school. Erik kept eating, but I realized all waited for me to speak. I chose my words as I would place a chess piece.

"I am interested as far as my family's profession is concerned. Father chose his career wisely and amply provided for his family."

"He did want you to attend law school," Mr. Washburn said. He ate like a bird and barely touched his plate. I wondered if Mother discussed this with him. Or Erik. I did not want to be a lawyer. I could be great if I so chose, but the choice did not agree with what I wanted.

"Mother reminded me of his will this afternoon. I have decided I want to be a professor."

It felt good to speak the truth, to say what I honestly thought. It was relieving, a burden from my shoulders. Mother stared at me with the same sharp eye she directed at the servants. Erik dangled his empty glass of sherry. He wouldn't have spoken in such a direct manner. He did things rashly, but not in an ill-thought way.

Catherine turned to her father. "I don't think Daniel understands, Father. You have a place ready, and Mr. Gage was to begin a private study with him."

"Thank you for reminding me, my dear," said Mr. Washburn. "It has already been arranged, Daniel."

Arranged? I hadn't seen the Washburns since Christmas, nor set foot in the law office for nearly a year. Annoyed, I managed a stifled smile.

"We'll see you tomorrow morning, then," Mr. Washburn said.

"Tomorrow morning, then," I echoed, trying not to sound angry. I might as well have never said a word, for all the impact. It was enough to see Catherine's smile, though. Oh, what would my friends think of this!

"I can't wait for the gala," Mother was saying. "We're having a tailor over on Saturday to fit Erik and Daniel. I thought of a string quartet, but Mrs. Tavington said a quintet would be far more suitable."

"We have the room for either one," Erik said.

"Have the extra servants arrive that morning promptly at seven o'clock," said Mother.

"I can offer two maids, three manservants and an extra housekeeper," said Mr. Washburn.

Catherine touched my foot under the table. I nudged her foot back. After twenty more minutes of discussion about Mother's birthday celebration, I was ready to retire for the evening. What did it matter whose invitation had been returned or when Erik and I would shop for supplies in Quincy Market?

"We'll ride in together in the morning," Erik said to me when we rose from the table and walked our guests to the door. It was late, and I was more exhausted than I hoped others realized. I helped Catherine into her shawl and Mother handed Mr. Washburn his hat.

"Thank you both for coming tonight," she said. "I do hope to see you before the gala."

"A pleasure, as always."

Mr. Washburn tipped his hat, and escorted his daughter out and into the carriage. I waved one final time and watched them pull out into the street and pass down the hill.

Mother grasped my shoulder and turned me towards her. "I am going to bed, Daniel. You have a good day tomorrow, if I do not see you."

"Good night, Mother."

"And you, Erik." She accepted his kiss. "Good to have you both home."

She passed up the stairs, in better spirits than I had first seen her. Perhaps it was the meal or the air, but her state of health had been frightening when I came home. Erik turned down the flame in the lamp at the bottom of the stairs. He reached into his jacket and pulled out a cigar.

"Care for a smoke outside, Daniel?"

I looked beyond the staircase, down the hall. "Not tonight."

"Suit yourself." He pushed open the front door. There was a whoosh of warm summer air.

I was alone.

The house settled into its evening quietness, the same familiar noises and creaks during my childhood. Yet, despite the familiar, I felt part of me came home a stranger to this life. For weeks I lived in close quarters with like-minded peers who supported my dreams and desired a more leisurely and high-spirited life. I never realized before how formal my early years had been. It was hard to fathom spending an entire summer here. Without Andrew's high temper, without David's funny remarks, without Matthew's astute observations.

Yet, there was one place that could not change. I went down the hall to the darkened rear door. I passed by the back staircase and heard someone quietly walking up the steps. I wondered if it was Mary. Perhaps Mother sent her on an errand for hot tea. I reached the rear door and felt around on the top door jam. A little golden key slipped from its hiding place into my fingers. I inserted it into the lock and pushed the door open.

The back garden was empty and quiet, moonlight glinting off the silvery leaves. I shut the door behind me and stepped out amongst the greenery. Deep breaths, gulping the summer air like a parched man. I calmed immediately. The rush of the dinner party, the excitement of ending school for the summer, the madness of seeing my family. All produced a state of nervousness in me that I wondered if others felt.

Well, no matter. The emptiness created a cushion of serenity. The rear garden was a place of solitude and occupation. I spent many an hour in here when young, pushing soil in a broken pottery bowl and helping the servants with rakes and hoes. I loved the barren way it looked in winter, the vines stripped of their leaves, and the aged brick dusted in white snow.

Tonight it was a summer bounty at its height. June was the ideal time for this small world to stream riotous color. An enormous old wisteria climber drooped pretty blooms by the doorway like a fragrant gate. Tiny golden-faced pansies peeped from the deep shade of the wall, twilight blue delphiniums waved their parasol-esque blooms, and tiny strawberry plants offered their harvest to me. I nibbled a jeweled fruit, exquisitely sweet, making my way towards the back of the garden.

An old wooden bench sat smothered in trailing vines. Arrow-shaped English ivy leaves wound between the rear slats and over the weathered arms. Briar rose bushes tipped full with blossoms as carelessly scattered as if a child blew them about. I reached down, caring little for the thorny stems, and plucked a pale bloom, as white as the inside of a shell. I eased onto the bench, unbuttoned my jacket, took off my shoes, and stretched bare feet into the cooled earth. Tucking my hands behind my head, I relaxed in the sweet summer air. From here, I could see the back of the house, square and shadowed. My garden was as beautiful as I remembered it those nights at school. June flowers would make way for the mid-summer vegetables, then I'd tend to August chrysanthemums before heading back across the Charles River to Harvard.

A small flame flickered in a top-floor window. A servant's room. I stared at it for a moment, and then a small face appeared in the glass. Startled, I sat up straight. The flame darkened, and the curtains swept the face from view.

I stood up and took the rose with me. I went back into the house, replaced the key, and climbed up to the third floor. It was stark up here, the plaster walls whitewashed, the floors bare. Servants' quarters. I found the room looking out on the back of the garden. I knocked on the door, but no one answered. I thought about leaving, but the door opened.

"Daniel!" Her hands flew to her mouth again. "Sir, I'm sorry. I keep forgetting."

"I saw you watching me from the window," I said to Mary. "Do you like my garden?"

"Aye, sir, I do."

I leaned my head down, but she wouldn't look at me. I held out the rose to her. She smiled and took it, inhaling the wonderful fragrance.

"Good night, Mary."

"Good night, sir."

I left and headed down the servants' staircase to the second floor. When I walked over to my bedchamber door, Erik poked his head out of his room.

"Visiting the maids again, eh, Daniel?"

"Leave me alone," I snapped, sharper than I wanted to.

"Not like Fiona, then?"

I walked over. "Drop the subject, Erik. I am going to ask Catherine to marry me. There will be no more talk of servants."

He grinned that insipid grin I hated so much. "Here comes the bride. Here comes the bride."

I made as if to hit him, but he blocked my arm.

"Good night, Daniel. Don't forget to be ready at seven."

I backed off and went to my bedchamber. I gave her a rose. What difference did it make? Mary was different. Catherine was different.

And how was I going to get through tomorrow?

· 3 ·

"Good morning!"

Window drapes were thrown back and a swath of new white light cut across my face. I groaned and pulled the bedclothes over my head. Erik tossed open the bed curtains.

"We leave within the quarter hour! Up we go."

He gripped the bed and shook it. I reached beneath me, grabbed hold of a pillow and threw it at him. He caught it easily, my throw clumsy with sleep.

"Nice try. We'll be late, Daniel."

Thank goodness for manservants. I was ready and even able to throw a splash of cold water on my face before I followed Erik down the staircase. Mother was waiting, in a bed jacket and cap, to see us off.

"I want you to help me with the guest list tonight," she said when we boarded the carriage.

"Guest list?" I yawned and settled into the seat.

"For her birthday gala. Drive on!" Erik tapped the roof of the carriage. "You are not that exhausted, are you?"

"Well, I remembered it yesterday. I even told some of my friends from school I could not attend a recruitment rally because of it."

"A rally?" Erik rolled his eyes. "Daniel, you are meant for better things."

"I don't think it would be a waste of time, if that was what you were implying."

"Certainly not, for the other young men of the city."

"The army has already raised and sent thirty-three regiments. And Massachusetts has a quota to fill, issued from the President."

Erik patted me on the shoulder. "You're my brother, and I stand by you. So I say with all respect, don't speak of regiments or war or rallies. Mother would banish you and I would –"

"You would what?"

He pursed his lips. "I would not support any choice involving fighting some ignorant southerners over some silly cause. As I said, you are meant for better things."

"Like a forced profession?"

He shrugged. "There are many ways to be a lawyer, Daniel. You could teach at the law school, if you wish. Despite the fact you and Father didn't see eye to eye doesn't mean the entire profession is, well, a hellish experience."

I stared out the carriage window. Andrew and Matthew had no money and no obligation to follow in a father's footsteps. David heard his spiritual calling amongst the drone of voices around him. It was not fair, in its usually illogical way.

"I won't speak of the war again, Erik."

"You're smarter than you look." He smiled. "We're nearly to the office."

The carriage turned the corner, and we drove down Washington Street. It was a beautiful summer morning, and the dazzling light glinted off the white windowsills, doors and starched gloves of those parading about the square. Boston's citizens were out in their finest walking suits and dresses. The traffic jammed and our driver restrained our horses from collisions. I laughed at the boys playing hoops in the street, remembering my happy days with old comrades. Several men walked about in their deep blue wool uniforms.

"The three-month-men," I said, referring to those who first signed up last April, and then were discharged after ninety days. I saw Erik's stern look and remembered I wasn't to speak of the war. Oh, well. Mother wasn't here.

"Ah, here we are." Erik thumped the roof of the carriage when we sidled up next to a large thick brick building with a blocky square front.

We stepped out onto the sidewalk. It had been more than a year since I'd been to the law office, though little changed. The law partners' names brightened the glazed front window, painted in a flourishing gold script:

STUART, WASHBURN, & GAGE, ESQ

Erik brushed past me and I followed him inside. The inner entry was a waiting room for clients, set up simply but comfortably with padded leather chairs and a small table for refreshments. In the rear of the waiting room was a large desk, and I recognized Mr. Gage's bent white head even before our eyes met.

"Good morning, Erik! And Daniel, too. Mr. Washburn mentioned you would come today."

I forgot how youthful he was, merrier than Father or Mr. Washburn, less rigid in his personal habits. I shook his hand with genuine congeniality.

"It appears I am to learn the profession."

"That's right, you completed the first-year at Harvard. Ready to enter the law school, are we?"

"Are we?" Erik repeated.

I removed my gloves. "There are many choices. It doesn't hurt to explore each option."

Gage was grinning like a schoolboy. "Well, glad to have you. Mr. Washburn is upstairs with a client, I believe. Erik, could you show him your office?"

"Ready, Daniel?" Erik placed his hat and coat on the little rack by the desk. I put my gloves in my pocket. As ready as I would ever be.

We ascended the little staircase in the rear of the entry. I stifled a yawn. It was quiet and warm, and those leather chairs looked quite comfortable. I was rarely up at this hour. Erik bounced along beside me, eager to show off his stature.

"The dinner hour is at noon, so I'll lock up the office and we can dine in the hotel lobby across the street. Did you know Mr. Washburn orders the same meal every day? He asks for 'the special' and the cook knows what he wishes. Father ordered his own special, too. Can you imagine, with the hundreds of guests, that they remember one meal?"

"Mr. Washburn barely eats a bite."

He ignored me. "That is how well-known I want to be. I want to walk into any restaurant on the street and they immediately know what meal to serve me."

We reached the second floor where a row of doors awaited, each stamped with an engraved brass nameplate. Father's door was on the far right, leading to the largest office. He founded the firm more than thirty years earlier, fresh out of Harvard's Law School, and his descending from one of the most prominent Boston families must have helped. It was difficult to contribute to his eulogy, like writing a paper on Milton.

Erik opened Father's office door and I stepped inside a room I remembered distinctly. Large round gas lights, thick patterned carpeting, those gloomy flat portraits that frightened me as a child, and the rows and rows of glass-clad books stretching all the way around the room. The place felt like an entombed library.

Erik went to Father's old desk, a massive piece of furniture with carved lion's feet and a matching throne-like chair. I didn't want to see him sitting there where Father had sat all those years. I loosened my cravat. Too little sunlight, too little air, not enough greenery to cheer the dark wallpaper. I would be buried alive.

"Like old times, right Daniel? I saw you looking at those portraits. I have actually gotten used to them."

"Can we go back downstairs? I would rather wait for Mr. Washburn there."

He sat back, tapping his fingertips. "You certainly do not want to be here, do you?"

"No, I do not want to analyze a client's troubles the rest of my days. I need to be amongst more activity, people of academic merit who seek more . . . well, more meaning in their lives. I don't know."

I sat down opposite the desk. Erik listened, for which I gave him credit. But it was plain from his quizzical look that he simply didn't understand. I did feel better on one account, though. Entering this office did nothing but reaffirm my aversion to this career. Some people never knew what they wanted.

But I did, and if there was going to remain such opposition, then I would have to work my way through it.

Mr. Washburn opened the door. "I hope I'm not interrupting anything, lads."

Erik rose. "We were waiting for you, sir. Are you at your leisure now?"

"Yes. I'll borrow Daniel, if you can spare him."

I left Erik sitting at Father's desk, using his blotter and his inkwell. I went across the hall to Mr. Washburn's office, a sunnier place with more windows and light. I felt a little better in this room. Not quite as cloying. We sat down and business commenced.

"Catherine mentioned last night that Mr. Gage would do a private study with you, Daniel. However, due to the war, he has an unexpected amount of work lined up for the summer and will be unable to assist you."

This was unexpected. If there was any man here I would rather have as a mentor, it was Gage.

"So, I have decided to have your brother take you on, as an apprentice."

"Erik?"

"He completed his Law School studies last year and is a capable and trustworthy young man." Mr. Washburn chuckled. "Reminds me of Edward, when he was young like that. Handsome, driven, compelled to succeed. I see more of your mother in you."

I flinched. I was often compared to her, though never under the best of circumstances. I reminded others of her indecisiveness, her fickleness, her impulsive ways.

"Daniel, you must overcome those tendencies to not make up your mind. Catherine told me of your attempts to leave school."

"That was only in the first semester," I said. "I wanted to do some traveling before settling into university life. For a time, I was thinking about perhaps going West."

"West?" Mr. Washburn laughed. "Yes, we've all heard stories of Indian raider parties and dime-novel shenanigans. But being realistic will serve you far better here in Boston. Catherine makes no objection to your advances, and neither will I, as long as I understand you are serious."

I didn't need it spelled out in a primer. "I am serious, Mr. Washburn, though it may not appear that way. I recognize the facts and I do make decisions. I merely live by a different schedule than others, at times."

"Well, for that problem, I have something you'll find useful."

He reached into his waistcoat and pulled out his pocket watch. After unhooking it from the fob, he handed it to me. It was still warm and ticked in my hand.

"Consider it an initiation gift," he said. "Now you can live by the schedule of those of us here."

"Thank you, Mr. Washburn. I am honored."

"I noticed you didn't carry one, and thought it odd. But, the clock ticks and I have work to do. Return to Erik's office, and let him know you will be his apprentice. He is efficient and will put you to work, I'm sure."

I stood and we shook hands. I placed the pocket watch in my pocket, and decided not to tell Mr. Washburn why I stopped wearing a watch.

"Oh, and ask Erik to give you twenty dollars."

"Twenty dollars? What for?"

Mr. Washburn laughed. "Your Father left it in his will that each of his sons should be paid in the beginning of the week."

How odd, I thought, but didn't question it further. Erik was not surprised to see me again. He was more than a little put out with my naiveté around the office, so I moved the chair away from the desk and sat staring at one of those crackled old portraits until he looked up from his paperwork and realized I was still there.

"Are you going to watch Grandfather all day?"

"Perhaps." I slouched into the cushion. "I'm glad I do not have to wear a wig like he did."

"I don't think you remember his stories about fighting in the War of 1812, do you?"

"Some, and he gave me that toy soldier set for Christmas when I was five."

"That's right." Erik took out a magnifying glass and peered at an open ledger-book filled with tiny numbers. "You played with those all the time."

"Until the paint rubbed off."

I stood up and went over to one of the bookcases. The glass was polished and the titles quite stuffy and uninteresting. I reached into my jacket and took out *Paradise Lost*. I stood beneath the light of the single small window and read the first few lines.

> *Of Man's first disobedience, and the fruit*
> *Of that forbidden tree whose mortal taste*
> *Brought death into the world, and all our woe,*
> *With loss of Eden.*

"A loss of Eden," I murmured aloud. "Why, Milton, I do believe I understand what you are implying."

"Daniel, I have something for you."

I put the poem back into my jacket and went to the desk. Erik handed me a small red book and a folder of papers.

"I am arguing a case next Monday against a textile factory owner who insists his Constitutional rights were affected. He claims, due to the rising costs of cotton, he has paid too much in taxes. Go through both his filed report and the Constitution, noting all discrepancies."

"I don't see why I shouldn't speak of the war," I said. "The reason cotton is so expensive is the South's secession."

"Don't think about the circumstances of the case, Daniel. Do as I ask, will you?"

If there had been more command in his voice, he would have been Father. Directing me with such authority. But his plea was strained. Maybe he didn't want me to be here, either.

"May I return to the lobby? If I have any questions, Mr. Gage is there."

He thought for a moment, and then nodded. With a smile of relief, I left the office.

· 4 ·

I took out the pocket-watch and opened the shiny cover, as bright as a coin. Eight o'clock. I'd been at the law office an hour? That was all?

Mr. Gage was still at the front desk. I walked up and rang the little brass bell.

"I didn't think we'd meet again before dinner," he said with a smile. "I see Mr. Washburn has given you some task to perform."

"Actually, it was Erik. I'm to have my private study with him."

"Yes, I am sorry I'm unable to help you. This ship-building case has me roped in." He laughed at his own joke. "You wouldn't believe how ship captains are, Daniel. Set in their ways and unable to chart any other course but theirs."

"What's going on in the case?"

"President Lincoln ordered a naval blockade of the Southern ports. Boston has responded, but many captains do not want to command ships only to block a port, you see. They would rather conduct their own oceanic business. It's been quite a mess the past month."

"I didn't know we were so involved."

"Most folks think the war will be over by Christmas. I have a hunch it will continue far longer than anyone wants to admit. You only have to speak to those who fought at Bull Run to gather that."

"And you have?"

"My cousin went to West Point and was one of the first on the front lines in Virginia. He sent a letter to me of the details of the battle. It has changed my view on the current situation." He paused. "I could let you borrow his letter, if you wish."

"No, but thank you for the offer. Mother discourages war-time talk and if she should find such a thing, it would not go well."

"I understand. I've kept you from your work long enough."

I looked down at the Constitution. "And I'm dearly looking forward to it."

Gage chuckled. "You come from a long line of men who strongly believed in that little document. I hope one day an amendment granting equal rights will be added. It's the only reason to fight, I believe."

"I assumed the laws would grant absolute equality, but with slavery, that obviously isn't the case."

"Daniel, laws are only a set of moral guidelines for us to follow. If nobody bothered to read and understand them, then this civil war would never end. And our country would never be whole again."

I nodded, not knowing what to say. I wondered why I wasn't to speak of such things at home, if it was such an immediate and pertinent topic. Perhaps it would create too much strain on Mother's nerves. She was already high-strung as it were.

I went over to one of the leather chairs and settled in with the paperwork and a pencil. I opened up the little red book and saw, on the list of contents, Article 4. The States. Maybe it was something Gage said, or the telegram Andrew showed me yesterday. Whatever the reason, I turned to that page and read:

Section 1   Each State to Honor All Others.

> Full Faith and Credit shall be given in each State to the public Acts, Records, and judicial Proceedings of every other State. And the

> Congress may by general Laws prescribe the Manner in which such Acts, Records and Proceedings shall be proved, and the Effect thereof.

I read it again, slowly. Then a third time. And I still did not understand how we could honor each state and still be in the midst of civil war. How could we both respect and fight our southern neighbors?

Familiar names covered the signature page – Washington, Madison, Hamilton, Franklin. It had only been eighty-six years since the days of revolution. Father mentioned old soldiers he'd met in his lifetime, so proud of their patriotic duty. As I browsed the signatures, what struck me the most was the listing of the states. North and South both included together, in complete agreement over these articles. Virginia and the Carolinas and Georgia signed.

I closed the Constitution. What happened last spring to give South Carolina the idea that it was not one of the states honored by these articles, and should thus secede from the Union? What happened for Virginia and North Carolina and Georgia to act the same way?

Those states must not have felt, in some way or another, that they were honored. They must not have felt the full faith and credit in the union of all the states.

I pulled out the case papers. This client also did not feel honored by the states. He was a textile factory owner whose livelihood depended on the states honoring each other and working together to keep costs down and supplies plentiful. But a war violated the sense of cooperation he depended upon. And not any war, but a civil war.

I couldn't argue against his position! How could I when I saw his side so clearly, as if it were my own? It was not his obligation to pay for the sins his state committed. He felt wronged, and I understood why. Gathering up the papers, I went back upstairs.

Erik stuck his pen in the inkwell. "Finished already?"

I dropped the folder onto the desk. "I can't find any evidence in the articles of the Constitution that proves this man is wrong, Erik. He doesn't feel honored by the states."

"There is nothing to argue against him?"

"I don't think he is wrong. I wouldn't want to argue against him."

He leaned forward. "It makes no difference what you want, Daniel. We are being paid to argue against his position. That is what being a lawyer is about. Any law student would have no problem arguing this case!"

"I am not a law student. I don't want to prove anybody wrong whom I think is not! How difficult can that be for you to understand?"

Erik shrugged. "Did you read his case?"

"I know enough about it!"

"But did you read it?"

I picked up the Constitution. "I read this, Erik. These are the moral laws we follow."

"Yes, they are. But they can be interpreted in many different ways."

"Well, I interpreted them my way."

"Fine." Erik organized the case papers in a pile. "I will do it later. You were told to help me, but you are being obstinate."

I couldn't help but agree with him there. I did have a strong opinion on such matters, but in this circumstance, I could not go against my convictions. Erik picked up the ledger-book and the magnifying glass.

"Tally these accounts. Calculate the totals for each column, match them with the income and expense lists, and compare them to last year's figures."

"Sounds fun."

"It isn't meant to be," he snapped. "It is a boring and tedious task. Do it downstairs if you wish."

I was no help to my brother, and now I was banished. Despite the fact that I had stood my ground, I felt worse. I was about to gather up the papers, when somebody knocked on the office door.

"Come in," Erik said.

"Has Father treated you well today, Daniel?" Catherine asked. She looked beautiful this morning, radiant in a walking dress the color of my morning glories.

"Quite well." I reached into my waistcoat. "He gave me his pocket watch, as a reminder to watch my time wisely."

"It will be put to good use, I'm sure," Erik muttered. He addressed Catherine, his tone a mixture of civility and urgency. "Was there a particular matter you with to discuss with me this morning, Miss Washburn?"

"No, nothing too pressing." She didn't take the hint and I tried not to laugh. Ah, my love did not understand business ways. "I am looking forward to your mother's birthday party."

"We draw up the guest list this evening." I decided to stall her for time. It would keep me from my awaiting boring and tedious task. "Have you any plans the Saturday after next?"

"I am not sure. I don't believe so."

"Then I suggest a ride around the Common. It is beautiful this time of year."

Erik was about to burst. "A ride in the Common would be a fetching idea. Daniel will be at your home around ten o' clock that morning?"

"Thank you, Erik." I smiled at Catherine. "Yes, I shall be there that Saturday. I have much to discuss with you, Miss Washburn."

"Erik. Daniel."

She nodded to each of us, paying particular attention to me, I thought. When she had gone, I turned to my brother. He was so relieved to get back to work I allowed myself a private laugh.

"Why, Erik, I must thank you. I now have the perfect opportunity for a moment alone with Catherine."

"Enjoy it," he grumbled, sitting back down. "Now, I must have that ledger completed by the end of the day. Do you think you can manage that?"

I took up the paperwork and went back downstairs. Father would have been pleased with my efforts, for I was able to finish Erik's task on time and with an added degree of focus. At the end of the day, when I handed it back to Erik, he muttered his gratitude and I made ready to gather my things.

We said good night to both Mr. Gage and Mr. Washburn when I

followed my brother out to the sidewalk. Our carriage was waiting. I yawned. Staring at those figures all day had cramped my hand and produced aches behind both temples. Erik looked at me sideways, a concerned look.

"I am almost sorry I assigned you that ledger book. Will you be all right?"

"I will." I looked up and saw an unmistakable figure approaching. The wide gait, the thick steps. My heart lightened immediately, and the long hours of my work day vanished at once.

"Afternoon, Daniel." Andrew nodded to my brother. "You must be Mr. Erik Stuart."

I smiled. "How goes it with you this evening, Andrew?"

He took half a step forward, staggering a bit. I couldn't help a chuckle. Twilight hadn't yet begun, and my friend already joined in evening festivities.

"I came to take you upstreet to pub, that's what goes."

Annoyed, Erik adjusted his gloves. "Apologies for the interruption, Daniel, but we have a prior engagement."

My brother's scowl dismayed me, and it was with great reluctance that I turned back to Andrew. "I am afraid I must decline the invitation. Mother wanted to draw up the guest list for the gala this evening."

"You say no, then? When you said no to the rally, too?"

"Rally?" Erik said, as if I'd announced I was going to muck the barn stalls. "You weren't going to attend an abolitionist rally, I hope."

"No." I tried to give Andrew a look of silence, but I could see my efforts were in vain. "There was a rally announcement for the war. It's the day of the gala, and I told my friends I was not attending."

"Indeed." Erik gestured towards the carriage. "Then, let's be off."

I tipped my hat to Andrew, trying to extricate myself as delicately as possible from his offer. However, it proved more difficult when Andrew leaned back with arms wide open and shouted:

"But we're celebrating tonight, Daniel. It's our summer out of the school! And don't you wanna wish me luck?"

I paused, embarrassed by the curious looks of others in the street.

Erik stood by the open carriage door, tapping his fingers. Turning to Andrew, I quickly asked:

"What luck am I to wish you?"

"Matty and me, well we're leaving. We're signing up for the war. So, you can't bother to see me tonight. It's the last you will see of me! Fine, then. Good." He gave me a slap on the shoulder, but it did little to dim my astonishment at his news. "Have a great night, Daniel Stuart. Don't want to enjoy paradise while we got it!"

The Pierce brothers were going to war? I half-believed him, but something about the fierceness of his tone moved me. Erik sighed impatiently and stomped over to my side.

"Daniel, Mother is waiting. Come along now!"

I took a step back. "If Andrew and Matthew are leaving for war, then I'd be a fool not to wish them off."

"If you insist on following your ruffian friends and neglecting your family, then I will not be surprised when Mother is grossly put out."

"Tell her, then. I am not going home."

He smacked his palms together in indignation and boarded the carriage so vehemently it rocked upon its wheels. After the door slammed and the great huff accompanying his departure settled, I made my way over to Andrew. He was looking smug indeed, as if he'd shot a prize trophy. He gave me an embrace so large and bear-like it buckled me in half. I crouched on the sidewalk and began to laugh, my knees grinding into the cobblestones.

"Whooee, you showed him!" Andrew hoisted me up as if I were made of twigs. "Let's enjoy the streets of North Boston!"

· 5 ·

"There he is! Hurrah!"

A pair of pewter tankards vaulted upwards from the corner table when Andrew and I pushed our way through the staggering crowd and fell into the benches. Matthew and David grinned, mouths foamy with beer, hair matted from the hot tavern.

"What is your business tonight, lad?" David tucked his little wooden cross inside his shirt and laughed. "Yes, the good Lord blesses our table!"

"Did Andrew tell you?" Matthew asked, then answered himself. "Of course, he must have."

I slid down the length of the slick wood bench. "About the war? You know Andrew!"

Andrew squeezed in beside me, bearing two additional drinks for us. We hoisted and cheered our arrival. Glasses clinked, and the ale tasted like honeyed mead from the gods. A twinge of regret at my ungentlemanly behavior threatened to destroy my good humor, but I shrugged it off. I was here to enjoy the evening.

The Bull and Boar filled early tonight, fishermen and factory workers in their tattered jackets and scuffed shoes. Scattered about were rowdy "Hullos" to their mates from the docks and the printing presses and the ropewalks and the coal fires of the city. Here was where Boston showed her true working grit, like the tough gravel that crunched beneath my carriage wheels. I ran a hand through my hair to muss its ends, to rid myself of the day's formalities. My pewter ale mug scraped the old table, the gas lights flickered above, the old daguerreotypes peered down from the walls. The Bull and Boar was the heart of the North End.

Andrew stood and leaned the massive bulk of his torso across the table. "I gotta toast tonight, you fellows. I gotta toast. To Matty." He ruffled his brother's hair. "This kid – don't he look like my little brother? He ain't. I'm the little one!"

I laughed at the old joke. I drank the ale and enjoyed the warmth in my veins, the way the lights began to smudge into a single glow. I hadn't felt this good all day.

"Hey you." Matthew nudged my tankard. "Andrew said he saw you on Washington Street today. They put you to work already?"

"It was a hell of a day, Matthew. A day that made me want all the less to be a lawyer."

David giggled. "I'll bet you were stuck doing the worst thing they could think of. Treating you like a – like a servant!"

I shrugged. "What I want to know is about this war business of yours! You both are going?"

Matthew looked to Andrew, but he was carousing with others at a nearby table. Then Matthew leaned in, his spectacles dripping on the edge of his nose.

"You know my brother, Daniel. Remember what we called it? Dead fish talk."

"Boy, I remember," David said. "Sitting on the wharves, listening to those captains and their tall tales of ocean beasts and mermaids."

I liked Andrew's dead fish talk. It was comical and somewhat endearing. But tonight, I did not see honor in it. It was not a mark of character to tell stories like that.

"Aw, there he goes." Matthew drained the rest of his tankard. "You got that look, Daniel. That look that says you ain't supposed to associate with us North End fellows."

I passed him my half-full tankard. "Finish that off, Matthew. And no more about it. Andrew can talk all the talk that he likes."

"I damn well can!" An enormous hand swooped up Matthew's empty tankard. "Anybody got a ha'penny?"

David passed him the money, and Andrew stumbled over to the bar. I wasn't interested in a second drink, but it was impossible to decline my drunken friend's insisting. So, I knocked back an extra swallow for him, and for his belief in his dead fish talk. They weren't going to war. It was all something of a fun game.

"Get over there!" Andrew pushed Matthew's shoulder, urging him towards a group of musicians reveling in the corner. "Tell 'em to play!"

I stood to help, and the warm feeling in my chest dropped to my knees. I laughed. The ale felt good, and I chugged another swallow. Then I grabbed up a second tray of drinks, assisting Matthew as we went over to the corner. It took little coercing before the candlelight gleamed on the shiny mahogany backs of the fiddles and the lustrous silver of the flutes. When the first piper rang out his thunderous reedy tone, I joined in the applause.

"Whooeee!" Andrew tipped an imaginary hat to the singer, a fellow with a little lap organ. "Play the Dublin Lass!"

A sprightly little jig twiddled from the fingers of the fiddle players. The front singer tapped his feet in a lively beat, belting out his tune in his strange Irish language.

"What is that?" Andrew shouted. "I can't dance to your gibberish!"

The singer stopped the song and laughed so hard his face turned purple beneath the lamps. He toasted a pint to Andrew, then began the song again.

When I had me lass in Dublin,
Such a fine lass there be.
I said to me lass in Dublin,
I'll buy a drink for thee!

Boots and shoes stomped upon the floor, the place vibrating with the lights and sounds of the players. Andrew passed off his tankard to Matthew and stepped right up in front, slapping his knee and parading around like a soldier. He gestured with both arms, and Matthew jumped right up with him, ale in hand. The two brothers linked arms and stomped and kicked their dancing around the back of the tavern. I stood sipping my ale, laughing, and sharing a smile with David, who applauded and whooped like an Indian.

She said to me, my lass,
"I cannot be with ye.
But I'll take yer offer kindly
So share a pint with me."

The tavern crowd roused and joined in the revelry. A couple of Irish girls in their tattered skirts stepped on up to the dancing brothers. They danced near them, all kicking up their heels. But then Andrew up and grabbed one of them! She shrieked, and we all laughed at her surprise.

"Hallo there, lass!" Andrew called out. "Share a pint with me!"

Her hands were on her hips, but she accepted his hand and they took center stage, dancing a complicated jig in front of us. A clear voice called out behind me.

"Excuse me, pardon me, I'm comin' through!"

I shifted to one side and a tiny Irish girl passed by me. She clutched her skirts in one hand and a full tankard in the other. She wove her way through the crowd, then went up to Matthew, who was still dancing around his carousing brother.

She tapped Matthew on the shoulder. He spun around, then she handed him the tankard and began to dance. He held the ale and drank some more as he watched her. I downed the rest of my tankard and accepted the rest of David's, too.

I couldn't take my eyes off her. She spun and danced with expert steps, a complicated jig old and true.

I said to me lass in Dublin,
"I'm off to war in the morn.
But I'll have a song to sing to ye
To sing when I do yearn."

Andrew spied the new girl and reached for her. She quickly danced out of his reach. He lunged for her again, but she danced away again. The crowd laughed at his brutish antics. Other young men stepped from the crowd, hands outstretched for the girl. I pulled on David's sleeve and pointed to her.

"She's an incredible girl!" David shouted above the din. "I heard she came over from Ireland not even a year ago. Can you imagine? To last that long after the famine?"

Andrew lunged for her again, tripped, and stumbled towards her. She wove her way through the tables and people like a fish. Andrew tried to push through after her, a clumsy enemy.

I stepped out and caught her arm. She didn't turn, but stood with her back towards me and laughed at Andrew. He balanced his heavy weight on the table and looked up at me, ale foam dripping from his lips.

"You got her, my friend. Now take her out to dance!"

"Dance! Dance! Dance!" The crowd roared in approval.

"Do ye think we should?" asked the girl in her strong and clear voice. She looked up at me. Dark eyes, a candle in the window, a small oval face watching me.

"Mary?" I sputtered. "Mary, is that you?"

"Come on then, Daniel. Let's dance!"

She tugged on my arm. I followed her through the tables and out in front of the musicians.

I'm lyin' now on a battlefield,
O lass, dear to me heart.
But I'll sing to ye in heaven,
An' we shall never part.

I followed her movements when we danced, matching her pretty steps and clasping her hands to swing our bodies like bells. I felt the ale, the warmth, the wetness of my shirt clinging to the back of my neck. The lights blended and the music coursed through our feet and our fingers. The reedy pipes chorused above, and the little singer with his organ sang for us when we danced.

When the song ended, the tavern crowd leapt to their feet, whooping and shouting for an encore. I felt as light as a sail. Mary stepped out before me and curtsied like a saloon girl. Another song started up, slower and haunting. I collapsed at the table.

Mary smoothed her hair. "I only came out for the evenin', sir. Ye aren't goin' to tell, are ye?"

I scratched my head. "No. But it is a long walk back to the Hill. I can call a carriage."

"In yer condition, sir?"

I held onto the edge of the bar when we gathered our things. Andrew wiped droplets of sweat off of Matthew's spectacles. I smiled. It was late and I had to return to the office in the morning. Perhaps a brisk walk in the summer evening would be a better alternative. I caught David's sleeve before he left.

"Will they be all right getting home?"

He nodded. "We don't live far. I only had a little ale."

"You are a good friend, David."

"Thank you for coming tonight. I'm sure the Pierce brothers did appreciate it, too."

I gathered my coat, wiping my brow. "I enjoyed myself. But you must tell Andrew to ease off the dead fish talk. For a moment, I thought they were both leaving for war."

"Perhaps someday, if it continues the way it has this summer." David shrugged. "And there isn't a whiskey shortage."

I laughed. "Good night, David."

Following Mary out of the tavern, I heard Andrew singing that Dublin Lass song. I'll sing to you in heaven, and we shall never part. He and Matthew held each other up, propped against one another like falling trees, stumbling down the street and disappearing into the night.

A light gray fog rolled from the nearby docks. It was the smell of the sea, the ships and the barrels of oil coming off the big whalers. I breathed deeply, glad to be enjoying the evening.

"Do ye know where we are, sir?"

I nodded and started off heading west, back towards Washington Street. She followed at a distance of several feet, walking steadily. I turned back once to see if she was still there, for she made little sound. When I made it back to Mount Vernon Street, I waited at the corner for her.

"We're nearly there," she panted.

"It would not look well for us to go inside together. Straighten yourself. You look a sight."

"I'm yer help, sir."

I glanced up the sloping street. "Mother will be in bed, but my brother may be awake. I'll go in the house first. Count to ten and come in behind me. Go into the carriagehouse and through the back garden. You won't be seen that way."

"I'm glad ye danced with me tonight, sir, if ye don't mind me saying."

I couldn't help a smile. "You are not to speak of it. We shall share this secret."

What a night we had shared. A night so needed after a long day.

The house was dark save for a lamp lit in an upper chamber. I stumbled under the portico and grasped the door handle. I was all right, not as far into a drunken state as I'd been in the past. I barely remembered those days after Father's funeral.

"A late hour for you, isn't it?"

I was startled. A glimmer of light from the parlor caught the rustling silk of her dress. I handed my coat to the valet. He held his nose from the smell and looked at me, but thankfully said nothing.

"Mother, I thought you were not well."

"Erik told me tonight how you disobeyed him to run off with your friends."

"I didn't disobey him."

I came into the parlor. Mother sat in the chair near the fireplace. Embers were lit, though the room was warm. She pulled her shawl tighter around her shoulders and turned the lamplight down lower.

"You said you'd help me with the guest list."

I sank into a corner of the sofa. For the first time that evening, I felt tired. "Has it been drawn up already?"

"Yes, and if you're not happy with it I'm not having it changed."

"That is fine with me."

"Don't be insolent!"

I did not need this. Not now. "Mother, I went to the law office today and I did what was requested of me. I answer to Erik and I am fine with that situation. When my friend from school invited me to an evening, I accepted."

"You humiliated your brother. In front of a North End ruffian!"

"Then why aren't Erik and I speaking about this?"

She rose from the chair. "It is going to be a long summer if you do not listen to your family. Erik said you were rude and lazy at the office. Perhaps you are selfish enough to think you should not be there, but he did!"

She stabbed a finger at Father's portrait. I was not angry, merely tired. Bone tired.

"Good night, Mother. I am going to bed. How can I be well rested for the office tomorrow?"

I strode from the room and up the stairs to my chamber. Footsteps padded up the back staircase, and a door opened above my head, on the third floor.

Ah, Mary. Such a fine lass there be.

· 6 ·

"Damn it!" Erik stuck his head out the carriage window. Wheels crunched back and forth on the packed street. "We'll be late."

"Do you hear that?" I yawned and stirred in the seat. My legs were falling asleep. "It sounds like band music."

He blew a sigh. "Another blasted war regiment? We must be trapped behind it."

I glanced beyond the window glass, startled to see another man peering straight back at me. Our carriage wheels were locked together, packed with dozens of others at the mouth of Washington Street. Others yelled inside motionless vehicles, and horses screeched from impatient whips. I reached for the carriage door.

"Then let's walk. It's not far."

People had lined the sidewalks, waving little flags and craning their necks down the road. Yes, we'd see the uniforms soon. Without waiting for my brother, I squeezed into the street. I shut the door and picked my way across, dodging wheels and ducking under a horse's muzzle. Mud and stones clung to my shoes. Erik leaned out and spoke to our driver, then navigated the street in a similar fashion and came to my side. He shook his sullied trouser legs.

"Of all the luck! Come on!"

We hurried down Washington Street. The crowd thickened until our 'excuse mes' and 'pardon mes' were useless. Suddenly, deep blue uniforms appeared from around the corner. I glimpsed their bayonets, glittering in the early sunlight. I stopped. The regiment was so close! Erik grabbed my arm.

"We are late!"

"I want to see them."

"Daniel, you can't."

I ducked into the gathering crowd, Erik's voice lost in the din. I pushed my way between the onlookers. I stepped on several skirts and bumped into a group of frowning gentlemen.

"I say!"

"Excuse me! Pardon! Pardon!"

Squeezing between them, I at last had a clear view of the street. Morning light streamed upon the approaching regiment. Their uniforms were magnificent blue wool, a true rich navy. Gold buttons polished like the sun. Their arms pumped when they marched in step with their comrades. I joined the crowd in a great cheer when they at last came right up before me. The captain, elegantly clad in a long frock coat, sat astride his horse, saber pointed towards the skies. He halted his men and shouted:

"Shoulder arms!"

One hundred men shifted their rifles to their shoulders.

"Present arms!"

The soldiers pointed their long rifles, spiked bayonets crowning the guns like shafts of straight silver. The captain turned his horse, presenting his well-trained men to us. I applauded, a great joy alight in my chest. They looked tremendous! And above us, the buildings were clad with bright bunting in red, white and blue. Little flags dipped in the hands of children and fabric rosettes pinned to their mothers' dresses.

"Ah! There you are, Daniel." Mr. Gage smiled at me amidst the crowd. "I have been sent to fetch you, it seems."

"Shoulder arms!"

The regiment shifted their rifles back to their shoulders.

"Forward, march!"

The captain again resumed his forward position and the great sea of soldiers began to move. Row after row of them passed by.

"They are leaving now," Gage said quietly. "Come along."

He was right, and it was time to go, so I resumed my journey to the office. Passersby dodged between us. We did not hurry, and all of a sudden he stopped me in the sidewalk.

"Daniel, did I ever tell you of the time when your father and I snuck from the office to wish the soldiers of the Mexican War a fair goodbye?"

I could not imagine Father forsaking his work for any reason. The law was his life, carved into him like rock.

Gage chuckled at the memory. "It is a fine thing to be enamored of the men who fight for us. I hear you are acquainted with abolitionists from the North End."

Andrew's dead fish talk. "They are my school-fellows and good friends."

"Your grandfather was about your age when he signed to fight in the War of 1812. Wars need seventeen-year-olds with too much youth and too much energy. Here."

He reached in his coat and handed me an opened envelope. It was posted from an interesting Virginia address.

"My cousin wrote again," Gage explained. "The Army of the Potomac is having a devil of a time trying to capture Richmond. Who knew the Confederates could put up such a fight?"

"So this talk of it being over by Christmas is not true?"

"Of course not." He put an arm about my shoulder and steered us towards the office. "Daniel, be your own judge of this war. Perhaps your friends are good men, but all men can be tempted to leave paradise. You must watch out for enemies."

I nodded, thinking of Milton. And my own garden, a place of beauty and rest. I tucked the letter in my pocket, and with a heavy heart, opened the door to the law office. The morning's excitement died, and for the rest of the day, I'd be shrouded in obligation.

"He appears!" Mr. Washburn greeted in the front lobby. "I thought we'd find you in a uniform by now."

Erik waited by the staircase, arms crossed like Mother when she was put out. "Are you ready, Daniel?"

Mr. Washburn shook his head. "You mentioned problems with punctuality, but an hour late to work?"

I brought out the pocket-watch. Indeed, it was half past eight. I walked past his disapproving eye and climbed the staircase, Erik right behind me. He didn't say a word, and as soon as we entered the office he went right to the desk, rummaged through papers, and found a fat leather-bound book. He shoved it at me like a hot ember.

"You'll be tested on the first three chapters. Read them and report back here to take the test."

It was a book on Constitutional Law. I thumbed through it, discovering the first three chapters were fifty pages.

"Erik, this is ridiculous."

I regretted my words immediately. He glared at me, angrier than I'd ever seen him.

"I don't care if it's the stupidest assignment you've ever received. If you don't do it, I'll personally take you home and inform Mother."

"That is unnecessary."

"Oh, is it?" He stabbed the book with his finger. "Then prove me wrong."

I took a pencil and left. Even if I was rude, why should I apologize? Alone in the upstairs hallway, I pulled out Gage's letter. I took it out of the envelope and tucked the envelope back in my jacket.

Mr. Washburn was still at the head desk. He could have continued his rant on my tardiness, but he said nothing. I found a chair near the window with my back to his desk, opened the book, and placed the letter on the page I was supposed to be reading.

June 19th, 1862

Cousin Johnny,

Your letter was three weeks late, but it arrived yesterday •

it grately cheered me. I dont get many letters now that the army is always moving. We are still near Richmond • still trying to outfox the rebs. But they got a new general now, Gen Lee, • he is tough to fight. He has dug in around the city • those dammed rebs wont move! Remember my friend the Sergeant? He got killed yesterday. I tryed to get him some help, but he kept saying he was thirsty • I couldnt find any water • I looked • everywhere were dead bodies. My shoes were covered in blood • shells had got so many of em • they were all torn up in bits and pieces. When I came back the Sgnt was dead. He got shot in the head. I am never forgetting his bloody face again. Nuthin but blood. I don't want to fight without the Sgnt. He was my best friend. Dont tell Mama about me fighting. She is thinking things are all right. Please write soon.

Gus

I hurried to the window, undid the sashes and pushed up the glass. I thrust my head into the fresh air and breathed deeply. My stomach roiled. All I could picture was my friends shot and bleeding in a smoky field. My God.

"Daniel, what is the matter? Are you well?"

Mr. Washburn stood by the chair, looking down. He noticed the Constitutional Law book. I gasped for breath.

"I am reading the first three chapters."

"Constitutional Law makes you ill?"

I pressed a handkerchief to my forehead and closed the window. "I am learning so many new things. It can be quite overwhelming. Did Father never mention how overwhelming it can be?"

Mr. Washburn picked up the book. "Of course not. He loved this profession."

I quickly took the book from his hand. At his surprised look, I sat down and opened to the first page.

"I must return to reading. I have a test to study for."

"Then I will leave you to it. If only you were as concerned with showing up on time."

Thankfully, he returned to the front desk. I removed Gus's letter and tucked it in my jacket, struggling to settle down and focus on the first three chapters.

But the words blurred, and I was shaken by a deep sorrow. I could not forget the wounded sergeant, crying out for water and dying alone without his best friend.

· 7 ·

"Well done today," Erik said when we removed our hats and handed them to a servant.

I wasn't as eager to return home as I thought I would be, given the time well spent with friends last night. If only every day could be spent in their company. Surprised at my own thoughts, I gave a half-smile. Six months ago I'd never have wanted to associate with North End men!

Voices drifted in from the front parlor, and we found Mother and the tailor conversing by the fireplace.

"Thank you," I said. "Oh, Mother? I think Erik has something to show you."

She came over and kissed my cheek. "Something good, I hope?"

Erik pulled out the test. On the top of the front page, scribbled in bright blue ink, were the words: "Perfect Score."

"I tested him on the first fifty pages of a Constitutional Law book. And, as you can see, our Harvard student remains an exceptional scholar."

"Wonderful!" She clapped her hands. "See Daniel, once you apply yourself, you are well-suited to law."

I chose not to argue with her, but it felt good to be celebrated. If only she knew the real reason I absorbed those chapters! Erik looked more pleased than he had in two days.

"He'll know the whole book by the end of next week."

"I don't doubt it." Mother gestured to the tailor. "Well, Mr. Barkins is here for your gala fitting. I visited Dunstan's today and found the most beautiful material for my gown. It should be ready by next Thursday. Come, Daniel. You first."

A servant set up library steps in the center of the parlor and pulled the sofa back several feet. Mother and Erik took a seat to watch the show. I stood beside the steps and the tailor opened his carpet-bag of needles, threads, and sewing accoutrements. Mother looked well, so I decided to smooth the strife between us. It would be a long summer if our arguing continued.

"So, what type of material did you select for your gown, Mother?"

She sat upright, looking pleased. "Oh, boys, you're going to love it. It is a gorgeous emerald silk, all the way from France! It is the newest rage in Paris, so the merchant told me. Oh, and I'll have matching slippers, too!"

"Speaking of the gala," Erik said, "we should think about heading to Quincy Market in the morning, Daniel."

"Oh?" I removed my jacket.

"For shopping, of course."

The tailor brought out pieces of black fine wool. I rubbed a section between my fingers. I would suffer in the heat, but it would do. The tailor climbed the steps, fitted me into the body of the jacket he was constructing, and then began attaching one of the sleeve-pieces.

Abruptly, there was a knock at the front door. The servant opened it, but nobody came in and I strained to hear the voices in the foyer. The servant entered the parlor, looked at me and announced:

"There is a Mr. O'Toole here to see you, sir."

"Mr. O'Toole?" The name was not familiar.

"He said he is from the Bull and Boar Tavern on Wharf Street."

Mother's face lost several shades. Erik looked puzzled, then angry. I quickly excused myself and went to the door. There stood one of the barkeeps I'd seen last night. He looked as out of place as if he'd been in the Arctic circle, peering nervously about our grand front hall. Annoyed,

I demanded:

"What is your business here?"

He dug in a pocket of his dingy trousers and pulled out a small book with a green cover. I snatched it from him.

"I found it on the floor of me bar last night," he said, then winked at me. "Hey, say hi to Mary for me. Quite a lass, I'll say."

"Thank you, Mr. O'Toole. Um, here. For your trouble." I reached in my pocket and held out coins, which he took without hesitation.

"This is a fine place you got here, mister."

My tone became firm. "Thank you, Mr. O'Toole."

I slammed the door. Well done, Daniel. Losing the book so carelessly. And now there was no way to cover up his purpose for coming here. Yet I must invent an excuse before I could go back into the parlor.

"Daniel? What tavern?"

It was Mother. I wanted to open the door and walk out of this house. I wanted to see my friends again and dance like last night. So much for dead fish talk.

"Sir?" Mary poked her head out of the kitchen, her face shadowed by the staircase. "I thought I heard Mr. O'Toole at the door."

Shoving *Paradise Lost* into my jacket, I leaned forward and grabbed her arm. She winced when I held her close, whispering into her ear.

"Please, Mary. Cover for me."

"I will sir, but ye let go!"

I hadn't meant to hurt her. I released her arm, pleading with her. She soon walked down the hall out in front of me. Smoothing my hair and lapels, I entered the parlor a step behind her. Mother rose from the sofa, her face a mixture of curiosity and annoyance.

"Daniel, why have you brought the maid? And who was that at the door?"

"He was looking for me, mum," Mary said in that strong voice of hers. "I'd left me handkerchief at his tavern last night. Ye saw me come in late, didn't ye sir?"

She turned back to me. I saw she had drawn out a little handkerchief and had showed it to Mother and Erik. Mother sniffed.

"Then why was he asking for Daniel, girl?"

I went back over to the tailor and climbed the library steps. "I don't think it matters, Mother. Let us resume."

"You did come in late, though." She was not going to let up. "And you cared nothing for the guest list."

I sighed and decided to tell her. "Mother, last night I went with some friends from school to the Bull and Boar Tavern. I know it is not a respectable place for a young gentleman, but they invited me. I left a book there and Mr. O'Toole was kind enough to return it."

"Yes, I told Mother you deserted me," Erik cut in, "and you are right. It is no place for a gentleman. Further, your behavior this morning in Washington Street is not indicative of that title, either."

Mother turned on me. "You had better start explaining yourself right now, young man."

Not before I'd collected myself and prepared my personal defense. I straightened the sleeve of the jacket. The tailor continued sewing the shoulder-seam. A grand ball we'd once held popped into my mind. A bal masque, all the dancers concealed behind grinning paper faces. I assumed a masked face now, staring straight at Mother.

"There was a Civil War regiment leaving the city and they marched in front of the law office. I lingered for a few moments to watch them. It was a grand sight, Mother."

"A grand sight, which caused him to be an hour late." Erik folded his arms.

"What does it matter?" I pointed to the Constitutional Law test on the side table. The movement jerked my arm and the tailor poked me with the needle. I grimaced. "You see I am doing my duty as best I can."

"Duty?" Mother looked at Father's portrait. "Is that all our family's profession is to you?"

During this pleasant interlude, Mary had retreated to the rear of the parlor. She began to quietly slip out into the hall, but Mother spied her.

"Girl! Come here at once."

Mary walked over, her head bent. For the first time in my life, I felt a sense of pity for a servant.

"Yes, mum."

"Report to the cook. I don't want to see you out of the kitchen for the rest of the week." Her eyes bore into the girl. "Daniel was right to discourage me from hiring the Irish. They are filthy, rude, and lying creatures."

Mary did not lift her head, but walked calmly and swiftly from the room. How I wanted to leave as well, not be forced into civility for the remainder of the evening.

"Mr. Barkins, you may proceed."

Mother sat back down and the tailoring commenced. A servant set a stand-up tilting mirror in front of me, and I observed the progress. The wool was fine, but itchy. I was warm and light-headed in the stifling parlor.

"I have received reply invitations from the Washburns already," Mother was saying. Though her displeasure at my actions ran deep, she lightened her tone as if all that mattered to her was the appearance of graciousness. "And it has been decided to have a string quintet instead of the quartet."

She and Erik spoke more about the gala – the refreshments, purchasing the wine and brandy, training the Washburn servants to assist ours.

I remembered Mr. Gage's letter from his cousin. Sorrow over his dead comrade. Would Andrew leave for war? Would his dead fish talk end and his actions begin? He would take Matthew, and David would, too. My friends would be gone.

"Daniel?"

I jerked awake. "Hmm. Yes, Erik?"

"Your jacket is finished."

The tailor was packing up his carpet-bag and the library steps were removed. I smiled sheepishly. So much for daydreaming fancies.

"Supper is ready."

Mother would not look at me, and she hurried off towards the dining room as if the room was on fire. I decided I would be courteous and cause no further arguments with her.

I followed her, but paused at the kitchen. Behind the door came wonderful smells, the banging of cast iron pots and the creaky swing of the fireplace crane. I pushed open the kitchen door. The hot smoky room was a boisterous place in my boyhood. I sat at that little table by the fire many winter nights sketching with charcoal crayons or enjoying a mug of cider. I still had a small scar on my right foot where an ember had leapt from the fireplace.

The cook bent over the knee-high stove stirring a soup kettle, her face and hands as pink as my roses. A scullery maid scrubbed mussels in the dry sink, and Mary stood at the chopping block slicing leeks and radishes. I cleared my throat. Without looking up, the cook greeted me. She'd been in the family since Father was a boy.

"Good evening, Mr. Stuart. We're nearly ready."

"Thank you, but I need a word with your help." At this, Mary dared to raise her head. I was glad to catch her eye. "If you would, please."

She wiped her hands with a rag and came over to the doorway. Though her fingers trembled, she looked at me steadily.

"Yes, sir."

I lowered my voice so the others would not hear above the clanging cooking pots. "Come to the back garden tonight, after supper. Do not let Mother see you."

She said nothing, but it was an order and she would obey me. I closed the door, reluctantly making my way to the dining room.

The evening meal, usually my favorite part of the day, was long and idle. I felt tired and anxious, the worst combination of emotions for social interaction. Mother's table conversation veered around the weather in England this time of year, the latest magazine issue of Lady's Godey's Book, and a local quilting contest to raise money for the Union soldiers. Erik feigned his own version of rapt attention. I learned long ago the more I encouraged Mother to speak of trivial amusements, the less likely she would involve me. Her extensive selfishness could be charming. Tonight, it worked to my benefit.

One advantage of being well-bred was knowing the right time to excuse oneself from an unpleasant situation. This skill I exercised to its greatest effect after the conversation lulled, plates emptied, and the mood quieted. I folded my napkin and rose to my feet.

"A lovely supper, Mother. It has been a delightful evening."

"Why, thank you, Daniel. I never can tell when you are pleased with me."

"I admire your graciousness." I went over to her place and kissed her hand. "But I must retire. I want to rise early for our errand tomorrow."

"Indeed." Erik swallowed the last of his wine. "See you in the morning."

"Good night."

It was rare to escape with both my pride and composure intact. If Mother tried to stop me, I might even have insulted her. It was exhausting to play-act when I merely wanted to leave.

The garden was unlocked. As soon as I closed the door behind me, all of the evening's unpleasantness dissipated as if by the sea wind. I couldn't help but smile.

Mary waited for me near the bench, by the roses. In the white moonlight, her face was luminescent and her dark dress made her look like a cut silhouette.

I suddenly felt foolish. What business did I have with a maid, when my heart belonged to Catherine? I was going to propose this Saturday, for God's sake.

I stopped several feet from Mary, tucking my hands behind my back so I wouldn't fidget. She remained silent, so I looked down at the strawberry plants and hoped my tone conveyed more authority than I felt.

"Um, I wanted to apologize for Mother this evening. You are one of our servants, but I don't think that warrants an insult."

"It's all right, sir."

"No, it is not!" I snapped.

She stiffened, startled by my curt tone. Embarrassed, I spoke slower and softer.

"Mother was angry with me. I am bound by Father's will to be a lawyer, which is not my wish. My friends, whom you know from the Bull and Boar, wish to fight. I'm not entirely sure what I do want, but I definitely know what I don't want. You understand?"

"Aye, sir, I do."

I nodded, feeling oddly relieved to have said it out loud. "Good, then. Perhaps someday I will know what I want, and then I can pursue it with energy and vigor."

She plucked a small pink rose from the briars. "Perhaps ye should stay here, in yer garden. Yer roses are beautiful, sir."

Her compliment unnerved me, for reasons I didn't want to think about. I walked this path with Fiona and it had nearly destroyed my reputation. I couldn't let that happen again. One's good name was too important in Boston.

"I must retire. I have an errand in the morning."

"Yes, sir."

She stepped past me and walked out of the garden.

You see, Catherine. My heart does belong to you. I will ask you to be mine and we will be happy together. Your father will understand if I don't pursue the law, won't he?

I reached in my jacket and pulled out *Paradise Lost*, opening to a random middle page.

> *Long is the way*
> *And hard, that out of hell leads up to light.*

The words nestled within me like a seed in soil. My restlessness since Father's death would consume me if I didn't direct it. With Catherine by my side, the compass could point with sureness.

Maybe Mary was right. I could stay here, surrounded by a beauty I had sown with my own hands. Perhaps this was what I wanted.

Or was it?

· 8 ·

We turned off of State Street and onto Congress Street. Traffic was light on Beacon Hill, but now thickened as the carriage approached Faneuil Hall. This beautiful building and its surrounding marketplace was one of my favorite spots in the city. A colorful medley of merchants, grocers, street-sellers, musicians, patriots, abolitionists, freedmen, servants, and all manner of patrons. We were near the sea and a pleasant breeze lifted the heat. I was excited by our morning's errand. The goods and foodstuffs we selected today would be delivered Saturday morning.

The driver let us off near Faneuil Hall, and we strolled over to admire its classic beauty. A spot of patriotic fervor for nearly one hundred years, playing a vital role in the days of revolution. I loved the old-fashioned blocky brick façade, the white cupola, and the gleaming brass dome. It was a gateway to all that was good and right about being a son of Boston.

"Let us complete this quickly," Erik said. "Plenty of work awaits us at the office."

I refused to let Constitutional Law discourage my enjoyment. We took up walking sticks and strolled the cobblestones behind the Hall. Quincy Market stretched up before us, its huge fluted columns reminding me of the Parthenon. This was a fairly new structure, built when I was at grammar school. Huge white awnings sprouted from its sides like flat sails, providing shade to those beneath hawking their wares.

"Oil for sale! Lamp oil! Get your whale oil! Fresh off the boat today!"

"Tinker here! Ha'penny for a piece! Tinker here!"

"The West is wild! Dime stories! Scalping Indians! Locomotive robberies!"

We skirted the marble columns, as massive as ships' masts. A festival of performers entertained the crowds. Jugglers vaulted bright rings up to the clouds and a merry traveling band tootled in the square. Children laughed and chased the pigeons around while their mothers nudged prams. Grocer stalls bulged with coconuts and plantains and bananas, brought from tropical places aboard the harbor steamships.

Erik paused at a spice merchant's stall to select cinnamon and pepper. I wandered over to the dime novel cart, stacked high with exotic adventures. The wizened old seller gave me a friendly smile when I picked up the latest Western territory adventure. He indicated a stack of new books.

"Hot off the press, sonny. All the way from London. Two for a nickel, special today."

"Why such a low price?"

"The war, sonny. You wanna see what's new?" He passed me a booklet. The cover read: The Union Song Book. "Get it before the rebs get us, what I say."

I shook my head. "Thank you, sir, but I'll take the Western ones."

He smiled at my two dimes. "You, ah, don't seem the fighting type."

"Fighting is for those who have no other alternative."

"Maybe, or maybe the ones who ain't got their skirts on fire yet." He reached underneath his cashbox and pulled out a sheet of paper. "Hope to see you there."

I took the paper and my books. Erik was arguing prices with a baker, so I sat down on a shady bench in the square.

When I unrolled the paper, I was in for a surprise:

TO ARMS!! TO ARMS!!

GREAT WAR MEETING IN BOSTON

Another meeting of the
citizens in Boston,
to re-enforce their brothers in the field,
will be held at

FANEUIL HALL

10 o'clock on June the 28th!

Speeches from:
Mayor Wightman, Governor Andrew, and Frederick Douglass

COME ONE, COME ALL!

GOD AND COUNTRY CALL!

It was a rally announcement! Yes, this would definitely set Andrew's skirts on fire.

Chuckling, I folded the paper and stuck it in my jacket pocket, right behind *Paradise Lost*.

Too bad the rally was on Saturday, the very day of the gala. It was also at the same time I would be taking Catherine for a drive. There was no way I could attend.

Erik gestured for me, his arms full of parcels. I gathered my books and realized the old seller shoved the little song book in with the other dime novels. Maybe my skirts weren't on fire, but it wasn't easy to pretend this war didn't exist.

Erik shifted a box aside. "Our errand is finished. Call the carriage."

I hailed our carriage from the edge of Congress Street, taking out the little watch. We had been here an hour. That was all the time I was granted away from the office. Damn our schedules. I wanted to take up my stick and stroll the rest of the morning away.

Erik and I loaded up the carriage, the driver strapping our parcels on the back. The morning light upon the Quincy Market columns was beautiful, shafts of warm summer sunlight alighting the square.

"Oh, and Daniel? I have something for you." Erik came around to my side of the carriage. He took out a small white box. "You cannot propose on Saturday without being prepared, can you?"

Inside was a gold ring. I stared at it, feeling nothing at all. My mind shut down, as if someone dropped a curtain on a tired play.

"Don't be afraid of committing your life to Miss Washburn." He snapped the lid shut and handed it to me. "She does care for you. I have seen it in her eyes and the way she carries herself. We are not all as fortunate, you know. To have found our future wife."

Oh, God in heaven. Wrong, all wrong. My eyes hurt. The heat, the light from the square. All I could do was nod.

"Struck dumb, are we?" Erik laughed the way he used to. "Well, if you meet any other pretty girls, you send them to my table next time."

"You know I will." I found my voice again. "It's time to go to the office now."

"Yes, we shall be even later than you manage to be."

I forced a grin at the joke, but barely kept up the conversation in the carriage. Erik was describing the desserts and fruits for display in the dining room. The little box sat beside me, like a mechanical engine that accelerated my life to a speed I did not want to take. Too fast, too fast.

Predictably, my brother had prepared more assignments. I studied chapters four, five, and six of the Constitutional Law book the remainder of the morning. I kept rereading the same paragraphs over and over. My mind was on so many other things, but one memory kept surfacing, like a buoy on the tides.

Deep blue uniforms, shiny brass buttons. And the songs of drum and fife, a heartbeat and a whistle.

At noon, I declined an invitation to join the law partners at the hotel restaurant. I grabbed some bread and cheese and a slice of dried beef, nibbling as I made my way down Washington Street.

The hazy sky turned gray, smoky, dense, and a light misty rain began to fall. I looked up through the buildings, up into the rain. It brought the scent of the sea.

Through the rain appeared the tall pointed cupola of the Old North Church. Drops of rain splashed on its red brick and churned the soil in the alley beside it. Several Union officers huddled beneath umbrellas at the entrance to the church, smoking cigars and dropping ash onto the muddy sidewalk. They were protecting a white sign that proclaimed: "Recruitments Here." I wondered if they would be present at the rally.

A familiar face appeared amidst the soldiers. I smiled and walked right up behind him.

"Fine weather, David!"

"Good grief, Daniel, you gave me a fright." David turned from the officers and laughed. "Don't stand out in the rain, now. Come into the church."

The officers waved to him when he escorted me up the church steps.

"Do you know those men?" I asked as we pulled open the doors.

"Some. They are the ones who encourage Andrew's dead fish talk."

We stood in the entrance to the church, a vast buttermilk-colored hall of straight-backed box pews, wide aisles, and a magnificent carved pulpit. An ornate gas chandelier threw smoky light upon the scene, while the rain tipped the windows and pattered the roof above. I hadn't been in here in years, and it was as beautiful as I remembered it.

"I know Andrew's dead fish talk can be compelling, but –"

"He is going to war. And I am going with him."

The firmness of his voice shocked me. My good friend, a boy merely. The solid weight of his declaration made me feel excited and uneasy. I shook my head and tried to laugh it off.

"You cannot be serious, David."

"There are three days before the rally. You think I shouldn't go?"

"None of us should fight. What reason have we?"

He left my side and started walking down the center aisle. "Look around you, Daniel. We live in a place of God's favor. We won the war of Independence. My great-grandfather fought as a young man right out of Germany. He believed so strongly in this country that he called it a second Holy Land. He spread the word of God the rest of his days."

"You will make a fine minister, David. As fine as your great-grandfather was."

"That is not my point." He reached the pulpit. He looked regal. "We anger God now. The North is losing. We can't win the fight against these southern heathens, these devil's men who believe in torturing others."

"You mean slavery?" I said, surprised at the passion in his voice.

"Of course!" He came down from the pulpit, a white leather Bible in his hands. "This Bible will come to war with me, Daniel. I have read the truth inside. If I am ever to be a man of God, then I must go to the men who fight for God. I must be there."

I felt the gravity of his words like no other. I had never seen anyone so certain, so intense about a cause. Father cared about law, but this . . . this was something different.

"So, I wager you're not continuing on to the Divinity School."

"School?" He laughed, a crazy laugh. "And what school teaches me about life, Daniel? What good am I in a desk when I could be in the field?"

There would be no shaking his opinion. I managed a smile.

"You told me an hour after we first met that you were going to be a minister. I honor where that path leads you."

"Thank you, Daniel." He looked up at the carved balconies, the light, the rain. "The battlefield will be my pulpit now, the place where I shall preach and help the soldiers. They endure such great hardships."

"The ones who fight think freedom is worth it."

"My father had a saying that I never forgot. Love is worth living for, but freedom is worth dying for."

I reached into my waist-coat and looked at the little watch. "It seems I must return to the law office."

He clasped my hand. "In God we trust, Daniel. He brings rain when He knows our garden needs it."

I almost could not speak. "You'll do good work, David. Take care."

"And you."

I waved to the Union officers, heading out into the rain. I wondered if Mr. Gage's cousin still believed in God after his friend died.

Did he think freedom was worth dying for?

· 9 ·

"After you, Miss Washburn."

I held the carriage door open as she swept in, faint summery perfume alighting the air. She looked beautiful, light as a confection in her butter-yellow walking dress and pearls. She peeked at me from beneath her straw hat, adjusting the satin bow at her chin.

"Are we going to spend all day in the carriageway?"

This was going to be a good morning. "Perhaps not, my lady."

I took my seat next to her and the drive began. I was tired from the past several days of harrowing hours at work. More Constitutional Law tests, more ledger-book figures, more studying of the local laws and Federal laws. My brain burst with all the information.

For three nights I tried to leave the house and speak to Andrew or Matthew, but to no avail. Mother kept Mary in the kitchen and me in the parlor. Both confined to our respected duties. It saddened me I would not see my friends again. There would be many empty desks at Harvard in September.

"Oh, look!" Catherine pointed a gloved finger at a passing scene. "It is Miss Tavington and her mother."

Thank God Fiona wasn't with them. After those days of fiasco she was sent out to be their new servant.

"Wasn't she an acquaintance of yours once, Daniel?"

It hadn't been a fiasco to me, only a brief affection, a misunderstanding. I was young and stupid. I still felt foolish about the entire incident.

"Yes, our fathers were old school-fellows. She hasn't called upon us since I've been back from university this summer."

"You are returning in the fall, aren't you?"

"To Harvard? Yes, Catherine. You need not fear I will run off to go West."

"I know you read those trashy little books. But I believe in your future, Daniel. You will go far in this world, as long as you focus on your dreams."

Well, this conversation certainly wasn't going as I'd hoped. I meant to propose and she lectured me. I was tired of others talking to me rather than with me. Funny how no members of my class desired to see me as an equal, while my North End friends saw me as nothing but an equal.

"Catherine, I have dreams the same as others. Why, this is a perfect time for big dreams. Look at the young men running off to war, for example."

"Oh, please. Your brother sent me a note the other day."

"He did? What did he write?"

"Nothing of true importance. But he did mention you have a tendency to speak of the war more freely than you should."

"And why not? It is happening now!"

"Because the entire subject is indecent, Daniel." Her eyes hardened, hands clasped firmly in her lap. "You indicated you'd be civil towards me."

"I am being civil. You are seeing it incorrectly."

"You know what, Daniel? I knew you would find some way of ruining this morning for us. I care for you, but I cannot be treated this way."

"Stop being so unreasonable, Catherine. Look at what is happening. My own Mother doesn't support my dreams and wishes."

"Perhaps you should listen to her. She seems to have more interest in your future than you do."

That was it. I grabbed my walking stick and thumped the roof of the carriage.

"Stop!"

My request was immediately granted, for we were on Tremont Street by the Common and traffic had swelled. I opened the carriage door.

"Daniel! For heaven's sake, what are you doing?"

"Good-bye, Catherine." I tipped my hat to her. "Consider our relation ended. I have no wish to see you in private again."

"Daniel, wait!"

Her shouts were lost in the noise of the traffic as I darted across the street and escaped beneath the leafy boughs of the Common. I did not turn back and knew then I never would. I didn't belong here and I didn't want to be a lawyer. I didn't want to have my dreams crushed any longer, mixed into the filth beneath the wheels of all those who thought they knew me better than I knew myself.

"Well, Daniel," I muttered. "This is it. Time to do what's right."

I yanked out the pocket-watch. It was twenty past ten. The rally had begun. But I could still make it. The gala was tonight, but I would be home before they set out the first fruit platter.

I felt light, buoyed by summer breezes, as I hurried through the park. The morning was gorgeous and some passersby paused to wave at me. I barely recognized their faces and sped up my steps. The city was busy today, the traffic sluggish like a brackish tide, the pedestrians slowly making their way about. My legs hurt with the exertion, but I kept going.

I reached the other side of the Common and met up with Congress Street. At last! I felt so joyous I began to laugh. Ah, my dear Catherine. I thought I was to call you wife, but I am not ready. And, I no longer cared what Erik or Mother thought. I had to do what was right for me, not for them.

Rounding the corner was Faneuil Hall and the marketplace. I smiled broadly, lungs breathing in the clear ocean breeze. Fat seagulls circled the square, squawking at me when I crossed the street and strode up to the wide double entrance. Several tables flanked the Hall where Union soldiers and raggedly clad Negroes shouted their causes.

"I fought with the three-month men!"

"Hear ye! Cast down the dragon of slavery!"

North End ruffians milled about and policemen chatted near the doors. I went past them and hurried up the steps. I threw open the doors and escaped inside the Hall.

"Am I late?" I asked no one in particular. A worker removed his pipe and pointed at a large brass band near the front of the Hall.

"You ain't late. They're getting started."

An officer in blue wool stepped before the band, and they struck up a marching tune I hadn't heard before. Some hummed along, several clapping in time with the music. The Hall was magnificently decorated in giant swaths of bunting, hung like curtains from the high rafters. The crowd inside was impressive, numbering in the hundreds. I squeezed between the workers, servants, sailors, shopkeepers, chimney sweeps, merchants, captains, and students of the city.

Large signs hoisted high, painted with exclamations. Free the Negroes! Kill the rebs! Stop the war! Many waved little flags. We all faced the rear of the Hall, where a twenty-foot table decorated with rosettes and flags sat upon a makeshift platform. More Union soldiers and officers, distinguished by their immaculate uniforms and gleaming sabers, stood at the table.

God, it was hot. I loosened my collar, but we were packed like sausages in casing. I was jostled and bumped, stepped on and nudged.

The band ended and a mild applause followed them when they retreated to a corner. Several fellows moved an impressive podium from the side of the wall over to the center of the platform. I squeezed along the length of the wall, searching amidst the masses. The orations were about to begin.

Mayor Wightman assumed the podium, stroking his beard and staring out at us. His speech began, an introduction to the rally. I couldn't hear much, for many members of the crowd whispered and chatted. I searched amongst them, but couldn't find the Pierce brothers or David. I sighed loudly, my efforts in vain.

I hadn't heard a word Mayor Wightman shouted to us, but now his time was through and Governor Andrew ascended the podium. The applause accompanying his entrance could have drowned out Vulcan's forge. He was popular and even removed his top hat to the masses before him. They waved hats and caps in return, fluttering little flags and whipping banners about in a frenzy.

"I am here merely as a mouthpiece," the governor began. "I serve to introduce the great man you have been waiting for. You are all sons of Boston, of the greatest city on this Northern soil. Eighty-six years ago, your grandfathers died for your independence outside these historic walls. And, within these walls, they spoke of democratic principles that we still swear our lives by!"

Principles, indeed. A great shout arose and he held out his hands to calm us. It was then I saw a familiar figure leap up, his arms raised in an Indian-like whoop. At last! I shimmied my way through the crowd and came up right beside the jumping heathen. I tapped him on the shoulder, and he nearly knocked me off my feet.

"Daniel Stuart!" Andrew grabbed my arm and yanked me into a tight embrace. "Damn the saints, it's good to see you!"

I laughed and freed myself from his crushing arms. "No more dead fish talk any longer, eh Andrew?"

"Don't mention it to him!" His skinny brother peeked from behind his massive torso. "He might change his mind!"

I felt a tug on my jacket. "And how goes it with you, David?"

"I am glad there is no rain!"

"So, what happened with the lady friend?" Andrew said.

I shrugged. "Let's say she was not the girl for me."

"Perhaps Lady Liberty will be?" Andrew pointed to the podium. "Look!"

Governor Andrew was leaving the stage to vigorous applause. Suddenly, the Hall became so quiet I could easily hear a chair in the rear of the platform scrape its legs backward. A man rose from the chair and walked across the planked floor in such a stately manner he seemed a grand king. Unruly black hair framed a wide craggy face. A face I had never seen before, a face the color of creamed coffee. His nose was wide and bulbous, his large lips pursed. He reached the podium and surveyed us with intense black eyes. Though he was a Negro, he was like no other Negro.

"Brothers!"

I jumped. His voice was like seaside rock, barnacled and weather-beaten. He held his left arm straight out, finger fiercely pointed.

"Free men! All who are here! You listen and you listen with your souls! I address you this lordly morning with a simple plea. You are capable of great things, but one thing I do fear. Our fellow soldiers feel no comfort in the soils of Virginia. They fight alone! They tremble before the shaking guns of the enemy. And this I fear!"

He clasped his fist. Those black eyes found me and I was like glass, as if I had no skin and he saw all.

"This I fear! I fear the cause will desert them, for they are deserting the army! The cause, men of Boston. The cause hungers for blood. The cause hungers for souls. The cause hungers for justice!"

He slammed that great black hand upon the podium. I felt weak, falling against Andrew, supported by my friend's steadfast body.

"I sailed an ocean of bondage. But others have yet to land! When, oh when will the hot sun beat down upon a new day? I awoke this blessed morn with my name and my life as my own. But others have yet to claim theirs! When, oh when will the bright shores of freedom be reached? When, oh when will you be the one to slay the tyrant of slavery!"

The crowd exploded. Hats sailed and flags waved. Bits of confetti and fabric rosettes littered the air like colorful petals. The Negro surveyed us like a benevolent monarch. His gaze enveloped me. I was dizzied by his words, overwhelmed as if my veins were full of golden ale.

Governor Andrew handed the Negro a piece of paper and a pen. He held up these objects like a master scribe. The room magically hushed again.

"I offer you a page and a means to sign thy name. Thy name was the first gift bestowed to you, before thine actions determined thy great worth. Who now, among the honored souls here, will be the first to offer thy name?"

Every single man in the first four rows leapt forward. Andrew vanished from my side, lost in the oceanic surge that stormed towards the platform stairs. I stayed near David when we joined the great tide of men eager to give our names.

A group of highly decorated officers sat at a table on the platform, receiving the lines of fresh recruits. I was squeezed behind David, part of the ascending line. I pulled on his jacket and pointed to the Negro standing at the end of the platform.

"Who is that?"

"Daniel, it's Frederick Douglass. He was a slave and now he is free. He wants all Negroes emancipated."

"You think that could happen?"

David turned around and replied as one who questioned no further. "I would die for his dream. For freedom."

My breath caught and I couldn't move. I . . . I wasn't ready to die. I did want to be with my friends, but I was not them. I couldn't go to war and face death. I didn't want it!

We were fast approaching the platform. The recruitment officers sat at attention, ramrod straight and brisk. I could hear their droning speech to the new recruits.

"Private rank only. Pay is thirteen dollars a month. You will be assigned a regiment at the railroad depot tomorrow. Private rank only. Pay is thirteen dollars a month . . ."

There was a line several men deep behind me. I began to struggle against the current, but the men were not happy and prevented me from leaving the platform. I tried to get beyond their outstretched arms, but it did no good. Some brute shoved me in the back and I pitched forward towards the table.

I faced a recruitment officer.

He was thin, thinner than a man should be. His teeth leached up into his gums like advancing waters and he smoked a half-dead cigar. The familiar Union blue forage cap was cocked on his forehead and his dusty sack-coat was unbuttoned, revealing a dirty white undershirt. I looked down at the sign-up sheet. The pen waited.

"Come on, Daniel!" Andrew grabbed the pen and signed with a

flourish beneath my nose. "Your turn!"

I stared at his grubby signature. "No. I don't think I can go."

A deep voice rumbled behind me. "What hath staid thy hand, young man? What prevents thee from fighting for the cause?"

Frederick Douglass, the great orator of the morn, reached my side. His eyes were quiet, deep, searching. I felt a wave of unexpected boldness.

"I wanted the adventure, but I don't think I can fight like my friends. I . . . I guess I don't believe in the cause."

He regarded me thoughtfully. "You have fortitude, young man, to be so honest. You are dressed well and speak well. You have had life handed to you."

"My family has been fortunate."

"It is a great thing to accept hardship. You must have faith, wisdom, and courage." He gestured to my friends. "You will be strong together."

"But it is war. We could die."

He picked up the pen, stroking the long white feather. "Yes, my brother, you could. But you always have the freedom to choose how you live."

My path. My friends. My choice.

And my life.

I took the pen from him. Douglass watched me, watched with those black, boundless, hell-deep eyes.

I signed my name.

Thy will be done.

· 10 ·

"Until tomorrow, then!"

"Tomorrow!"

Andrew's farewell echoed into the night, a jubilant shout that rustled up the pigeons and stirred the joy within me. I stuck my hands in my pockets and pulled out a small white box. It was the little ring I wanted to give to Catherine. Well, it was not meant to be. She loved me for my future, not for me alone.

I looked back towards the North End, towards my friends. They were my comrades, for we headed into a future glory. I longed to be with them, and the final hours before our scheduled rendezvous at the train depot tomorrow stretched like a desert. God, I didn't want to go home.

Might as well get through it. I looked a sight, having spent the remainder of my day engaged in a game of town-ball. My coat and trousers were dirty, my shoes scuffed. With Andrew, though, my team won the game. Andrew was the best man to have on a team, I thought while ascending Mount Vernon Street. The Hill was lively tonight, carriages rumbling up and down the cobblestones, laughter in open doorways, plenty of lighted windows. A cheery scene.

I headed up the carriageway and entered the house in a servant's fashion, through the stables. Passing through the coal-shed, I came into the dark, smoky, and crowded kitchen. Cook shouted orders from the side-board to the dozen girls-of-work scurrying about. I pulled my hat a little tighter about my ears and hunched my shoulders when I made my way through. At the rear of the kitchen I managed to squeeze towards the door and grab the handle.

"Mr. Stuart!"

I nearly shut the door in her face, Mary almost dropping her empty plate. She looked back down the hall.

"Yer brother is upstairs, sir. Ye might not want him to see ye like that."

I brushed past her and disappeared up the hall before Erik could come down and find me. No guests had arrived, but the parlor was filling with servants and chairs were moved into a corner for the musicians. I pardoned a servant for an extra stick-pin and left the parlor before anybody could see me. I encountered no-one else in the hall, either, and shut the back door behind me with a great sense of relief.

The garden was quiet tonight, a prelude to the evening's festivities that I so desperately needed. Blessed silence, quiet and low breeze. I walked to the back of the garden, over to the bench. Would I see my home again? I pinched a small white rosebud from its stem and weaved the stick-pin between its thorns. Soon enough I'd ready myself, but I was grateful for these moments alone. The final rays of sunset disappeared and I was bathed in shadow, the roses luminescent like stars.

"Sir?"

"Good evening, Mary."

She came into the garden, her plate full of little fruits and cheeses. "I thought ye might like some refreshments."

"Thank you." I looked up into the night sky. Airy masses of dark clouds splayed across the constellations. "Are the guests arriving?"

"Aye, they are."

"Mary, you remember my Bull and Boar friends, I'm sure."

"I know Andrew, o' course. He goes regularly."

I laughed. "I suppose he does. They're good fellows. Andrew, his brother Matthew, and David. Well, this morning I broke off an engagement with Miss Washburn, and joined at Faneuil Hall."

"So, ye went to the rally with 'em, then, sir."

"Yes." I paused, fingering the little rose. "Yes, I went to the rally and I signed up. I shall be a private – a soldier – in the Union army."

"If ye'll pardon me, that sounds like madness, sir."

"I am mad, I know it. Mad to realize I did something like that, but maybe also mad to realize I can't be here anymore. I don't want to be a lawyer, I didn't want to marry Catherine."

"But sir, ye have it all here. This is yer life."

"I know it's hard to understand. You have no choice in life and I have every choice and . . . I'm leaving tomorrow. I meet my friends at the train station at dawn. We're going to war."

"No sir, ye can't be leaving. Ye're wrong."

"Wrong?" I felt angered. "I am not wrong. I signed up today and I am going, Mary. You can stay here with my mother."

I was more definite of my decision than I'd been all day. I walked past her and towards the back door of the house.

"Daniel?"

I turned on her so quickly I nearly knocked her over. "You are out of your place. Return to the kitchen and assist the cook. I will never see you again."

"Wait." She grabbed my sleeve, a gesture so impertinent it froze me. "I want to come with ye."

"You can't come to war. Please . . . leave me be."

I went back into the house. It was a great relief to close the door behind me, shutting the garden for the last time. The sense of peace surprised me. I assumed the garden brought me peace. Maybe it was only an escape from the wretchedness of the rest of my life. I'd sat on that bench and taken comfort in the beauty of the landscape at so many times of sorrow and desperation. But, what if I could journey forth into a new life? One where I never needed a place to escape?

I strode down the hall with great purpose. I made the right choice when I signed my name. I made the choice to follow my life and live it fully, never needing a place to escape from its wonders.

"There you are, brother!"

Erik appeared from the china closet, a pair of champagne flutes brimming with sparkling golden liquid. I took one and tossed it back quickly. Erik laughed.

"Starting early, are we? Mother is looking for you. You are quite the young devil, you know that? I stalled the Washburns in the parlor."

Oh, Catherine. I'd nearly forgotten. "She was not right for me."

"You didn't have to leave her in traffic, you know."

"Thank you, Father. Appreciate the tip."

"Don't talk to me like that," he snapped. "For God's sake, go upstairs and get dressed. And stop being so rude and uncivil. We are hosting this evening, so act like it."

"As if I wanted this stupid party, anyway."

He shook his head. "What the hell has happened to you? For the past two weeks you've been the most ungrateful louse I've ever seen. Why? You don't want to be a lawyer; that much is plain. So teach law. But look at your life as it is now! Not two blocks from here is the dirtiest slum in the city. We have it made, Daniel."

"Oh, we do, do we?"

"Yes!" He clapped me on the shoulder. "Find a way to be happy with your current situation, no matter what it is. Otherwise, what's the point of success?"

I handed him the champagne glass. "I'll be ready shortly."

I could feel his puzzled gaze on me when I slipped past the parlor door and climbed the stairs. What was the point of our success, of our good name? Surely not to bask in our greatness while others suffered. While others fought and died.

When I reached my chamber, it occurred to me I might understand why my friends wanted to fight.

My manservant helped me into the black formal dress suit, scrubbed my face, oiled my hair. I ignored his comment that there would be plenty of laundry on Monday. I wouldn't be here, and the thought made me smile. After the rose was pinned in place, I gazed confidently into the mirror. I did pass for a gentleman, no matter how ill that title described me now. When a knock sounded at the door, I knew exactly who it was.

Mother regarded me with an approving, but critical eye. "Mr. Barkins does exceptional work."

"So does Dunstan's," I said, admiring her deep green ballgown. "You are more beautiful than any other lady of Boston."

"No buttering me tonight, Daniel. Erik told me what happened between you and Miss Washburn this morning. I'll discuss it with you tomorrow."

"I'm looking forward to it."

She reached her hand back and slapped me. "You disgrace your family, Daniel. You disgrace me."

I said nothing. All I could think of was that I had to be at the railroad depot at seven o'clock in the morning. There would be no discussion. I didn't take another breath until after she stormed from the room.

Carriages pulled up the cobblestones, and the house was filling with guests. When I came downstairs, the valet greeted Miss Tavington and her young charge. I hoped they wouldn't look up, but I was not so lucky. Fiona's eyes on me were enough to make me want to run past them and go right to the depot. Tomorrow morning could not come soon enough.

A pretty waltz began in the parlor and I squeezed in between several male guests to watch the dancers. Mother and Mr. Gage floated past, smiling fixedly at one another like younger lovers. Mother seemed to have forgotten her anger. But the portrait of Father remained above the fireplace, Catherine whispering to a female friend beneath it. I felt nothing when I looked at Miss Washburn, her beauty suddenly revealing a cruel twist to her lip, a harshness to her whisper. How strange I had not seen that before!

Mr. Washburn stood by the sideboard, helping himself to the array of dainty sweets. Though I had displayed ungentlemanly conduct towards his daughter, he motioned me closer. Surprised, I made my way over to him.

"Good evening, Daniel." His handshake was warm and his smile genuine. "A fine party, I must say. Care for a bit of sugar?"

I accepted and we stood silently, watching the dancers and the string quintet seated in the opposite corner, dressed finely and playing well.

Several servants traversed the room, offering wine, sherry, and brandy on silver trays. I helped myself to several. Washburn chuckled.

"When a man drinks like that, he's either enjoying himself or wishes to forget himself."

"I think you are right on both accounts, sir."

"One thing you may wish to forget comes to mind."

If he meant Catherine, he didn't say so. I felt uneasy, half-expecting him to slice my words into ribbons. But I could not think of something to say that would smooth our acquaintance. I stared into my empty wineglass.

"Mr. Washburn, I must apologize –"

He shrugged, a gesture that astounded me. "I have tried to point you in the direction you are meant to go. I am telling you this since Edward is not here to convey it."

"I fully appreciate Father's choice, but I say now, and have felt for some time, that it is not what I want."

Washburn swallowed his wine. "Daniel, are you sure what you want?"

I gave an exasperated laugh. "I am seventeen, sir. Do I have to decide right now?"

He put his arm about my shoulder and spoke low, too low for anyone to hear but myself.

"Losing your father was not easy, and you took it the hardest of all. It is your grief that makes you hesitant, not your youth, Daniel. You wanted to drop out of school and run out West. I think you should follow Edward's will, and be grateful for his choice."

A sudden surge of angered energy coursed through me. I plunked the wineglass down on the sideboard.

"I am entitled to free will, Mr. Washburn."

The waltz ended and guests applauded the dancers. I was more alone than ever in my convictions, but my faith did not waver.

I retreated to the library. A few gentlemen milled about, and I performed the customary greetings and polite bits of conversation. They soon finished their cigars and wandered towards more social rooms, so I was able to enjoy the quietness. I reached in my jacket and pulled out

Paradise Lost. There was a line I read, that I turned to again:

*What in me is dark
Illumine, what is low raise and support;
That to the height of this great argument
I may assert eternal Providence,
And justify the ways of God to men.*

Grief did not make me hesitant about the path I chose, though I did miss Father terribly. But my family did not understand me, their lack of insight wounding me like a bullet. Why should I justify my choices? If I followed their rule, I'd be doomed to a stuffy office, away from soil and light and sun. All the natural world would be lost, and I'd wither.

I tucked the book back in my jacket. Some part of me felt comforted by Milton's poem. Perhaps I could begin to understand it after all.

The rest of the gala proceeded as well as could be expected. I stayed near the library, smiling and chatting amiably with whomever chanced to walk by. I caused neither additional fuss nor insult to the Stuart name. At one time, Mr. Gage sought me out, but I merely thanked him for coming and hoped he had a safe drive home.

Thus, my evening passed and the hour grew late. I was tired and the wool suit itched. Musicians packed up their violins and retired for the night. No other guests remained but the Washburns. I stood in the parlor doorway, surveying the remains of the food trays and the empty crystal glasses. A maid appeared from the kitchen and started gathering the plates.

"Well, I wanted to thank you, Mrs. Stuart, for such a lovely evening," Mr. Washburn purred when the valet helped him into his great coat.

"I am so glad you came," Mother said. "You both made it a wonderful event."

Catherine tied her bonnet. "Yes, the evening was definitely the most enjoyable part of my day."

I ignored her snooty look and reached into my waistcoat. The little pocket-watch ticked in my hand, smooth gold face like a coin. I held it out.

"I appreciate your gift, Mr. Washburn, but I will not be needing it any longer."

He was surprised. "I beg your pardon, Daniel? It was to help you remember to get to work on time."

"I have learned the value of time, Mr. Washburn. Thank you for assisting me."

He gave me a smile, and I suppose he assumed I'd accepted Father's will. He took the watch. Mother looked far less than pleased, but Erik smiled.

"So I won't have to wake you on Monday morning?"

"Absolutely, Erik. You needn't bother yourself any longer."

The Washburns left and Mother headed up the staircase without a goodnight to either of us. Erik gestured for me and I followed him outside. We waved the Washburn carriage good-bye and stayed for a moment underneath the portico.

Erik brought out two cigars, struck a match, and we enjoyed a good smoke in the summer night. I inhaled the sweet, spicy scent and looked up at the stars. The night was clear, bright, a moon of great fullness.

I looked over at my brother and felt I would weep. I couldn't tell him. He loved me, and I sensed that beneath his decisions he desired my happiness. But I couldn't tell him.

"You think Father watches over us?" he said quietly.

I nodded. "Yes, I do."

"And grandfather with him, the crazy bastard."

"He was, wasn't he?" I gave him a slight punch in the shoulder. "Like his grandson."

"Indeed!" Erik laughed. "You angered Mother tonight, for her to not even wish us good night. I would be on my guard tomorrow."

"Thanks for the tip. I sincerely mean it."

He stubbed out his cigar. "Well, good night Daniel."

"Good night."

He started to go into the house, then reached over and took my shoulder. "She doesn't believe in you, but I do."

I couldn't look at him. "Thank you, Erik."

When he went back inside, I was alone. I looked up at the stars and saw each one was ringed with a slight aura, like petals around a blossom. And they, in turn, grouped into the shaped constellations, turning across the sky with the seasons. With them guiding me, I could join my friends and journey from home.

Though I leave my garden, I am never alone.

· 11 ·

I slept an hour, and then was awake with a candle, packing my leather bookbag. I grabbed the clothes I'd worn to the rally, brushed dirt into the lavatory bowl, and straightened the wrinkles. Into the bag went an extra white shirt, wool socks from last winter, and as many handkerchiefs as I could find.

A small daguerreotype of my family in its tintype frame nestled in the clothing, a smoky gray portrait taken when we realized Father was dying. I added matches, stamps, several sheets of writing paper, and my favorite stylus pen. Oh, and the forty dollars from my two weeks of work at the office.

No need for shave balm or hair oil. I struggled to think of what else I might need – what were a soldier's possessions? I had to admit my ignorance, but I did remember a bar of soap, a comb, my dime novels, and *Paradise Lost*. Matthew would chuckle.

At the chiming of the six o'clock hour, I put on a faded bowler hat, took up my bookbag and closed my chamber door for the final time. Quiet footsteps descended the back staircase. I was awake with the servants on a Sunday morning.

The stable-groom was brushing horses when I happened upon him. My request for the train depot came as a surprise, but he complied and readied the open-air brougham.

Presently, the little carriage drove down the carriage-way. I turned in the seat and stared at my home on the Hill, a single candle flame in an upper window. I wondered if it was Mary. Did she still want to join me?

Within a moment, the bricks and columns of my home vanished behind its bow-front neighbors on the street. I wondered if I would see it again.

Boston was quiet, a hazy summer dawn. It was like the morning after a storm. The mist carried the smell of the sea, and my breath caught.

I was leaving. I was leaving my home and my family and I hadn't said good-bye. They would wake in an hour to ready for church and I wouldn't be there.

A few minutes later, the train depot appeared through the mist. I was more nervous than on an exam-day in Rhetoric class. Perhaps I might have tugged on the driver's coat and asked him to ferry me home, were it not for a familiar figure standing on the platform, a jacket thrown over his shoulders. He was the first one I saw, but then others approached the depot from the opposite side and by the time we pulled up, a good-sized crowd assembled.

Andrew sidled up to the carriage door as if he was strolling about the Common.

"Fine morning, ain't it Mr. Stuart?"

"Indeed," I smiled. "Are you here to regale me with more of your dead fish talk, Mr. Pierce?"

"You want some?" He laughed. "Hey, Matty! David! Look who showed up!"

I turned to the driver. "Should Mrs. Stuart or Erik Stuart ask of my whereabouts, tell them you brought me here."

The driver nodded, and I swung down to the platform with my bookbag. All three school-fellows gathered about me, inspecting my plain clothes and plain bag.

"To think Daniel Stuart, Boston's golden boy, is down to nothing but socks and soap," Andrew guffawed.

David showed me a Bible, the same one I'd seen him with at the church. "You don't need much, right Daniel?"

Matthew fingered my jacket. "We'll receive uniforms at the training camp, so you won't have to wear this for longer than six weeks."

"Six weeks?" I repeated. "I've never even owned the same jacket for six weeks!"

The three of them laughed, and Andrew gave me a playful slap on the shoulder. When the carriage pulled away, I didn't look back. Andrew's teasing, David's smile, and Matthew's wry jabs cheered me, and excitement crept into my heart. We *were* going to be soldiers!

"What camp are we going to?" I said.

"Fort Ellsworth," Andrew answered. "I think it's in Virginia."

I stared at him. "We are going to Virginia?"

"Where did you think the army was?" David could barely speak, he was laughing so hard.

"Attention! Attention!"

Quieting our amusement, we looked to the end of the platform. A single officer in full dress uniform stood beside a small table.

"Gentlemen, I am Captain Gates. Welcome to the first part of your journey as soldiers in the Army of the Potomac. The train, destination Washington city, arrives in five minutes. Anyone who wishes to be a passenger must line up and sign your name."

He tapped a paper tablet with his finger. The crowd, which had now grown to thirty men, more or less assembled into a line with Andrew being the lucky one directly in front. He turned back and snickered to us. Captain Gates frowned.

"Sign, if you would."

One by one, we all signed. It was different than the rally, with the growing light and the sea-scented fog. I wrote my signature beneath David's and joined my friends in peering down the line of tracks.

We didn't have long to wait. A shrill blast cut through the fog like a lighthouse bell. The locomotive belched up the tracks, drowning the smell of the ocean with its coal odors. It eased beside the platform like a weary draft horse and sighed with a great hiss. The conductor peered down from his sooty perch and gestured to the crowd.

"Aboard for Washington City!"

I felt a rush of adventure as the hot, pushing crowd clamored to get on the train. This was no luxurious conveyance, but a livestock cattle car complete with a straw floor and rickety boarded walls.

The four of us squeezed into the far corner of the cattle car and took up residence on hay bales. Andrew stood while the rest of us sat at his feet, our luggage tucked against our knees.

Matthew pulled the collar of his jacket around his chin. "Tell me we're not going to go the whole way in a cattle car."

Andrew snapped a loose board in the corner. Through this window appeared the platform and the depot, outlined clearly in the morning light.

"Say good-bye to Boston, boys," Andrew said. "Some of us ain't going to see her again."

I will, I thought. It was nearing time for Mother and Erik to wake. Would they come swinging up the road in a flurry of dust?

I sat in the cattle car and the train blew the whistle and we pulled down the tracks, jerking to life like a mechanical contraption. My family did not come, and we were on our way.

Soon the platform and the depot vanished and we passed from streets I knew into the South End, chugging by rows of skinny homes, boys playing games in the dirt, men and women on their way to the churches. We were off. I swayed on the hay bale and kept rhythm with the beast.

Through Andrew's board I looked out at the pretty farms and villages. Church bells rang out in the towns and, when the hour drew closer to noon and sunlight brightened, the bells sounded again. In one village we saw a wedding and in another we saw a funeral. I hadn't realized how central the church was to village life, but David knew. He enjoyed our trip and hummed some hymns to pass the time.

At noon, the train pulled into a small village depot, we got out and stretched and walked around. I sat on the edge of the platform with the Pierce brothers and shared some of their bread and cheese. David took off his shoes and enjoyed the summer grass. I felt much better, confident of my decision and still excited. We boarded the train again and resumed our journey. Southward, ever southward.

After tiring of the view, I dragged my hay bale to the wall and dozed for a bit. I only slept an hour last night and rested more deeply than I thought I could. I guessed my companions felt similarly, for we all slept the rest of the afternoon.

I awoke in the evening, cramped in the neck and sweaty from the heat. The rocking of the train was jerkier, pitching back and forth like a boat on windy seas. My stomach roiled, and I stood up and managed to stick my head out of the little board before I spit up. The wind ruffled my hair and my throat burned. A strong hand yanked me back inside.

"Ain't got your sea legs yet, sailor?" Andrew said.

"Don't listen to him. You weren't awake an hour ago, when he was doing the same thing," Matthew yawned.

I returned to my uncomfortable seat. The train was picking up speed, so we weren't going to pause for the night. I shared a little more food with my friends, leftover meat and dried bread.

Straw was scattered about in the floor of the cattle car, so I gathered up a bundle and constructed a makeshift bed in the corner. My companions scoffed at the frivolity, preferring the hard wooden boards with their jackets beneath their heads. David said something about life in the wilderness, but I paid him no heed and spent my first night away from home lying in the damp, crunchy straw, looking up beyond the boards to the stars, shifting and swaying with the motion of the train.

Many hours later, Matthew woke me. The train was slowing, it was a little past dawn, and we were pulling into a station in New York City. I was stiff and achy from my rickety bed, and saw when I stood that my body created its own long impression in the straw. I brushed off my wrinkled trousers and straightened my shirt as best I could. David crouched, peeking through the hole in the boards.

"I can see the city! It's much larger than Boston!"

"The population is greater," Matthew remarked when he cleaned his spectacles. "Andrew and I haven't visited since before the war."

"Summer of '59." Andrew rummaged through his bag. "We need to get some food."

"What were you doing in New York City?" I asked.

Matthew shrugged. "We had an uncle who lived here, but he died at Bull Run."

"Oh. I am sorry for your loss."

Andrew laughed. "He was a sour son of a bitch, anyway. I think God needed him."

"Andrew!" David stood up.

"My apologies, Father David." He grabbed the boy and locked him in a head-grip. David struggled, then began to laugh. It wasn't easy to stay angry with Andrew for long.

The train stopped, and we were told we'd be here for only an hour. I was in no mood to leave the car, not knowing quite where anything was in the city, but Matthew wouldn't stop whining about his hunger. So he and Andrew took off for some food. I stayed with David near the train, walking around and exploring.

The rail station was enormous, the grandest I'd ever seen with marble floors, several coal-stoves, and thick wooden columns. I felt uncomfortable in my tattered wear. A well-dressed gentleman reclined on a bench with a newspaper, and I marveled at how things changed in twenty-four hours. I wanted to speak to him, but the hour was drawing to a close.

"Come, Daniel."

David ushered me back to the platform, where I stood in the sunshine and gazed at the substantial city laid out before us. It rose from the hazy morning like a many-headed beast with tall buildings and rows of clapboard houses that sagged so greatly they looked like they were melting. Glass was broken in some windows, and the streets were dirty, small urchins and downcast women hurrying about.

Andrew and Matthew came back with paper sacks full of unusual foods from the neighborhood grocers. Andrew pulled out a strangely shaped bread twisted under and over itself in a bizarre design, with salt grains sprinkled on top. He tore off a piece and handed it to me.

"The Germans call it a pretzel."

It was doughy and warm and salty. I liked it, and enjoyed listening to their tales of wandering about the streets, hearing the many languages spoken.

"Even Irish," Matthew said with his mouth full. "They're everywhere, aren't they?"

I thought of Mary. "Let's get back on the train."

"Don't be in such a hurry," Andrew said. "Hey, look!"

A good-sized crowd of men hurried towards the depot. The train whistle blew and the crowd hurried faster. They carried all manner of luggage.

"More recruits!" said David.

If I was to fight alongside these fellows, it would take a great deal of composure. They were brutish, rough-shod, covered in soot and ink and dust, working-men from factories and printing companies and foundries. They had large chests and arms and thick calloused hands.

One of them stepped from his comrades and gave Andrew a mighty slap on the back.

"Welcome aboard, Jimmy," Andrew laughed. "Get up on the train, you slimy sack of dog feces."

"Nice to see you too, Andrew." Jimmy tossed his bag into the cattle car, then took a running start and vaulted in. "Never thought I'd find your sorry arse back in the city!"

The newcomers crowded our cattle car and the two behind it, grabbing up the straw and hay bales before we could reclaim our former perches. Disgusted, I took off my jacket and sat on the floor, knees tucked under my chin. David noticed my sullenness and tried to cheer me, but I was tired and out of sorts.

A fresh whistle blast pierced my ears, then the locomotive started up and we resumed our journey. I sat by myself, my legs cramping. Andrew, of course, greatly enjoyed our new companions and regaled them with stories of being a student at Harvard. The more rough-and-tumble ones thought it curious, and he held their attention for several hours.

I moved over to the small window where the missing board was, a shaft of sunlight squeezing through. It was enough light, and I took out

Paradise Lost. Matthew, propped against the wall with his skinny legs jutting out before him, whistled to me.

"That isn't *Paradise Lost*, is it?"

"I'm just passing the time."

"You barely passed the exam!"

I chuckled. "I guess I decided to give it another chance. Without a professor's tests."

"Didn't you say something about wanting to be a professor?"

The thought was like a half-remembered dream. I tucked the book in my jacket.

"You know, Matthew, I wanted to drop out of school that first-term."

"Andrew mentioned you wanted to go West."

I rummaged in my bag and pulled out my favorite dime novel. "You ever read these?"

"Daniel, are you serious!" Matthew laughed. "They're nothing but tall tales. No better than Andrew's dead fish talk!"

I elbowed his arm. "It's a short read for being a tall tale."

"Funny. Stick with *Paradise Lost*."

"These tales inspired me, Matthew. I wanted to see our Western territories, head out from the cities and sleep under the stars."

"You wait. There aren't feather-beds in soldier barracks."

I rubbed my back. "I admit I miss my own bed right about now."

"You could have stayed there." He looked down at his hands. "You had it all, Daniel. Why did you come with us?"

I thought about his question for a long while, so long that Matthew was falling asleep. I stared out the little jagged window of the cattle car and watched the world roll past.

Maybe I didn't have it all.

· 12 ·

The conductor's shout floated from the front of the train. "Disembark for Washington City!"

"Chipper fellow," Andrew remarked as he gathered up his things.

I swung my bookbag over my shoulder, cracking several bones in my back. David laughed, and Matthew made some sort of joke about it. I was glad we'd arrived, but I was tired, hungry, sore and weary from traveling. Our uncouth New York neighbors made it difficult to enjoy the last leg of our journey, but we were here.

The cattle car doors threw open, exposing us to the dazzling sunlight. Washington was far cleaner and brighter than New York, the wide streets busy with the morning traffic. The rail depot was beside a half-constructed building, and some men working upon it gazed down at us curiously. It was far warmer than Boston, and I loosened my collar. Upon approaching the South, the June air was damp and humid, without the sea to cool it.

My friends and I stepped down from the train and crossed the platform. A makeshift lean-to was built right across the street from the depot, a hand-painted banner dangling across the front.

ARMY REGISTRATIONS

"That must be for us," Andrew said and promptly walked right over. We followed him, several of the other train passengers joining us.

In the shade of the lean-to was a skinny desk, a man in Federal uniform smoking a pipe and reading a book. He cocked his head at us and stroked his scraggly beard. He looked no cleaner than the officer at the recruitment rally. Several other men in uniform lazed about, chatting and squinting in the sun. Andrew stopped and surveyed the scene, perspiration beading his brow.

"Good morning, sir," he greeted. "Colonel, sir. My comrades and I have arrived from Boston on our way to the fort in Alexandria to learn training for the army, sir."

"Which fort, son?"

Matthew reached in his bag and pulled out some paperwork. "Fort Ellsworth, sir."

"Ah, then you'd best be getting the ferry 'cross the Potomac. Leaves at noon."

"Thank you, sir," I said before Andrew could. "We appreciate your time."

He saluted me and, for the first time, my hand went to my brow. I stood up straighter, locking my knees.

"That settles things," I said. "We need to get to the river."

Andrew cleared his throat. "Matty?"

His brother was far more prepared, for he dug around in his bag again, and pulled out a map. We walked a little ways from the lean-to, gathered around and realized we were a long way from the river. The train depot was on the outside of Washington.

"Let's get started, then." David shouldered his bag. "We wouldn't want to miss the ferry."

Washington reminded me of Boston, with the same large square Federal homes lining the streets and similar post offices, general stores, taverns and blacksmiths. It was not as rowdy as New York, but it was definitely busy. One of its many purposes was made all too clear.

"Damn you, stupid pigs!" Andrew shouted as the umpteenth wagon of soldiers careened past us.

Matthew covered his nose. "I wouldn't want to get sick here."

On most front stoops sat a wounded or recovering soldier, uniform in tatters, a stained bandage on a leg, on an arm, wrapped about his face. Dozens of soldiers milled in various styles of uniform, including many curious fellows with red pants and funny round caps.

"Zouaves," David explained. "They were quite the heroes at Bull Run."

"Make way!"

We scrambled to the side of the street, clearing the way for a large assembly of marching soldiers. These were not the great shiny warriors I'd seen in the regiments of Boston. I saw something in their eyes I hadn't seen in years, not since the famine ships brought the Irish to our shore. Hollowness, deep sadness and sorrow. Alarmed, I caught Andrew's attention.

"What has happened to these men? I see no wounds!"

He shrugged and spit in the dust. "We're losing the war, Daniel. Don't you read the papers? The Richmond campaign is a dastardly mess of things."

"The rebels have a new commander," David said. "They call him the gray fox. He dug in around Richmond and he won't let any Union soldiers through."

I thought of Gus's letter, which I had not forgotten to tuck in amongst my things. He had mentioned a general.

"His name is Lee, right? General Lee?"

"Right, Daniel!" Matthew folded his map. "Robert E. Lee, to be exact. A West Pointer, perfect record and no demerits while there. He fought in the Mexican War and did extremely well. He took command a month ago when Johnston kicked it. It looks like he gives Johnston a run for his money."

He pointed to the soldiers. Nobody laughed or even spoke. The Union Army was near Richmond when Gus wrote. And they hadn't moved since? That was not a good sign.

We soon came upon the river docks and enjoyed drinks and a small meal in the hotel across the street. I sat at the table in a half-awake stupor, sipping warm beer. I had been so excited, but now I was weary to the core. All I could think of was Erik bragging about how Mr. Washburn ordered the same dinner at the hotel. Uneasiness crept over me, and I tried not to think of home.

I set down my empty beer glass and stood from the table. It was noon, yellow and dusty, the sun cutting through the cloudless blue. My shirt stuck to my skin at my collar and sides. The hot heavy moisture in the air made it hard to breathe.

The river was laid out flat and glassy, a wide ribbon of slowly moving gray water curving around the city like a beribboned brim. A large white ferry paddled up to the docks, massive wheels churning the sluggish waves. Thick smokestacks belched smoke like a train. Men onboard grabbed ropes and lashed the great boat to the pier. A gangplank extended out and slammed the wooden boards of the dock. As the horn blew, we gathered our things and made our way down to the dock, gaping at the huge steamship.

"That's her," Matthew said. "Next stop is Alexandria, Virginia."

"I think I see it on the other side of the river," David said.

A tanned, burly man with a torn jacket lounged on a barrel at the foot of the gangplank. All four of us approached, but I stepped out in front a few feet. He stirred from his perch and peered at me.

"Where you lads heading?"

"Alexandria." I stood straighter. "This ferry does cross the river, does it not?"

He regarded me. "Lemme see your hands."

"My hands?"

"Come on, fish. Yer hands."

I held out my hands, palms up. He took one look at them and laughed louder than I'd ever heard anyone in my life. I drew back my arms at once.

"Why, yer as pink as the day you dropped from your mama's quinny, ain't ya?"

"I beg your pardon?"

I made as if to move past him, but he stuck out his leg. I tripped and landed on my knees. The man laughed harder. I rose to my feet in time to see help arrive.

"Hey, you!" Andrew went up to the man. "You let my friend board or I'll throw you in!"

"Ho ho! Those rebs better watch out!"

Andrew's green eyes clouded black and he made as if to shove his cocky opponent, but Matthew held him.

"We're soldiers in the Army of the Potomac," Matthew explained calmly. "We must cross the river."

"Nobody boards my boat until they pay. Hand over the coin."

David stepped between the Pierce brothers, pulled open his small leather purse and handed the ferry captain four dollars. The man examined the money with the glee of a pirate.

"What have we here! I ain't seen this kind of money since the war started!"

"You jest," I said.

"You callin' me a liar, pretty boy? You're stupid. You're all stupid. But I was in Mexico." He leaned closer to me. "You see fish, these notes is rare about here. Dollars hard to come by. Whatever hoighty-toighty place you layabeds come from, it don't matter. I seen you all, with your clean hands. And I seen you on the way back, on stretchers with yer insides laid wide open. Be one of the lucky ones comin' back in a wood box, eh? Get your arses on the boat and ferry across. But 'tis the land of the dead on the other side."

"Step aside," Andrew declared. "I'm going first."

The man chuckled, but he let us by. I felt ill again, but when I stepped onto the ferry and felt the tilting of the boat beneath my weight, I was more at ease. I'd spent a lifetime near the ocean and was familiar with boats. I skirted the side deck and went to the front of the ferry. My friends followed and we sat down on old wooden crates. Matthew shook his head.

"That fellow, he's a loony one."

"He doesn't think we'll make it," said David.

"He's not right," Andrew said. "In the head, you know."

I went to the railing, leaning out over the river. Crazy old man. He saw too much of war. But it was hard to forget his squeaky laughter.

Our passage was uneventful. Andrew played with a small wooden disk attached with string and sprung it across the deck. David also brought an entertainment – a tiny rendition of the popular draughts game, complete with miniature game board and miniscule red and black painted pieces. He and Matthew started up a game.

I strolled about the ferry deck. The sun was hot, and the river smelled fresh and earthy, like the soil in a forest. The breeze lacked a salty tang, but it cooled the sweat at my brow.

Presently, the other bank came into view, a rolling ledge of straight brick homes lined up side by side. Like soldiers, I thought. The dock stretched out and we eased up beside it. A mellow bell clanged, and several men rushed forward to grab up the ropes and anchor the vessel. The ferry captain swung down from his perch.

"Just so's you know, I'm the only way home."

Andrew banged Matthew in the ribs. "Come on, Matty. Let's get off this durned ferry!"

"I'll be seein' you soon, in a box or on yer two feet, fish." The captain tossed a rope to a fellow on the dock and walked down the gangplank. "There's only two ways you gonna get back home to yer Yankee mama."

"I'd rather be in the box!" Andrew huffed.

My feet touched upon Southern soil, a strange red dust like the planet Mars. My breath caught. I looked back at the ferry captain. He belonged in a madhouse. I'd pay fifty cents to watch a scuffle between him and my hot-headed friend.

But I knew enough to realize he was right. I was at war, but I could leave. I could still walk away, and the captain could take me home.

"The captain is right, Andrew." I looked at my friend. "We are in the South now. You really want to go home in a wood box?"

Crossing his arms, Andrew glared at me. "Don't you be catching the yellow!" he spat. "I ain't got friends like that."

The ferry captain gestured up the gangplank. "I seen yer hands," he called. "You don't have to do this, fish!"

Andrew suddenly grabbed my jacket and half-dragged me away from the ferry. I struggled against him.

"Andrew, let me be!"

"Damn you, Daniel! You're too soft! Is that what money does to a man, eh?"

I wrestled from him and spun in the dirt. The resulting cloud got into my nose, my eyes. I coughed and leaned against my knees, sputtering into the ground. I stood up, wiping my nose. Andrew was smirking.

"I know you, rich boy. You were gonna leave us, gonna go right back on that boat."

I kicked dirt at him. "And so what if I was? You had no right to stop me!"

He pointed straight at me. "Then I call you a coward. What, you wanna go home to that cur of a brother and your stupid cunny mother? Ha!"

I ducked his first blow, but caught his second on my shoulder. He easily pinned me against the red dust, and smashed my face into the ground. My throat crushed beneath the weight of his massive forearm. Andrew's eyes were like green fire, the red dust licking my arms and legs like flames. My throat burned with dust. I blinked back tears.

His voice grated in my ears, hot breath rasping. "So cry about it, you spoiled bastard. Why would I want to fight beside a useless whelp like you, anyway?"

"Andrew!" Matthew's voice echoed through the hot red dust. "He heard you. Leave him be."

Andrew eased off, his face a glorious triumph. He wiped his hands and stood up, ignoring Matthew's scolding. David leaned down, giving me a sympathetic smile. I accepted his hand and gingerly got to my feet, spitting up dust and dirt.

Resuming our journey into Alexandria, I couldn't look at Andrew. I walked behind my friends now, my eyes burning with shameful tears.

I did want to go home. I wanted to run back to my garden, to stretch on the bench in the cool shade. I wanted to answer the siren-call of home, of comfort, of featherbeds and walks by the sea and elegant dinners.

But every step took me farther from any Paradise, real or imagined, I had ever known.

· 13 ·

"We're here." I pointed to a flat-fronted wooden building, its banner prominently displayed.

"You've found it," David said.

We stood before yet another recruitment office, the largest and busiest. Dozens of soldiers milled about, some staring at us. Others practiced drills, cleaned their guns, or stood motionless with flags near the door. One brushed past Matthew and shoved him rudely. At this gesture Andrew sprang to his brother's aide, only to be calmed down and told to keep his temper in check. David chuckled at the incident. I was getting tired of their antics and ignored them. I wanted rest, a change into clean clothes, a decent meal, a hot shave. I felt more soiled than a day's work in a garden.

The office also turned out to be headquarters for the military telegraph. A group of men in spectacles and jaunty neckties clamored about the large contraption.

"God damn it, Murphy!" One of them shouted to the operator furiously tapping away at the telegraph. "Don't send that!"

I pulled on David's sleeve. "Wait. Did you want to send a message home?"

David shrugged. "Let's go. I can write home another time."

"Have you asked how to get to the fort?" Matthew peered inside the telegraph office. David was ready to find the way to Fort Ellsworth, but I had a small errand to run.

"I will be return momentarily."

I headed over to the telegraph. The operator was still tapping furiously. As I pushed past one of the surrounding fellows, he pushed me. I ignored his glower and addressed the operator.

"Excuse me, sir?"

The operator didn't stop. Perhaps he hadn't heard me?

"I'd like to send a message home!"

"Get out of here, sonny!" roared one of the other men. "This is for the army only!"

"Then you should treat one of its members nicely!" I shouted back.

"What, you think you're a soldier boy, now?" He peered into my face. He was shorter than me, with a thin face and the bushiest eyebrows I'd ever seen. "What battles have you served in?"

"Bull Run." I pulled it out of memory, the only one I knew. "So I would appreciate you gentlemen letting me telegraph to my family before I am sent to the front lines again."

"Ha!" The telegraph operator laughed. "You wanna send a message to the President, too?"

"No, to my family. Please, I . . . I left and I didn't tell them where I was going."

"A runaway, then," the teasing short man said. "You got something to hide, boy?"

Andrew stuck his head in the room. "Daniel! The fort is outside of town! We follow the railroad tracks!"

"One moment, Andrew!"

"Come on, will you?"

The telegraph operator laughed again. "Yer comrade-in-arms there ain't in uniform. Get out of here."

"Murphy, you say your name is?" I put both hands on the table and leaned down. "There's twenty dollars in your pocket if you let me send a message to my family."

"I got another message for the President, Murph," the teaser said. "You take this weasel over the President?"

"What fort are you boys going to?" asked Murphy.

"Ellsworth."

"Good training camp they got there." He stood up and offered me the chair. The others groaned, dispersing from the office.

All save one.

"Now, you listen to me, you fresh fish!" The teaser grabbed the chair and threw it out of the way. "Give me the twenty dollars and I'll send your God damn message."

The operator stuck out his hand. "You got it, or not?"

I reached in my knapsack and pulled out my wallet. The money inside gleamed for my greedy audience. I took out twenty dollars and reached out to hand it to Murphy.

All of a sudden the teaser reached forward and grabbed for my wallet. Bills fluttered to the floor. Murphy scrambled to pick them up, while the teaser grappled with my arm. I was shoved against the wall, but hot strength bubbled within me. I shoved the teaser back and he stumbled against the telegraph machine. The table tipped and the machine fell. I heard a tremendous crash when it burst into a heap of metal and ink.

Murphy stared at the teaser. "You fucking idiot!"

He rushed forward and pulled the man off me. I caught my breath and stumbled out of the room. At the huge commotion, my friends came quickly to my side.

"What was that?" Matthew asked. "Who are those men?"

I shook my head. "Let's get out of here!"

"How many fights you going to be in today?" Andrew cuffed the back of my head. "And why wave your wallet in front of a bunch of spies?"

"Spies?"

We scrambled out of the office and took to the streets of Alexandria, half-running down the street. My temple hurt, and I gingerly touched the bruise. David pulled me down lower.

"That one fighting you was a Confederate spy."

"How do you know?" I said.

Matthew pushed up his spectacles. "He had a flag inside his shirt pocket. I couldn't see it at first, but before you left it was there."

"I guess he did want to send a message to the President after all," I wheezed. "Only, it was to President Jefferson Davis and not Lincoln."

"Stay the hell away from everybody but us, will you?" Andrew laughed. "First that loony ferry captain, then you're being all yellow, and now tussling with reb spies! I say, Daniel, you're giving me quite a day!"

I'd been in more scrapes in the past twelve hours than the past twelve years. It was as if I'd stepped right into one of my own dime novels, dodging ruffians and hooligans. All I needed was a pistol and I'd be whooping and hollering my way through these rough towns. But the adventure was wearing out its welcome.

Alexandria was similar to Washington in its clamor and busyness, but there was no mistaking we had entered a different world. Slave pens and auction blocks lined the streets. Negroes crowded around us, most of whom had no shoes and regarded me with a look of anger. An old Negro woman sat outside a hospital building, selling small pots of flowers. The side of my head hurt, and I was so thirsty I stopped to drink from a horse trough.

Matthew soon guided us out of the city and we found an enormous train depot on the outskirts of town. It was a roundhouse, built like a wheel of cheese with different railroad tracks heading out and away from the city.

"We'll be on one of those someday," David said, "heading down to the army."

We left the town and traveled along a gently curving road dotted with trees and a few small shops and houses along the way. We'd been walking for nearly an hour and our shadows were lengthening. I had no pocket watch and was getting hungry.

"I see it!" Andrew shouted.

The fort was large and brick and round, built into the side of a hill. Enormous cannons jutted from its walls like strange metal snouts, hanging empty and sunny in the evening light. The entire structure resembled a castle, with a large pair of wooden gates blocking our entrance. A line of soldiers stood outside the fort. Their deep blue uniforms gleamed like new, dressed as finely as the ones in Boston. I felt a great sense of relief. At last we had made it.

A soldier approached us. He stopped three feet away and stood ramrod straight. He saluted. We lined up before him, all four abreast, and saluted back. He looked pleased and announced in a cordial tone:

"Colonel Peters, commander of the 3rd Illinois Artillery. We are stationed here to protect Fort Ellsworth."

"Sir." Matthew kept his hand to his brow. "We are recruits from Boston, Massachusetts, here to be trained and mustered into the Army of the Potomac."

"We could definitely use you," said the colonel. "General McClellan has been calling for reinforcements all summer."

"Massachusetts is to offer three hundred thousand volunteers," I said. "Sir, we are here to fight."

"Yes, we are, sir," Andrew added. "We're glad to serve."

He stepped forward. "Checks."

I was confused, but then realized he meant to look us over. I stood with my arms raised and legs splayed while he felt down my jacket and trousers. Several other soldiers rummaged through our bags. They were thorough and brief, and the whole affair went smoothly.

"Open the gates!" The colonel ordered to his men, then turned to us. "Report to the officers' headquarters, and you will be assigned to the barracks."

"Thank you, sir." David lowered his eyes.

Artillerymen left their positions and went over to the front of the fort gate. They grabbed the gate and pulled it open.

"We've arrived at last," I said.

"No, Daniel." Matthew pushed up his spectacles. "This is only the beginning."

The doors of the gates opened wide and revealed a busy arena of great activity and preparation. Not since the morning in Quincy Market had I seen such a hustling gathering place. Hundreds of small white pointed tents dotted the inside of the fort, and tall wooden barracks lined up like rows of grocer stalls. Long columns of uniformed and plain clothes men marched back and forth, and the air filled with the muffled sounds of their footsteps and their shouting officers. Horses dragged enormous wooden carts and fat cannons with their snouts pointed backwards. Each cannon looked like a tree mast encased in iron and hollowed. More artillery officers, dressed like Colonel Peters' men, followed the horses and kept the carts at ready.

Scattered musket shots pocketed the air. It sounded like rocks being clashed against one another, muffled deep booms. Small puffs of smoke rose into tiny feathery wisps. Some soldiers laughed, others stood quietly in the shade. Some chatted, some squatted on upturned boxes or before small ground fires. I caught the scent of fresh coffee, frying steaks, and soups. My stomach growled.

I could already tell which ones were veterans. There was ease in their movements and gestures; they were comfortable in this place. I'd seen the same look in Colonel Peters's eyes. A gravity, a weight, as if they'd lived more than one lifetime.

My vision blurred and then sharpened in the summer heat. I had my future marching before me, drilling before me. I had never seen my life in so clear a way, as if a magnifying glass had clamped over my eyes.

"Now this!" Andrew gave me a hearty slap on the back. "This is war, gentleman!"

A nearby soldier wearing a slouch hat started to laugh. He threw his cigar in the dirt and came over to us. "Fresh fish, eh?"

My hand went to my brow. "Yes, sir. We're to report to the officers' headquarters."

"That building yonder." He pointed to a small white hut a hundred yards off. "Be that as it may, you might not want to shout yer ignorance around here."

"Who are you calling ignorant?" Matthew demanded in as demanding a voice as he could muster.

The soldier laughed again. "Better keep that boy in line. He's got a Greek sense of pride."

Andrew nodded. "Sir, I got him."

The soldier acknowledged him with a nod, and moved on. I gaped at Matthew.

"I would have thought Andrew would get his dander up, not you."

"Calling me ignorant," Matthew muttered.

Andrew ruffled his brother's hair. "Don't be getting us into more scrapes than Daniel, will you?"

David started to chuckle. "I think that's the first time I've seen a resemblance between you two brothers. What a marvel."

"I agree," I said. "It wouldn't take anything but a minor insult to end up in a fight with either one of you. It is quite the similarity."

I shouldered my knapsack and started off in the direction of the headquarters. If either of the Pierce brothers let their emotions cloud their better judgment, this was not the place to exercise such rash actions. The other three caught up with me, and we skirted the perimeter of the fort.

Four soldiers stood sentry in front of the hut, bearing flags with a stoic sense of duty. Nearby several musicians practiced. The drums beat to the rhythm of my own steps when I approached the headquarters. A tall soldier with much gray in his beard guarded the entrance. He greeted me with a salute.

"State your name and business."

"Daniel Stuart, from Boston. I am here for training. As a private in the Army of the Potomac."

I detected a small smile beneath the beard. One by one, he greeted my friends and they had similar responses. But when the soldier reached over and opened the door, he gestured for me alone to enter.

The headquarters was small, but highly decorated with flags, bunting, various statues of eagles, and a small bronze bust of President Lincoln. I became nervous and couldn't think. A large soldier sat at the desk, his uniform as decorated as his office. A pair of white leather gloves rested beside him and he wrote with a steel pen, marking some sort of account book. He popped the pen in the pen rest and rose to meet me. His face was ruddy, tanned, and lined like rock. His beard was orange streaked with white, and his eyes were colorless and fierce. I saluted him immediately.

"Daniel Stuart, sir, from Boston, sir. Reporting here for training at Fort Ellsworth."

He nodded. "That quota from the President has been very effective. You are not the first Massachusetts man I have seen this week."

"I answered the call for volunteers and traveled down to be here."

"Well now, Mr. Stuart." He eyed me. "An educated young man, I wager. Why do you feel you are qualified to be a soldier in my army?"

Feeling foolish, I took a second to breathe. God, when was I going to learn to be prepared for such meetings?

"I am inexperienced, sir," I admitted. "Yet I couldn't follow a life at home without honor. I offer myself in complete and total service to the army. I fully accept that we are at war with the Confederacy and that it may cost my life. I am willing."

"So it seems. That was quite the textbook answer."

Surprised, I blurted: "But it is how I truly feel, sir."

The commander sat back in his chair and laced his fingers. "If you want my honest opinion Mr. Stuart, you are over-qualified to be a grunt soldier in the lines. You come from money. I can see that plainly. You have choices most fellows don't have."

"Sir," I said, my voice faltering. "I choose to be here."

He spoke deliberately, each word fired like a bullet. "Go back home, to the good land of Boston, and make a real change there. This be a devil's playground."

I reached in my knapsack and took out my wallet. The remaining twenty dollars gleamed. I took out my last dollars and put them on the table.

"You see, sir," I said. "Without a dime, I'm just like everyone else."

He didn't look at the money, at the bills sitting right under his nose. Instead, he slowly stood up and raised his hand in a perfect salute.

"I am Colonel Becker. Welcome to the Army of the Potomac, Private Stuart."

· 14 ·

"Daniel, wake up! Get up!"

"Erik, stop! I don't want to go to the office today." I turned and snuggled further under my arm, blocking the light.

"Come on, Daniel!"

"Go away," I muttered. I didn't want to move. Stiffness in my legs was overpowering. We must have drilled for a hundred miles yesterday. Muscles screamed in protest when I attempted to move.

"Hey, that's not funny. Get up!"

I lowered my arm, squinting in the sunlight. "Andrew?"

His big smile lit up the room. It was an early dawn, earlier than those mornings in Boston when Erik awoke me.

"All right, all right." I slowly raised myself to a sitting position. "Thank you for the lovely wake-up call, Andrew."

"Better than the bugle, eh?" He cupped a hand to his ear as if to listen for it. "We've only been here a month and you already dreaming of home. Pathetic, if you ask me."

"Leave him alone, Andrew." David appeared at the end of the bunk, dressed in his civilian clothes. We had not yet received uniforms. "I hear we're going to train with rifles today."

"Excellent choice," I managed a smile. "Seeing as how I can barely move."

"Hey, listen to this!" Matthew ducked into the room, bearing a large map, his spectacles bouncing up and down on his nose. He stopped and looked at me. "Daniel, what are you doing?"

I twisted my back and heard several bones snap. "What news do you have for us?"

"I thought we'd be here for weeks, you know? But Pope's army is moving away from Richmond and trying to draw out the rebs."

"Rebs?" I laughed out loud. "You have been around the colonel too often."

The morning bugle call punctured the air like Morse code. Deet deet deet. I rolled my eyes and made as if to fall back on the bunk, but Andrew grabbed my leg so hard the pain jolted me awake.

"Argh!" I slapped his hand away. "I should wrestle you for that."

"Oh ho! And we all know what happened last time you tried." He leapt off the bed and started away, followed by David and his jumpy brother.

I reached for my shirt and buttoned it, then pulled the chamber-pot out from under the bunk. When I finished I threw the contents out the open window, where they sloshed into the spongy ground beneath the barracks. I was hungry and sore. The men marching out of Boston hadn't looked as weary as I felt. And I hadn't enjoyed a decent meal or a better drink than tepid coffee since the gala.

The mess hall was crowded with soldiers and officers, some in uniform, others still in civilian clothes. I was no gentleman here. Without polished shoes, a tailor-made jacket, and macassar oil in my hair, I blended in.

Twice, I had thought of myself as due better treatment than others because of my station. But it was a former class and a former station. I had no longer a penny to my name. Our first payroll was due in three weeks. Until that time, the United States Army provided for all aspects of my life.

"So, when are we going to wear the blue?" Andrew pointed his fork at the colonel, enjoying breakfast with other officers at the head table.

"Quit talking back to the captain, and I'm sure he'll give you a uniform," Matthew said.

For the past three days, Andrew had said something profoundly stupid in drill. Of course, he then drilled an extra hour one-on-one with the captain. It was quite humorous. Andrew with his dead fish talk again.

David snapped his fingers in front of my face. "Daniel's dreaming about home again. I can smell the Boston pie."

I looked down at the colorless mass on my tin plate. "Why, this is the finest oyster stew south of the Mason-Dixon! And this" – addressing my cup of bland coffee – "is the most precious cask wine all the way from France. How could I fault the sommelier for his fine choice?"

My friends laughed. They loved it that I had no carriages, no gloves, no servants. I was one of them.

The drill call came all too soon, and we left the mess hall with half-empty bellies and half-full hopes. I heard David muttering a little prayer and hoped God also listened to me. Any excitement and newness had worn off within the first forty-eight hours of constant drilling. Sometimes it felt like I'd been at Fort Ellsworth for one hundred years.

"It's glorified walking," I said to Matthew. "That's all drilling is. Learning how to walk and how to turn."

"If it was so damn easy, how come David is having a hard time?" he whispered. "You struggled with epic poetry, remember?"

I was going to retort, but I kept my mouth shut. David was not having an easy time, and I did feel empathy. Drilling was mindless, especially after the first two hours. But that was what the army was about. Moving together as one man, an automatic industrial machine.

"Attention company!" The captain stood before us, his boots impeccably polished, sword gleaming like a silver knife. "Look to your left!"

We all did so. Andrew was on my left, and he in turn looked at Matthew.

"Look at that soldier. He could be you! He could get shot! He could get shrapnel from shell! He could fall!"

My stomach started to slide lower into my belly, and I flexed my knees to keep them from locking in place. The captain strolled up and down before us.

"You want courage? You want glory? You want fortitude and strength? Then look at the soldier on your left."

Several moments elapsed, agonizing quiet moments. Nothing stirred, and a trickle of sweat snaked down my neck.

"Attention company!"

We all faced forward again, and I nearly groaned with the pain of my stiff muscles. The captain raised his saber.

"Privates! Look to your right!"

David was on my right. I stared at the back of his head.

"Look at that soldier. He could be you! He could get shot! He could get shrapnel from shell! He could fall!"

My breath caught. I felt dizzy, lightheaded, and a little jittery. Maybe it was too much coffee, or the sun was too bright. It was a hot July day.

"You want service? You want selflessness? You want God's blessings? Then look at the soldier on your right."

Yes, David did have God's blessings. I wondered if he thought better of coming here, rather than attending Divinity School.

"Parade rest!"

We faced forward yet again, but didn't have to stand so stiffly. I relaxed and felt a little better. I wanted a drink of water. The barrel was not too far off. The captain pointed his saber at each of us.

"You are soldiers in the Army of the Potomac! You are not cowards! I don't train cowards! I train men! I train men to be soldiers! I train men to be brothers!"

Brothers. I thought of Erik, of how it was a Wednesday morning and he would be working at the office. He might as well be on the other side of the universe.

"Your soldier is your brother! Repeat! Your soldier is your brother!"

"Your soldier is your brother!" we shouted back to him. "Your soldier is your brother!"

"As you were." He saluted us and we saluted back. "We are in a brother's war, soldiers. Brother against brother. You fight for glory. You fight for service. You fight for God. You may even fight for a woman. But out there" – he pointed his saber towards the south gates where we had first entered the fort – "is the enemy. And you must kill the enemy."

All of a sudden the gates pulled open and a large wagon came rumbling into camp. The wagon was enormous, pulled by a team of six. It circled around the back of the fort, then came to rest near the officer's headquarters.

"Attention company!"

We faced forward again, at attention. I marveled at how I'd automatically stiffened, straightened.

"Rank and file!"

I turned left and the soldier behind me – David – shifted to my right-hand side in one swift move. In one command we'd gone from a line of two into the column of two, a pair of soldiers marching side-by-side. I was pleased to see David remembered the move and executed it well. I gave him a slight jostle in the ribs and received a smile in return.

"And march! Left! Left! Left, right, left!"

I stumbled a bit, having stepped off on the wrong foot. But I quickly regained my stride and joined my comrades in moving the column across the wide field of the fort, heading towards the large wagon. A table had been set up in front of the headquarters and several men were unloading the wagon and setting its contents onto the table.

"Uniforms!" I heard Matthew say, marching directly in front of me.

"No talking in rank!" The captain scolded.

After weeks of drilling, marching, and dining in the same set of clothes I'd brought with me from Boston, it would be unbelievably enjoyable to don the wool jackets and trousers of a real soldier. Despite the drilling and the army meals, I didn't feel like a soldier.

The captain ushered us in front of the table, then shouted his command and we formed back into two parallel lines. One by one, he called out our names and we stepped forward to receive our uniforms.

"Private Olney!"

David left my side and then returned with his brown paper parcel. He regarded it as if he held a ceremonial robe. I smiled at the look of wonder in his eyes.

"I didn't think I could do it," he whispered.

"Of course you can," I whispered back.

"Private Andrew Pierce!"

Before Andrew could go back to his place, the captain held his arm and kept him out in front next to the table. He looked dejected and, for a moment, I thought he was to be punished yet again.

"Private Matthew Pierce!"

The captain gestured for him to stay as well. And the two brothers clutched their uniforms, standing next to one another in front of the rest of us. The captain pointed his sword at each of them.

"Your soldier is your brother!"

The brothers repeated: "Your soldier is your brother!"

"Let their example of strength and wisdom be a model for the rest of you!" And the captain let the Pierce brothers return to their places.

I felt a small pang of hurt in my throat. If only Erik were here, standing beside me with the same degree of honor. The Pierce brothers were as opposite as could be imagined. One studious and cautious, questioning motives, reasoning decisions. The other rash and impulsive, brawny and energetic, breaking obstacles, charging gates. Yet, I had a brother, and I could see the same admiration and regard the two had for one another.

"Private Stuart? Private Stuart!"

David pinched my arm. I started and realized my friends were staring at me. I felt the hot rush of blood to my face.

"Colonel Becker has high hopes for you, Private," the captain muttered when I received my uniform. "Don't waste it with your head up God's arse."

"Yes, sir." I saluted and he returned the gesture.

I returned to my place in line, embarrassed and ashamed of my daydreaming. Must I continuously think of home and my family? I resolved to keep my head out of the clouds, lest I fall out of favor with the officers. I could get myself killed if I wasn't paying attention in battle. That was too big a price to pay for nostalgia.

The mess bugle call came, and we hurried to barracks to get into our new uniforms. We were quite the sight as we filed out of our barracks and down the stairs to the mess hall, to eat for the first time dressed as soldiers in the Army of the Potomac.

Though the wool was hot and itchy, though my trousers were an inch shorter than Mr. Barkins would have tailored, and though my wool forage cap was more shapeless than any other hat I'd donned, I felt prouder to be dressed in the deep navy blue sack-coat and sky-blue trousers of the army than any other suit in my life. It also felt unbelievably good to wear a clean set of clothes for the first time in days. I was happy to pack my civilian clothes away.

"We look like soldiers!" David laughed as we gulped down our noonday dinners. "We are good in God's eyes today. I think we please Him when we are dressed so finely."

"You said it, Davy," Andrew smiled. "I can't wait to meet the rebs looking like this! Say, Matthew, when are we going to get to play with guns?"

"Receiving our rifles is definitely the next step." Matthew fingered the shiny brass buttons on his plain sack coat. "However, I'm going to be more interested in decorating my shoulder than shouldering a rifle."

"General Pierce, I presume?" I bowed to him. "Where shall the army be headed next?"

He brought out an imaginary map and consulted it. "On to Richmond, boys! The Confederacy won't know what hit them! Let's outfox Bobby Lee and save Washington!"

I put my hand to my breast, but there was one piece missing from my new uniform. "Can any of you fellows whip a stitch?"

Two shrugged, but Andrew did not. He looked at Matthew and David in a mockery of surprise, and then quickly muttered, "What needs be done for you, Daniel?"

Andrew could sew? I started to laugh, and that, unfortunately, was the stone needed for the ripples. It took several minutes for the rest of us to wipe our tears and halt our chuckles long enough for me to address my friend. He, as I could well imagine, did not find it humorous and glowered at me, his eyes as dark as a forest at night.

"I'd . . . I'd like a pocket sewn inside my jacket, please," I requested with as much composure as I could summon. "The particular size for a small book."

"That's right, you did bring *Paradise Lost*!" Matthew exclaimed.

"What? Daniel, you cannot be serious."

David banged his hands down on his tray, and his physical clumsiness transferred from drilling. A piece of dried cornbread took flight and sailed across to the next table and bounced off of an officer's cheek as if it had been targeted to that spot.

This was exactly the wrong thing to happen, for Andrew began his unmistakable guffawing and soon all four of us were roaring with laughter. The officer, a sergeant none of us knew, rose from his table and speared a ferocious look at poor David.

"You! Private! Report to your captain at once!"

"Sir," I rose from the table, my expression immediately grave. "Sir, it was my error. I provoked Private Olney."

"I'm Sergeant Falls," the non-commissioned officer sniffed. "I will not proceed with reparations, but I know your faces. And those on my enemy list do not admire me for mercy."

"Thank you, Sergeant Falls." I sat back down at the table, and the sergeant left the mess hall. David, mortified and silent, did not even offer thanks. I leaned over.

"It was a perfect shot, David. I can't wait until next time we play town-ball."

"Aw, cheer up David," Andrew said. "I'd have grabbed up that Sergeant and gotten a real wrestle out of him."

"Yes, we all know what you would have done," Matthew said dryly.

Of course, there was none to stop us from enjoying the humor once more. David's mood cheered, and we strolled out of the mess hall as new men.

As soldiers in the Army of the Potomac.

· 15 ·

A summer-autumn morning misted into camp, unsure of which season to hang her hat upon. We'd been drilling for more than six weeks and the long sticky days of July gave way to the shorter, warmer hours of August. Trees dotted the inside of the fort and their limbs were full of a loud buzzing sound like fingernails tapping against rocks. When I stepped closer to see what was making the racket, an enormous grasshopper twitched at me. It lay flat against the trunk, as brown and gray as the mottled bark.

"Cicadas," said a curt voice. We hadn't exchanged words in weeks, but I knew exactly who it was.

"Indeed, Sergeant Falls," I remarked. "Quite an annoying buzzing. They sound like hornets."

"Yes, they're all about this area of the south. Pennsylvania, Maryland, Virginia." He took off his forage cap and ran a hand through his red hair. His eyes were the fiercest blue I'd seen since my father's. He was hated vehemently by many of the others.

"Return to your drilling, Private." He saluted me and I returned the salute. "You are to be mustered in soon."

Reports of General Pope's movement floated in and out of camp for several days. Some New York and Washington newspapers confirmed the

Army of the Potomac had been divided into Pope's and General McClellan's command. The President appeared confident in his decision to appoint both generals, so the mood about the fort remained optimistic. I was learning many new things about the army. The different ranks and names of the generals and other officers were common as if I'd known them all my life.

Twice I tried to sit down and pen a letter home, and twice I watched my ill attempts turn to ashes in the campfire. I continued drilling, training, firing, marching, and loading my gun until the side of my hand was raw from reaching into my cap-box. The weight of the rifle surprised me; it was heavier than two cast-iron skillets and felt like a leaden lance tossed up onto my shoulder.

"Shoulder arms!"

I was once again assembled into rank file with my comrades. We stood at attention, mute as tombs, our guns cradled in our palms.

"Good, good," the captain muttered as he perused us. He was particularly picky, as the time drew closer for our mustering. "Shoulders square, Private Olney."

David couldn't have squared his shoulders more than if he'd been made of wood, but his rifle's heft was often too much for him to handle. I feared for his slight frame, his jerky movements, his obvious struggling.

"Present arms!"

At this my hands automatically placed my gun across the center of my chest, diagonal and at a perfect angle to my belt. In front of me, a small line of wooden targets was set up, crudely painted with circles.

"Company load!"

My heart beat faster. Would I execute this command swiftly, or still feel like a fresh fish recruit, raw and naïve? Thankfully, the weeks of drilling ingrained in my muscles a memory of their own. I took the cartridge from my cartridge box, tore the paper with my teeth, spat the empty cartridge away, loaded the bullet and powder, took off the rammer and shoved it down the barrel of the gun and replaced the rammer. My Springfield rifle was loaded.

"Better than yesterday," the captain said, eyeing Matthew when he walked past. If David struggled with the physical aspects of marching, Matthew's manual dexterity left much to wanting. Only Andrew and I grasped all aspects of soldiering easily.

"Ready arms!"

We were to fire as one company, as we might in battle. I raised the loaded gun to my shoulder in one swift movement, removed a small cap from my cap box, placed it on the cap nipple, and cocked the hammer. The recruit behind me pointed his rifle next to my shoulder.

"Aim!"

I stared down the length of the barrel, peering at the target as if through a telescope lens. We'd practiced with rifles for two weeks, and at first the strange line of sight baffled my vision. Yet I'd grown accustomed to it and now focused on the small colored circle sixty feet away.

"Fire down the line!"

One by one, the soldiers fired. After Matthew, I squeezed the trigger and the gun fired, jerking me backward slightly. I felt a reverberation through my shoulder as if someone had knocked a mallet inside me. It was both unsettling and powerful. David fired after me, and so it continued down the line.

"Shoulder arms!"

I cradled the gun in my palm and its weight curved into my hip, resting against my shoulder. I looked straight down towards the targets. A small hole appeared on one of the inner rings. I was a decent shot, but I would improve with time. In any case, the one-inch diameter circle I'd carved would cause enough damage to severely wound an enemy. Minie balls shattered bone, a fact Andrew was fond of repeating.

"Company, right face!"

We all turned right. I faced the back of David's forage cap, and Matthew stood directly behind me.

"Company, march! Left, left!"

I followed David as we marched along the fort's outer path, a well-worn dirt track cannons often lumbered across. Usually, we went to the barracks, were given final instructions, and then issued our dismissal.

But today, we veered off the outer path and marched straight across the entire fort, right towards the officer's headquarters. I couldn't help but smile as we pulled up alongside, paused, faced right, and stopped.

Colonel Becker, whom I hadn't seen since that first afternoon so many weeks ago, stood at attention before the officer's headquarters. The fort's quartermaster sergeant sat at a little table beside him, a large cloth-bound book open to blank pages.

"Attention, new recruits!" Colonel Becker announced. "You have shown fine form here at Fort Ellsworth, training for the fields of war. You will soon be joining Generals Pope and McClellan in their respective armies. Now is when the call of duty commands you to answer!"

Andrew whooped a loud cheer. Embarrassed, I looked down the line at him, but others let out hurrahs. I grinned.

"I appreciate your enthusiasm, for you will need it. General Robert E. Lee of the Army of Northern Virginia is proving a worthy foe, and his troops amass forty miles southwest of here, outside the old battlegrounds of Bull Run. Tomorrow the locomotive will arrive to take you to join the Army of the Potomac under General Pope's command. Your company will be added to the Massachusetts regiments."

My friends and I were part of an assortment of Massachusetts, Connecticut, New Hampshire, and Vermont volunteers, a mixed New England company of about sixty men.

"Gentlemen, it is my great honor to invite you to come and sign your names into the muster-roll."

"Excellent!" Matthew whispered.

By alphabetical last name, each volunteer walked up to the quartermaster sergeant's table, signed his name, shook the colonel's hand, and returned to our assembled company. After all of my friends had gone, it was my turn.

"Daniel Stuart!"

I approached the table and looked down at the muster-roll. There was David Olney's writing, and the Pierce brothers. I thought of the weeks from home, hot hours of drilling and horrible meals. I thought of the nights I'd wept into my pillow, burying my face so no-one could hear.

After I signed my name, I could hear Frederick Douglass's voice of approval. Though I still had trepidations about the unknown we were to face, I could not go home.

"Congratulations, Privates. You are officially mustered into the Army of the Potomac!"

I joined my friends in cheer, applauding their efforts as well as mine. We would leave tomorrow. So fleeting our time here, but fall beckoned and the summer was gone. In scarcely a fortnight, our peers would be back at Harvard College. How fast the weeks had flown!

"Tomorrow, fellows!" Andrew exclaimed as we made our way to the barracks for our final night at Fort Ellsworth. "We're soldiers now!"

"Not quite," David said quietly. "We have yet to be tested."

"God tests us in many ways," I said. "Some are easier than others."

"Very true," my spiritual friend said.

Of the three, David understood and respected my silence. I received a kindly smile, and after our final mess bugle and the lamps were turned low, I lay in my bunk and looked up at the shadowed ceiling. I could already smell autumn's crispness in the night air.

I wondered if Mary still went to the Bull and Boar. I wondered if she still danced. I could see her now, a vision in her tattered skirts with ale flowing and fiddlers twiddling. Her face, illumined like a blank sheet of paper, talking of madness. Yes, Mary, perhaps I was mad to leave you and come here. But how could I have ever known? How could I have ever lived?

We stood abreast outside the south gates of Fort Ellsworth the following morning. Dawn splayed across the Virginia sky, awash in ribbons of purple and rose. I was packed and ready.

The crossed tongues of the railroad tracks trembled with the great rolling wheels of the locomotive, black as Morpheus's embrace. Blasts of smoke chugged from its chimneystack and blotted the sky with cotton fingerprints. The cars passed by me, rickety and bumping. I felt the wind of the cars, the force passing. The beast slowed, lagged, metallic screeching, at last at rest. Something about its lengthy pause made me reach over and tug on Andrew's jacket. He shrugged me off, but something was wrong.

We approached, peering on tiptoe. Necks craning, mouths gaping. Several men jumped down from the train and threw open the wooden gates of the cars. I made as if to mount, but soon stepped back in horror.

Dripping, limbs askew, bandaged all. The soldiers inside reached for us and struggled to stand, holding their bloodied faces from the morning light. They clutched at their bodies, contortioned and twisted to unhuman shapes. Rising from straw-strewn blackness, they stank of manure.

"This . . . can't be!" David's eyes were filling with tears. "Who are these poor souls?"

I heard Sergeant Falls's sliding footsteps, the snappish tone. "They've come from General McClellan's failed campaigns around Richmond."

I shook my head. "Why are they delivered here?"

"This is your conveyance south. And your first order, as soldiers, is to empty the cars."

The four of us stared at him. He could not be serious! These men were in need of medical attention, not the aid of new recruits. I opened my mouth to protest, but Matthew's words halted me.

"This is why we should not underestimate General Lee."

"Shut up, Matty," Andrew hissed. "Let's help them."

Sergeant Falls motioned for us to enter. I was frozen, as if a cold North wind had blown icicles into my veins. Andrew yanked me past my horror-stricken comrades, many of whom had forsaken this macabre task. In a mechanical fashion, I unloaded my haversack, my gun, my cartridge box and cap box.

After I climbed into the cattle car, I was bathed in a fearful dimness. Hands reached for me, voices cried out. I felt the wet wool of their jackets seeped into my skin. Wet blood, wet sweat, wet spittle dribbled from wet lips. Matthew was hoisted up beside me and for several moments we stared at the mess at our feet.

"God in heaven," he said. "They must have been traveling for hours."

"Some aren't moving," I said.

"Hurry yourselves!" Sergeant Falls shouted.

I reached beneath a pair of boot-heels and lifted. The man was still alive, but barely conscious. Matthew took up his shoulders and we handed him down to other members of our company. I lifted again and again, pulling each rag-doll body over to the entrance of the cattle cars, where they were rolled onto shoulders and carried into the fort. Matthew worked beside me, and we formed a united pair. I took the feet. He grabbed the shoulders. We swung and heaved, rolled and lifted. Within moments I was wet and hot, as if I lain in dirty bathwater.

By and by, the cattle car emptied. All that remained was the smell of the manure, and wet straw clung to my boot soles.

"Good, boys. Good."

Sergeant Falls wiped his hands as if he wiped the ordeal away. He was pleased with our effort, if he could be pleased. What a mongrel bastard.

"Help!" croaked a faint voice. I shaded my eyes from the sun and peered into the darkness. Matthew had climbed down, but there was still one man remaining!

"All right," I muttered as I made my way over to him. "I'm here to assist you, soldier. Where are you wounded?"

"The leg," he managed to say. His face was streaked with manure, the dirt forming long brown lines about his eyes like furrows. "Name's Augustus Gage, but you can call me Gus."

"Gus!" I was so surprised I dropped his hand and he slammed onto the floor with a mighty thud.

"Private Stuart!" Sergeant Falls shouted at the cattle car entrance. "Get him over here!"

"I'm sorry," I mumbled as I helped the soldier up. "Gus, I know your cousin. I know John Gage."

Gus's head lolled and we tipped against the slatted wall of the cattle car. I braced my weight and pulled him against me. In this half-bent fashion, I dragged him over to the doors. It was like helping a drunken man.

"Yes, John Gage of Boston. The lawyer," I said. "Gus?"

"Johnny, Johnny." In the light, his cheeks were pale. "I wrote to him, but he don't write back. Gotta have friends in war, sonny. Friends is all you got."

"I know what you speak of," I said as we reached the open cattle car door. "I read your letter about the sergeant. I'm sorry, Gus."

He said no more, for he was taken from me and lifted down to the other members of my company waiting by the tracks. I couldn't believe it. I had Gus's letter in my haversack not twenty feet away. I could recall the details of his familiar scrawl as clearly as a memory of my own.

A terrific explosion resounded beneath me. I pitched to my knees on the edge of the cattle car. A pistol fell to the ground.

"Dear God," Andrew murmured. "The bastard shot himself."

Gus's feet. I held his living feet in my hands not two seconds earlier. The back of his skull gaped open and his body dropped into the dust.

"No!" I shouted. I leapt down from the cattle car and began to run towards him.

"Private Stuart!" Sergeant Falls stepped before me. "Orders to clean the cattle car. We depart in one hour!"

Gus was dead. I shouldn't have said anything about the sergeant. I shouldn't have mentioned his dead friend. I watched with sickly horror as his body was dragged away, then reluctantly returned Sergeant Falls's salute.

"Yes, Private Stuart. I am assigned First Sergeant of this company. Clean out the car."

We were given brooms, mops, rags, and buckets. I mopped blood and straw and bits of bandage and buttons and pieces of leather and fabric scraps. Debris floated in a dammed mass at our feet.

It was time to leave. We grabbed haversacks, canteens, cartridge boxes, cap boxes, bayonet holsters, rifles, belts, packs of cards, Bibles, eyeglasses, looking-glasses, razors, combs, *Paradise Lost*. In the brilliant sun rays, our Union blues were gold-tipped.

We lined up like children and waited to board the newly cleaned cattle cars. I didn't want to grab the stiffening arm, the slippery boot, and the heavy body of a wounded soldier ever again. After we boarded, I leaned against the walls of the car and rested upon my forearm. I could still feel the weight of Gus's body against my own. I could still smell death. I may as well have been standing in a grave.

· 16 ·

I dozed against my slatted bed. Dreams and wakefulness intertwined like rivers. Flies buzzed around me, peeked through the boards and whooshed out into the dark. Andrew rested on a hay bale, Matthew snored beside an upturned crate, and David curled at my feet.

"Daniel? Wake up, private. We are here."

"Here?" I mumbled.

It was Matthew, his insistent grip on my arm. "Warrenton Junction."

The cattle car had stopped. There was muffled shouting from beyond, orders to sleepy troops. I squinted in the dark, my neck stiff. It was before dawn.

The regiment poured from the cattle cars like dark water from a vessel. We formed into our lines, and in the dark I could make out Andrew's burly form, the glint of light from Matthew's spectacles, David's slight, bird-boned body. Half the buttons were undone on my coat and my rifle banged against my shoulder.

Sergeant Falls shouted to the orderlies scattered in the pale field. We were in a low-slung valley. It was too damn early for conversation, so I heard nothing but our familiar marching sounds. Tin cups banging, brogans plodding through the grass, swishing and bumping of the bayonet holsters. Andrew stepped lively. I felt mired in fog.

"Reports of cannons in the rear!" Falls shouted. "Follow in step, boys!"

His voice was eerily high-pitched. I took one step forward and stubbed my toe hard enough for my eyes to water. I grimaced in pain. My first march out and a God damned stubbed toe.

Warrenton Junction disappeared behind us and we followed the railroad tracks. The first few steps were clumsy, but I found the rhythm and moved along. Beside me were the rail ties, half-buried in the grass like forgotten pieces of kindling.

My toe throbbed with each step. I attempted to turn my foot, then rested more weight on my heel and hobbled forward, but I only succeeded in getting out of step and nearly suffered a twisted ankle. God damn rebs. God damn war. Our first real march and all I wanted was to sit on a rail tie and take my shoe off.

What a soldier I was!

The chill vanished and dawn peeped over the land. Next to the tracks appeared the bluish outline of a squat building, and we reached it at a steady pace. An acrid scent of wet burnt wood wrapped its arms around it. Singed bridges over two runs sent billows of smoke into the blurry morning, and the building's perimeter was shrouded in a misty vapor.

"It must be Jackson." A New Hampshire volunteer, curly red hair peeking from under his cap. I didn't know the man's name. He poked Andrew in the shoulder. "He up and come through here, ye know."

"Jackson? From Bull Run?" Andrew spit a wad of tobacco juice. A fitting breakfast for him.

"This is Catlett's Station." The New Hampshire man cast a haughty glance at it. "Welcome, my friends. Ye know, I ain't been here in nigh on a year now."

"You fought at Bull Run?" Matthew's eyes bulged.

"I done my share," the recruit lobbed back at him.

We skirted the remains of the wreckage and continued, keeping those railroad ties in view when our division followed the track. Sunlight burned the remainder of the dew and we fell into a rhythm. An easy, toneless rhythm of marching. Our band began a joyful ditty, but the brassy sounds grated my ears.

"If only they'd shut up," Matthew muttered, and I liked him even more.

"Easy, boys! The enemy has been sighted!"

The column veered towards a distant grove of pretty clumped trees. We were heading into a painting, for all the danger it possessed. The railroad tracks disappeared into the gold-tipped meadow. The sun was bright, the field was bright. I winced from my throbbing foot and loped along.

We reached an orchard, the trees hung with green fruit that would be ripe within weeks. A fresh and earthy scent of ripening apples. My mouth watered, but we soon passed into a cornfield. Papery stalks brushed against the blue wool on my chest, and the Indian corn ears bumped against my rifle and my knees. We kicked through the stalks, the fallen ears, the sticky strands.

We came at last to a little brown creek, a tiny river. Nearby a bridge burned, and its smoldering wood crackled over the brown water and the green grass. It smelled good, like an autumn bonfire.

"It must be a raid," the New Hampshire man was saying. He spit in the grass. "Well, what do you think, boys? Ain't so bad, now is it?"

Fireworks exploded over his head. His cap flew by me and sailed like a wool bird into the grass. I stumbled backwards, caught David's arm, and we tumbled.

Strong arms lifted me, pulling me above the body at my feet. The fallen volunteer stared from the grass, shrapnel embedded in his jaws and cheeks. He stared, shocked by the fireworks that killed him.

"Daniel!" Andrew righted me upon my feet. David was up, too, looking shaken but not hurt. "Daniel!"

I wanted to say his name. I wanted to say something.

And the world erupted into a concert of thunder and fireworks. Shells burst overhead, spraying their deadly spittle upon us. I stumbled again and couldn't keep my balance. My rifle felt like a leaden lance.

Somebody shouted: "Forward!"

My palms stung with the slapping of my rifle, and my legs were weighted with rocks. And the noise! The roaring music of grape shot and cannon. It drummed into me until I felt the bass through every organ of my being. My throat burned with labored breath. I licked my lips and tasted powder.

"Form a line! To your ranks!"

The order was far off, as if heard from a deep well. We stopped. I panted, dizzy and lightheaded. I braced my foot to keep my balance and the intense pain of my toe brought the world sharply into focus.

"Ready, boys!"

I grabbed a cartridge, tore the paper. My lips were dry and the paper stuck to my lips. A man near me poured powder down his gun, paper on his lips, too. He looked at me, and a red star bloomed on his forehead. White eyes rolled skyward. He fell, crumpled like torn paper. Shaking, I poured the powder down my gun and shoved the bullet in deep.

"Aim!"

I swung the gun to my shoulder, using its weight for leverage. It was like tossing a poker. I spat the paper away and cocked the rifle.

"Fire down the line!"

I squinted into the smoke, aiming into vapor. I pulled the trigger. The blast shuddered through me, the groaning jolt of the weapon.

"Ready again!"

I switched my weight to my other foot, propping my throbbing toe upward. Blood streamed towards the rear of my shoe. I loaded the cartridge, rammed the bullet, put the cap on, cocked the rifle.

"Aim! Fire!"

My bullets disappeared into the shroud of smoke before us. If I hit a man, I didn't know. If I hit a tree, I didn't know.

"Advance on them, boys! Steady now!"

We started to move, a shifting moat of crouched blue wool and jabbing rifles. My toe throbbed like a drum banging in my brain. I tore another cartridge and rammed another bullet.

When I replaced the ramrod, something squished beneath my pained foot. I looked down and screamed. It was a hand! The bones crunched beneath my brogan. I pulled my foot away quickly, too quickly, for I tripped and stumbled again.

"Keep firing, boys! Pour it into them!"

I bumped into a tree and steadied again in time to see the soldier directly in front of me take a bullet to the groin. I stepped in front and away from him. My heart slammed, but I couldn't stop. Forward. Forward. Ground inched beneath me.

The smoke cleared and I spotted Matthew. His hands moved faster than I had ever seen. In the thick of battle he could load! He was driven by the singular intent to load and shoot as humanly fast as possible. A bullet zipped into a nearby sapling. I gasped so loud I shrieked. I turned from Matthew and fired into the trees and the smoke. My throat burned, my eyes burned.

Soon, I was in the cover of shade, cooling my neck, my cheeks. I reloaded the gun and jammed a fresh bullet down the shaft. Strange light speckled upon my chest. I could see little red dots, like red stars on a midnight sky. My sweaty temples were chilled. We had reached the clump of trees.

All of a sudden, I saw a splash of gray. The enemy. I fixed the cap on my gun. I would try for this one. I dropped to my knee, slapped the gun into my palm, aimed, waited.

Fire.

The gray disappeared, swallowed by smoke and blood and screams. Did I hit him? I strained, leaned forward. I jammed another cartridge in the gun. I saw nothing. Nothing but the round arms of advancing smoke.

Suddenly, like the parting of a sea, the woods split open. Beyond was a huge sunlit field sprinkled with men. The scene was one of utter chaos. Several Union regiments chased a mass of gray troops out into the open. Officers on horseback shouted and waved pistols at the advancing blue soldiers. Cannon lumbered across the field, pulled by men the size of mice. They loaded and fired, shell bursting into a thousand invisible fragments.

"We've got 'em!" Sergeant Falls screamed.

The rebs were fleeing! We were winning! Matthew loaded his gun. Blood flecks colored the vision through his spectacles. He wiped the lenses and the red smeared. He pointed to a shadowed building beyond the field.

"It's Bristoe Station!"

"Onward! Follow those men!"

I coughed dust and plunged into the sunlight. Sweat collected around my collar and ran slick and salty down my temples. Forward. My armpits and thighs rubbed wet and raw against my wool coat and trousers. I felt pain in my groin, a dull pinch. I shifted my rifle as best I could and tugged at the wool. Forward.

We double-quicked across the field. My toes throbbed and my feet squelched bloody socks as I charged across the golden valley. I ran after the gray men. Some turned and shot at us. Some pitched forward and never moved again. Our line broke into pieces, clumps of blue. Smoke draped like a fog. Our pace slowed when the field blurred and grayed.

Andrew was excited, his wide grin leering. Matthew gripped a paper cartridge, squeezed the nose of his rifle. David was breathing so heavily his entire body shook. I joined them and we all looked at each other.

"The rebs are gathering over there!" Andrew pointed to the left of the field. "We've got to get them!"

Sergeant Falls screamed from behind us: "Regiment! Form the line!"

We stood shoulder to shoulder, lined up abreast.

"Ready now!"

The smoke dissipated and swaths of blue light sliced through. The field was wide.

"Pour it into them, boys!"

I slapped my rifle into my palms. I tore the cartridge, poured the inky powder, rammed the gun, fumbled for the cap, cocked the hammer, hoisted it up on my shoulder. I stared down the snout and squeezed an eye shut.

I saw grass. Startled, I yanked the gun away. I was staring at land. The ground sloped upwards! And the enemy had that ground! I tilted upwards and aimed at the top of the slope. I yanked the trigger.

My bullet blasted upward. The solid weight of the gun shook. It tingled through my fingers. Beside me Andrew shot up towards the slope.

Rebs were up there, perched like falcons on that ridge. They stared greedily down upon us and their rifle mouths aimed down upon Andrew.

They wouldn't hit him. They couldn't hit him.

"Andrew!"

He dropped his rifle, grabbed his canteen and held it in front of him. The bullets rained upon him, a thunderstorm of lead. He hit the sod and scrambled for his rifle. I screamed and bolted in front of him. My rifle jutted like a flag.

Andrew was on his knees in the grass, the mangled canteen falling to the ground. Tears streamed wet and dirty down his face, but his green eyes blackened.

To my shock and utter amazement, he grabbed his gun, bolted up the slope with the energy of the Furies, and launched into the gray mass.

I seized a cartridge, spat the paper, rammed the ball. My knees were soaked, my feet hurt, my back in pain. I smudged dirt across my face and went after Andrew. Matthew and David were beside me.

We were outnumbered and alone. The officers left, the cannons too slow, the horses gone. I stumbled up the slope, sliding on soil slick with blood. I tripped and fell over the dead and wounded. Forward. Forward. Andrew shoved his bayonet into the soft underbellies of the enemy. Bristoe Station stood guard above the yellow smoke. The wounded fell. The rebs pushed back, harder and stronger and louder and fiercer. The river of gray multiplied, as if every dead spirit morphed into two living.

I took a step back. No! Forward! Took another step back. Forward! We were losing. Retreating.

"FALL BACK!"

No! Sergeant Falls was wrong. Were we regrouping? Would we push again! I aimed and fired a desperate bullet. Damn it, no!

"Daniel!"

David's bloody face appeared in the smoke, floating near me. Blood smeared his cheeks and the blue wool of his coat. He jabbed me with the butt of his gun, jabbed until it hurt. Toes throbbed, my fingers cramped on my rifle.

"Fall back!"

I squeezed a helpless trigger and the click was hollow, a click of nowhere. Step back. Step back. We were soon running, double-quicking back across the field, away from the slope. Loss bubbled up within me, a fount of desolation. I wept as I retreated.

Breezes cooled my face. Again I was in the shade of the trees, the edge of the dappled forest. I plunked my rifle in the grass and knelt against it. I felt a hot pounding in my ears.

"I can't find him, Daniel."

Brogans paused next to me, sky blue trousers. It was Matthew. He took off his forage cap and let it dangle by his side, fingers brushing the speckled band. His hair was wet, plastered to his skull. His cheeks were streaked with sweat, his spectacles and eyelashes sprinkled with droplets. He looked away and out at the field.

"I can't find Andrew."

I immediately rose to my feet, a cold knot of anxiety gripping my stomach. Words evaded me and I searched the field in vain. Matthew was frantic.

"He ran right into their lines. He must have been hit. There's no way he couldn't have been hit."

The fighting weakened and a feeble scattering of musketry fire pocketed the scene. Cannons shuffled across like sleepy cattle, the gray troops had slowed their swarm, and the fallen lay like ink splatters on a grassy canvas.

I stumbled from Matthew, found a sapling and retched dry heaves into the grass. Foul-tasting water bubbled from my stomach, burning my nose and throat. I coughed and gripped my knees.

"Well, if it ain't the mighty Daniel Stuart."

I rose and wiped my mouth. Smirking, Andrew held my rifle out to me. I glowered at him and snatched my gun away. I hoisted it up onto my shoulder in one perfect motion and cradled its hot end in my palm.

Matthew stared at his brother, then suddenly burst into sobs. "You stupid bastard!" he screamed. "You could have been killed!"

Andrew propped his rifle against a tree, walked over to Matthew, and gently wrapped his enormous arm around Matthew's thin shoulder.

David and I looked at each other, both in awe. Matthew soon quieted, and Andrew gave his hair a ruffle.

"Attention regiment!"

Our regiment gathered its scattered troops. The field looked like a messy child's nursery, dead and wounded scattered like dropped dolls. And we lost this field. We ran from it like dogs.

The regiment formed back into columns and began to march, ending up on a roundabout path. I smelled wood burning when we passed Bristoe Station. Flames licked up to the late-afternoon sun. The enemy had abandoned this place, nowhere to be seen. The regiment skirted the edge of the trees and came at last to a clearing. In the near distance, perhaps a hundred yards from our new path, cornstalks waved their yellow leaves.

Matthew pointed in the grass. "Look."

The railroad tracks! We had come back to the railroad? I craned my neck down the snaky black tracks. Bristoe Station burned in the distance and a line of scorched baggage cars lead away from it, like a fiery tail. Somebody had been busy while we were fighting.

Twilight descended and we rested in the clearing. Blankets unfurled like wool flags in the grass. I was hungry and glad to sit before a small fire. I took a seat next to David, too tired to put up the shelter tent. We sat on the blankets in the orange shadows of the rail cars. Crimson flames were silhouetted against the periwinkle-hued sky, faint scent of wood smoke, buzzing cicadas. I looked over at my schoolmates. Their faces were bathed in orange light.

"We made it," David said.

"Of course we did," said Andrew. "I say we do it again tomorrow."

"You can't be serious," Matthew said. But then he started to laugh because he knew that his brother was definitely serious.

· 17 ·

It had been two days since the Bristoe Station assault. When we squatted around campfires and chatted amongst ourselves, the gray soldiers disappeared into our stories. None of us could believe what we'd seen on the field. Even Andrew couldn't tell us why he'd run up the slope, a single soldier in front of thousands. We just knew he'd done it and were in awe.

In a dream one night, I was back at Harvard with my friends. It was an oratory class, and we were lined against the wall, awaiting the podium. But when each youth stepped up, the professor handed him a gun. I woke smelling blood.

After drills on the third morning, I spread out a game of checkers with David. Matthew had disappeared following role call, but Andrew sat near us in the dewy grass, cleaning his gun. He ran the pad of his thumb up and down the barrel. Up and down. It had been windy, but the air was hot and heavy. I removed my cap and yawned and settled. David clicked the checker pieces together. He tapped one against his teeth.

"I am good at this game, Daniel."

His little red pieces lay out on the squares of the board like soldiers in drill. David picked up his piece and leapt over two of my black pieces. He scooped them up and looked at me with a startlingly devilish grin.

"I'm winning, Daniel."

I plunked a finger on my piece and zig-zagged it to an end square. "King me, David."

He stacked one of my pieces on top and smiled.

"Andrew! David!"

Matthew's voice was strained and hoarse. He hurried over to us. His countenance spoke of one ill, and our laughter died as quickly as if it had been slain.

"I've come from the captain's tent. I asked him for the report on the battle. I only wished to know. The rebs beat us, Andrew. Pope couldn't hold it. We . . . we lost the field."

"I knew it," I groaned. "I knew when we ran from that damned meadow. We shouldn't have run with such haste!"

Andrew fingered the ramrod on his gun. "With Pope and McDowell at the helm and that bastard fool McClellan? Our loss was not in haste!"

David tugged his coat. "Look."

A section of blue men marched by, unknown to us. Another regiment we hadn't met. Matthew muttered something to Andrew and all I heard was, "Pope." I poured the checker pieces back into David's haversack. Hoofbeats clumped in the road, and we scrambled out of the dust.

"Onward!"

Sergeant Falls rode past our temporary encampment. His arm stretched straight out towards the column of soldiers. He looked like Frederick Douglass, pointing beneath the bunting of Faneuil Hall.

We gathered our accoutrements for a new march. Haversack, cartridge box, canteen. Matthew struggled with his belt and I pulled its stiff leather.

"Left. Left."

My foot fell into step and I felt the weight of the gun against my shoulder and the rhythm of a thousand bodies marching. I trusted in my feet and the tautness of my shoulder and the blue and brown figure of Andrew in my periphery. He kicked at the red dust.

It was hot. Damn hot. I marched in a sea of red dust, kicked up by hooves and boots. My toe was healing, and the hardened skin knocked against the walls of my brogans. The sun was an orange eye, as if the gods shone a telescope from the heavens. The nights were pretty enough to sleep beneath the stars, but my exhaustion deepened until I could hardly sit down without nodding off into half-recalled memories and nightmares of strange colors.

"Doesn't seem that long ago that we were fighting," David said one evening at camp.

"Funny how marching makes me more tired than fighting," Andrew said, and I nodded, licking dusty lips.

Matthew spread his map upon the ground. He pointed to the various landmarks of railroad tracks, depots, villages, streams, towns.

"I think we're heading north. Did anybody notice we changed direction?"

I gnawed crumbly bacon, squatting by the small fire we'd made. "Go speak to Sergeant Falls about our movements."

"I don't think he wants to talk to me anymore."

"Why is that?"

"He told me I ask too many questions. I think I scare him."

"Form lines!"

The red dust turned yellow when we marched further north and crossed the Virginia border in the early afternoon. Maryland was open country, as if someone had unbuttoned the hills and laid them flat. Grassy mounds softly crested like waves, and we marched past scattered farmlands. Between coughs, I saw the array of scattered and abandoned articles by the edge of our road. A shiny pocket watch glittered in the light. I smiled, thinking of Mr. Washburn's face when I handed the watch back to him.

Our supply wagons were several regiments ahead of us, like slow-moving clouds on the horizon. The cannon were dragged backwards, their snouts heavy and stiff. I had heard their roar, but they were silent now, lugged by the mules.

We came to a hill and marched up its slope, squeezing more strength out of our strained limbs. Andrew helped us up the hill, and I heard not a sound of agony issue from his lips. Our climb increased its steepness until I feared my kneecaps would give beneath the sheer weight. More than once, I felt the anxiety of losing my balance and tumbling backward. But we at last made it up the hill and I was so dizzy with the exertion I removed my cap.

Sergeant Falls leaned over from the edge of our marching line and poked me with a piece of hard bread.

"He should lay off you," Andrew grumbled when I replaced my cap.

"It is nothing, Andrew," I said, surprised he even noticed.

"No talking in formation!"

Falls moved away, a snarl curling his lip. How he loved his mighty position on high. I had not pulled out *Paradise Lost* in more than a week, but it look little for me to recall a line. It popped into my head as surely as if someone shot it into me:

A mind not to be chang'd by place or time.
The mind is its own place, and in itself
Can make a heav'n of hell, a hell of heav'n.

Tinny notes blew in the distance, the sound like an old harpsichord. It was the evening bugles. I lived by the bugle call now. Those weeks at Fort Ellsworth had instilled so many regular, orderly calls I could barely remember what it was like not to know reveille or taps or the mess bugle.

We were to make camp here, halfway up a hill overlooking a beautiful valley. I spread out my blankets, while the regiment grouped into little blue bunches. Andrew made our fire and supper foodstuffs were passed around. The hard marching rendered our tongues mute and barely two words were spoken. I lay beneath the stars and counted six white pinpricks in the blackness before the hours slipped away into sleep.

I awoke to a bugle call. They were like brass gulls, cawing raucously each morning. I felt around for my jacket and pulled the wool on. A wave of mustiness hit my nose full force and I wheezed, causing David to poke me in the back. I reached for my brogans. The bugle cawed again. Andrew grumbled something and Matthew coughed. Mornings were the hardest. Not knowing where one was, poking around in the dark like some no-eyed creature, skin recoiling at scratchy fibers. My leg cramped from a strange sleeping posture, and I walked as one afflicted with a disease of the spine.

"Shut your mouth, Matty," Andrew snapped after Matthew tried to give us more information on our position, the movements of the other brigades, and even General McClellan's thoughts.

I managed a weak smile at my academic friend. "Perhaps General McClellan should read *Paradise Lost*, Matthew."

"*Oh?*" He swigged from his canteen, and began to quote: "*Others apart sat on a hill retired in thoughts more elevate.* That is a fitting line for our army this morning, is it not?"

Nodding, I continued the poem: "*They reasoned high of Providence, foreknowledge, will, and fate.*"

"Massachusetts! Form lines!"

"*And found no end,*" David said quietly, "*in wandering mazes lost.* I remember those lines well. This army is lost in mazes, too."

His eyes were sad and heavy, as if he bore the weight of all of our sorrows. I wondered at his downcast mood and stumbled into formation with the rest of the men. We were to march higher into a more aerial position. Would the Confederates charge this hill? I shuddered and forced my legs to move.

With daylight came the first sound of cannon fire in three weeks. It boomed up from above as if a giant stirred beneath the hills. I scrambled quicker up the slope, disregarding the immense groans as saplings and bushes shook to the roots. There were half a dozen blasts, then a long silence and the march slowed. A muffled shout floated up from the valley below, and I craned my neck around a tree for a better look.

"What's down there?" David said.

"It's either us or them," Andrew said.

Matthew gave an exasperated sigh. "If you listened to me, you'd know it's the Confederate army. They're apt to yell like that."

His prediction was not verified, so we marched to a fairly large open clearing on the far side of the hill, where we were told to wait. I had unloaded my things and stacked my rifle before I realized how advantageously positioned we were.

"This is a damn good spot," I said aloud.

"Quite so," David said. "Though we are not the ones damned."

I didn't know what he meant, but his gloomy countenance was unnerving.

Orders were to rest, but that could obviously change at any time. I liked our position. Our location was like a side-box at the theatre, private and unobstructed. Union cannons dug in right beneath us like balcony patrons. A beautiful tapestry spread out below, showing a cornfield and a pretty valley and a little stream in the distance. Puffs of smoke dotted the edges of the cornfield and troops moved on the far side of the valley.

Matthew pulled out a pack of cards and David chewed some hardtack crackers. I rested in the grass, propped against my knapsack, and settled in. A nap would be in good order, so I removed my cap and placed it over my face.

"Private Stuart!" No, not now. "On your feet, Private!"

I shoved my cap on in a haphazard manner, rolled onto my knees and pulled my aching, tired body upwards. My feet burned in the hot shoes, Maryland sun beat on the itchy wool, and all of the items dangling from my shoulders and belt felt as if I were Atlas burdened with the earth. I raised my hand in salute.

"That is the second time I've caught you removing your hat," Sergeant Falls began. "If you think, Private Stuart, I am going to tolerate such insubordinate –"

Artillery rattled our perch with booming shot and shell. I wavered on my feet and nearly pitched forward down the hill. Sergeant Falls caught the back of my sack-coat and yanked me back from the slope.

"Sergeant! Sergeant Falls!" Colonel Blaisdell hurried over from the front of the regiment, on foot.

No matter the reason, officers were needed elsewhere. Sergeant Falls abandoned his daily practice of torturing me and left. I leaned back against a tree, bracing my brogans in the dirt. The Pierce brothers abandoned their card game and joined me in realizing that watching a battle was a hell of a lot different than being on the stage.

Transfixed by the scene below, I could only sit in mute horror as the morning's battle began. Troops charged from the sides of a large golden corn-field. I heard the immense swishing when their bodies brushed against the papery stalks, the squeaky cries of the wounded, the clashing when they met in the center of the harvest.

"God damn it," Andrew kept muttering. He paced the slope like a chained dog. "Matty, let's go speak to Colonel Blaisdell."

"You can't," his brother retorted. "We are obviously in reserve."

I, too, brushed off his rash proposition. "Andrew, you'll be punished for insubordination. We'll move when we move."

He growled at my answer and pouted near the edge of the hill. As the hours passed, no other regiments helped the ones fighting in the cornfield below. I had no appetite for dinner after I beheld the mangled forms of the dead as they lain side by side. Andrew grabbed Matthew's map right out of his hands, and stabbed his finger at the grisly setting.

"So, are you going to put that on your precious map?"

"Andrew, that's enough!"

He dropped the map and gave up. David remained quiet.

Fighting shifted to the side of the valley, the low-slung grassy level meadow near a small white building that reminded me of the little older homes in Massachusetts. Cannons spat into the reforming lines, a thick trench lined with bodies of the fallen. It was easy to see our armies in blue, and the dead were the enemy. Again and again the lines formed and charged the trench in the middle of the field. Again and again the rebs shot into them. Buckled kneecaps, blasted groins. They fell by the armful. Flags dipped as they pulled back. Reformed, regrouped.

My eyes stung and the sun bore into my skull. How voluptuously greedy were the hungers of men. We spilled so much, too full of the murderous wanton. Spilled blood, spilled lives. David's face mirrored the despair I felt as we sat like fat kings and watched the pieces battle on a gigantic checkerboard. I began to understand why he'd been in low spirits.

When the lines in the meadow pulled back, they left behind their wounded. And the noises that came from the earth when the trench piled with the dead! The smoke formed a half-raised curtain above them, as if we were on Olympus and Aries toyed with the soldiers burning with his wrath. I was dulled into a stupor by the lullaby of the cannons and the rocking of the blasts.

"God damn it!" Andrew roared, hours later. Hours after we had been positioned like lords over all. "Why are we still here! Those men are dying and we're in reserve! Get me off this fucking hill!"

This time Matthew did not quiet him, but he couldn't shout obscenities and draw the officers' attention. I rose to my knees, but David had reached him first.

"Kneel, Andrew."

Andrew shook his head. "Let me alone, David. Your God does nothing for those boys. Go away!"

Though a full three inches shorter, David stood his ground. "Kneel, Andrew."

I don't know why he obeyed that time, but he did. He dropped onto his knees and bent his head low in frustrated agony. He wouldn't want me to, but I pitied my friend. Yes, we were in reserve, but what could we do?

David knelt beside Andrew, reached in his haversack and drew out his little Bible. Together the two friends sat at the edge of the hill, eyes closed against the war around us.

By afternoon the valley was cupped with the dead. They lay in perfect rows in the cornfield, seemingly asleep were it not for their twisted forms. Some crawled across the meadow; others remained face-down and perfectly still. They heaped in the trench, sleeping upon one another in a bed-like grave. From the hill, from this little clearing above them, it mattered not which color they wore. The air smelled strange, a rank mixture of metallic blood, smoky powder, hot earth. Flies swarmed amongst the dead, and the noise reminded me of the cicadas at Fort Ellsworth.

Battle lines shifted towards a small stone bridge far off to the side of the valley, right beside an adjacent hill. There must have been sharpshooters hidden on the side of that hill, for when the blue men and the tiny flags started to cross the bridge, they were picked off and fell into the skinny creek below. I heard the splashing, the pocketed cries. Again and again they started to cross that flat stone bridge and again and again they were picked off.

"Do you know the name of that little creek, Matthew?" I asked.

He hadn't spoken for hours, his map folded closed in his lap. We watched the fighting for a few more minutes. I assumed he was ignoring me and decided not to press him any further.

"Antietam."

"What, Matthew?"

"The creek. It is called Antietam Creek."

The Union troops on the bridge crossed the little creek, swollen with dead, and scaled the hill where our enemy hid. We watched them swarm the incline like flies around a carcass, and burst onto the crest.

"Ha!" Andrew shouted. "I knew they could do it!"

All four of us scrambled to our feet. I pulled the brim of my cap lower and stared out as far as I can see. Had we won? Were we going to secure the victory today?

Setting sunlight scorched an orange glare over the battle. Federal lines appeared at the top of the hill. Scrambling, stumbling, falling down their hard-won ground, tumbling into the creek below, spilling on to the bridge.

"They're coming back!" Matthew shouted hoarsely.

A vast chorus of triumph resounded behind them and enemy guns appeared and rained down upon them as they fled.

"No, dear God," David murmured. "No."

Men in blue huddled in pocketed groups on the other side of the bridge. Those who lagged, who slowed, were shot and lay still. The creek brimmed red like wine, and the Confederates on the hill rejoiced. I felt dull and sick, as if it were my blood flowing out and painting Antietam creek.

"Damn it! The rebs got the hill."

Andrew could do nothing. None of us could. We were in reserve today. We were not used. I wondered what General McClellan thought of the fight in the valley today. What of the cost in blood, bone, and muscle laid out this evening. There were thousands. Too many thousands.

David's face was pallid in the darkening light. "There was nothing we could do, Andrew. This fight was God's will."

I didn't know if I believed him. God did not order the blue troops in the field, nor did He order us in reserve. No divine hand caused a death today.

Under the stars, we retreated. Darkness bathed the dead and bits of moonlight illuminated their white hands and faces. We climbed down the hill, following the road back. I felt a mourning pity tonight. If I had one candle for each lost life, I could light up the sky.

Nobody spoke when we left the valley, found the main road again and marched towards a little white town. Faces appeared in dark windows. I saw women for the first time in weeks, rushing in and out of houses with their aprons full of bandages. They threw dirty water into the streets and directed the wounded where they needed to go. Bandaged men passed us and disappeared into the houses. Houses were hospitals, the dirt road washed in muck and blood.

We marched until the early hours. At last we found an open field free of the wounded. It was time to stack arms and rest.

The following morning we moved again, and Matthew returned to his map. We had crossed back into Virginia and headed southeast.

"They're calling it a Union victory," he said at dinner.

I sizzled a mixture of cornmeal and flour over the fire pit. It was the first time I'd ever cooked in my life, and I struggled to keep the mixture from burning.

"From where I was sitting, the Confederates took the high ground."

"That they did. McClellan should have pursued Lee. Lord knows he has the troops. Yet politicians are still calling it a victory."

"My father knew many politicians," I said, "and you can't call a weed a flower because it smells pretty."

Andrew returned from a nearby tree, hiking up his braces. "If we don't win one by Christmas, I'm marching right to the White House and giving Mr. Lincoln a shake in his boots."

"Then ask for bullets in your stocking, and maybe Santa won't bring coal!" David teased.

Andrew scooped a huge plate of my cornmeal hash. "Hey, coal is a great gift. Winter's coming!"

· 18 ·

One afternoon, my head opened with thoughts of home. I had not written since I'd been to war. I returned from drilling, sat on my cot, and my gaze fell upon a half-upturned hardtack box. My writing supplies sat forgotten on the box top - a pen and plain inkwell, paper sheets, envelopes, stamps.

A slat balanced on my knee and I dripped ink into the dirt next to my shoe. I stared at the paper for a long time. A song played in my head, the light waltz from the gala. Around and around went the dancers. Mother's fixed smile, Erik enjoying a cigar, Catherine's oval face. Around and around.

29th September, 1862

Dear Erik,

I have stolen moments from our monotonous daily ritual of drilling, eating, and marching to write to you. The battles have quieted and I can sleep without my ears ringing from the cannon fire and the rifle shots. This is not to say I find it a measurable alternative to home in

Boston. But I am here, and here I shall remain.

How is the office? I admit I do not miss Constitutional Law. I think of Harvard sometimes, but it is here that I truly live. Please pass my regards to Mother. It would be of great service if you would reply, and her as well.

I expect we will stay in Virginia for some time, as General McClellan is not famous for his aggressiveness. I send you several dollars from my pay, to let you know I am earning. Thirteen a month is little, so any financial compensation would be appreciated. I am not one to garnish my wages.

The hour grows late, and supper time is near. Forgive my lack of relating battle experiences. Memories are fresh, but the dead have been buried. I will write again soon.

Sincerely, Daniel

It is strange, my brother.

My whole life had been about our family. Our family, our name, our fortune.

But Father was dead and Erik worked at his desk. They had their own gravity, whilst I floated like a lost star. I should find a coursing path and light upon it. Perhaps it was here, amongst the wool and the powder and the bullets.

"Daniel?" David poked into the tent. His temples were wet and his cap askew. He still did not march well, and practiced more than any man I knew. "They're serving at the cook's tent."

"I'm coming."

"What's that?"

"I have written to my brother."

"Oh. Good. You're lucky to have plenty of stamps. I keep losing mine when we change places." He yawned and rubbed his neck. "Come on."

I followed David out into the sunshine of our latest temporary camp.

Virginia had been dry and bland for a week. The cicadas ceased buzzing and the soil looked washed out, like faded brick. Nature headed into the golden month of October at a brisk pace, which was more than anyone could say for McClellan.

When the summer turned into October, we received a new assignment. We disassembled the tents, gathered our things and our guns, and left the rural countryside behind. I knew, even when we kicked up the red dust, that I trusted the movement. I knew, even when my remaining cartridges rattled in the leather pouch at my waist, that we would be called back to the land to fight again. What did it matter, though? Perhaps we should spend the winter back in Alexandria, and that would be a renewal for all of us.

"Massachusetts! Form lines!"

I cupped my rifle and stood at attention. Sergeant Falls walked up and down the lines. Were it not for the dusty sack-coats, the weariness, the looks in our eyes, it was like we were back at Fort Ellsworth. Falls stopped in front of me.

"Private Stuart!"

"Yes, Sergeant!" I shouted.

"Are you proud to be a private in the Army of the Potomac!"

"Yes, Sergeant!" I shouted again.

"Are you prepared to fight and die for your country!"

"Yes, Sergeant!" Why did he single me out every damn day?

"Then why the hell haven't you tied your God-damn shoes, soldier! And why do you sit down on picket duty!"

My brogans were tied and I hadn't sat down on picket duty last night. This was starting to annoy the hell out of me, and I wanted to cuff him right across the ear. But my desires were cut short when all of a sudden a nearby bugle broke into a call I hadn't heard since we assembled for mustering. Sergeant Falls abandoned his position in front of me and quickly ran to the front of the regiment. I took the moment to steal a peek at my feet. Andrew snickered.

"He does love you much, doesn't he?"

"You were there," I whispered to David. "I wasn't sitting last night."

"You're like his camp follower," Matthew teased. "Hey. What's going on?"

Other regiments were marching up to line abreast along with ours. Half a brigade was assembling, moved into huge long rows. Colonels and brigadier generals on horseback rode up and down the lines, inspecting the colors, shouting at the regiments.

"This looks like a grand review," David said.

"The President was present after the Antietam creek battle," Matthew whispered, "but not this far south in Virginia!"

"Attention! Attention First Brigade!"

Brigadier General Joseph Carr rode out in front, surveying his assembled troops. I hadn't laid eyes on our brigade commander since the last day of the battle of second Bull Run. I'd admired him that day for his courage, but today there was something different about his erect carriage, the way he held himself on his horse. He exhibited the fierce side facial hair of General Ambrose Burnside, but I hoped he would speak of anything but the Maryland battle.

"Thank you for your attention. The Army of the Potomac has been reassembled into new Corps! We are now part of General Joseph Hooker's Third Corps! You may well remember the General who fought bravely in the cornfield at the battle in Maryland!"

A cheer rose up. I remembered sitting on the side of the hill, staring down at that bloodied cornfield and the bodies. I did not cheer.

"We are honored to be under General Hooker's command. Yet there is a greater victory than the one the Union secured at Antietam! President Lincoln has seen it fit to grant the Negroes in the south their full and complete emancipation!"

"What!" Andrew shouted when the cheer again sailed from the mouths of our fellow comrades. "Full abolition?"

"Can it be?" David stared at me, wide-eyed. "Does God smile upon the slaves this day?"

I could do nothing but shake my head. Brigadier General Carr removed a letter from his coat, unfolded it and read:

"I, Abraham Lincoln, President of the United States of America, and Commander-in-Chief of the Army and Navy thereof, do hereby proclaim and declare that hereafter, as heretofore, the war will be prosecuted for the object of practically restoring the constitutional relation between the United States, and each of the states, and the people thereof, in which states that relation is, or may be suspended or disturbed. That it is my purpose, upon the next meeting of Congress to again recommend the adoption of a practical measure tendering pecuniary aid to the free acceptance or rejection of all slave-states, so called, the people whereof may not then be in rebellion against the United States, and which states and may then have voluntarily adopted, or thereafter may voluntarily adopt, immediate, or gradual abolishment of slavery within their respective limits; and that the effort to colonize persons of African descent with the consent upon this continent, or elsewhere, with the previously obtained consent of the governments existing there elsewhere, will be continued. That on the first day of January in the year of our Lord, one thousand eight hundred and sixty-three, all persons held as slaves within any state, or designated part of a state, the people whereof thenceforward, and forever free; and the executive government of the United States including the military and naval authority thereof will, during the continuance in office of the present incumbents, recognize and maintain the freedom of such persons, as being free, and will do no act or acts to repress such persons, or any of them, in any efforts they may make for their actual freedom."

Carr pulled the letter down from his eyes. He read well, his voice clear and able. But it was plain he was greatly affected by this strange new document.

"If you wish to read the full proclamation, it is to be printed in Union newspapers across the states!" Carr continued. "I thank you all for your national sacrifice and praise be to God for the glory we have reached! Regiments dismissed!"

When the brigade dispersed and Sergeant Falls once again called us to line, he did not single me out. I had great interest in the emancipation of the Negro race. I would never forget how Frederick Douglass's earth-deep voice shook me to the core. But, for now, it was enough to have

Falls excited about anything other than my humiliation.

"It is only done to garner votes," Matthew said as we broke for a noonday dinner before resuming our march. "Lincoln's a politician same as any of the Whigs were."

"Of course he is," I said. "And he was a lawyer as well, so his strategies have been well-planned and executed."

"I don't care about votes or strategy," Andrew declared. He boiled water for coffee over the small fire. "The darkies will be freed now. Can you imagine it?"

"They are children of God, too. They are human, so different they may appear on the surface," David said.

"Human, yes." I shook my head. "They won't live brutish lives at the hands of tyrant slave-owners any longer."

"We are all sheep, Daniel. The Lord remains my shepherd and I follow Him."

David pulled out his little Bible and started to read Psalms. I played with the grass, looking out on the land. The greens were dying, turning colors. Not as vivid as a New England autumn. But the days were shorter, and I would soon face my first winter as a soldier.

"Up! On your feet!" Falls's order echoed down the lines. We gulped the rest of our meal and scrambled to ready ourselves.

It wasn't until we were assembled and on the move that the destination rippled down through the ranks.

Washington. I was returning to Washington.

· 19 ·

Rutted from heavy caissons and wagon wheels, the roads gradually straightened and became more passable. Traffic increased as well, and fortifications rose from the surrounding hillside. At last we came upon the city of Washington, approaching from a different angle than when we departed its shores in July. The October wind was chilly, and I burrowed further into my sack coat collar on the boat ride across.

Andrew pointed across the Potomac River towards the hazy gray line of the city. "I knew I'd cross this river again on my own two feet! Now where's that crazy ferry captain?"

"You said you'd rather be in a wood box," I said sullenly.

"All in good time, rich boy. All in good time."

Matthew rubbed his eyes. "After the ferry docks, we are to go immediately to our posted station. I don't think Daniel would like us to dally any further."

"You don't look so good, my friend," David said.

My belly was empty, and I struggled with heaves. Washington was how I'd remembered and yet not how I'd remembered at all. We passed makeshift fortifications, drilling troops, soldiers lounging in doorways, seated on barrels in the streets.

Our posted station turned out to be an ugly lean-to on the shores of the Potomac River, right beside the muddy banks of the rushing gray waters. My hopes faltered when I realized we were not a hundred yards from the dock. I wanted to forget our former time in this city.

We approached a stilted cabin half-sunk into the reddish mud. Were it not for the blue uniforms milling about, I'd declare we had come upon a place of Uncle Tom.

The regiment spread tents on patchy brown grass. It was after role call, a gray morning. The air tasted of late autumn, a November day six weeks early.

"Privates!" Sergeant Falls shouted. "You four!"

Of course we would be singled out again. It occurred to me that war might be easy were it not for the officers. The four of us trudged over to the shack and lined up abreast in front of its tilted opening. We stood at parade rest, quietly and sleepily, for nearly an hour. Somebody tooted a bugle, and regimental flags flapped. Lulled by the waters of the river, I looked up at a V of migrating geese. The birds honked, disappearing into the mist.

A dark skinny line appeared on the road from the city. The line moved slowly, escorted by officers on roan horses. Approaching our station was about the sorriest group of men I had laid eyes upon. Chains clinked on their gaunt wrists. Few wore caps, and the gray light revealed sunburnt foreheads, ugly crusted skin, thick hands and chests. They wore the remnants of uniforms, flat dirty gray and stained brown wool. None had shoes.

"Prisoners," David breathed. "Rebel prisoners."

Andrew clicked his tongue. "I'll be damned."

My friends and I moved to the side when the prisoners arrived. With little grumbling or cursing, they filed into the shack. Not one met our eyes. Sergeant Falls executed his orders swiftly, and within a quarter hour the forty prisoners were convened beneath the crooked roof of their temporary dwelling. Most sheltered within the walls, a few sprawling hairy legs beyond the shadow of the roof.

How this seeming bunch of bedraggled convicts possessed a threat to the vast armies of General McClellan, I couldn't claim to know. They picked their teeth, ran hands through their hair, coughed, tended to old scabs. It was like watching mangy cats clean themselves. Sergeant Falls shouted:

"Right face! Forward march! Halt! Left face!"

My friends and I faced forward, our backs to the prisoners. I felt uneasy, their nauseating noises hovering behind me. After Sergeant Falls had moved away, David leaned towards me and whispered:

"Our backs to the enemy?"

I shrugged and indicated other soldiers. Several stood at attention nearby, armed at the ready. David licked his lips nervously. We were a woolen shield, a fourth wall to the shack.

My skin crawled. Chomping teeth, endless scratching. The smell was awful, like a vegetable barrel on a warm day, rotting and over-ripe flesh. The morning stretched as long as a cold day at church. We were relieved for a noonday meal and then promptly returned to formation. My calves and shoulders ached from standing, fully clad in all my equipment. I rolled my neck and heard bones twitch.

"I didn't know we'd be put on prisoner detail," Matthew complained.

Andrew tapped his fingers against his rifle muzzle. "Knock your whining, Matty. I bet none of you yellows could last another day of this."

"Go tell that to Sergeant Falls," I muttered.

"And you, Daniel. You ain't superior either. You go to Sergeant Falls, but I'm staying right here."

Let him boast, let him brag. I gave my money away before donning this uniform. I had as much a right to be here and prove myself as any other. With that, I straightened my shoulders and concentrated on the river.

To keep our bet and our pride, we guarded the prisoners the next day. The rebs were fed at dawn, so had nothing to do all day but sit and stare at our backs.

After three days of agonizing guarding, Sergeant Falls relieved us and replaced us with comrades. My muscles were so stiff I felt like a three-day-old corpse. I could tell Andrew's pride was getting the better of him when he snapped at Matthew. Nobody spoke during our cold supper.

The following morning, Sergeant Falls called the regiment to attention and informed us four prisoners were seriously ill. Andrew's disposition had not improved after a night of sleep, and his sloppy posture attracted Falls's attention as fast as a minie ball found its target.

"Private Pierce! Look presentable, soldier!"

"Yes, Sergeant! I am an obedient soldier!"

I was none too surprised when Andrew's retort brought more than he bargained for.

"Private Pierce! I have a task even someone as thick-headed as you will obey!" Falls pointed to the sick prisoners. "Bring Private Matthew Pierce, Private Olney and Private Stuart! You ladies are to escort these prisoners to the Georgetown Union Hospital! That is an order!"

I inwardly groaned. Standing motionless for hours was one thing, but having to take these mangy enemy soldiers into the city was too risky a proposition.

"Privates, form up!" shouted Falls.

Andrew straightened. "Sir, with all due respect, I do not think we should take them to the hospital. I mean, what's one less reb?"

He had a valid point, but in true Andrew Pierce fashion, the delivery was less than ideal. Sergeant Falls scowled but, to his credit, did not say another word. We were given directions to the hospital and formed up beside the men, two on each side.

It began to rain, sprinkling our shoulders and the sandy bank. The river dulled to a flat metal gray. Washington huddled in a sorry state beneath a colorless sky. I shivered and pull up my collar.

We started up the path towards the city. The prisoners walked between us, their toes squishing in the mud, their clothes sodden rags. Andrew jabbed one or two and David grumbled of their slow pace, but there was no need to prod. They were not the fierce yelling barrier I met at Bull Run, nor the rows of tempered steel I saw from the hill in Maryland.

Washington provided shelter, but rain coaxed the city's smells and the entire environs stank like a sty. All of us gagged and held sleeves to our noses. The prisoners didn't seem to mind, and I wondered if they had been held in one of the run-down tenements.

"Where are you from?" David asked the prisoners.

"Tennessee." Although, to my ears, it sounded like "Tinisee."

"Georgia." A longer drawl came from the man beside him.

"Virginia." Quite the sophisticated accent, I thought. Soft and refined.

Andrew poked the man on the end. "You! Where are you from?"

"Ireland."

"Ireland?" I repeated, startled.

"What are you doing in the Confederate army?" David asked.

"They pay more'n me job."

"Damn it, he is a mick." Andrew laughed. "Remember that Mary Daley? What a pretty lass she was."

"She was more than a pretty lass," I said. "If you ever cared to know her."

"And who made you my mother?"

"Shut up, Andrew." Matthew pointed in the distance. "I think this is the main road."

We had come upon a bustling street, lined in ashen light and gray buildings. Horses and wagons drove by, and the city was alive with movement. It had been a long time since I'd been in a city, and I was surprised at the strange feelings of anxiety. The constant bustling provided quite a contrast to quiet Maryland hills and muddy Virginia valleys.

David rubbed his nose. "We turn left here?"

Matthew nodded. So we escorted the bedraggled quartet around the corner and down a similar street, no less noisy and even more crowded with wagons. Andrew cursed aloud when one nearly ran him over, dashing past with the speed of Apollo's chariot.

"What the hell was that!" He rubbed his leg. His hand smeared dark red, and he looked up in startled horror.

"An ambulance," David said. "We must be heading in the right direction."

I reached in my haversack and gave Andrew a handkerchief. He tarnished the fresh white linen with blood from the wagon. Another drove by at a slower pace. The wheels clipped along the muddied streets. Rain fell on the wounded limbs and bloodied faces dripped from its rear. A sickening cargo.

"Hey, Grady! Grady!"

The "Tinisee" prisoner glanced about in excited elation. So bizarre was his change in manner that I prodded him with my rifle. He ignored me and called out:

"It's me! It's Grady!"

A man appeared from the crowds, darting in between wagons and pedestrians. He was dressed well, a nice suit, cravat flapping in the wind. He came right alongside us, heaving like he had been running all morning. David was bumped aside, but held his rifle high. The stranger tipped his wet bowler hat, talking so fast I could barely understand a word.

"Grady, I thought you was dead! You heard the papers yet? Awe man, there's this Yank named Grant who's comin' after us. I thought you was killed! Too bad you were nabbed at Shiloh, eh? Why, look at ye! Where are you fellers going?"

"Excuse me!" Andrew jabbed his bayonet in the air. "We are escorting these prisoners to the hospital."

"Indeed," I said confidently.

"Well, indeedy do. I'll be catching up to there hospital. You take care yourself, Grady. They're building some prison down in Georgia for the Yanks!"

"Get out of here!" Andrew growled.

We were all ready to tear into him. He backed off, hands up in mock innocence. "I don't mean no harm, fellers. Don't mean no harm. See you, Grady. Bye!" He bobbed away into the crowd, colorful as a fishing float.

"The Union got you at Shiloh?" David said to the Tennessee prisoner.

"Don't speak to him," Matthew said. "This must be the place."

It had been, in no polite terms, a hell of a morning. I was glad to get out of the rain, out of the muddy street. Georgetown Union Hospital was a large square brick building that looked like it had been an armory. A flurry of activity swarmed about its front doors. Wagons rolled up to its doors, unloading their wounded and dying passengers. Nurses appeared and dragged the men inside. Others lolled about the front steps, sitting on wooden stools with amputated legs and arms wrapped in dirty bandages. I felt a stomach heave and clasped my mouth. Andrew patted me on the shoulder.

"Keep your bacon, Daniel. Let's get these rebs inside and get the hell out of here."

I couldn't agree more. Fortunately, the prisoners were too weak and sick to make much of a fuss. With a little pushing and shoving, we managed to get them up the steps of the building. Wounded Union men serenaded us with a chorus of angered jeers.

"Get them outta here!"

"What the hell are you doing with rebs!"

"Go away!"

"Wait, I think I see Bobby Lee!" A one-armed man at the doorway taunted.

My patience snapped. I broke from the formation and jammed the man's collar against the wall of the hospital, his empty coat sleeve dangling.

"I don't care who you are and what you've sacrificed," I hissed into his ear. "But you don't go making this war more hellish than it is. You got that!"

He winked. "Ain't you pretty, huh? I still got one good hand for you!"

He grabbed at my trousers, but I knocked him against the wall and would have provided another patient for the hospital were it not for Andrew's hand on me.

"Leave him be, Daniel."

I slowly let the man go and walked away. His laughter burned into my back. David gave me a comforting smile.

The entry hall of the hospital was a madhouse of bedlam, slamming doors, screaming, weeping, soldiers and nurses and doctors rushing in and out of adjacent rooms and up and down an enormous central staircase. Matthew, Andrew, and David wanted to leave the prisoners, but I suggested they find fresh beds. After they left, I stayed with the prisoners near the doorway. The rebels slumped against the wall, dripping and exhausted. I was grateful they wouldn't give me any trouble.

For ten minutes I waited, but no sign of my friends. The halls smelled of metallic blood and my head began to ache. I signaled a nurse, a girl of barely twenty, carrying a bowl of bloody water.

"Excuse me, nurse!"

She glanced at the prisoners. It was dark in the hall, little light from the windows. I couldn't see her face. She started to hurry off. It was too much. Too much to be laughed at, to march in the rain, to be forced into these tasks. I grabbed her arm.

"Look, nurse! Are there beds available?"

She struggled with my grip. My fingers twisted, and I grunted in pain. My haversack tipped, and I rolled my eyes as its contents tumbled to the floor. Damn it, clumsy girl.

The nurse picked up *Paradise Lost*, regarding it like holy water. I snatched it away from her. Her voice was so soft I could barely hear above the din.

"Follow me upstairs."

"Thank you." I wiped my brow and signaled to the prisoners. Matthew and Andrew returned. David soon joined us, shrugging his shoulders.

"Everyone is too busy. There is no help."

I pointed to the staircase. "I found a nurse. We are taking the prisoners upstairs. Why don't the three of you wait here? It will only take a few minutes."

"Glad to oblige." Matthew gripped my shoulder.

The nurse and I ascended the stairs, dodging other nurses, wounded soldiers, doctors, surgeons. The prisoners were weak from fatigue, hunger, illness. It was a struggle, but we reached the second floor. Thank God the nurse was right. Here were fresh beds, clean white linens, washed floors. I could weep with relief.

Several other nurses helped me with the prisoners. It was not until the Tennessee man, Grady, was tended to that I felt I could leave. I had taken too much time, and my friends waited. Soon I'd be free of this awful place. I started down the stairs.

"Sir?"

The nurse who helped me stood at the top of the staircase, framed by light from a window behind her. I smiled.

"Thank you again for your trouble."

"Yer mother's here, sir. Mrs. Stuart is here."

My heart gave a sudden jolt, like a lightening jag. "What did you say?"

"Ye don't . . . know me, sir?" She leaned closer. "Daniel?"

What – could it be? I stepped up, catching her face in the light. Dark eyes, roses, a face in the window. Long ago days, no longer my life.

"Mary," I breathed. "What are you doing here?"

Her cheeks were hollow, her skirts sullied from work, but her eyes shone through like a beacon. She had wanted to follow me to war. Good God, she had come!

"Sir, I had nowhere to go. Yer mother can explain. Aye, though she's not Mrs. Stuart any longer. She married Mr. Gage. She needs to see ye."

"Mother is here! Why?" Her face was sad, and I felt queasy, as if upon a roiling ship. "What has happened!"

She was silent, her eyes mirroring a sorrow I never wanted to feel.

"Mary!" I took her shoulder. "You must tell me."

"Let me go. I am not yer servant any longer, Daniel Stuart." She shook me off, her voice clear and strong once more. "Ye should thank me for even tellin' ye!"

"Oh, you damned Irish!" I smacked the top of the banister. "Were you sacked, Mary? Is that why you're here as a nurse and not as my mother's maid? Why did you come?"

Her voice broke. "Ye have no maids, Daniel. Ye have no servants! Yer mother married Mr. Gage so she wouldn't be in the streets!"

"How dare you speak of my family that way! You are lying."

"She's at the Federal Hotel down the street. Ask her yerself! If it don't grab yer pride too much, that is."

Another nurse poked her head in the corridor. "Girl! There are four new beds!"

Mary wiped her eyes. "I hated being yer maid! I'm better off here. Leave me be, Daniel. I don't want to see ye again."

She hurried off. I clung to the banister, my head reeling. I had to go to the Federal Hotel and speak to Mother. Something was wrong. Erik had never written to me, but perhaps there must have been a valid reason . . .

What the hell had happened to my family?

· 20 ·

"Daniel, we have stayed here too long," David urged when I had fled back downstairs. "We must return!"

"I cannot, not yet," I gasped. "Sergeant Falls may be angry with my tardiness, but I must go to a nearby hotel."

"Hotel?" Matthew pushed up his spectacles. "That makes no sense!"

Andrew rolled his eyes. "Forget about him, fellows. I'm leaving. Like we were ordered to do."

He strode from the hospital. The sky, gray as the Potomac River, greeted us with a torrent of rain. Andrew started down the road to the prisoner shack, but I shook my head.

"No, Andrew! I must go!"

David pulled his cap down to shield his face from the rain. "Then I will wait for you, Daniel. But do hurry!"

I mustered a smile, then ran down the crowded street, splashing mud. I found my destination easily, for it was the only hotel within the block. A droopy banner lay sodden against its clapboard face.

My heart was pounding horribly, the way it had at Bull Run. I chewed crusty bits of cracker, took a deep breath, and walked up the stairs. The lobby was brightly lit and cozy, a fire humming with two chairs pulled up before it. Months had passed since I sat in such a chair, warm before a glowing fireplace. I tenderly caressed the firm satiny fabric. Glasses of sherry, crystal twinkling in the firelight. Oysters and peach iced cream!

"Excuse me, sir?"

The desk clerk looked up. "Can I help you, soldier?"

My soggy woolens left little to shine beneath a glorious sun, but I was glad I wore my uniform. Mother would be proud.

"Find the room Mr. and Mrs. John Gage are in. Can you ring them?"

He eyed me haughtily, but had the decency to do my bidding. I rushed to the staircase and, within a quarter hour, Mother descended. At her arm was her new husband, John Gage. His white hair was wet, plastered to his head from the rain.

Mother wore the plainest dress I'd ever seen, naught more than a country calico. I couldn't have been more startled than if she showed up in nightclothes. Her simple bonnet framed her face in a tired oval, her hands bare of jewelry. She clutched a frayed brown shawl. I had spent months picturing her in the green silk from the gala, dancing like gossamer with the string quintet and bowls of luscious fruit.

I stood rooted by the fire. I had dreamt of rushing into a happy embrace. Yet she held back and I found myself not wishing to dampen her cheap dress with my wet coat nor sully her cheeks with my stubble and sweat. I merely kissed her hand.

"Daniel." Gage accepted my handshake. His voice was reedy, as if it had been hollowed. "It is good to see you. Now you may call me Father."

"Yes, sir. We are family now." I had never uttered a more vacant sentence. "If I may call you fortunate in your happy match. Mother is well under your care."

"We try, Daniel. We do try."

I hadn't known the war crept upon them like this, stretching sad gray fingers up to Boston. My disappointment mixed with confusion and a surreal sense of purpose. I had to know how our circumstances had altered so greatly.

"I regret that I take my leave," Gage said. "Mrs. Gage has news for you that is a family matter of great importance. We have not been married long, and you have been missed."

"I am sorry to see you go, but I am delighted that we have met up again this night."

He nodded. I felt more formal than in my dinner suit and starched collar. Such an affected difference. His suit was a little worn, but that could be from traveling. Maybe he knew of his cousin's death, but I had no time to ask him. He vanished up the stairs.

"Please sit down, Mother. I saw Mary at the hospital, and she told me you were here. I came straight away."

Mother and I took our seats by the fire. I reached across, but she drew her hand away. She looked down at her lap when she spoke.

"I had been trying to get word out for a week about the army's position. I knew your regiment from Erik's letter."

The one I sent after Second Bull Run. So my family had received it. They hadn't wanted to reply, or cared to. I leaned back in the chair, not quite knowing what to think.

"It was your letter, Daniel. Your letter that started everything."

"What?" I looked into her eyes. "What did my letter start?"

"Erik is innocent. He is innocent of all charges brought against him. You must take my word on that."

I shook my head. "Mother, I know your journey here was long and the rain does little to lift spirits, but I beg you to explain whatever it is that you're talking about. You have me at a loss, I'm afraid."

"We thought you had run out West, Daniel."

I felt a streak of pride, deep and strong within me. "No, Mother. I didn't go West. I came to Virginia to be a soldier."

"Mary tried to tell me. I had her beaten for her lies. Oh, but it was my own shame upon me when that letter arrived . . . and you were here."

No wonder the little Irish girl hadn't regarded me in quite the same light as before. I had entrusted her with the truth of my absence, only to have her doubted by my family. I wanted to see her again, to apologize for the conduct she had ungraciously received. A damn fool, Daniel. Must you be such a damn fool?

"Erik found it a decision of ridicule, to abandon your life and leave for war. He had it in good faith to come and take you home."

"Drag me home, more like it. A soldier's life is for commoners, is that it, Mother?"

I stood up. How could I have forgotten so easily? How could I have shoved these displays of falsehood from my memory with such expediency?

"I wish both you and Mr. Gage all the happiness in the world. But I have made my decision, the same when I made it months ago."

She reached out and clutched at the hem of my sack coat. Her fingers squelched the wet wool and droplets of rainwater ran down her wrist.

"I will not lose you, Daniel. I have lost so much already."

Her frantic manner startled me. "Mother, why are you dressed so poorly? And where is Erik? Why didn't he come?"

"Because he is still in Boston. He is imprisoned there on false charges."

"Brought about by whom?" I demanded, for there could be no doubt that Mother was speaking truthfully. Her eyes had met mine and I saw fearful hollowness in them.

"Mr. Washburn." She let go of my coat.

"That cannot be." I slowly settled back into the chair. "Please tell me what has happened."

"When Erik received your letter, he at once set about organizing a party to bring you home. To hold you accountable for your actions, he said. To bring you to justice for abandoning your family for foolish notions. I am not sure of the details, but I know he went to Mr. Washburn's residence at five o'clock the next morning. He didn't come home for two days, and no one could give me any news. Mr. Gage came to the house and said that Erik had been thrown in debtor's prison."

"Debtor's prison!"

She took a deep breath and let it out slowly. "In his will, your Father declared all his property to be divided between you and you brother in the event of his death. But, should either one of you find yourself unable to contribute to the family's welfare, he decreed that Mr. Washburn should be the supreme owner of the holdings."

"So, why is Erik in debtor's prison?"

"Mr. Washburn took our home, forcing us to declare bankruptcy. He stated it was on the grounds that since you were at war and had admitted in your letter that you would remain at war, that you were unable to contribute to the family's welfare."

"What gives him the right to say such a thing?" I demanded. "I assume this has gone to the courts!"

"Mr. Gage is currently fighting the case. But the courts care little for our family's ordeal when troops are fighting. The date keeps being postponed."

"I imagine so."

"You can imagine nothing!" She glared at me. "I am penniless! I married Mr. Gage to keep from starving. We are using his income to fight the courts and save enough money to free your brother. I was thrown out of my own home, by my own friend."

"Mr. Washburn will not let you in the house?"

"No, he and Catherine have already moved many of their belongings in. Mr. Gage and I live on Tremont Street. I have not been in that house in a month."

"Oh, God. Mother, this is a huge misunderstanding. He was Father's most trusted friend. How could he have done this?"

"I am glad my husband never lived to see this God forsaken war and his son's actions. You left your brother and you left me, without a word. You are far crueler than Mr. Washburn if you choose to remain here."

I thought of the forty dollars I had brought from home. Dollars fluttering in the telegraph office, dollars plunked in front of the colonel at Fort Ellsworth. The money was gone. And my garden was, too. I felt the world lost to me inside. I stood up in front of the fire, shaking.

"Have you seen Erik since . . . since this occurred?"

"No. I pray he will be released. But the paperwork has not settled."

"And if I were to come home?" I turned to her. "If I were to come, could I be instated as a member of the law firm and settle the accounts?"

"The only assurance Mr. Washburn has of keeping our home is that you wrote in your letter you would not return. But it would be quickly disproved should you decide to leave with us."

"I am a soldier now, mustered into the Army of the Potomac. Mother, your situation is more dire than I ever could have foreseen."

"Then, will you return to Boston with us?"

I offered my hand to her, but she did not take it. "I do not know how long we are to be stationed in Washington, but I will return soon with my answer."

"I don't understand. Why can't you come now?"

"If I left, I would be a deserter, Mother. And the honor of our family would mean nothing, if I do not uphold it here as well."

I bent to kiss her cheek, but she recoiled from me. "I thought you cared about me, Daniel. I even thought you cared about that precious garden of yours. What, you never wish to see it again? You never wish to see your brother again?"

I faced the red blaze of the fire, watched the dancing flames. "I knew when I signed up for war that there was a chance I could die. I have lived with this reality, and I have seen much death here."

"Erik could die, too." She pulled out a handkerchief. "He could rot in that jail the rest of his life. You have no idea how he has been broken."

I shook my head. "Erik will not break. I know him. He is stronger than I. But you need to see him. Please let him know that I have thought of him often and I wish him well in his circumstances."

Mother rose from the chair. "You are, indeed, lost to me, Daniel. I feel you no longer care for me."

"That is not true, Mother, but I guess that is how you see it."

"Good-bye, Daniel."

She went up the stairs, mustering as much pitiful dignity as I'd ever beheld. I wanted to make her understand my choices! Perhaps she had wanted something larger in her life at some point, some long ago dream that haunted her in quiet, infrequent hours.

Oh, Erik. I had seen the outside of a debtor's prison once. A tall blocky building like a fortress, tiny slitted windows like cat's eyes. I tried to imagine him locked in a cell, barred from the light, but I couldn't. Erik, you were too strong for that.

And Mr. Washburn, to be the snake in our midst we never saw. To seize upon our home and burrow into it, casting my mother and brother away like slop water. I made many choices, and perhaps being more aware of their consequences might have helped my family.

It rested upon me, a fault entirely mine.

Out in the rain, I felt the cold trickles easing down my neck. I stopped in the road. Nobody would have my garden.

Nobody but me.

· 21 ·

"Daniel, come on! We are late!"

"I'm sorry, but I had to see –"

"Let's go!"

The four of us made a desperate pursuit back to the little prisoner shack at the edge of the river. It was fast approaching night and we had been so detained my friends feared serious consequences. My heart sank, my breathing fast and labored in my ear. It was as if we were in that Bull Run forest again, the weight of the war upon me.

We came over the crest of the hill, glimpsing our regiment lined up near the shack. It was empty. Where had all the other prisoners gone? I had no guess, so we stayed silent, slowing our pace when we crested over the hill. Matthew paused to wipe his glasses. He looked at me with those brown fish eyes. I couldn't bear his stare and turned to David.

"That was a stupid thing to do," he whispered.

"I'm sorry, but I had to make that errand," I whispered back. "We have not done anything too ill, have we?"

"Wanna bet?" Andrew griped.

Sergeant Falls strode violently up the hill. He stopped before us in the rain, his figure sharply defined and his eyes like piercing blue coals.

"Private Andrew Pierce!"

"Yes, sir!"

"Private Matthew Pierce!"

"Yes, sir!"

"Private David Olney!"

"Yes, sir!"

"Private Daniel Stuart!"

"Yes, sir! Let me explain, sir!"

This time I received a nasty glower. "You are not given permission to speak! It was your responsibility to get those prisoners to the hospital and return immediately! Was that order clearly understood?"

"Yes, sir!"

"Did I tell you to speak!"

I stood as mute as a lamb. My stomach dropped to my knees, and I felt weak and stiff.

"The rest of you may go! But your rations are halved!"

David slunk beyond the sergeant, and I'd never seen Matthew look so relieved. They quietly returned to the regiment like sand rejoining a beach. I stood firmly, my gaze straight at the river. It looked like undulating metal, cut with white shards. It was the color of the sea.

"This is unacceptable, Private! Son, where the hell have you been! I sent Sergeant Dougherty to fetch you, but he said you had been down the street at a hotel!"

"Sir, I was seeing –"

"Silence!"

Suddenly, his expression changed to one resembling realization. He twisted his moustache thoughtfully, his voice oddly calm.

"I know it's hard being a soldier. Not many chances around here for a man. But don't you forget orders for a whore!"

What an accusation. "Sir!"

"You are dismissed, Private! I'll not report, but you know I'll be watching you. Send Private Andrew Pierce into my tent!"

I stared at my shoes. "Order understood, sir."

"Good!" He leaned closer. "And if I catch a whiff of those strumpets on you while you are on duty – well, God is the judge of that! But I will carry out the necessary sentence!"

"Yes, sir!" My voice echoed painfully, a cry of pride.

He waved his hand at me, then stalked back down the hill. The man thought I saw a prostitute. Oh, the indecency! And now I wouldn't get a moment's peace from Falls, for a break in orders that was unavoidable!

I could still leave with Mother. But Sergeant Falls would be watching me. I was surrounded by enemies who not only wished me harm, they wished themselves profit. If it wasn't Sergeant Falls, it was Mr. Washburn.

David and the Pierce brothers were putting up shelter near the prisoner shack, their tent half-constructed. I fell in to help, driving the stakes in the ground, spreading the fabric. Not one would look at me. When I tried to go over to Andrew, he pushed me aside. I blocked off his escape with my arm.

"Sergeant Falls wishes to see you, Andrew."

"Move, rich boy."

I acquiesced and brought my arm down. "I believe he has good intentions for you."

Andrew's arms hung by his sides. I waited, but he was silent. He walked away from me and up the slope towards the sergeant's tent. I assumed his place with our tent and helped get settled. It was a relief to sit beneath its wet canvas, out of the rain.

Supper was cold and dry, a few chips of beef and half a cracker. I had gotten used to the hunger, the cold, the wet. I barely noticed it and my sleep was so deep I woke stiffly the next morning.

I walked out of the tent and the sun beamed down upon me. My head felt full of iron nails. The red dirt at my feet was blindingly bright, a rich terra-cotta of carmines and scarlets. I stumbled over to the line where the rest of the regiment awaited.

"Morning, Daniel." Andrew smiled a broader smile than I'd seen in weeks. "How goes it?"

"Attention, company!" Sergeant Falls shouted. "I wish to announce the new positions of several of our ranking privates. Private Andrew Pierce is now Sergeant Pierce, in recognition of his exceptional bravery and courage displayed at the second battle of Bull Run. Come, sergeant, and receive your honor."

Andrew accepted his new stripes and the medal. He and Sergeant Falls saluted, then he rejoined our company. His pride and immense satisfaction gave him the look of a gorged lion. I pursed my lips. That's all Andrew needed – a new excuse to swagger about.

"Private Matthew Pierce has displayed exceptional ability as a navigator and general informer of troop movements. He shall be trained alongside the company adjutant. Come forth, adjutant assistant, and receive your honor."

Matthew received the adjutant book and its contents, and returned to the line. His face was set with the seriousness of his new position. Matthew acknowledged for his intelligence. It would have happened sooner or later.

"Private David Olney has also demonstrated excellent resources as a spiritual presence in our regiment. I hereby declare him the official chaplain of his company, to be consulted on all matters religious and sacred."

Made chaplain? David walked forward, received the little Bible from the regimental chaplain, and returned to the line. His eyes were cast to the ground, in typical David humility.

"I have no doubt you will bring pride to the regiment. Thank you gentlemen, for being assembled here today. The cook will prepare a fresh breakfast. We are to head out from Washington and are reported to camps at Fairfax Seminary in Virginia. Regiment dismissed."

A resounding cheer rose up from the crowd and everyone burst into shouts and cries of happiness. I unbuttoned the top of my sack coat. David showed me his new regimental Bible.

"It's the best one I ever had."

"It is of good quality. I know you'll enjoy using it."

"Well, well, well. If it ain't the mighty Daniel Stuart! Oh, should I say Private Stuart, eh?"

"Leave me be, Andrew."

"Who's the sour pickle?" He elbowed me in the shoulder. The

shoulder with no new stripes. "You know, I ought to thank you. If it weren't for your stupid antics on the battlefield at Bull Run, I wouldn't be a sergeant. But I get to gloat, since I saved your useless arse."

"I would not expect you to repeat that favor now."

"Now don't you insult me. It wasn't my fault you came back late."

"I had to ... do something."

"Sergeant Falls sure doesn't care, and I don't either. And you know what? I have spent enough time listening to how you are better than me and Matty and David because you grew up in some hoighty-toighty mansion —"

"Shut your mouth, Andrew!" I cuffed him across the arm. "You don't know anything about me. You don't know that my brother is in jail. You don't know that Mr. Washburn took our home and forced my mother into bankruptcy. You don't know, and you wouldn't care, either!"

"My, my. What a spot the Stuarts have gotten themselves into. Kinda makes me want to cry." He mocked my sadness in a sickening pantomime. "To see the codfish aristocracy brought down. What a shame."

"Get the hell away from me."

He laughed out loud. "I am fifty pounds more'n you are. And I'm a Sergeant now. Don't be stupid, Daniel."

"Well, if you enjoy your new rank so much, then I have a favor to ask you. I need to return to the hotel before we leave Washington. Can you grant me an audience with the captain?"

"How much money you got?"

I reached in my breast pocket. "Two dollars."

"Ha! I'd do it for ten, my friend. But not for two."

I pocketed the coins. "It's been pleasant, Andrew. Excuse me."

"Welcome to real life, Daniel Stuart. How sweet and simple it is."

I pushed past him and headed for the captain's tent. Andrew kept sniggering, and I could still hear him when I crested over the slope. Sergeant Falls stood in front of the headquarters. He stepped right in front of me, but I felt too determined to have him sway me.

"Good morning, Sergeant. I would like to speak to the captain."

"Purpose?"

"Permission for a short leave of absence, sir. Into Washington."

He scowled. "Haven't you had enough fun in the city, Private Stuart?"

I took a deep breath. "I was not with a . . . a woman of ill repute, Sergeant. I had to see a family member."

"Of that I'm sure."

But, to my surprise, he disappeared into the tent. I waited by the stone fence. It was not long before he reappeared.

"The captain will not grant you permission to leave camp, Private Stuart, and I am to escort you back to your quarters."

"What, sir? You gave him my reason?"

"You are dismissed, Private."

I pointed to the tent. "You will ask him again for me, Sergeant. I believe the captain is mistaken."

Falls turned and beckoned another officer. They flanked me, one on each side like jaws.

"There is no need, officers," I said quietly. "I will not cause any other trouble."

"That is for us to decide," said the second sergeant.

Escorted like a silly girl from a party, I was returned to the shelter tent. Matthew raised his eyebrow, David concentrated on his new Bible and Andrew couldn't help smirking. Falls spoke directly to Andrew.

"Sergeant, I'm making you responsible for this soldier. He doesn't seem to know his place."

Andrew saluted him. "Yes, sir."

The two officers headed back up the hill. I felt a cold weight on my shoulder. Andrew held his rifle out to me, the muzzle inches from my eyes.

"You have nothing here, Daniel Stuart. You gotta know your place. And I'll always be here to remind you."

"Oh, you think so?" I snapped. "Not if your stupidity and rashness get us all killed."

I ducked inside the shelter tent. God, I felt this exhaustion at home. A bracing against tides that spilled upon me. I fought against this suffocation, this slow drowning. It only made me more determined to cling, like a crabbed creature, to the jagged rock.

For if I did not fight, then Paradise would be forgotten to us all.

· 22 ·

"So Lincoln wants Little Mac to move, eh?"

Andrew polished his bayonet. He held out the long shaft before the firelight, glinting like an icicle. I yawned, tired on our early morning march.

"Ole Abe's gotta figure out something," Andrew continued. "McClellan ain't had us do a thing since that Antietam creek battle. What of the reports, Matty?"

His brother sat on his haunches, papers tilted near the small fire, studiously peering over the figures.

"These accounts are so muddied, it's like they were written backwards!" He crumpled up the pages and threw them into the fire. "Sergeant Pierce, you have to bring this regiment up to Army regulations and standards!"

I laughed. I couldn't help it. I hadn't seen Matthew this frustrated since school days trying to explain *Paradise Lost* to me.

"Oh, you think that's funny, Private?" Andrew stood up.

"I can't tell who is sick, who has deserted, who has leave, and even if we're fighting for the Union!" Matthew took off his spectacles and scratched his eyes. "Oh, leave him be, Andrew. I'm tired of your fighting. Go pick on Sergeant Falls."

Andrew shrugged, but not before giving me a sly wink. "I got you for extra drilling soon as we camp, Daniel. I'm ordered to watch you."

"Then follow me to the chamber pot," I muttered. "It's quite a show!"

Matthew stood and grabbed Andrew's haversack, which was around his neck. His brother stumbled backwards.

"Sergeant!" Matthew shouted. Andrew's hand went immediately to his brow. "I'm also a private, you ridiculous ignoramus! Leave Daniel alone, find Sergeant Falls and ask him when we arrive in Fairfax Seminary!"

Andrew pointed at his eyes then at me. Yes, Andrew. Everybody knows you'll keep an eye on me. God, even the Confederates know! After he had disappeared in search of Falls, I took his seat by the fire and started chuckling.

"It speaks poorly of your conduct that you insist on making him angrier." Matthew kicked the soil. "He's got stripes on his shoulder."

"I imagined us in battle again, but the Confederates weren't firing. They were sitting on the ridge, watching me!" I laughed harder.

"We will all be in the grips of madness if we don't settle somewhere," Matthew said. "The army is scattered and unfocused."

"Those reports were from the adjutant?"

"The man is frightfully disorganized," he complained. "I'm not just his assistant – I'm his clerk!"

"Company C! Fall in!"

I pushed some sand and heaped it on the dying fire, swigged the last of my coffee and tucked the cup into my haversack. A small figure moved amidst the stirring troops.

"How is David with his new chaplain duties?"

"Took to them like a duck to water," Matthew said. "I cannot wait until we cease this endless marching. You know, it was mighty wrong of McClellan not to go after Lee. The General complained to President Lincoln that we're fatigued and our horses are tired, but I am ready for another encounter with the enemy!"

We shouldered our rifles and joined the columns. The weather was perfect for a march in wool uniforms. A cool breeze played with the leaves and swirled bits of dying grass at our feet. The dust had settled, the sky a brilliant October blue. I enjoyed the familiar clinks and swishes and hoof beats and footsteps as we passed through Virginia's countryside. The cicadas had stopped buzzing, birds honked above us on a winter flight, and the leaf colors blended and melded into a palette of muted tapestry. Now and then I caught the unmistakable whiff of wood burning, of stoves lit in the scattered farmhouses. I loved autumn.

Yet even the beauty of the days did not cover the uneasiness I felt each evening as we stretched blankets beneath the skies. Mother still waited in Washington. Each step away from the city brought me closer to the Confederate army. If my heart had made the choice to go with Mother, my feet made the choice to carry me from her.

"Well, you wanted to know when we'd arrive," Andrew said to us one evening a week after leaving Washington. "Tomorrow we camp at Fairfax Seminary, to await further orders."

"It's in Alexandria," Matthew said. "We are returning to where we started. How fitting."

He was right. On October seventeenth, one month after the Maryland battle, we crossed King Street in Alexandria and came in sight of an enormous brick building with a cupola on its roof. It was a fancier cousin to Faneuil Hall, in its resemblance to that patriotic center of Boston. The grounds were neat and trim, the lawns well taken care of, and the entire appearance was one of tidiness and order. It was easy to share David's excitement.

"If this is to be our winter camp, we are blessed," he murmured. "This place of God will shelter us from the cold."

We circled Fairfax Seminary, ordered to set up shelter tents on a large lawn several hundred yards from the main building, named Aspinwall Hall according to Matthew. A sweet little chapel, a library, and several other halls and buildings created the feel of a university. I was reminded of Harvard more than once as we settled into our new home. It had been months since I'd felt so comfortable in our strange, ever-shifting life.

Aspinwall Hall watched over our drilling, and our daily routine came to resemble the days at Fort Ellsworth to such a degree I fancied we had returned there. Again we were in the vicinity of Alexandria, again on the other side of the river overlooking Washington. Autumn set in and we drilled beneath a plush blue sky amidst swirling golden and scarlet leaves. I kicked them softly when I marched, crinkling beneath my feet.

David pulled out his checkers game, Matthew devoured the books in the library, and I started reading my dime novels. Their wild adventures, the pleasant setting, and the increasingly optimistic morale cheered my spirits and reinforced my convictions. Soldiers laughed again, Andrew's prideful temper softened, and even Sergeant Falls managed to let me alone. Darker days faded to memory, and, save for an occasional cannon burst or a startled horse's whinny, I thought little of battle.

Seven miles separated me from the hotel. I thought of Mother and was so confused over the strange nature of my conduct towards her I knew I had to reach Mary and ask her to pass along a request for my family. I doubted she would open my letter, but I had to try.

One afternoon between drills, I addressed an envelope to the hospital in care of Mary, and penned a note.

20th Oct, 1862

To Mary Daley,

Thank you for telling me about Mother at the hotel. I am in your debt. I have a note to pass along to her, if you would be so kind to oblige me. Please let her know that I wish to hear from my brother, Erik. I know he is doing poorly, and wish to know of his exact condition. You were a good servant to me and I apologize for any ill conduct I may have displayed.

Daniel Stuart

I reached in my haversack and pulled out a little tintype frame I had carried since the morning I left home. It was my family. Mother, Father, Erik, and myself. I remembered the day the photographer visited our home, for it was a day of April Fools and Erik had played a joke on me. I smiled to think of it. The outlines of an ink stain were still visible on my shirt. Disappearing ink, eh? He dumped half the contents of an inkwell all over the front of me. Mother was furious, but that was the last time I heard Father laugh.

He died a week later.

His funeral was the prettiest spring day I could recall. A warm sun broke through the cold and the dying earth awoke again. When I visited the garden, a golden crocus greeted me where none had bloomed before. I parted the snows and sprinkled a tin cup of water on her jeweled petals. Such tiny, aching beauty.

"Private Stuart? Don't you realize –" Andrew leaned down and stuck his head in the tent opening.

I took my hand from my face, wiping the tears away. Embarrassed, I put the little daguerreotype back into my haversack.

"In a moment, Andrew." I struggled to keep my voice from cracking.

"Sergeant to you." He dropped to his haunches, cocking his head at me. "Your family?"

I reached for my handkerchief, wiping my nose. "The daguerreotypist took our portrait in the parlor. I . . . I think we all knew Father was dying, but I still had to help Mother choose a mourning gown. Now she is penniless, and my family's fortune is in shambles. Our home has been usurped, and my brother sits in a prison."

"Is that letter for him?"

I shook my head. "It is of my concern, Andrew."

But he had the envelope before I could blink. "Mary Daley? Pretty little mick lass from Boston?"

"Give it back to me." I tried to take it from him, but my position was awkward and I tipped over onto the gum blanket.

"Sergeant Falls was right! You did see a woman that day in Washington!"

I crawled out of the tent and stood up. "She is a nurse at the hospital.

I didn't know she was there. She helped with the Confederate prisoners!"

"You leave her be, Daniel. She was your servant, but she's free now."

Confused, I reached for the letter again. "She told me about Mother and Erik. Why do you assume I want her to do my bidding?"

"She told me things about you and your family."

I stopped. "What of it, Andrew? She's my maid. My family's servant."

"Aw, come off your high horse, Daniel. So what if your daddy is gone, huh? We sat on the hill and watched thousands die. Your old life is gone. Mary ain't your servant. Don't send her any letters."

"It is not your concern!" I snapped. "I can write to whom I wish!"

"Sergeant Pierce! Private Stuart!"

It was Sergeant Falls. I could barely believe what had happened. One moment I was telling Andrew of my family and the next he was stealing my letters. And now he would go to Sergeant Falls and tell him I was writing to a woman of ill repute or some other such nonsense. It was childish and cruel. I couldn't imagine my friend would do such things.

But I hadn't foreseen Mr. Washburn's behavior, either.

I joined the rest of the regiment at drill and the day was beautiful, but the glorious fall afternoon mocked me. I had wanted to help Mother and prove to Mr. Washburn I was capable of helping my family, but what a foolish notion. Stop being so idealistic, Daniel. What can you hope to do?

How can you possibly help?

Well, if I was not going to be able to write to Mary, then I had to find another way to reach my family. Six months ago I was giving her orders, and now I begged for her company. Matthew could help me. He was the only person Andrew ever listened to.

I took *Paradise Lost* out after supper, opened it to a random middle page so any passerby would think I was reading, and penned a new note to Mary. My scribblings went unnoticed by the sergeants, for they were carousing with bottles of hard apple cider freshly brought from Washington. After addressing the envelope, I quietly slipped from the jovial group clustered around the autumn bonfire and crossed the long lawn, over to the building where I knew Matthew would be ensconced.

A single candle was lit in the library windows, small flame dancing on the Gothic arched panes. I wondered if it had been a smaller chapel at one point, for the stones were large and blocky, and the bookshelves as massive as Medieval pews. I couldn't help but smile when I found my scholarly friend, bent over an enormous book that looked old enough to be encased in hide. He peered up and down the rows of letters, magnifying glass in one hand, pen in the other. I did not think I would startle him, but it was inevitable.

"Holy Mother, Daniel!" His voice echoed off the thick walls, the old books. "Not one to enjoy the hard cider tonight?"

"I had my share." I took out the envelope. "I have a dear favor to ask of you, Matthew. Can you please see this envelope delivered?"

He took it, noticed the address, cocked his head. "Mary Daley. I know the name."

"The girl from the Bull and Boar. The one who . . . danced with me the last night we all went together."

"Ah!" He chuckled. "My goodness, Daniel. She is at the hospital in Washington?"

"Under no circumstance must Andrew know of this letter. It's important."

"I cannot lie if he asks me of it, Daniel. That is my only stipulation should you choose to use me as a passenger pigeon."

"I don't intend to use you for anything, Matthew, besides a lecture!" I playfully pushed his shoulder, but my clumsy friend couldn't hold his balance and toppled over the huge book. When he righted himself, a thin film of dust had settled upon his brow.

"To dust we return," he muttered.

"That is what David would say." I paused. "You will mail the letter, then?"

"Come off it. I'm smarter than you think. Now, if you'll excuse me, I must return to Homer."

I held up the cover, reading the title. "*The Iliad.* My goodness, Matthew. You can't just fight in a war. You must read about it as well?"

"If this torn country of ours is to ever cease war, we must know of its historical origins, its current ideals, and its future causes."

"The past can't be altered, but I am afraid I grow too cynical to believe the coming years can change," I said. "If only we were the ones inside the great wooden horse, for the unsuspecting Trojans to find."

"It was a brilliant maneuver, but not respectable warfare. It should be as Napoleon dictated: lines of men facing one another across an open field, chivalry and valor at their finest." He shook his head. "I fear this war grows too tainted by its own bloodlust, its own need to squeeze the South from her resources, block her naval ports, cut off her railroad supplies, and employ back-door tactics."

"Yet, the end result was accomplished." I tapped the cover of the book. "Troy was sacked. Would you fight an extra battle, with ten thousand more casualties, to preserve valor? Or would you employ these back-door tactics and annihilate the enemy?"

He met my gaze with one of unusual intensity. "I care not for the numbers of the dead. It is as war logically ought to be. But I can never argue against qualified tactics."

"My friend, you are alike to Andrew." I gathered my things and tipped a salute. "Be sure to get some cider before it's gone. We'll be back to green coffee before you know it."

He smiled and picked up the magnifying glass again. I was pleased with myself for enlisting his postal services. Andrew's promotion had not only advanced his military rank but had swelled his head to sizable proportions. Preventing me from mailing a simple letter was comical. Well, if he thought to discourage me in so petty a manner, I would employ my own tactics. Unlike Matthew, I did care about the numbers of the fallen.

As the days bled into weeks, the army gradually became woundless. No battles were fought, no pawns shifted into place. Instead of the game against the enemy, we were immersed in a lulled inertia. I had spent more time at Fairfax Seminary than any other place in my life save my home. I came to know its mossy clover in the shade, its lines of trees we picketed beneath, its high stone walls shadowing us from Alexandria.

I loved being close to town and so near to Washington. Fresh bread and vegetables came from nearby farms. I was even startled one wondrous evening when mulled wine was passed about, and I wouldn't have traded a glass for all the bottled sherry in a Parisian wine cellar.

Our Irish comrades in the regiment brought out a playful side when they carved turnips and pumpkins the last night of October. We had little in the way of costumes, but Sergeant Falls had enough of the famed trickster in him to enjoy scaring us. I enjoyed the pranks, the jokes, and the special cakes baked by the Christian Ladies Union of Washington. As they passed the rounds about, I sought a friendly face and asked if she knew Mary Daley.

"No, sir, I am sorry I don't know her. Your wife, sir?"

"Wife!" I blurted so loudly I caught Andrew's attention. He shook his head at me. The startled girl moved off, and I was left yet again with no word.

The next day was cold, gray, and the Seminary resembled a giant prison. I nursed a headache for hours, annoyed and snappish towards my comrades. Matthew left me well enough alone; he scurried about with rumors of a winter battle. I grew weary of him, avoided Andrew, and neglected my supper. David found me in the tent, wrapped in blankets and curled against the canvas wall.

"Daniel? Are you ill?"

I sat up, rubbing my eyes. "I was thinking of my family. I fear I have abandoned them, but I thought I had done the right thing."

"God gives us rain when he knows our garden needs it," David said. "You did see your mother in Washington, didn't you?"

"Yes, of course. I did happen upon one of the girls from the Bull and Boar. Do you remember Mary Daley?"

"I remember you two dancing." He laughed. "Come with me to the chapel. I wish to show you something."

I followed him across the Seminary lawn. Long navy shadows stretched across the land. Fires sprang up among the men, bright bits of orange and red mixing with the darkening twilight. The night was cold, and I snuggled further into my collar. My breath curled like smoke. It wouldn't be long now before I slept within a wintry cradle.

Beside the library, right next to Aspinwall Hall, stood the tiny chapel. Built in the Middle Age Gothic style, it had heavy dark pews and narrow slitted windows. The center aisle was barely wide enough for my friend and I to walk abreast. The pulpit was the simplest I'd ever seen, a slanted top crowning an unadorned podium. I was reminded at once of Frederick Douglass, eyes bearing upon me, fist slamming with each syllable. Behind the pulpit stretched a window of stained glass, featuring a design of a cross and nothing more. David lit several more candles, and tiny flames illuminated the humble scene.

"We will not be at this seminary for much longer," David said. "General McClellan will move us southward again, back to the jaws of the enemy."

"Yes, we are soldiers." I fingered the hem of my sack coat. "It's quite remarkable they have made you chaplain."

He surprised me by shrugging his shoulders. "It is not the title I find interesting, Daniel. Only insofar as others truly see me as an instrument of God. I am His voice for them, and for you."

I looked up at the stained glass. "I appreciate your talents, but I am in no need of any services."

"Yet we are a part of a holier story. Children hear the tales of David and Goliath, and Daniel in the Lion's Den. There is a St. Andrew and a Gospel of Matthew. We play a larger part than we think we do."

"Hard to remember at six in the morning when we're called to drill."

"Absolutely!" David laughed. "I still cannot march as well as you. Sergeant Falls has more than enough enjoyment when he reminds me. I guess what I wanted to say, is there is meaning to this."

"To the war?"

"Yes, but not war alone."

He stood and walked to the podium, as he did in Boston so many months ago. Again I was struck by the gravity of his words, the firmness of his gestures, and the conviction haloing him like an angel. He spoke to me from the pulpit.

"Do you still want to leave, Daniel?"

"What?" I said, caught off guard.

"You were ready to leave when we stood on Alexandria's shores. You were ready to turn around and go home. Do you still want to?"

"David, I don't know. But I would be a deserter, and that is a crime I cannot commit against the Army and against the country."

"Unless your family paid for another to take your place."

"I am not sure if that is something they could do, given their circumstances."

"You would say yes, should that question arise?"

I rubbed my face, staring down at the large blocks of stone in the floor. "I do fear for my family's future. My brother sits in prison for debts and I am the one responsible. I am tired of the fighting, David. I am tired of fighting inside myself. We will move again and we will fight again. I am tired of not being able to do anything."

He gave me a little smile, then stepped down from the pulpit and extinguished several of the candles. We were soon in near darkness. He went to the foot of the stained glass cross, then knelt beneath, head bent. I stood and walked over to him. He pulled me down beside him.

"Dearest Lord, grant your servant Daniel the courage he needs. The courage for the lions he faces. The courage for the lions within and the lions without. He fights to please You, and in honor of his own Father. He fights to free our brothers in chains, and for his own brother. He fights for Your son and as a son. Grant him courage. Amen."

"Amen," I breathed.

I lowered my eyes in shame. If the ones who fell at Second Bull Run and Antietam faced their last moments with courage, then I could do the same. When David offered me his hand, I shook it with more reverence than I had ever felt.

"Your prayer was an incredible gift. Thank you."

"Daniel, the punishment for desertion pales in comparison to the dishonor of your soul. It is easy to run away. I have dreamt more than once of Boston. And you come from luxuries few here have ever known."

"It seems like a long ago dream. Like a life not even mine."

"But it was. You should be proud to come from such an accomplished family. But it is each man's God-given duty to follow his own course.

Yours led you here. I'm giving you a little help, that's all."

I chuckled, my laughter echoing off the stone walls. "I appreciate it."

He pointed to the final lit candle, the tiny flame flickering with the energy of a greater blaze.

"You will be able to see the way, so long as one candle burns. Or one star shines."

I clasped his shoulder. "And so long as I have a guide to help me."

Leaving the chapel, I made my way back to the tent. It was a long while before I fell asleep, but it wasn't because of the November chill or the rumors of the army moving.

I lived a larger story. Hard to remember during its smaller moments, but I was part of the great Army of the Potomac. A single drop amidst its steely tides. I needed courage to remain, but I belonged here.

I belonged here.

· 23 ·

The final summer flowers died, and it must have been the sign General McClellan awaited. The Army of the Potomac stirred from tents and barracks, ashes swept from fireplace sites, and blankets rolled. Regimental bands dusted off their drums, and fifes twittered like spring birds. I felt lightness in my heart and whistled my way through preparations.

Matthew scrambled about like a headless chicken, papers fluttering. I jostled his elbow, and his grumblings about the army made me smile as he recounted his sixty rounds.

"Took Little Mac long enough. We've been here nearly two months."

He asked to borrow a stamp, and I felt a twinge as I handed him one. I hadn't heard from Mary or Mother or Erik in the long weeks. I didn't know what to make of their silence and tried not to assume the worst.

"Regiment! Form up!"

I shouldered my rifle, adjusted my belt, and joined Matthew and David once more in the ranks. Our brigade had rested here so long, the grass was stamped down and trees on a nearby ridge had disappeared. Horses were restless, and cannons shuffled by us. I hadn't seen their long snouts and full caisson wagons in weeks, since they'd been practicing at nearby Fort Ward. I stamped my feet to keep warm. The November breeze was chilly, and I moved stiffly.

David had greatly enjoyed our time at Fairfax Seminary, so I gave him what I hoped was an encouraging grin. He returned it with a sad smile. Sergeant Falls escorted the color-bearers to the front of the column, then returned to where Andrew was stationed at the head of our company.

We stepped off, marching as one. It had been a strange autumn, and I was more than a little fearful of winter. I'd spent a lifetime of winter evenings curled up by the fire in the parlor, sipping hot teas under thick quilts. I braced myself for the hardest months I had yet to face as a soldier. Woodcut images of the Valley Forge Revolution soldiers starving in their winter camps did little to alleviate the anxiety. Well, if General McClellan was as conscious of his troops' suffering as Washington had been, we'd see through the snows and attain victories.

The march was slow, due to the sheer numbers. We met up with the remainder of the Third Corps beyond the boundaries of Alexandria and marched south. Washington was clearly visible across the Potomac's gray waters. I didn't realize I'd been staring so long at it, when I tripped and nearly toppled David down with me.

"I am marching better than you this morning," he said. He glanced at the city, then his expression changed to one of realization. "You must take care, Daniel. I fear Mary may have bewitched you."

"Nonsense!"

I hadn't meant to utter it quite so loudly, and Sergeant Falls relished the opportunity to berate me for talking in the ranks. I ignored his tirade and, after he had moved off, I sought David again.

"She never wrote to me. It was weeks!"

"Calm yourself," he whispered. "Do you not realize we are heading into an encounter with the enemy?"

"And this time, we will fight," Matthew added. "I fear for the strength of the Confederates' position. They have had more than enough time to recover from Antietam."

Bigger picture, Daniel. I silenced and continued the march. Matthew had scouting reports in his head, David devoted himself to God, and I merely wondered about a former maid. I felt as foolish as I had when I first left home.

Within several hours, we'd marched away from the iron waters of the Potomac and veered west. Gray skies hid the sun's warmth. Some skirmishing interrupted another regiment in the brigade and delayed our supper for an extra hour, but my comrades and I were not engaged. We'd barely progressed ten miles by the time we stretched out blankets in the Virginia countryside. The landscape was misty and soothing, rural farmlands and hills and great stretches of trees. In the distance loomed the Blue Ridge Mountains. I would have liked to settle here, the weather milder than Boston and the natural contours of the land pleasing to the eye. I could see why Jefferson and Washington and Lee all loved their beloved home state.

Marching continued the following day. I was lost in thought, fancying a Thanksgiving dinner spread out on the dining table, when all of a sudden we stopped. Nobody knew what to make of our abrupt pause, until a strange order rippled down the ranks:

"Make way for the pontoons!"

Andrew and Sergeant Falls lost no time in ushering us to the side of the road, bunching the ranks and confusing the captains. I had heard of pontoon boats, but had never actually seen one. Matthew sniffed the air.

"If I remember my map correctly, we must be near the Occoquan."

"The what?" David said.

"The Occoquan is a river. We crossed it by locomotive on our way from Fort Ellsworth to the Bull Run battle in August. It seems we are to cross by foot today."

"Is there nothing but rivers in this state?" I yawned.

"Hate to disappoint you, Daniel, but this is not the last river we'll see in Virginia."

"I'll wager."

We stayed by the side of the road for such a lengthy while I took a seat in the cold grass. The ground was stiff with winter's frozen breath. I wrapped my arms around my knees and pulled them to my chest to keep warm.

"They're coming!" David said.

A great rumbling shook the earth, then the pontoons came into view. An enormous assembly of wheeled wooden contraptions rumbled by. Resembling gigantic slices of wooden fruit with flat tops, they sat on wagons pulled by horse teams, like caissons. Were these boats?

Andrew came over to join us, smoking a cigar. "They're pretty funny lookin', aren't they? The engineers lash 'em with ropes and they create a bridge."

"When are we expected to cross?" asked Matthew.

He blew a smoke ring. "Eh, maybe tonight. Most likely tomorrow. There's so many regiments, and you can only march a column of two abreast. So hold your horses, Matty."

What I wouldn't give for Mercury's winged feet right now. Disgusted, I remained sitting by the side of the road. David's unearthly patience annoyed me, and I said no to a checkers game. Matthew chatted with the sergeants about our position, what the Confederates might be doing, the latest issue of *Harper's Weekly*. He secured a copy of the issue from October 25th, featuring a comical wounded Garibaldi on the cover. I cracked a smile at his pathetic state, but gained a true amusement when David quoted from an inside section:

"Hear you this, Daniel. 'Of all the vanities and fopperies, the vanity of high birth is the greatest. True nobility is derived from virtue, not from birth. Titles, indeed, may be purchased; but virtue is the only coin that makes the bargain valid.' "

"Quite so?" I pulled *Paradise Lost* from my haversack. "I never had to purchase this title, did I?"

The men laughed, but my spirits truly heightened when at last we got to our feet and prepared to cross the Occoquan River.

I leafed through the *Harper's* issue, stunned by a particularly gruesome image from Antietam. The dead and wounded piled near the little white house, the gallant charge of the 20th New York, the enormous two-page spread of the fallen rebels under moonlight. In the center of this horrific tableau knelt a girl with wild hair and rolled-up sleeves, tending a soldier in the throes of agony. Ugliness reigned around her:

dead boys slumped over tipped barrels, men fishing corpses out of the creek, soldiers grabbing up the limbs of their comrades. I shut the covers. Matthew gave me a strange look when I violently shoved the magazine back into his hands.

"You all right?"

"I look forward to crossing this river."

It was my first experience marching upon this strange, swaying path of pontoon boats. Our brogans clamped upon the boards, and our breath made tiny white swirls in the colorless air. We crossed over the river and rested beneath the cover of trees on the opposite bank.

Andrew was eager to keep going, but our strength was massive and we waited for a week. The whole long, shuffling mass of the army slowly, ever so exquisitely slowly, made its way across the pontoon bridge. I grew weary of the sounds of the shoes on the boards, and rubbed my temples. At last, we were to move again. Andrew stomped his feet against the cold, blowing on his hands.

"Seven days! It took us seven days to cross the damn river! God, what the hell are we waiting for?"

He was our sergeant, but he was still the same man I knew. Our regiment formed into columns and we continued.

The next afternoon, Colonel Blaisdell called a halt to our march and we gathered around him, mutterings and mumblings quieting when we squeezed together. The colonel looked at the piece of paper in his hand, folding his arms across his chest.

"Though I myself have remained divided on the subject of politics, there will be a few of you today who without a doubt will surely miss General McClellan. Two nights ago Major General Ambrose Burnside replaced our former commander."

Matthew and I were hardly surprised. Of course McClellan was replaced. He did not move fast and he had lost an opportunity after Antietam to pursue Lee. Who was Burnside?

"We are not in the Third Corps any more, gentlemen. Burnside has renamed us the Second Grand Division of the army. He has reorganized us."

The men dispersed. I asked Matthew about our new commander.

"General Burnside? There have been reports of his gallant action at Antietam, which could have made him a likely candidate for battle."

"I do not remember him in Maryland."

"He brought the men over that little bridge at the creek. He made it across, before General A. P. Hill came up from Harper's Ferry and his rebs drove us back."

"That I will never forget," I said. "I thought we had secured the victory, only to watch our troops fall back."

November departed into the cold grayness of the mornings, and December dawned with new vigor. There was crispness to the air, smelling of snow. During drill, the earth was solid and cold beneath my brogans.

At last, after a slow but steady progression, we camped in the middle of a grove of stunted pine trees. The balsam smell drifted sweet and piney. The call to set up tents and settle into camp life occupied us for a few hours. While gathering dead branches for firewood, I gazed across the meadow and saw a huge and impressive brick mansion. Union officers and soldiers milled about, obviously a headquarters.

"Someone said it was the Lacy House, I think," Matthew mused. "Look, Daniel. It's a plantation. That darky girl is one of theirs!"

A Negro girl, toddler in tow, appeared from a nearby wooden shack and crossed over to the main house. She looked robust and rugged, even from a distance. The child was crying, so she had to half-drag it by one of its fat arms. Surely the child should wear a coat in this weather, I silently admonished. It wasn't until I'd returned to the tent when I realized slaves wouldn't have coats.

Some citizens in the vicinity visited the camps to purchase salt and other articles of food. They were from a town about a mile away named Fredericksburg. I paid them little mind and went about my own business, alarmed at the dropping temperatures. Mornings I pried my hands from my cold rifle to get a fire going. Matthew was as stingy with matches as he was with stamps.

For three days there was no combat, no sign of movement, nothing to convince us we might be called to action. Winter smelled like death, cold dead ground and branchless timber. I huddled around our supper fire with Matthew.

"I think Lee's going to wait for us to come to him this time." I blew on my hands. "The Confederacy is not going to attack us. They do not have our numbers. Lee wants to test us next time, to see what's going to happen. I think you are right about General Burnside, Matthew. He will be tested."

Matthew swigged from his canteen, making a face at the water's biting coldness. "I fear you are correct about General Lee, Daniel. He has shown himself to be a marvelous offensive commander, but as a defensive general, his position is even more pronounced. And if we should blunder into a similarly disastrous encounter such as what we've already seen . . ."

He didn't finish the thought. I recalled the humiliating march back to the railroad tracks, the burning baggage cars. Leaving the scene at Bull Run like whipped dogs.

Though we'd crossed a pontoon bridge scarcely a fortnight ago, a similar bridge was to be constructed opposite us, across the Rappahannock River. According to Sergeant Falls, pontoon boats had been ordered early in November, but day by day went by and none appeared. Andrew cursed their slowness, and Matthew turned fretful. As each frosty morning woke us with cold bugle calls, the Confederates strengthened their earthworks on the opposite hills.

It was even harder to wait than at Fairfax Seminary, for the enemy was so close! A new regiment joined us in Falmouth, boys from New Jersey. Andrew spoke to their men and came back to tell us similar expectations of the coming battle. Matthew withdrew further into his paperwork, calculating forms and counting and re-counting rations. David eagerly made his way around the regiments, touching his fingers to their hats and blessing their rifles and cannon.

"Will he be joining us in the coming battle?" I asked Andrew.

"He doesn't have to, but he will. Matty tells me you're gloomy about our chances."

"Well, the pontoons have not yet arrived and –"

"Oh, we all know that, Daniel." He brushed me off. "If you want to think we are doomed from the start, then I refuse to believe you. And don't you dare take hope from my men. They've got it before we fight and they have a right to keep it."

"Andrew."

"Sergeant to you, Private."

I hadn't been as supportive of his new rank as he wanted. "Aren't you paying attention to our enemy's army? Every day we don't move is another day they reinforce their position!"

He bent down so close I could see tiny cracks in his chapped lips. "You overstep your boundaries, Private. I think it's your bed-time."

I did not offer another observation, however true it may be. There was no sense in trying to convince Andrew of anything beyond what was in his immediate vision. As soon as the order to march and fire arrived, he'd be ready. Speculation was an airy-fairy occupation.

So the next day, I joined Matthew and David in a walk to the farthest edges of camp, where we could plainly see the huddled, cold town of Fredericksburg. Bleeding its inhabitants in a long steady line of fleeing masses, they followed a road across a wide vast plain sloped gray-brown. Far beyond the town, on the distant ridge, soldiers moved about. Matthew let me borrow his spyglass and I peered at the toy-sized cannons rumbling into place, the settling of the caissons, the horses and infantry dashing back and forth behind a thin gray wall. Fleeing citizens loaded miscellaneous belongings haphazardly into wagons, dropping debris as they struggled with mules, children, frozen earth. What a frantic, strange scene.

"The whole town prepares for our arrival," Matthew said. "It's going to be a hell of a fight, and I think even David would agree with me."

"Not my choice of words, but General Lee is a formidable foe."

I scoffed. "Our greater numbers will win the day. So long as we get this over with quickly, I don't care how it's done."

"You don't?" David shut his Bible with a slam. "How can you be so damn dispassionate?"

My mouth dropped at his outburst. He colored for a moment, then lapsed into silence, playing with a rip in his sleeve. Impatience seized me, like a red fist.

"David, don't try and convince me of your own compassion. If those citizens all grabbed up a rebel gun, you would damn their souls like the rest of them. Maybe we're all damned, whether we camp or fight or leave. We're all damned whatever we do."

He did not answer. I would have raised my voice again, let the anger consume me until it darkened lit spaces within. I was lightheaded, frozen from cold, hungry, weary. I hated how I felt, burning and burning inside.

It was two weeks into December. My comrades and I waited on the bluffs opposite Fredericksburg, separated by the Rappahannock's brown waters like a moat before a castle.

Nine days after arriving in Falmouth, the preparatory orders arrived. We were given wool winter coats, extra cartridges, three days' cooked rations.

And we readied for an assault on the Confederates across the river.

· 24 ·

BOOM!

I was thrown back against a tree. My breath caught between lungs and throat, and I winced at the pain along my spine. Two cannons thundered like trumpets along the ridge of Stafford Heights. Burnt powder tinged the air, drifting along our side of the ridge. I had not smelled it in months.

"They'll never finish that pontoon bridge now," Matthew muttered. "General Burnside is a fool."

A volley of musketry sliced through his mumblings. The crackled remains of a railroad track bridge stood silently in the rippling waters of the Rappahannock. The dead bridge lay like an amputated arm in the water. An engineers corps lay the unwieldy pontoons in the water, steadying them in the winter mist. Then, when stars parted for the gray sun, the order to march fell upon the First Division.

Confederate artillery skipped shot through the town, sending puffs of dirty smoke into the air. Wooden house splinters rained down upon the enemy troops when they made their way over to the river and towards the approaching men in blue. I realized, with a sense of forlorn disappointment, that our extreme rear position might prevent us from even being sent over the pontoon bridge.

But we became part of the march to follow the First Corps, our skinny blue column snaking its way along the bluff even while hundreds of artillery wheels rolled by us and were positioned along the Heights.

"It's about time," I said.

"That's what I was thinking," Matthew said. "They're getting reinforcements."

We concealed ourselves among the woods and gullies of the shore opposite Fredericksburg, cocking rifles and digging feet into the ground. My knees ached from the crouched position between David and Matthew. Matthew sniffed and wiped over his spectacles.

"They won't be needing us," he called out when his brother walked by. "We might as well still be in Washington."

"Yeah, Matty. This is much better than that prisoner shack." Andrew laughed and moved away.

By late morning, the pontoon bridges were complete and a great stream of winter-clad Federal troops made their way across the river. The long winter coverings hid their navy coats. Many wore fingerless gloves or mitts, and their breath puffed in the air. They were quiet and deliberate, the light bouncing off their tin mugs.

"Hancock's men." Matthew pointed to their colors, then gestured to the ridges beyond the town. "I think they're heading straight for Marye's Heights."

The regiments double-quicked across the pontoons. Fighting spluttered in the town and volleys of musketry shot back and forth, mixing with the screaming of people foolish enough to have remained. We waited on the hill, same as we did at Antietam, waiting to change position or move or perform any other duty. But we were not needed, and our only movement was a break to nibble dried pork and hardened bread.

Burnside must have been annoyed at the piddling attack, for his orders unleashed the artillery. An enormous thunder roar of cannons above our heads fired upon the town. Raining murderous hail of shot and shell upon those doomed rebel homes. The devastation was immediate and horrific. It was like Zeus hurled thunderbolts at the helpless streets. Matthew vaulted to his feet.

"The glass, Andrew!"

"Get down, damn you!" He handed it to Matthew. "Sharpshooters will see you!"

The sudden artillery barrage did not clear the town of the enemy. We stayed hidden on the upper banks of the Rappahannock, watching the scene until into the evening. The town appeared destroyed and dusty, save for madly rushing blue troops. We bivouaced among the trees.

By morning, the Confederates had advanced towards the river, encasing themselves behind shelter on the banks. Hunting us while they camouflaged themselves. Deeply sloped rifle pits of Confederate artillery dotted the opposite ridge. Blue hooded columns formed into lines near the edge of town.

"This is like Antietam," Andrew grumbled as he stared longingly at his rifle. "Held in reserve. God, why won't they let us fight?"

David scowled. "Sergeant, must you ask this of the Lord?"

"Enough out of you, Chaplain."

The sun burned through the mist with a beaming yellow eye. The sergeant's grumbling was cut short when we formed our lines and marched out beyond the wooded slope. We marched southward along the left side of the embankment and, upon a new spot of cold dead ground, we were ordered to cast tents. Nothing but brief cannonading and bouts with skirmishers in the streets whiled away the hours.

I kicked a brogan at the stiff land, stubbing my toe. Hot white pain seared up my leg. The pain reminded me of Bull Run and it was all I could do to keep from weeping. The charcoal evening clouds laced with spider-web branches and tiny white stars. Soft dark wind trickled among the men. I breathed deeply and my breath intertwined with the breeze until I did not know whether I inhaled my own breath or the wind.

Fredericksburg was dark, eerily quiet after two days of artillery barrages. Beneath the moonlight, a courier rode up to Colonel Blaisdell. An order coursed through our regiment. The first three companies slipped from its place and headed downhill. The long line of pontoon boats softly rocked in the cold waters of the Rappahannock. I cocked my rifle, holding the cold muzzle close to my body. My feet thumped on the rocking bridge and I felt as if I was upon a ship.

Along the evacuated docks, Confederate bodies draped over spilt sacks of moon-white flour, jagged slabs of quartz brick, crumpled clothing. They had fired upon the bridge engineers, the cries of the wounded muffled by fog and water.

"I am cold," Matthew said.

His brother came up to us, helpless. "Wood is gone, Matty. Hancock and the rebs took everything."

Our regiment stayed near the bridge, as our duty required. We took turns crossing and recrossing the pontoon bridge. We were ordered to guard, though the only enemy we met was the cold. Matthew cleaned his spectacles out on the Rappahannock, his skinny frame silhouetted against the shapeless water. Fireless and frozen, we waited for dawn.

Morning brought strange sounds, sensations. My vision blurred with a smoky haze from sleeplessness. Coughing, tinny tinkle of tin cups, a tiny orange spot when someone lit a single candle. Popping musketry, scattered and indistinct, intermittent, sounded like slate tapping against a desk. Whap. Whap. Somehow the cold pink rays alighted us, and Andrew cracked his knees in earnest.

"All right, boys." He stretched his arms, using his gun as a brace against his back. A big yawn, loosening and twisting his torso.

Matthew yawned, too. He stuffed his haversack of the contents he removed last night. Not a comfortable pillow, but comfort was a memory.

"Never thought I'd be sleeping near a bridge in Virginia," I said.

David stirred, the last of us to awake. He rubbed dust from his hair, scratched his head, looked at me.

"You getting on well, Daniel?"

I nodded. "Yes, I believe I am."

His gaze drifted from me to beyond my shoulder. I turned. The sun climbed. It was distant, its circular orb a pale sickly yellow. The sky brightened to a morning glory hue. Only a winter sky could be so blue. We wrapped ourselves in our winter overcoats. Other regiments stirred and Confederate cannon awoke on the far hills. They burst buildings into powdered dust and splinters, smoke lolling into the streets. We paid them little heed, save to sleepily step aside when bricks fell and verandas toppled. Here and there was the tinkle of punched glass, wagons creaking through the streets.

"Damn civilians." Andrew straightened his coat. "Regiment! Line up!"

Incensed by the opening rabble from the enemy, our own cannon answered joyfully. Their screaming taunts flew above us like burning eagles. On a crowded stage of sharpshooters and stray citizens, we were to have an audience of shot and shell.

We turned our backs on the pontoon bridge and loaded our rifles. Sunlight reflected off the billows of white ambulance wagons careening in the distance. The street was wide enough to march eight abreast. Homes, factories, storefronts, all erupted into splinters and bricks when the cannon targets dropped from the heavens. Several regiments of the First Corps marched out in front of us, and their blue coats ascended the hill and into the smoke.

"Where's the Confederates?" David said.

A flash of movement in an upper window caught my eye. Above! They shot down at us from above!

"Forward men! Press on!"

The First Corps regiment ascended into the mist, swallowed up by the hill's elevation and the murderous sharpshooters. Their flags turned dusty, yellowed by the dirt and debris. Then they were gone, and the street was empty.

"David, the sharpshooters are in the upper buildings," I coughed through dust. Smoke entered my mouth and I coughed again. "David, did you hear me?"

"Regiment! Forward! Up the hill!"

Andrew pointed his rifle towards the empty street. It was like target practice from Fort Ellsworth. Keep an eye above, Daniel. An eye above.

We moved slowly, the street one long dusty passageway. I squinted upwards. Sunlight so bright, sky so blue. Our shadows were clear and black.

Shooting began. A soldier two rows ahead screamed, spraying blood.

He clutched at his face, and went down in the dirt. A man beside me stepped on him, gasped, pulled his foot away. I shuddered, kept going. An eye above. Keep an eye above.

Another man, hit in the shoulder. He grabbed at his arm, his rifle fell, he tripped, down in the dust. Then another. I heard the scream, sprayed with speckled drops. Another, slammed against the brick wall of a store. He left a huge red welt of blood as he slid and dropped, a muffled thump in the cold street. Keep an eye above.

Soldiers raised their rifles, shot holes into upstairs windows, onto porches, tearing curtains. A balcony cracked when some clustered Confederates received a barrage of bullets. They tumbled against the sides of the homes. Horses screeched and whinnied nearby. A wagon burst right out in front of our regiment. Bullets rained down upon us as if the blue sky turned to black clouds of a storm.

The soldier right behind me suffered a wound to the torso and flailed, grappling with my coat when he toppled in the dust. I landed on top of his hard warm stomach, his blood squidging between my fingers. I struggled with him and grabbed his fingers.

"Let go!" I screamed.

He grunted, fighting with me as he died. I pried his hands from my coat. Other Union soldiers tried to reform the line. I struggled to my feet. Rebs jumped down from their perches and formed a haphazard line. The regrouping Union line had advanced less than twenty feet. I could still catch up. Rebs crouched in the street, loading their rifles and screaming at us like a row of rabid dogs.

"CHARGE!"

The Confederate line launched towards us and clashed with my comrades. Matthew, Andrew, and David locked in hand to hand combat with the enemy. Artillery shells burst into the street, smoke consuming the attacking lines. I grabbed my rifle and charged towards them.

Our line disintegrated like paper in water. Screams and groans erupted all about me as the men fought. My lungs heaved like the mighty Atlantic, my throat burned with screaming and smoke. I skewered a reb on the tip of my bayonet, the metal jaws slicing in as neatly as a hot knife into butter. His blood leaked onto my gun and I ripped his flesh when I pried the rifle loose. An enemy soldier charged towards me, aiming a pistol. I raised the rifle, aimed and fired. But the hammer clicked and no shot! My stomach dropped. I was done for. He would shoot me.

"FIRE DOWN THE LINE!"

The reb pitched into the dust, his bloodied back blooming like a rose. Union infantry! A fresh line approached! We were reinforced!

Andrew shouted: "Fall aside! Regiment regroup!" He crouched beneath a large shelled home on the side of the street. He raised his rifle wildly, gesturing towards the buildings. "Fall aside, men! Fall aside!"

I rushed to the side of the street. Fresh blue lines halted in the dust, loading. Their captain brandished his pistol.

"Fire, boys! Fire at will!"

I ducked next to Andrew as the bullets exploded up the street. Shells burst buildings and the world tilted and spun. I was thrown against a wooden wall. I banged my head awful against the wall, slumped to the ground. Debris rained upon me like falling petals.

"Daniel!"

Andrew shook me. His dirty face appeared through the smoke. His teeth were black, his eyes a startling green.

"I can't find David!" he shouted. "Get up!"

I licked my lips, tasted dust and metal. I got to my feet and grabbed my pounding head. My hand was red, coat sleeve smeared with blood and dirt. The blue lines screamed and rushed up the hill. Their brogans pounded the dust. Hot sun and white smoke poured upon our ascending comrades, rifles at the ready and teeth bared like charging lions.

"They're taking the streets! Andrew?"

He stormed into the street, brandishing his rifle at the running blue lines. Enemy cannon spewed murderous mortar. A giant hole erupted in the middle of the lines and the men flung to the side. I cowered against the building, my bleeding head in hands.

Andrew screamed like a strangled beast. I grabbed up my rifle and dashed into the street. I ran between the regrouping blue lines, the row after row of blue and blood. Andrew screamed and screamed. God! Stop!

I stumbled through the men, knocked by them when I pushed past and came upon Andrew. Small blue-clad legs in the dust, an awful choking sob.

"Andrew!"

I grabbed his huge shoulder with both hands, bloody handprints on his blue jacket. I slipped and dropped to my knees. David lay wounded, bleeding, a dirt-streaked face in the dust. Andrew ripped off his cap, pressed it to David's chest. A perfect red shot. David gasped, his eyes huge and round, gripping handfuls of dust.

"REGIMENT!"

New lines were coming! Slick sliding of metal, muffled shouted orders.

"Get him out of here!" I screamed. "Andrew!"

David looked at me, eyes seeing and not seeing. "Daniel. Daniel."

I grabbed Andrew and brought my mouth right next to his ear. I coughed and screamed: "Andrew! They're coming!"

"FIX BAYONETS!"

More blue lines about to charge up the street. We were alone in the middle of their path. Get David out before they trampled him! I took David's feet. So tiny, little bird bones, twitching and stiffening in my arms. I wept, my face hardening with crusty blood and dirt.

"Andrew, help me!"

"CHARGE!"

Andrew shoved his hands beneath David's arms, his bloody cap sliding into the dirt. God, no! He would not be trampled by his own comrades! Together, we lifted the boy. We carried David to the side of the road.

Matthew reached us when the lines crossed the street, charging like ferocious warriors, eyes aflame and guns at the ready. They flocked into the sunlight, their feet churning and trampling the corpses in the dust.

"David! Where's he hit?"

Matthew shoved me aside. David was hurt badly. I leaned against the wall, choking and bleeding. Andrew wept, his nose dripping. He wiped with his hand. Matthew shoved his cap into the boy's chest. David groaned.

Somewhere within me the hurt bubbled over and I leaned down and grabbed David's hand. No, not David. Not David.

"Stay with us," I choked. "Stay with us. You'll be all right, I'll get you home. I'll get you home."

His head lolled to the side, cupped by Matthew's arm. Andrew bent over his twitching feet.

David looked up at me. "You'll get home, Daniel."

His lips closed, then his arm fell loose and his hand was limp in my own. The popping of musketry came from far off, billows of smoke rolling down the street, the cries and screams of other blue lines.

Andrew held David's shoes in red hands. Matthew's jacket was doused in blood, cutting a large wet swath across his side. Matthew took the boy's hands and arranged them on his chest. Andrew pulled his jacket closed, buttoned it. The earth was pulling me down, pulling me into dark soil. I'd never stand again.

Our regiment gathered towards us, dragging comrades' bodies from the street. They slumped, dusty and unkempt, into jarring heaps beside the boy. I was too tired to weep. I could collapse in the sunlight, stretched out beneath the sky.

Andrew reached in his cartridge box, and re-loaded his rifle. He raised the barrel high, parallel to the ground. His shadow was fierce and mighty.

"Regiment! Form up!"

I couldn't stand. I couldn't get to my feet. Matthew approached him. Andrew swung the gun onto his shoulder, aimed it right at his brother. Matthew stared down the long smooth muzzle.

"Sergeant!"

Sergeant Falls approached, barking in Andrew's ear. "Drop your rifle, sergeant. We are ordered back to reserve on Stafford Heights."

He surveyed the grim street, the bodies of reb and Federal alike dragged to the shelter of the buildings.

"Sir!" Andrew gave a strangled cry. "Sir, permission to –"

He indicated David, tiny, bloodied. Falls nodded.

"We'll take him across the river. We'll take them all with us."

David, we'll carry you. We won't leave you here. I coughed, slowly rising to my feet. Andrew handed his brother his gun and reached beneath David's elbows. Matthew moved to help, but Andrew gently placed the boy over his shoulder, as sweetly as a child.

Something fell from David into the dust. I reached down and wiped dust from the cover of the little Bible. Stained with David's blood. I'll carry it, David. I'll keep it safe for you.

Fredericksburg lay fallen in our wake. Shelled buildings gaped, splintered glass like icicles, smashed furniture and mirrors and cracked paintings. It was like some giant child threw a tantrum and wrecked her dolls' houses. Blood drips splattered front steps and porches, like an artist dripping paint. The houses had become hospitals, crowded with moaning wounded.

Down to the river, we crossed the splintered pontoon bridge. The hills of Stafford Heights beckoned, and we climbed. I shut out all thoughts, but I carried David's Bible. My cheeks froze and my feet hurt and my head stung with pain.

On a gentle slope near the top of the hill, Andrew selected a pretty spot beside a grove of trees. He laid David in the brown grass, and several men dug the grave. Beyond Fredericksburg, in the long wide valley, waves of blue lines charged the heights. The Confederates blew holes into the lines, littering the grass with small, still shapes.

The men finished the grave digging. Our regiment gathered around the small grave. Streaked faces, murmured prayers. Andrew stepped from us and knelt in the grass. The way he had knelt at Antietam. The way I had knelt at the Fairfax Seminary chapel.

I stood beside David, his book of faith in my hands. I didn't know what to say. I looked out at the valley and the charging blue lines falling. A song blossomed in my mind, tender as a new leaf. A carol. I softly sang:

What child is this,
Who laid to rest

On Mary's lap is sleeping?

Whom angels greet
With anthems sweet
While shepherds' watch are keeping.

Around me, the voices arose. My comrades joined me in song. Our regiment sang as one. A final song for our faithful boy. Forgive us, Lord, for what we do. Watch over our David.

This, this is Christ the King,
Whom shepherds guard and angels sing.
Haste, haste, to bring him laud.
The babe, the son of Mary.

Night dropped like a cold curtain. I sat before a weak fire that shed neither light nor warmth. Matthew stuck his hands in his armpits and stamped his feet. Andrew poked at the fire and said nothing.
I could have. Been there. Done something. Watched over him? I could have, it could have been. Different.
It began to rain.

· 25 ·

We remained on Stafford Heights three more days. For three mornings I awoke and role was called and I drilled. All in sight of the quiet and burned town of Fredericksburg, and the little grassy mound on the crest of the hill.

The land was quiet.

No more cannons, no more rifles. Smoky mist draped like a cobweb over the Fredericksburg valley. Burnside's assault on the far hills was over. The Confederates held Marye's Heights and reports revealed a sickeningly lopsided battle. Twelve thousand casualties to the enemy's five thousand. I didn't need Matthew's adjutant skills to know the battle was lost. The gash in my forehead was healing.

I clutched a mug of cold coffee, standing on the edge of the ridge. Wintry sun shone on the dead. They lay stretched and stiff, as though somebody laid them there. This world, this terrible damned insufficient world. Playing host to its own macabre gala.

On the third day, a letter arrived. It was posted to Fairfax Seminary, so I knew Mary had found me. Regiments stirred, and we would leave soon. The men struck tents and scrubbed their uniforms free of the blood from the battle. I walked over to where David rested. The place was beautiful, removed beneath the woody pines.

1st Dec, 1862

To Daniel,

You will undoubtedly be pleased to hear from me, as I have not been able to write to you. Prison is too terrible a circumstance to commit to narrative. Mother and Mr. Gage have visited, as per your request. Mr. Gage is saving a nominal amount for my release, even as our family faces financial ruin. I pray for their swift action in this time of falsehoods!

Mother says that you are changed from your time in the army. I can only imagine what torturous circumstances you have put yourself into, but rest assured they are but little compared to how we suffer. Daniel, you must return to Boston immediately. Mr. Gage will wire you three hundred dollars for the discharge. It is no small sum, but you are greatly needed at home!

Once here, you will assist Mr. Gage in raising money for my release. We could open our own law office and be rid of the ones who betray us. I refuse to hang my head in shame. Let us both be free of our past sins!

Forget the army and come home. Do you wish to be a soldier or a son of principle and duty to his family?

I eagerly await your reply.

Erik Stuart

I folded the letter and tucked it in my haversack. I would not read it again. Somehow, in the months since Boston, I'd forgotten many things. I felt such deep fondness for my brother, but never had our differences been clearer than when I finished reading his letter.

We are family, Erik. But if you ordered me to choose between being a soldier or a son of duty, then I could not answer in your favor. I played the role of the dutiful son, as surely as a Booth on the stage. No one tried harder than I did to escape beneath that mask. I wanted to believe that I could be happy.

You write of Mr. Washburn's falsehoods, but I, too, lived a lie. I smiled when I wanted to weep. I stayed when I wanted to run.

Now, I lived my truths. War ripped away masks and pale, real faces gleamed beneath the harsh light of hellish chaos. The brave acted foolishly, the weak saluted heroes, the homes evaporated, the streets turned into corpses.

You could not know the depth of my true duty here, Erik. I laid my best friend in the earth four days ago, a bright seed that would never bloom. Your letter changed nothing.

"Form up, regiment!"

I put the letter in my haversack and joined the line. Our regiment was broken, reduced, many wounded and sick. I recognized remaining faces. They were with me when we drilled at Fort Ellsworth, bivouacked among trees, sweated under the Virginia sun, watched Antietam in the valley, drenched under Washington rain. And they knew of my dead friend, he who had soothed their fears and lifted their spirits. We all mourned for David.

Fredericksburg faded in our wake. We returned to Falmouth, marching past the Lacy's House once more. Retracing the path of a fortnight earlier, I could still find the spot where I'd stood with Matthew and David overlooking Fredericksburg. If it had been a victory, we would be on our way to Richmond. I ignored the Pierce brothers and kept to myself, not uttering a single word on the uneasy march back to Falmouth.

"Make winter quarters! We are encamped until spring," Sergeant Falls announced.

The two days it took to build a winter cabin seemed an eternity, but I welcomed the activity. It was easier to focus on mundane tasks. Chop wood, nail boards, start a fire, launder our uniforms. I ate little, and rarely spoke. The surrounding area stripped bare of wood as little wooden huts sprang up all across the land. Our home was crude and slightly tilted where the Virginia red hill sloped down on one side. The dirt floor was uneven, the wind howled through the windows, the blanket-flap door whipped about. Andrew and I built flat bunks for sleeping against the walls, and Matthew added a board that could be a shelf or a table.

For ten straight days there was no movement, no word, no news, nothing to change the gray and blue. I breakfasted, drilled, dined, and slept. Matthew retreated into paperwork, and Andrew volunteered for every detail Sergeant Falls summoned. Camp turned rowdy and irritable, men grumpy with the ridiculous Fredericksburg battle and the dropping temperatures.

Other structures of camp life appeared – a post office, a daguerreotypist's tent, a news wagon, and several enormous hospital tents. When at last the doctors and surgeons began their tedious work, I calmed my stomach and assisted the ill. Sergeant Falls tried to discourage me, accusing me of wanting to fall sick. I paid no heed to his warnings and stopped at the open operating tables as often as I could. Inside the hospital was as close to the chaotic storm of battle as I'd ever seen. I did what I knew to do, washing an invalid's clothes, applying medicines, changing bandages.

I slept with David's Bible beneath my pillow, but my dreams were of Mary. Again and again she appeared, dressed in white, haloed by flowers. I lay beneath warm bedclothes, and she bent over me. Tipping a silver cup to my lips, and singing in her strange Gaelic tongue. I woke with a deep peace, but it was not until my appetite returned that I realized she was healing me.

One evening after drills, Andrew entered our hut with a smile, the first I'd seen in weeks. He gathered Matthew and I together, to read a copy of a telegram he received from Sergeant Falls. It was a message from the President.

"The courage with which you, in an open field, maintained the contest against an entrenched foe, and the consummate skill and success with which you crossed and recrossed the river, in the face of the enemy, show that you possess all the qualities of a great army, which will yet give victory to the cause of the country and of popular government. Condoling with the mourners for the dead –"

He stopped; he could not go on. I took the telegram.

"Condoling with the mourners for the dead, and sympathizing with the severely wounded, I congratulate you that the number of both is so comparatively small. I tender to you, officers and soldiers, the thanks of the nation. Signed, A. Lincoln."

I gave the telegram back to Andrew. He gripped my shoulder, but the look he gave Matthew was tender. I tried to smile.

"It will have to do for a Christmas present."

"I had forgotten," Andrew said. "It is the twenty-fourth, isn't it?"

I nodded. "Let's go sit by the fire. It's cold in here."

The brothers joined me, and we stepped outside our hut. A light snowfall last week had all but melted. We took our seats on upturned boxes and crates, warming fingerless gloves and cold toes. My damp coat slapped against my skin in the wind.

"This reminds me of our Christmas Eve reveal we would have in the parlor," I said quietly.

"I read about a reveal in a magazine story once," Matthew said. "What was that like?"

"It was held in the front parlor on Christmas Eve. Mother and Father would close the parlor doors, and Erik and I had to wait outside while they and the servants lit all the candles on our Christmas tree. Then, they opened the doors and we were delighted by the magnificent tree all decorated with foil rings, small toys, wrapped candies, and rolled sheet music."

"I got a game of Quoits one year," Andrew said. "We didn't have a tree, but it was the best present I ever got. Beat you all the time, Matty."

Matthew smirked. "Yes, you did."

I was starting to warm up a little. "Mother sat at the piano and sang her favorite hymns, then Father gathered us all together and read the birth of Jesus from the Bible. We would stand in a circle before the mantel, hands held. Each of us would say a prayer for the past year, and a prayer for the year to come. Then, we blew out the candles and went to bed."

"Did you get a stocking at the foot of your bed?" Andrew asked.

I chuckled at the memory. "With an orange and candied nuts in the toe."

"We did, too," said Matthew. "Whenever I smell oranges, I think of Christmas."

"What was the best present you ever got?" said Andrew.

Christmas memories passed through my mind like a picture flip-book. Then I remembered, long ago, the happiness that could only come when a child's greatest dream became real.

"Father caught me helping the servants with the harvest that fall, instead of attending to my studies at grammar school. I was five or six years old. He scolded me, but that Christmas he presented me with a set of garden tools. You can bet that was the longest winter of my life! The following spring I planted my first rosebushes."

Andrew laughed. "Quite the man of cultivation."

"Indeed." I smiled. "That same Christmas, Erik got a bound copy of the Constitution. Father groomed him for the office from the cradle."

"Fathers are all alike," Matthew said. "Our father wanted us to work the textile mills as he had done and his father before him. But Andrew and I were not made to be factory workers."

"No, we were not." Andrew blew on his hands. "Lowell held no future for us, to be sure. It was Matty's idea to go to Boston, try to get into college."

Matthew reached over and playfully smacked Andrew on the shoulder. "I turned you into a right scholar, didn't I?"

"You ran away from home?" I said. "I hadn't known that."

"We did." Matthew looked proud. "Best decision I ever made, to take Andrew and I away from Lowell."

"What of your family?"

Andrew shrugged. "Mother got a lung sickness when I was two. Father died at the factory a year after we left. We got a box in the mail with two dollars and a pair of socks Mother knitted. So much for parents, eh?"

I wondered what Mother would have left if we lost our home. Would I get a box in the mail someday? I smiled at the brothers.

"So much for parents."

From somewhere far off, carried by the chilling breeze, came tinny tapping from the drums. Drilling on Christmas Eve. Somebody coughed in another winter hut and somebody else laughed. All sounds were eerie tonight, forced. The drums were closer. Rat-a-tat. Rat-a-tat.

"They're singing," Matthew said. "I think they're singing carols."

I listened through the cabins, beyond the outer tents.

"Well, I'll be," said Andrew. "It is Christmas."

Matthew was right. The regiments were singing. The song rose above the drums and fifes. Their voices rose in chorus together.

God rest ye merry gentlemen,
Let nothing you dismay.
For Jesus Christ, our savior,
Was born upon this day.

To save us all from Satan's power
When we were gone astray.
O, tidings of comfort and joy,
Comfort and joy.

O, tidings of comfort and joy.

· 26 ·

"I'll see to him now, Private."

A hand rested on my shoulder, pulling me from sleep. I stirred and wiped the spittle from my mouth. My chin had three weeks of stubble. I cleared my throat and looked up into the kindly face of a surgeon.

"It's all right, Private. You can go back to your bunk."

I lurched to my feet, gripping the hospital bed for support. Beneath wrapped blankets the sick soldier coughed, covering his chapped lips. A stout nurse with a pewter bowl of water approached the bed, extra towels tucked under her arm.

I yawned and made my way out of the hospital tent. My legs were stiff, my old stubbed toe aching. I must have broken it in August, and when the wind howled it ached. Reminding me winter had set in.

Pausing at the door, I looked out among the Falmouth camp. Curls of smoke drifted here and there, and lamplight illuminated the huts, so it looked like embers glowing in a dying fire. Somebody was playing a fiddle, and my breath caught. I hadn't heard fiddle playing since that night at the Bull and Boar. Since those boys in the corner of the tavern took up their instruments and sang for us.

I rubbed my hands together. God, I couldn't remember the last time I'd been so cold. I bundled into my winter coat and made my way around the hospital tent. I wanted to write to Mary. I had to see her again. These endless days were bleeding my enthusiasm to such an extent I felt myself slipping, falling, into some dark place. I couldn't sleep, my brain numb. If only she could be here, to be near me, her little hand in mine.

Snow began to fall. The flakes were enormous, the size of petals. I stopped to watch them drift by the fires and the lamps. A horse nickered nearby, and I smelled the straw and manure of the stables. Rounding the edge of the hospital tent, I stopped, struck motionless by the sight.

Tucked against the hospital wall was a small bench, shadowed beneath the empty limbs of a large tree. The way it looked in the night, with hospital tent lamps glowing on the wall and the snow falling softly, I could have been standing in my garden. I loved the way it looked in the winter.

Damn you, Daniel. Damn you for being such a fool. She wanted to be yours, to come with you. And you pushed her away. You told her she was out of her place. You told her to leave you alone. Then, when you had the chance in Washington to restore amends and win back her favor, you pushed her again!

Well, I would be like that no longer. I would never treat her like a lesser being again. She deserved nothing but my respect and gratitude for anything she ever did for me. I must make it right by her.

I returned to the winter cabin and lit a candle. Matthew snored softly in an upper bunk while I wrote.

4th Jan, 1863

To Mary,

    I pray that you read this letter, though I have done little to deserve your attention. If you are still in Washington, and if I have anything in my previous conduct to allow for favors, then I place a request. Please come to Falmouth. The hospital is in need of your capable hands.

    If you are predisposed to stay at Union Hospital,

then I merely wish to offer you the sincerest apology for my conduct when last we met, and also for being so hasty in ignoring your request to join me at war. I have not forgotten.

    Grant me this favor, and I am <u>your</u> humble servant.

Ever yours,
Daniel

    I sealed the letter, rocking the little stamp back and forth in the wax. If she would come to Falmouth, I could show her how much I tried, how much I wanted to be better for her.

    The army took and took, bleeding pieces of me to its hungry depths. I gave my time, my energy, even my demeanor and habits. A lifetime of social cultivation disappeared like stalks of hay beneath the sickle.

    I slipped out to the post office tent and delivered my letter. When at last I lay on my bunk, wrapped head to foot in my wool uniform, winter coat, and army blanket, I still shivered. Nights were long, and all I did was stare up at the underside of Matthew's bunk, tracing the wooden boards and studying the knot whorls. It looked kind of like the slatted walls of that cattle car. I remembered David sleeping beside a hay bale. I saw him marching, tripping, stumbling, ever on the wrong foot and ever at the wrong time. Forgive me, David. I could have been there.

    In the morning, my cheeks were frozen with icy tears. Matthew rolled off his top bunk and straightened out his sack coat. Andrew was already up and out, presumably with Sergeant Falls, preparing the morning's drills. I pulled out a match and had lit the candle when Andrew burst through our door-flap in such a rush he looked like he'd run a hundred miles.

    "Have you come to fetch us for morning drill?" Matthew asked, confused.

    "Good God, no!" Andrew stepped forward and clapped his brother so hard on the shoulder he pitched forward and banged into the wall.

"Matty, we will have a happy new year! A happy new year for this blessed army!"

I began to chuckle, but for once this did not anger my friend further. "It is, Andrew, if one pays attention to –"

"Hurry out at once!" He bounded back to the doorway. "Polish your buttons! Straighten your rifles! We are to have the grand review! Quick and sharp now!"

I frowned at my burnt-out candle, snuffed by the morning's chill.

"What could he possibly mean by such exuberance?" Matthew yawned. "He is a regular oaf at times."

Andrew may have been an oaf, but he was correct. By the time Matthew and I readied ourselves and emerged from our hut, the vast Army of the Potomac had wakened and assembled. I gasped at the stately rows and rows, perfectly spread out upon the fresh dusting of snow. Flags flapped in the steady breeze, and colonels sat on horses, blowing frozen breath into the January morning. I nudged next to Matthew in our regiment, and even Sergeant Falls smiled at me. He'd not done so since the days at Fairfax Seminary. Well, we were ready. What was the occasion?

The regimental bands started up and again, I felt the stirring within my breast. God, I thought those feelings, those strange emotions of awe and wonder had died in the shelled streets of Fredericksburg. I didn't know they lain dormant, now reawakened with new vigor. I felt alive, shaken up inside me. The drums. Rat-a-tat. Rat-a-tat. The fifes fluttered whistling notes.

"Attention!"

My knees locked together, I cradled the butt of my rifle, staring straight ahead. Before us was erected a makeshift platform, a larger cousin to the one in Faneuil Hall during the rally. And ascending upon it, in full military regalia with sword drawn, looked to be the Major General himself, Ambrose Burnside. I had never seen the man so close; we were less than fifty yards from him. His gigantic facial whiskers obscured a round face, but his body was stout and his voice remarkably clear. It was this man who commanded these thousands of souls at his feet? This man, who stood legion above us all? I fancied our flawless formation offered more testimonial to the greatness of our army than this person could embody.

"Good morning! I have great news to relate, all the way from Washington!"

"It's only fifty miles," muttered Matthew. "Does he think we're on the moon?"

"The victory held by General George B. McClellan upon the field at Antietam, Maryland, secured a historic proclamation. President Lincoln decreed emancipation for all the Negroes in the Southern states!"

"If we manage to win this war," Matthew whispered. "If not, they're still slaves."

"Therefore, I carry the utmost honor and respect for the sacrifices of our comrades-at-arms in the Army of the Potomac! Our vast numbers and superior strength have much to commend us when we face the foe!"

I doubted this whiskery, fat general cared a whit for the dead boys he left behind at Fredericksburg. No matter what kind of victory or loss had been secured, he only received the reports at the end of the day. My friend became another casualty, another number. Maybe you think you carry honor, General Burnside, but I carry my friends.

"And it shall be announced, that President Abraham Lincoln's Emancipation Proclamation, as of January the first, 1863, has officially gone into effect!"

Now I knew the true reason for Andrew's elation, for he joined the throng in whoops and cheers. An enormous hurrah arose from the ranks, and one of the artillery cannons shot a single shell. Well, the event was commemorated. I tucked my rifle against my shoulder and clapped. Save for some contrabands in Boston and that strange Negro girl at the Lacy House, I'd never seen a slave in my life.

David could remember the larger picture, the story behind the battles, but I needed something more solid. I needed my friends beside me, their voices urging me, their guns firing alongside mine in the lines. Without them, I didn't have any stories to tell.

"How about that, eh?" Andrew ribbed me after we had been dismissed.

The huge army slowly disassembled, the perfect rows muddling into a veritable stew of flags, horses, cannon, and regiments. Back to winter camp, and back to drill. I blew warm breath on my mittens, plodding through the snow.

"If he'd hoped to lift my spirits, then his aim was accomplished."

"We been wanting this for a long time, right Matty?" Andrew tilted his shoulder, displaying those sergeant stripes. "I'm going to be like Burnside one day."

"No, you won't." Matthew shook his head. "You're more like Fighting Joe Hooker of our own corps. You remember him at Antietam?"

I didn't, until Matthew reminded me of his gallant charge in the cornfield. Even after a wound to the foot, the general mounted his white horse and galloped back to the fray.

"He's a blond war god, like Achilles of *The Iliad*," Matthew declared. "I'd like to see him in command. He'd bring real change to our cause. I have faith in that."

Nobody said it, but I knew we were all thinking of David. Andrew's expression soured a bit, but it was evident he still kept a good cheer about him.

"Looks to me like Sergeant Falls awaits. I'll be off, gentlemen, but I shall see you tonight! We must celebrate!"

"It's been a long time since I heard him say that," Matthew admitted after he'd gone. "Not since the Bull and Boar, perhaps."

"Dead fish talk," I murmured. "If I was still at home in Boston, and he'd written to me that he had stripes and was a sergeant by now, I'd assume the dead fish talk!"

Matthew laughed. "God, you're right on that account. But between you and I, it is good to see Andrew back to his normal, blustery self. Moping about and being too cruel to the new recruits is an evil side to him."

I hadn't realized I was thinking of *Paradise Lost* until later that evening, after a day of predictable and monotonous drilling. I pulled the poem from my haversack. It had lain closed for weeks, its lines encroaching too much into my real life. I could no longer read it as a thing apart. Maybe it was David or maybe something else, but it had become a part of me. As if to answer my thoughts, my eyes fell upon these words:

To reign is worth ambition though in hell;
Better to reign in hell than serve in heav'n.

If I reign here, it is masked by others who hold more sway. I would serve in heaven, if it were to serve Mary. For her alone I could bear a lifetime of unalterable devotion. Ah, if only Mercury were here to carry my message to her on silver-winged feet. Fifty miles to Washington, Matthew had said. It would be fifty feet if I could will it so.

"Daniel? You in here?"

Matthew entered the hut, carrying a brown paper sack. I put the book away and reached up to snuff the candle.

"No, no, don't put it out." He reached in the sack and produced a large bottle glistening with golden liquid. "Andrew's off to find more, but he said we could start the celebration!"

I chuckled. "Sometimes the two of you can be alike. What, we have whiskey only?"

"This is the army, Daniel, not the Bull and Boar."

"Well, then if we can't go to the tavern, you brought the tavern to us."

By now, he'd succeeded in pouring enough in each of our tin cups to satisfy the most ardent tippler. "To President Lincoln and the Emancipation Proclamation!"

"To Lincoln and emancipation!"

We clinked. Though Matthew did little more than sip, as soon as the fiery gold scorched down my throat, I swallowed mouthfuls. It was like drinking hot embers, each one ablaze in a strange mixture of chemicals like a druggist would stock. I soon downed the cup and demanded another pour. Matthew toasted again.

"To General Burnside and his ridiculous plans for this ridiculous army!"

"Ah, yes!" I held my cup high. "To General Burnside! Why? 'Cause my sides are sure burning!"

Matthew laughed. I laughed, too. My legs were tingling and my mouth tasted like cast iron. I replenished the metallic taste with another hearty swallow of whiskey, wrinkling up my nose as it burned its dragon's tail down my throat. I coughed and pounded my chest with my fist.

"It's an excellent vintage, Matthew," I wheezed.

He laughed harder. I wiped my eyes and had already downed a second cup when a great shout came from outside.

"Helloooo in there!"

"There's my brother!" Matthew said. "Damn fool!"

He stumbled over to the door-flap and managed to let it aside. But it was not Andrew who entered our celebratory domain. I slammed my cup down on the little table as a woman stepped in.

Her face was heavily painted, her voluptuous hair spilling in red curls. She swished past Matthew, giggling at his dropped chin. For a moment I was so confused I thought she was Andrew in disguise. But the sloppy kiss she planted on my friend's cheek immediately dispelled that notion.

"Ain't you a luvely boy, darling," she purred.

I slid off the seat. Irish. God in heaven, she had to be Irish. She reached for Matthew and plucked the whiskey bottle from his hand. She poured into my cup, downed a hearty swallow, then handed it to me. I was too astonished to do anything but drink.

Andrew swept aside the door-flap and came into the hut. He'd brought a second girl with blond hair, quieter and not as brazen as the first. Andrew's half-empty bottle dangled from his hand. He swigged from the open bottle, wiped his mouth, and held it out to Matthew.

"Happy emanthipation, Matthy!" he slurred. "Ain't I caught myself a fine lass tonight?"

"Aye, Sally dear, give the boy yer luve!" cajoled the Irish girl.

Sally swished like her friend and made her way over to Matthew. She slithered up next to him, snaked her fingers through his hair, and pulled his head down for a real kiss. I downed the rest of my cup. The Irish girl took up the bottle and poured more. She bent down so low I could plainly see that beneath her winter cloak was a flimsy dress with an indecently low neckline. I coughed, years of gentleman breeding bubbling inside me. I had to cover her! For modesty's sake!

I stumbled to my feet, but my stomach had dropped to my knees. The candlelight smudged, and my head was as light as a balloon. I knocked against the table and pitched towards the girl. My hands caught in her cloak.

"You should be covered, miss," I slurred at her. "Cover you up."

She grabbed my arms and righted me. "Aye, ye are a luvey, ain't ya?"

Andrew pulled Sally away from her embrace with Matthew. "That's my brother, Sally darling. My flesh and blood brother. I'd die for that soldier, you know it."

"Die for that soldier," Matthew repeated in a heavy voice.

Red lipstick smeared across his mouth, his spectacles askew. He reached for the bottle and drank heartier than all of us. The Irish girl entwined her arms around my neck. She was short and stout and soft, curvy bulging flesh that warmed my hands and stirred my trousers. I struggled against her, but she was surprisingly strong. She held the whiskey bottle to my lips.

"Give it a good 'un, luvey," she purred.

I had three good swallows before she shoved the bottle into Andrew's hands. He and Matthew were enjoying Sally's company, passing drinks back and forth. She lifted her leg and Andrew started untying her shoe. Matthew kissed her again. The other girl giggled.

"Aye, we'd best be leavin'! Come along now, boyo."

I was trying to sit down, but she had me entangled again. She supported me and I leaned into her warm curves. Laughing, she dragged us over to the door-flap. The Pierce brothers were so occupied with their honey-haired catch they paid me little heed.

Out into the cold night we went. The chilly wind whistled in my ears, but my belly was on fire. I could barely move, but we somehow made our way along the edge of the cabin. I sloshed heavily through the snow, stumbling. She held me and guided us both. I felt strange and good and warm and wrong.

My head bumped a wooden wall. She'd brought us to the rear of the cabin. My body pushed up against the back wall, and she pressed against me. Her cloak was parted, her ample bosom heaving. I was mesmerized by her and reached for the cloak. I accidentally grazed her soft flesh with my hand. She tilted her face up at me, dark eyes alight.

"Ye are ready for me, darling." I shook my head, but she was laughing again. "Ye are a pretty boyo, ye are."

She pressed her hips against mine. I couldn't do this. I wouldn't do this. I lolled my head to the side, staring into the hazy darkness. Biting wind whipped against my face and I shivered. She moved against me, and I caught the rhythm, like we were dancing.

"Dancing," I murmured. "Dancing."

"Aye, luvey." Her hands were at my waist. "I'm yers tonight, luvey."

She unbuttoned my trousers. I buried my face into her neck, smelled smoke and whiskey and acrid hair pomade. She snaked an arm up and ran her hands through my hair. She brought my head over to her mouth. She kissed me, struggling with her skirts. I helped lift her dress, her warmth so close. So exquisitely close. She rocked against me, then onto me and around me, and I gasped.

She groaned, seeking my mouth again. I kissed her, our bodies pressed, rocking like a ship at sea. I matched her rhythm, her breathing quickening. I was warm and tingling and sweat beaded along my neck, at my temples. I grabbed the folds of her cloak and gripped the cold wool. Her warm neck muffled my moans and I clutched her when I settled and was still.

She lay against me. Her hand sought my chin, and she bent my head. I shivered, though not from pleasure. My stomach felt heavy, my legs burning. She tried to kiss me, but I lifted my head. I shivered again.

At that, she frowned and rocked her body off of me. A blast of cold air caused me to frantically straighten my trousers. The sweat chilled my neck and I realized she had unbuttoned my coat, too. She was straightening her dress, tying her cloak over her sweating bosom. I reached for her, but she slapped my hand away.

"I wanted to cover you, for modesty, for modestly sake."

She shook her head and laughed. "Come on, boyo."

My head ached and my back was sore from rubbing against the cabin. I was exhausted, on the edge of sleep. Lurching, she helped me back to the door-flap.

When we entered, a funny sight beheld my eyes. Matthew was fast asleep, sprawled across the bottom bunk. His trousers were on the floor, and Andrew, shirtless and sweaty, was helping Sally into her dress. He saw us and toasted an empty bottle of whiskey. The other empty bottle rolled on the floor, along with both overturned cups.

"Wait, boyo," said the Irish girl. "Where's my coin?"

"What?" I said, my tongue made of stiff leather.

"Payment, boyo. Ten dollars ye got?"

I stared at her. A lady of the night. It must have been the whiskey. Ten dollars. Ten dollars. I made my way over to my haversack, on the edge of the bed where Matthew was snoring. I dumped the coins on the bed. Andrew chuckled.

"Nearly a month's pay, my ladies. High price for breaking in the boys."

Andrew wasn't going to pitch in, so I reluctantly handed my money to the girls. Matthew never stirred and Andrew made quite a show of kissing Sally good-bye. The Irish girl flashed a friendly smile, then covered herself with her cloak's hood and left the cabin. The door-flap whipped closed, blasting cold air on my sweaty face.

I sat down on the floor, stiff and tipsy. Andrew knelt beside me. His breath stank.

"We should celebrate more, eh?"

I shook my head. "Ten dollars, Andrew. Ten dollars."

"It ain't nothing. Up you go, rich boy."

He grabbed me and lifted. For the second time that night I was hoisted to my feet. My stomach surged and I grabbed my mouth. Andrew quickly brought me to the door, where I retched into the snow. My hands stung with the cold. We then somehow managed to get back into the cabin and over to the bunks. Andrew laced his fingers and held his arms down. I stuck my foot in his hands, and he half-threw me into the top bunk. I crawled into the unfamiliar bed. My mouth tasted like three-day-old corn hash. I mumbled a good-night to Andrew, and he replied with some sort of joke.

The whiskey pulled me towards sleep, but I stared into the darkness. I could hear her voice over and over. I could feel her body against mine. I didn't know her name, hadn't asked.

I was afraid it would be Mary.

· 27 ·

"We move out tomorrow!"

Sergeant Falls disappeared from the cabin doorway and was gone, calling to other winter huts. Matthew sprang up from the table where he'd been repairing his trousers and hurried after the sergeant. He returned scarcely ten minutes later, his expression crestfallen.

"Damn Burnside," he muttered. "We aren't going to get paid this month."

"Don't trouble yourself too much about it," I said.

I lay on the bottom bunk, trying half-heartedly to read my dime novel. I gave up and perused the little Union Song Book the old bookseller gave me in Quincy Market. Matthew, still fuming about our lack of pay, brought out his map.

"So we're to march upriver, cross the Rappahannock – near Bank's Ford I am guessing – and take Bobby Lee by surprise, turning his left flank." He smacked the map on the table. "Ridiculous plan. If there's one thing Burnside can't do, it is surprise General Lee."

"You said he had no demerits at West Point? Lee, I mean."

"That's what I heard. A perfect student of war. Not to mention General Thomas Jackson taught at Virginia Military Institute. I am beginning to think Lincoln will never supply us with a commander worthy of our foe."

I returned to my reading. Matthew fretted with a nervousness bordering on female anxieties. No word yet from Mary, and I privately admitted I was glad of it. We had never spoken words of affection, nor had I demonstrated any undue regard. But my evening, my moments with...

I was awake these past ten nights and my mood soured. I was annoyed, restless, and eager to have something to do besides drill and eat and sleep. Never had I wanted for amusement, and now a vicious sense of boredom courted me.

So it was with renewed vigor that I prepared for the march. Our army rumbled awake again, stirred from its winter sleep. Wagons loaded up with rations and caissons hitched to their resting cannons. Horses were fed and watered, saddles polished, and officers trotted through the camps.

"The army isn't ready," Matthew complained as he recounted his food rations. "Our regiment is down by forty percent, and you know how full the hospital tents are!"

I filled my cartridge box with fresh rounds. "It will keep both Andrew and I in good spirits to do something more than drill."

"Andrew would never *not* fight."

I'd seen little of the other Pierce brother in the past week, save for the hours at drill. He preferred Sergeant Falls's company to ours now. The two created quite a pair, rustling up the younger members and haggling recruits with nonsensical duties.

The next morning, several divisions started upriver, away from the road that led to Fredericksburg. On a Tuesday afternoon, three days after issuing marching orders, my regiment was called to attention while part of General Franklin's Grand Division passed. I shouldered my rifle, my haversack brimming with rations, cartridge box jammed with fresh bullets. After Franklin's men had passed, the band struck up a marching tune and we proceeded towards Bank's Ford.

A pleasant breeze invigorated me, and I even thought of discarding my winter woolen coat. Never would it be this unseasonably mild in

January in Boston! The land smelled crisp and dry. We advanced down the rutted road, through a wooded section of dead brown trees and snow-capped rocks.

Within an hour, the sky resembled the rocks, ominous granite. Rumbling broke through the flat and blurry clouds. Matthew groaned, but said nothing. Late in the afternoon, it began to rain. I pulled up my collar and hunched my shoulders to prevent the trickle from chilling my neck, but the drizzle steadied. Matthew looked equally downcast, droplets snaking down his spectacles.

"Of all the luck. We should never have moved until spring."

"Quiet, will you?" I snapped. "Matthew, all you have done the past three weeks is complain and fret and –"

"Shut up, Daniel!" he hissed.

Andrew walked by us, his gun tilted to keep the rain from pouring down the barrel. He nudged Matthew in the shoulder, grinning. How could he be so damn happy? I had no idea, and he began to whistle. It was the little Irish ditty from the Bull and Boar.

"Oh, I had me lass in Dublin," Matthew sang softly.

I ignored him and buried deeper into my coat. Nobody saw my tears in the rain.

We trudged beneath the downpour for several hours. The ground rolled slowly beneath me, the Virginia red soil churning beneath my feet. It mixed into a paste, like cake batter. My feet made funny sucking sounds as I whomped through the muck. Suddenly, a shout came from up the road:

"Regiment, halt!"

The line paused. I shifted my weight from foot to foot, trying to keep my soles from sinking into the mud. A high-pitched scream of horses and mules drifted from further up the road. Wind whipped the flaps of our capes, rain pelting like wet bullets. The road was flooding, and water soaked into my shoes. Adding to my enjoyment, my toe started throbbing again.

Matthew sniffled, wiping his arm across his spectacles. His brown hair was plastered around his face, thick strands roped across his forehead.

Andrew clomped over to us, his brogans sinking into the muck. He pointed up the road.

"Artillery wagons are stuck in the mud! We've orders to assist!" he shouted. "Company C, move out!"

I tilted my rifle, slick rain running down its cold nose. Sergeant Falls cupped his hands around his mouth, and repeated the order to the rest of our company. We broke from the column, formed a crooked line, and moved beyond the regiment. Andrew led us to the side of the road, where slick grass protected our feet from the mud. I shook the water from my brogans.

Ten minutes later, we came upon the cannons. Illuminated against the skeletal winter trees and the shooting rain, the Massachusetts artillery was stuck in the mud. A dozen head of cannon sank into the muck. The wheels were buried and stuck out like wooden half-spheres. Horses screamed and strained, a dozen soldiers trying to calm them. I pursed my lips. Good God, was there anything we could do?

"Company, to the cannon!"

I rushed forward. Matthew and I each grabbed a spoke of the cannon wheel. Several men assisted the artillery soldiers, grabbing the horses' reins, and the rest of Company C clustered around the caisson.

"Company, heave!"

My hands locked around the wheel and my feet braced in the muck, I pulled with all of my strength. Matthew struggled beside me, and we pulled and pulled. The wheel rotated through the mud, but did not break free.

Suddenly, my feet slipped, and both Matthew and I toppled next to the cannon. I knocked my head against its fat metal body and hot pain seared across my vision. A tiny crunch, tinkle of glass in my ear.

"Daniel!"

Matthew stared at me with huge frightened eyes, his hands off the spokes of the wheel. I lifted my hand, wiping mud on my trousers. His spectacles lay twisted like a contorted insect, the glass in tiny fragments.

"I'll get you a new pair!"

I helped Matthew up. He rescued the twisted wire frames and

jammed them in his cartridge box. Ashamed and exhausted, I grabbed the wheel again. The soldiers at the horses and caissons heaved and grasped. Through the rain other soldiers helped other cannon.

Andrew came over to us. "Matty, what happened to your spectacles?"

"Daniel broke them."

"We fell!" I jabbed his shoulder angrily.

Andrew pushed past me and grabbed the wheel beneath the cannon. My head throbbed, my throat heavy and full.

"Go help the horses, Daniel!"

He braced his shoulder against the wheel. I stood in the rain, Matthew groping like a blind man. I stepped away from the cannon, each sucking step threatening to take me down, lose my balance, suck me into the muck and the grime and the ooze.

"Heave!"

Andrew and Matthew pulled the cannon wheel. The men at the horses heaved and the soldiers at the caisson heaved and the screams of the beasts competed with the rain for a brilliant torrent of noise.

The cannon slowly lumbered out of its sticky hole. It moved forward, inch by agonizing inch. Another, then another. I moved around to the back of the cannon. Its massive snout eyed me. I took up the other wheel and we moved the cannon forward. Rolling, rolling, sloshing through the mud and the rain.

We rested a few minutes, then took up the wheels and moved the cannon again. Stop and start and stop and start. The pattern continued for hours. I had never been so God damned tired in my life.

By the time the artillerymen called a halt to the evening, we had moved the cannon less than ten feet. I sat against the wheel, nestled in the mud. My shoulders screamed in pain, my toe throbbed, and my arms hung like dead weights. Several artillery officers detached from helping the horses and came around to thank us. Company C was weary, bedraggled, soaked to the core. My rifle was useless. Even if we happened upon the Confederates, I had little but insults to shoot at them.

Andrew helped Matthew up out of the mud and I followed them to the side of the road where we hung up our tent. It was nothing but a rope staked between two trees and a sheet of wet flapping canvas covering us. I crawled inside, pushing up against the cold canvas sides. Mathew wriggled in next to me.

"I can't see, Daniel."

"I'll get you another pair," I said, more irritated than I meant.

I pulled my elbow up to keep the canvas from whacking me in the face. I took off my cap and squeezed the water from it, shaking and slapping it against my leg. Matthew rubbed his eyes. God damn my clumsiness. The army never quieted and my dreams teemed with screaming horses, soldiers cursing, the plink and plonk of metal against metal.

Andrew woke me at dawn. It was still dark and still raining. Someone had propped up the cannon with some loose boards and sticks, so it looked like oars hanging askew.

Sergeant Falls caught up to us. He gathered us together, inspected us, helped us back into our columns. Another regiment was to assist with the cannons. Some brigade commander decided we were needed elsewhere.

I marched along, ripping my feet from the mud, making steady but pathetically little progress. Andrew guided us like an Indian, picking our way amongst the trees and following the roadside. It took the better part of the day to march two or three miles. We were held up by other regiments, passing horses and wagons and soldiers and cannons and caissons and mules stuck in the mud. The Army of the Potomac struggled to free itself from the red Virginia muck.

Matthew and I huddled beneath a large tree and ate our biscuits and cold dry ham. It was too wet and rainy for a fire. After dinner, we continued our march.

"We're ordered to assist the pontoon bridge," Sergeant Falls explained. "We're heading towards the river."

"Clear the way! Move, men! Move!"

Pontoons on caravan wagons rumbled by us, each like a fisherman's dinghy on wheels. I hurried to one side of the road, Matthew and Andrew to the other side. Tucking beneath the branches of a tree, twigs poking me in the back, I watched the pontoons. They weren't heavy enough to become horribly stuck like the cannons. After the final one was gone, I could hear the river. The mighty Rappahannock River.

Our regiment buttoned itself back together like a wet coat. We moved like a many-headed beast, our heads tucked down against the storm, our feet sinking into each other's footprints. Through the darkness I saw the wild river, like the churning waters of a swiftly moving cauldron. I broke through the trees and became stuck in the soft slippery muck at its banks. I halted, aghast at the scene.

Pontoons swayed like tormented riders on the back of a wild horse. Some soldiers rushed towards the raging waters, while others tried their damnedest to guide the pontoons. Half of a pontoon bridge jutted into the river, whipping back and forth like a ferocious serpent upon the choppy waters.

Andrew dropped his rifle and it disappeared into the mud. Matthew bumped into him from behind and tripped, falling at the river's shore. The soil at the banks was slick and icy. My feet anchored and I pitched forward like a rag doll. I ripped one foot free of the mud, but the other held fast.

Ropes snapped and the pontoon bridge fell apart. A mad lone pontoon swept down river like a speeding hawk. Men grabbed the ropes, heaving against the Rappahannock. Andrew started for the river, moving as fast as he could through the slick muck.

"Stay here!" he shouted at us. "I'm going to help them!"

Matthew picked himself up and tried to go after his brother. I was mired, helplessly watching him grope for tree trunks, branches.

"Matthew!" I cupped my hands around my mouth. "Wait!"

Andrew had reached the shore. He waded into the wild river, heading towards the broken pontoon bridge. I jammed my rifle into the mud for leverage and pulled against the earth. My leg popped free, my shoe entirely encased in mud. I managed to yank the other shoe of its slimy prison. Gasping against the incredibly strong power of the mud, I advanced towards the mighty Rappahannock.

Matthew was already knee-deep into the river. More soldiers came up from behind. Their cold woolly bodies jammed past me, and they entered the river to go after the pontoons. The waters flooded with men, horses, pontoon boats.

Andrew reached the pontoons and clung onto the ropes. Angry currents swallowed men, horses, pontoons. I braced myself against the rain and the river and started to wade in. The river was like an icy dragon, eating my feet and legs. I gasped so loudly I shrieked.

"Matthew, wait!"

Pale faces surrounded me, dripping brown beards, blue woolen caps. The rain stung my back, my shoulders, my eyes. I advanced into the water. My calves froze, trousers clinging to my legs. The river was rising, rising. It was gripping me, roaring in my ears. God, it was cold!

Andrew broke away from the pontoons. Rope tore out of his hands and he screamed in pain as it sliced his palms. The brown boat sped off down the stormy river.

"Get the rope!!"

Andrew lunged for the rope and tied the pontoons. The enormous curved bulk of another slid into the waters. Andrew reached out and grabbed it, tying it to the rocking bridge. I waded over to him. Rope lashed around his huge white hands.

"Daniel!" He wiped his face with his shoulder. "Fine weather we're having, ain't it?"

I managed a weak smile. "Where's Matthew?"

Andrew cocked his head. Matthew was with some other soldiers, near the pontoon bridge, holding the rope together. I started to wade out further, around Andrew. The waters were up to my waist, and I couldn't feel anything anymore. My legs were numb and muscles ached. I heard a popping sound like musketry. Whap. Whap. My teeth chattering. Like firing bullets in my mouth. Moving with the river, moving with the ferocious current.

Matthew hunched by the side of the pontoons, pale and blind, both hands wrapped around the knots between the lashed pontoon boats. I reached his side.

"Matthew!"

He didn't look up. A huge dark shadow fell over us. Another pontoon boat's great wooden bulk slid across the choppy waters. Andrew guided it carefully. There was room for several more, but it would be a hell of a tight squeeze.

Suddenly, the mighty river opened its cavernous mouth and roared as loud as a cannon. The soldiers on the other side of the pontoon bridge lost their footing and splashed into the water. I ducked to keep from getting hit in the face. Matthew was drenched in full force. He lost his grip on the ropes and tumbled backwards, dragging the rope as he fell into the river. I tried to hold on to the rope, felt it loosening, slackening, the horrible untwisting.

Pontoons were coming apart. Matthew popped up out of the water, spluttering and coughing. I grabbed his coat and lifted him onto his feet. He vomited down the front of his coat, spit and stomach fluid and river all mixing. I propped him up. Andrew let go of the pontoon bridge, started wading up towards us. The knots were coming undone. Andrew reached his brother's side and smacked Matthew's back once, then twice.

"You all right?" he shouted.

Matthew nodded, pale. Andrew held his chin up. He smiled.

The rope suddenly snapped. The pontoon bridge broke free and the enormous wooden boats bore down on us.

"Look out!" I screamed.

The pontoon boat rammed Matthew squarely in the back of the head. His head slumped forward and his body slipped beneath the waves. Andrew dove beneath the water. I waded out as fast as I could. No, no. Not Matthew. I could barely move. Andrew emerged from the water, his arms gripped around Matthew. Blood poured dark and thick from the back of his head. God, he was too pale. His face floated like a ghost. My stomach churned. I reached beneath the water and hoisted his feet.

We half-dragged, half carried his body towards shore and pulled him from the river. He shivered and moaned. Andrew took off his winter coat, reached under his sack coat, and ripped fabric from his shirt. He put his coat back on, then wrapped the wad around the back of Matthew's head.

"Daniel, help me!"

I pushed the heavy wet fabric into the back of his skull, his hair matted. From across the river, the jubilant shout drifted across.

"There is Burnside, stuck in the mud!"

God damned Confederates. I squeezed back tears, pushed the fabric in deeper. Matthew's blood dripped through my fingers.

"We must get him back to camp, Andrew."

"I'm fine," Matthew murmured. "I can walk. I'm fine."

Andrew reached down and gripped his hand. My legs were freezing, my trousers like wet clapboards against my skin. Rubbing raw, chafing. I gingerly stood up.

We were separated from our regiment, but the Army of the Potomac was a tangled mess. Pontoon boats whipped down the river as the bridge collapsed. There was no possibility of crossing the river. Andrew and I slowly brought Matthew to his feet. Little to do but take him back to Falmouth.

Andrew disappeared to find Sergeant Falls, while I supported his brother. Bile dribbled from Matthew's lips and down the front of his coat. I wiped him as best I could, as if caring for an infant. Too pale, too cold. My feet sank further into the muck.

I pulled us both away from the river and into the trees. I rested against a tree trunk, the cold solidity welcoming and stable. I propped Matthew up beside me and we waited.

Within an hour, Andrew returned with Sergeant Falls. No stretcher, first aid kit, or medical supplies could be found. We had to return to camp. I wearily followed them back up the road. I was too tired to help, too tired to think. It was worse than running from the enemy at Bull Run. Defeated by rain and a raging river.

We staggered back to camp. I felt like a burst star, cold and unlit in a vast darkness. Andrew took his brother to the hospital. The army was as scattered as if cannon blew holes in the lines. Diffuse, dropped here and there, stumbling into Falmouth.

I found my winter cabin, pushed the door-flap, and dropped into the chair. I slumped at the table, too cold and frozen to move any further, and fell into sleep like a stone into water.

· 28 ·

"Worth dying for," I murmured and turned my head. A distant ache, a feeling of immense pressure on the back of my head. I groaned.

"Daniel? You awake?"

Bright sunlight lit the cabin wall, a blinding yellow square on the chinked boards. My head hurt so greatly it was difficult to focus in the light. My mouth felt stuffed with cotton. Andrew stood in the door-flap. He had bandages around his hands, where the rope had sliced his palms.

"God, I thought you were dead. You didn't move, you know."

I leaned back in the chair. My trousers and sack coat were stiff and musty, like hundred-year-old rotting bedclothes. Wool saturated with river water and slimy mud. My feet made horrible squelching sounds in my shoes. I had never in my life felt more repulsive.

"What's worth dying for?" Andrew was saying.

I ran a heavy tongue around my lips. "What?"

"That's what you said when I woke you. Worth dying for."

"I'm ... not sure. Good Lord, my head hurts. What's the time? I must be late for drill."

He shook his head. "Men are still making their way back to camp. Half our regiment is missing, and the adjutants are, pardon my humor, having a field day trying to count heads. Burnside's army is a mixed pack of cards this morning."

I reached for my canteen, wincing at the frigid metal. "Matthew is still at the hospital?"

"Yes, that's what I came to tell you. Some girl was there, asking for you. She looked so damn familiar –"

"She was?" I interrupted. "Was she short, with dark hair?"

Andrew smirked. He snapped his fingers, and I felt a horrible sickening in my stomach.

"Mary! The Irish girl from the Bull and Boar! That's right, I do remember her. You wrote to her before Fredericksburg. I see, I see!"

"Andrew, she came at my request –"

"I'll bet she did. Took a fancy to her old master, eh?" He laughed the way he used to during his dead-fish talk. That half-sarcastic, half-amusement laugh. I lurched to my feet, determined to end this as quickly as it had begun.

"Thank you for informing me she is at the hospital. I can visit Matthew and give you an update on his condition, if you wish."

"Nah," he shrugged. "If them other nurses is as good as the little mick lass, he'll have a speedy recovery."

I stepped past him and was pushing aside the door-flap when a memory stirred.

"It was what David had said."

"About what?"

"David said love is worth living for, but freedom is worth dying for."

Andrew gave me a thoughtful smile. "Is that what our friend believed."

Our friend. When I looked again at Andrew, unshaven, doused in river water, frayed sack coat and rumpled trousers, I was startled by a mad rush of memories. In the weeks since David's death, I hadn't remembered anything. I hadn't thought of our days at Harvard, or drilling at Fort Ellsworth, or our first battle. Not of the hill overlooking Antietam, the days at Fairfax Seminary, the long cold march to Fredericksburg. All had darkened, like an empty stage.

As long as one candle burns. As long as one star shines. David believed I lived a larger story.

The hospital was in an uproar. Soldiers spilled out of the doorway and crawled on the frozen grass. Yellow piles of sick mess littered the entrance like ink drops. I held my stomach and pushed past the ill and wounded. The stench was intolerable, a rank stew of musty wool uniforms, strange medicines, tangy blood, and putrid bowels. Bedsteads creaked with the new patients, soiling their bedclothes and the floor. I nearly fell in a faint. Only the sound of the shouting nurses kept me upright. I had to find her. I had to see her.

My stomach felt horribly twisty. I couldn't find Matthew, and I couldn't find her, either. I'd ask Sergeant Falls for a leave from drill. Come back when it wasn't so crowded . . .

"If ye would, please! Don't stand about!"

When I turned, she had gone. I knew that voice.

"I've got 'im. On three, Hannah. One, two, three. Aye, there he goes!"

A bedstead clattered against the wall. I heard the soldier's groan. A glimpse of her, smooth dark hair, bent over the bed. She was tucking in the sheets. She reached for a tin cup filled with water, and held it to the patient's trembling lips. Knocking the cup aside, he grabbed her and brought her down close. He was shouting at her, hurting her. I tore through the melee and reached her side as soon as I could. She struggled against him. His eyes bulged.

"Hoist the nets! Hoist the God-damned nets!"

"Jesus, Mary, and Joseph!" She wriggled free. I caught her as she stumbled backwards. She was a beating little bird in my arms.

"A sea-farin' man," she muttered. She still hadn't turned around. "The surgeon'll be here by the by. Keep yer head about ye."

She bent to retrieve the little cup. The sheets were doused. I reached for it, and my fingers clamped on hers. I moved clumsily, and she swiped the cup from under me and turned.

I met her dark eyes, fierce and wild. She had come. She had come for me.

"Will ye move, now." She could not hide her look of recognition, but it was wrong to see her now, an ill-timed moment. "I've work to do."

I stepped aside. She started to walk by, then paused and said in a low voice: "Leave me be the rest o' the week."

"Mary, I can help you."

She brushed past as if she didn't believe me or didn't want my help. Too many soldiers froze outside, waiting to be seen. I found a tin cup, filled it with water and took it to those who could not move inside. As the men passed the cup around, I found a stray broom and swept the vomit from the walkway. I went to different cabins, finding old blankets, extra winter coats, candles, anything to keep them warm.

Andrew was right about the army. No rain fell and not a single shot was fired, but we were a mess. As soon as I helped one soldier, three more appeared, disoriented and muddy from their battle with the Rappahannock. Darkness was falling when some of the cannons and artillery caissons finally rumbled back into camp. Dozens of dead horses and mules, killed by the strain. Falmouth reeked with rotting horseflesh.

Andrew helped Sergeant Falls collect the ill and aid other regiments. I wished more than anything I could see Matthew. He was not dead, but some part of me felt he was. I hated seeing his empty bunk at night.

"So, ye did pay me heed, Daniel."

She wiped her hands with a rag. I returned the broom to the corner, exhausted from my long days of working. She shivered beneath her thin blue shawl, but her eyes were clear. She came at my request, and six months ago I would have found it ordinary.

"Can you tell me where Matthew is?"

She indicated a bed by a far window, and I realized it was the best location in the hospital. I turned to thank her, but she was tending the patients again. Light poured in from the window, a pale curtain draping her hair, her face.

Through the wintry windowpanes, drill had begun again. Thin reedy fifes and tapping drums. I felt like I was in a dream, like I had slipped on somebody else's life. I slowly approached my friend's bedside.

His bed was clothed in white, dark metal frame. Matthew lay straight, head tipped to one side and swaddled in bandages. He looked strange without his spectacles, his heavy-lidded eyes closed.

"The river! The river!" he suddenly shouted, delirious.

I came quickly around the side of the bed and grabbed his cold hand. I could smell the metallic blood seeped in his hair.

"Matthew, it's me. It's Daniel."

He awoke, breathing hard. When he opened his eyes, I felt sick. His gaze was off-kilter, his eyes rolling around in his head like cloudy marbles. He cried out like a bleating lamb.

"I can't see! I can't see!"

I leaned my head down, fierce shame in my throat.

"I gave him laudanum. 'Tis all I could find."

Matthew settled, as if soothed by her voice. Mary placed fresh rolled bandages on the bed. His breathing slowed and he soon slipped into sleep.

"Thank you for your care, Mary."

"Have ye heard from yer family?"

"Yes, Erik wrote to me. He is still imprisoned." I paused. I hadn't spoken of it aloud in so long. "It must have . . . God. To think if I'd stayed in Boston!"

She unrolled the bandages. "'Tis naught but a fancy, so clear yer head o' it. An' what of yer brother being in prison? Ye can't desert and go to 'im, so ye'll stay here. That's the life ye've got now."

"I appreciate the reminder," I said sullenly. Anger pricked my eyes. How dare she speak so callously! "I have no money, no home, and I've already lost one friend to this God-forsaken war, so believe me, Mary, I'm not caught up in anything fanciful!"

I was crying, but I didn't care if she saw me. She was a good nurse and she would do her best for Matthew. I was what I always was. A damned fool. A fool for leaving, a fool for trying. I tried to follow David's faith and I tried to be a good soldier, whatever that meant. I'd never been a good son and I'd never be a good friend, either. I couldn't save anyone. I couldn't do anything but be a fool.

Outside in the cold, I welcomed its wintry slap. Yes, stir up the winds. I don't care! Every time I try I fail, and everything I do is foolish.

"Daniel!"

God, leave me be! I stumbled away from the hospital, wrapping my arms about me like a woolen shield.

"Will ye wait, boyo!"

I turned on her so quickly I nearly hit her. She shivered in her shawl, her eyes tender and scared. I pointed to the hospital.

"Leave me alone! Care for them!"

She reached for me and clasped my cold shoulders. I bent towards her and the wind shrieked between us.

"Daniel," she murmured in a lullaby voice. "Come away. Come."

I slid my arm beneath hers and around her tiny waist. I brought her close, my feet disappearing beneath her skirts. She stiffened, but at last turned her head and rested upon my cold woolen breast. I gently tucked my chin against her hair and closed my eyes. Her warmth seeped into me, trickling and spreading like the sea.

"Private Stuart!"

Damn, it was Sergeant Falls. I stepped from Mary, composure masking my harried manner. She bowed her head to the approaching officer, and then, without another glance to me, quietly turned and walked back to the hospital. I could not help watching her leave.

"Private!"

I straightened and saluted, but when our eyes met he knew. I could not hide what I felt for her.

"That Miss Daley's a pretty girl, eh?"

I furrowed my brow. "You know her, sir?"

"She informed me of Private Pierce's condition when I visited him yesterday. What's left of the army has found its way back to camp. We drill in one hour."

"Are we to try another march, sir?"

"In this blasted weather? Not a bloody chance!" he shouted into the wind. His coat flapped furiously. "I will grant no special requests for hospital visits, Private!"

"But, sir!"

"This regiment is lazy and undisciplined! Not to mention lustful! Yes, Private Stuart, I know of your shenanigans with the camp followers."

I colored to think of it. "It was Sergeant Pierce, sir!"

His eyes narrowed to icy blue slits and he bent close to me. "You dare accuse an officer of unlawful conduct?"

He could not frighten me. I had to see Matthew, had to see Mary. "I withdraw my accusation, Sergeant Falls. But leave Mary be! She needs to care for Private Pierce!"

My courage startled him to silence. Though he did not speak again, his salute confirmed his opinion. He knew as well as I there were plenty of witnesses and not enough of a case to bring charges against any soldiers in regards to camp followers. I smiled grimly after he had gone.

When I returned to the hospital, a stern nurse relayed the message that I was not to see Mary while she was working. Cursing our situations, I returned to Matthew's bedside. He breathed evenly, but his skin was a sickly yellow, high flushed cheeks.

I lit a candle and sat on a stool. I stayed by him for a long time, listening to his labored breath, the footsteps behind me, the moans of others wounded and ill.

"Mary will care for you," I said softly.

Her warmth cheered the dying flame within me. I feared the fire would burn out, and I did what I could to save it. But I felt myself slip into darkness, away from all that was light and sun. I clung to her in the wind and the snow.

I needed her to care for me.

· 29 ·

She reached for my hand. The warmth of her fingers flooded into mine. The smell of her hair, small hands pulling up the bedclothes on the hospital cot, her quiet footsteps. Arms laden with supplies and tokens of her trade. Pewter bowls, sullied rags, buckets and water, glass vials with peeling labels, tin cups, spoons of gruel, shots of morphine and laudanum and extracts of heroine and cocaine. Fingers brushing her apron, soothing a dying man's fevers, stirring the waters of a bloody bowl.

I caressed her little fingers, reached up and quietly touched her cheek. Her skin was warm and soft, a welcoming after the cold rain. I felt empty, like a tree after the last of its leaves fell.

Shivering in my blankets, I opened my eyes. My dreams were so real they were painted in portraiture across my mind. I could still feel Mary's fingers in my own. For a long while I didn't move, cocooned in blankets like a spring bud.

I rose and lit a candle. The cabin was so cold my breath smoked in the dimness. Troops stirred outside, a horse nickering. The burning wick was the only smell in the stale air.

There was a knock on the wall. "Private Stuart?"

I blew out the candle, gathered my mittens and stepped outside. I saluted Sergeant Falls and stood at ease. He cupped a tin mug of coffee and kept licking his chapped lips. It was a horribly cold morning.

"In thirty minutes, we're assembling for a grand review of the army. General Burnside handed in his resignation, which the president accepted yesterday."

I nodded. It was to be expected, given the Fredericksburg and mud march debacles. I had never thought much of the skinny Illinois lawyer, but now I prayed he would find a worthy general to lead us. Someone to bring even one victory, someone to awaken the earth. In all my months as a member of the Army of the Potomac, I had yet to rise on a victorious day.

"And the new general is to be our old corps commander." My ears perked up. "General Joseph Hooker himself. Ole Fighting Joe."

I broke into a grin. "Matthew said he'd bring change to the army."

Falls looked off towards the hospital. "He'd better. I fear another Southern victory will bring Europe to the side of the Confederacy. Then we'll be fighting the damned French."

An uneasy feeling settled in my stomach. I'd never thought of the Confederacy gaining favor overseas. What if they were recognized as a new nation? Full faith and credit, to the states so honored. For the first time, I felt the secession was dishonorable.

"Private Pierce fares no better than last week," Falls said. "I fear he has fallen seriously ill."

I had to try. I had to. "Permission, sir, to –"

He held out his hand and grasped my shoulder. His eyes were tender, his smile sad. "Your soldier is your brother. We are all brothers here, are we not Private Stuart?"

I blinked unexpected tears. "Yes, sir."

"You can thank Sergeant Pierce." He waved me away and walked towards the captain's tent.

I stood for my friends in the grand review. It was the twenty-sixth of January. Our regiment was riddled with holes like a piece of hardtack. Jackets were unkempt, buttons dulled, edges frayed. War had tarnished us. Yet, perhaps because of our veteran state, I felt honored. Honored to be among them, those who had fought beside me. We saluted the same officers, smiled upon the same flags, answered to the same commands. I had full faith and credit for the men I fought beside, for the men I fought for.

Rows and rows and rows of regiments all present at attention. Drums started. Rat-a-tat. Rat-a-tat. Fifes chirped patriotic melodies. The old familiar songs, ones I had heard at Faneuil Hall and now so dear to me.

Regimental officers appeared at the end of the line and strode quickly past us. I caught Andrew's smile. He was proud, too. It was been a tough endeavor, extracting a terrible price. But even with one friend buried and another fallen ill, I could not think of any other place I'd rather be.

An entourage of men on horses with flags and swords rode by and then our old corps commander himself, perched on his white horse. The winter sun peeping over the hills cast a glow upon the scene, tipping the bayonets and the outlines of our uniforms in gold. Major-General Joseph Hooker removed his hat, revealing a head of cornsilk-colored blond hair, and waved his sword high in spotless white gloves.

"Attention company!"

My hand went to my eyes in salute, the gesture copied by thousands of soldiers. Hooker rode by us, nodded courteously at our flags. There could be no doubt he remembered our actions at the second battle of Bull Run and Fredericksburg. He was clean-shaven and his ruddy skin burned with the wind like a heating teakettle. Curled breath in the chilled air, a sense of formality in his movements. He was from Massachusetts, too. There was that unmistakable air of good breeding, of virtues associated with the proper knowledge of action. He would bring us to victory, the tidal surge of the ocean engulfing the shore during a storm. A cold, sweeping mass of men to bear down on our enemies.

Morning light glowed in a yellow rectangle on the floor of the hospital. I waited inside the doorway, casually watching the activity of the nurses. Mary took a broom from the corner and brushed beneath the beds. Several nurses tended beds, their faces bent towards patients. A surgeon poked his head in from the back room and motioned for Mary.

"I'm needed at the operatin' table." She reached into a basket and handed me a small brown bottle. "'Tis hard to find, ye know."

"Thank you."

She smoothed her apron. "Three drops in water on th' hour. I'll be back soon."

Her eyes were red and puffy. She'd probably been awake all night. I gave her a tender smile.

A tarnished silver bowl sat on the little table by his bed. It smelled horribly, for Matthew had been ill many times. I breathed a heavy sigh and sat down. He was bathed in light from the window, and through the wavy glass regiments drilled. They looked like distant phantoms, moving dream-like between worlds.

"Mmm," Matthew murmured. "Daniel, I think it's you."

I tucked my cap on my knee and scratched the back of my head. "Yes, Matthew. I've just come from the grand review. The blond war god is now our Army commander."

"Hooker." His breath was thin. Like David's had been those final moments. He held up a hand against his face, blocking the light. When he at last opened his eyes, I had to bite my lip to keep from crying out.

His gaze was dead. Blank as a wiped slate. Were it not for the steady rising and falling of his chest, I'd not think him alive. He reached out for me, and I took his hand. His fingers were cold, pale against my own.

"I'll have Andrew get you some spectacles. I'll make sure of it."

He began to cough, a hoarse wracking convulsion that shook his limbs. He gripped the bed and sat up. I grabbed the bowl and held his head as he was sick. His body shook like a dancing toy I'd once had. When he was at last finished, I helped him lean upon the pillow. He clutched at his forehead beneath the freshly wrapped bandage.

"Oh, Daniel. Thank you."

I uncorked the small brown bottle and measured three drops into a cup of water. I guided it to his lips and coaxed him to drink. His face contorted and he grimaced, complaining of the bitter taste. I didn't tell him the label read laudanum, but it was what Mary could do for him. He needed rest, free from pain.

"Hooker won't move the army until spring. If he goes on the

offensive and attacks the Confederates, then our sheer numbers should, by any logical account, do the trick."

"Hey, you're starting to sound like Matthew again," I teased. "You are the smartest of us, you know."

"No, you are." His tone was serious. "But you were so damn stubborn when it came to epic poetry."

"I had no problem with *The Iliad*!" I said, laughing. "I could even read *The Aeneid* again, if one required me to do so."

"Andrew was never for book learning, either. I adore books. I could lose myself in them, word by word, page by page, until the days melted away."

I patted his shoulder. "Then I shall have to bring *Paradise Lost* and read to you. But I fear that must wait for another day. I only received an hour's respite from drill."

"That, Daniel, I do not miss."

I rose from the stool and stretched. "God, sometimes I feel I've been fighting in this army for a hundred years. Other times it is like I arrived yesterday."

"As David would say, we fulfill our heavenly duty with earthly matters. I guess drill is an earthly matter."

I chuckled. "Mary will be by in the next hour with more medicine. She is a good nurse. You will recover."

I squeezed his hand one last time and left his bedside. Peeking into the back of the hospital, I quickly had to step back, for the floor was washed with blood like someone had dumped a bucket of paint. The back flap of the tent was open, and beyond, a stack of human limbs sat casually in the snow, like frozen firewood. I bit my lips, glad my meager breakfast stayed in my stomach. The surgeon lifted his red hands from the operating table, Mary ready with a soaked towel. He grunted something to her, and she turned and saw me. A look of great annoyance crossed her features, and even amidst the macabre scene I smiled. The last time I'd seen that look she was telling a drunken Andrew she wouldn't dance with him. She wiped her hands and approached me in a huff.

"Ye believe they're still gettin' gangrene from Fredericksburg?" she said. "Ye're looking peaked, Daniel. Come back when ye can."

I sat down on the cold bunk in the cabin and dumped the contents of my haversack on the bed. Dime novels, the tintype of my family, *Paradise Lost*. And David's Bible, still stained with his blood. I opened the small leather book, flipping pages. I tried to have courage, David, but I was so damn tired of the monotony. You won't understand, but I can't sit by Matthew's bedside and watch him grow weaker.

Days passed, and I could do nothing. Nobody could. A gripping ache wrapped around my chest. I couldn't sleep. I spent a small fortune on candles, and when my coins disappeared, I sat at the table in the dark cabin. I didn't want to see Mary. I was ashamed of my dirty uniform, of my uncouth manners.

When I drilled, I spoke to no one. Andrew was gone most days to see his brother. He sometimes mentioned reports to me from the adjutant's tent. I nodded and my mind slipped to blank again. I slept during drill, eyes awake, staring straight ahead, hands automatically shouldering my rifle, moving in rank and file. I was awake all night. Passing clouds made strange shapes in the night sky, a daguerreotype of shadows and filtered moonlight

On payday, I received my thirteen dollars for January, plus another twenty dollars in back pay from December and November. I hadn't carried so much money since I'd come to war. I sat at the table in the cabin, counting and recounting the bills.

Andrew came back to the cabin that night, and he was not alone. He'd brought that blond girl again, that lady of the night. I grabbed his whiskey bottle from him and demanded he let me be.

The blond girl offered to bring her friend back for me. I struck her across the cheek. Andrew cast me out into the snow.

"Get your ass out of here, ye lout!"

I sat on the cold ground, the snow soaking into my trousers, spreading up my backside and seeping into my shoes. It felt good. I patted the snow. A golden square illuminated its bluish mounds. Andrew had pushed the door-flap open again.

"I should burn this! I should have burned this!"

He flung an envelope outside, then disappeared back into the cabin. What the hell had he done? I reached for the envelope, wrinkled and nearly torn in half. God, it was addressed from Boston! I moved closer to the light, ripped open the envelope, and brought the sheets up to my face.

2nd January, 1863

Dear Daniel,

I have been released and am now in the care of Mr. and Mrs. John Gage. They relinquished the ownership papers to our house, but the sale was only enough to cover the debts that Mr. Washburn fraudulently exposed as my own. I felt my strength fail me when Mother relayed the news. I would have been imprisoned for years without the payment of that false debt, though what could have been done? Oh anguish! Despair! My trust resulted in this betrayal! We must recover, and we shall. But only if you return can we restore the Stuart name.

If you remain in the Army of the Potomac, then you are indeed lost to me. You choose a nameless glory instead of your brother! What, you would rather be the doomed Achilles than a prince on Olympus? That is a decision of mortality!

No man can serve two masters, Daniel. You had it all here in Boston with me. Consider these my final words. I have no home to banish you from, but I turn from you.

Seek benevolence elsewhere.

Erik

Your loss, Erik? Your despair, your anguish, your benevolence? You think you feel it!

"You think you care!" I shouted.

Muffled cursing, and a sound like a broken bottle from inside the cabin. Glass shattered inside, burst into a thousand colorless fragments. Scattered petals, shaken from a dying tree.

I sat long enough to hear the whore's moans, then leaned to one side and vomited onto the ground. I mumbled an apology to the earth, then heaped snow where I was sick. A small dark spot appeared beneath all the whiteness. Soil! A garden! I pushed more and more snow. I was uncovering my garden. I was coaxing blossoms from their wintry blankets and bringing them up into the light . . .

Wake, gentle earth. Wake for me.

· 30 ·

"So this is why ye didn't come see me."

Warmth, softness, a white canvas above me, blank as fresh-fallen snow. I smiled and tried to reach up, but let out a cry in pain when my shoulder muscles screamed vehemently.

"Aye, ye'll be in bed for a bit. Naught I got for that, but rest. Ye can be so daft, Daniel, ye know that?"

I remembered snow and Andrew and a letter. Mary stood by the bedside, a curved silver bowl resting against her hip. She picked up a tin of salve and laid it on my chest. Despite the soreness, despite the shooting sparks of pain galloping up my arm, I reached for her hand.

"Mary, I can't . . ." My throat caught.

"Ye'll be fine if ye don't go trying to kill yerself," she said softly. "Sergeant Falls found ye this morn, nearly dead from the cold."

Her warm lips eased my frozen fingers and palm. Her face was close, her eyes glowing from the lamps. She kissed me on the forehead, then rested her cheek against my fingers.

"My home. My – my garden. It's gone."

"Hush now," she said quietly, firmly. "I need to see to the others. But listen to me, Daniel. Look at me now. Ye did nothin' wrong, ye hear? I've saved many lives because of ye. Whatever home in Boston ye had, ye can't return there."

She slowly unbuttoned the top collar of her dress and reached inside. She pulled out a black cord, dangling with a thin gold light. Tears pricked my eyes.

A key. My garden key. She saved it. She folded its small solid form, still warm from her body, into my hand.

"But, there are some things this war will never take from ye."

I closed my fingers around the key. "Rest here with me. Don't leave. I've lost so much. I lost my garden. I lost my home . . ."

Her voice was tender. "I lost mine, too. Lost it to hunger. I lost my father when the potatoes rotted, and I lost my mother on the wild seas. Ye can't live for loss, Daniel." She stroked my hair, her eyes tearing. "Ye must keep dancin'."

She promised to check on me later that day and disappeared, her skirts swishing away. Matthew was on the other side of the room, and I could not go to him. I opened my palm and saw my little garden key. She had kept it for me. The night of the gala, Erik said that he believed in me. But he only did because he thought I would eventually come around to seeing things the way he did. Mary had seen my garden. She had known the best of me.

I slipped into sleep and rested until Mary woke me at dusk. She had food, salve, a small pillow full of lavender she had heated over the hospital stove. It smelled heavenly, a musky sweetness of spring. She told me to rub the salve on my sore muscles, and after I ate I felt better.

"How's Matthew?"

She straightened my blanket. "He does poorly. A lung sickness, I fear. He sleeps for hours, then wakes screaming 'cause he can't see. I tended a man, blinded by shrapnel, in Washington. He cut his wrists with a whiskey bottle."

"I'll be well enough to see to him soon, won't I?"

"Within the week." She must have seen the frantic look in my eyes, for she reached for my hand. "I look after him, Daniel. Ye rest now."

When I awoke the following morning, a wrinkled envelope sat on the table by the bedside. I looked at it for a long while. I marveled at how such a simple thing could carry so much meaning. I, who had spent a lifetime surrounded by luxury and opulence, now had the balance of my life reduced to three hand-written pages, a key, a Bible, a poem. What I carried was all I had.

    I drifted in and out of sleep for days. I dreamed of David, his face floating in a constellation. I dreamed of Erik, sitting at his desk in the law office. I dreamed of Matthew and Andrew, dancing at the Bull and Boar. I dreamed of Mother and Father. Strolling about the Common, getting into a carriage, applauding at a theatre. I dreamed of the garden, my fingers brushing rose petals, releasing the scent like a flock of doves, soaring above me, disappearing into the blue.

    My dreams of Mary were real. Bending over me, dark hair catching the glow of the lamps. A metallic taste, cold water from a tin cup. She whispered and kissed my forehead and the warmth of her hand renewed me. I wept silently, tears trickling to my wet pillow.

    Andrew fetched my haversack, so Mary could read my dime novels to me. I sighed with pleasure to hear her clear, lilting voice add color to the Indian and Western adventures. The hospital gradually emptied as those from Fredericksburg and the mud march were buried or healed. Mary kept at the ready with chamber pots and bowls for those still afflicted with dysentery and lung fever.

    "I think ye're well enough, now," she said one morning several weeks into February. "Ye'll be seein' Matthew soon."

    I flexed my shoulders and arms. The pain had gone, danger of frostbite and weakness fading with the salve. I enjoyed a full stomach and deep rest, luxuries that hadn't been mine in months. Slowly and with great care, I rose to a sitting position. I swung my legs out and put stocking feet on the cold wood floor. My brogans were under the bed, my coat dangling from the bedpost. When I'd dressed I was able to stand, stretching my sore limbs. I felt like I'd recovered from a hit with a locomotive.

    I picked up Erik's letter. If I left, David's death would be in vain. A single shot and that boy's pious beauty was gone. If I left, Matthew's fall in the river would be in vain. Andrew's anguish, the terrible charm of war, the land stripped.

Near Matthew's bed was a little black potbelly stove. No home, no garden, no words. I walked over to the stove, lifted the grate and tucked the envelope inside. Flames cradled and curled around my brother's letter.

I looked out the window, at the quiet activity of the camp and the distant hills and slopes of Virginia. Patches of snow lay here and there like dropped petals, and several regiments drilled. Horses nuzzled the snow and smoke curled from the cabins. Matthew breathed in his bed, his chest wheezing like a broken bellows. I reached down and took his hand. He stirred and smiled.

"Mary said you were recovered."

I sat beside him. "I wish it could stay this quiet forever. I like the army like this. No fire, no rivers."

"Andrew blames the river for what's happened to me. He blames what shouldn't be blamed. A river is what a river is!"

He launched into a coughing fit and I held his wracking body, as bony and shrunken as a starving man. I was glad he couldn't see my anguish. He soon quieted and lay back upon the pillow. I poured a cup of water, added the medicine drops and gave it to him. He sipped, making a face at the bitter taste.

"Daniel, did you ever notice we walked the same roads? At Bull Run, we came in on the Hagerstown Road following the Orange and Alexandria railroad tracks. After the battle we returned. Same with Fredericksburg. We marched on the Fredericksburg Road and returned on the same road. I can't seem to make anything of it, but it strikes me as peculiar."

"I hadn't thought of it," I said, trying to make light conversation if that was what he wished. "There was something David said to me, while we were at Fairfax Seminary. He said we live a larger story. Maybe he was right."

"He would have been nineteen this spring." Matthew turned his face towards the ceiling, his blank eyes full. "He was the best of us, Daniel."

A tear curled down his cheek. I leaned down, reached inside my haversack, and brought out *Paradise Lost*.

"Well, I think both you and David would be pleased with how well I understand this poem now. It is one thing to read these lines and try to memorize their meaning for an exam."

"It is another to truly know them," Matthew said. "To be there in the words, walking beside them, guided by them. I am glad you understand, Daniel."

"Has Andrew been to see you?"

He sighed. "Not for several days. When he did come, he had been drinking. I could smell it. He said he was trying to secure a furlough. Oh, to think of it, Daniel. If we could go home!"

He coughed again, was sick again. He clutched at his torso. I helped him over the side of the bed, loud groans and cries of pain.

"It hurts! It hurts!"

He strained against the inner torture, gripping the metal bed frame. I held the bowl beneath him and steadied him while he was sick. The attack was long, painful. He ceased his struggle, collapsing upon the pillow. His hair was damp, his lips bubbling with vomit. I wiped his mouth, his forehead. I rose from the bed, poured more drops of medicine into the cup, helped him to drink. He coughed, spluttering water down his shirt, onto the sheets.

"God damn it, leave him alone!"

Startled, I dropped the cup. Water splashed onto my lap, lukewarm wetness seeping through my trousers. Heavy footsteps clopped over to the bed. Andrew lurched against the bed frame, his weight creaking the metal bedposts. He wiped his mouth. He hadn't shaved in days and his coat was stained with large patches. He stank so heavily from whiskey I was surprised Sergeant Falls hadn't caught him.

"What the hell are you doing to my brother!" he roared at me.

Angered, I snapped, "He's sick, Andrew. I've been helping him."

"Well, your duties are officially ended. Get out of here."

Matthew cleared his throat. "Andrew, come back when your breath doesn't smell like the Bull and Boar. I am not going anywhere."

"Oh, but you are!" He produced a wrinkled yellow slip and waved it before his brother's blank eyes. "For I have secured a furlough from good ole Joey Hooker himself. That's right, Matty. I am taking you home."

"To Boston?" I said.

He gave me an insipid look, but Matthew was shaking his head. "I can't go to Boston. I can't even see. I'm too sick."

"You're well enough to go and I say it's so." Andrew craned his neck around the hospital. "Where's that damn mick nurse?"

"Watch how you speak about her." I gave him a hard poke in the shoulder. "She's done more for your brother than you have!"

"Shut yer mouth, Daniel. Hell, nurse or no nurse, I'll do it myself. Let's go, Matty. We got two weeks. I've got you. Come here."

He started towards the bed and managed to grab Matthew's hand. Matthew cried out in pain as his brother yanked his upper half towards him.

I stepped between the brothers and shoved Andrew with as much weight as I could muster. He sprawled backwards against the bed frame, tearing his grip from Matthew.

"You can't move him, Andrew. Leave him be."

I was close to tears. I stepped closer to him, leaning my head down and speaking in a low voice so Matthew wouldn't hear.

"I . . . I think he may be dying."

Andrew's thick elbow hit hard beneath my jaw and knocked my teeth together. I groaned and stepped back, gripping my aching jaw. Pain. Honest, fresh pain. Andrew straightened and pushed past me so roughly I lost my footing and landed hard on my seat on the floor.

Mary came rushing over, her apron pockets bulging with glass bottles. Puzzled she looked at both Andrew and myself, but it took nothing but a second for her to realize what happened. I put a finger to my lips. My opponent was not to be punished, rash and stupid though he may be.

Andrew knelt at Matthew's bedside and reached for his brother's hand. His voice was tender, breaking with each word.

"Matty, I got the furlough. Let's get you out of this place. Let's get you home."

"He can't be moved. Ye already know, sergeant." Mary reached in her apron and brought out the medicine bottle. "'Tis for the lung fever."

When I got to my feet, I picked up the cup. There was nothing else we could do for Matthew. He was too ill. The furlough, the ticket home to Boston, was on the blankets. I picked it up, my heart beating faster and faster.

"Take it, Daniel," Andrew said bitterly. "We ain't going."

Two weeks to be home. Two weeks . . . I could see Erik and Mother. I could help the court case. I could appear before a judge. And then to come back – would my family let me leave? I had the garden key around my neck, a couple of dollars. Mary quietly nodded. I couldn't leave her.

"Take it and go!" Andrew shouted.

I took a deep breath and slowly ripped the furlough. Matthew began to weep. Mary said nothing, but I saw a faint smile.

Andrew was astonished. "That was your one chance to get back to your family!"

I dropped the torn pieces into the empty cup.

"Andrew, you are my family. You too, Matthew. I say the same for David. Your soldier is your brother."

· 31 ·

A horse nuzzled a patch of slight snow, as thin as a slip of silver. Like a hidden pocket, a tiny stretch of green appeared. The horse lifted its head and its ears twitched. I heard its nicker as I came back from picket duty. Spring was coming, easing into the army. Winter had quietly slipped away, like a servant leaving a room.

Sergeant Falls had moved three new recruits into my cabin — two young men and an older veteran who wouldn't stop talking about Shiloh. The veteran kept mumbling the name of some drunken general from Ohio. I was uneasy around my new bunkmates. They reminded me of spooked cats, and their jumpy movements made me glad the weather warmed.

During picket duty I spent my nights staring out into the Virginia wilderness. Sometimes I'd doze, but the nights were still chilled and I spent those hours thinking.

"That's the Army of the Potomac for you," Sergeant Falls muttered one morning around the end of March. "Gives you too much time to think."

I gave a half-smile and went back to washing my clothes. The tiny stream was freezing, but the water was refreshing. I dipped my shirt in the water and scrubbed the wet fabric. I could smell the loamy bottom of the little stream, could smell spring coming back to the land. This time of year I felt happier than at Christmas. The gardeners and the cook would start laying out seeds. It was these last few weeks before the ground would break open and all would start alive again.

"Daniel?" Sergeant Falls was watching me. "I mean, Private Stuart."

Most of the snow had melted and small patches of faded red soil sprung here and there. The stream quietly trickled past us, the trees beyond stretched up above us, their empty branches intermingling with the morning sun.

"I never thanked you," I said. "For saving my life that night in the snow."

He shook his head. "You know, Stuart, you were different from us. I could never understand it. I knew you came from money but I never asked about your past. I believe each man has his own."

I drew up my wet shirt. I wrung the water into the soil, trickling into tiny rivulets that ran back into the stream.

"I guess it was odd to me. Your head was somewhere else, somewhere I don't think I could ever go. Maybe it was about that nurse, eh?" He gave me a friendly jab in the shoulder.

"I have Mary to thank for many things."

"You heard that Hooker will have us moving again."

"He's been putting this army back together for weeks."

"I'm not confident in Sergeant Pierce's recent judgments, given the tender state he finds himself in. I believe you will keep an eye on the men in your company. You can perform that task, I am sure of it."

I remembered the day he'd dragged me from the captain's headquarters in Washington. Falls still made me as uneasy as a sleeping lion, but he could trust me. Somehow, I felt a bit lighter inside, an easing off. General Hooker would have us moving again soon, and I'd be in the ranks.

Several days later, Andrew was ordered to collect firewood, and he didn't want to do it alone.

"How's Matthew?" I said as Andrew swung the axe. The rail split easily beneath the weight. I bent to gather the broken bits of wood and heard a muffled sniff. When I rose again, Andrew had a mittened hand over his face, a gesture so startling I nearly dropped the firewood.

"Andrew?"

He turned slightly away. The axe dropped into the thawing soil. When at last he looked at me again, his eyes were red-rimmed. I at first thought he'd been drinking, but he was more sober in that moment than in all the days I'd known him.

"You'll see him," he said. "You'll know."

I bit my lip and looked down at the axe. He was not recovering. God, the things I couldn't do. The things I couldn't lift were becoming heavier and heavier, the things I couldn't change and couldn't right were growing with astonishing and disheartening frequency.

"A bit of good news for us," he said as he picked up the axe again. "Hooker's got his head on straight about money. We're getting pay tomorrow."

Good, I was glad he changed the topic. "It's been, what? Four months since we've seen any pay for our time here? I am sure many will be pleased."

"Them gray boys up the river ain't getting much, so I'm glad we are."

I looked away, across the lines of tents, laid out like beds of white flowers. Beyond the soldiers, beyond the horses and caissons and artillery and sutler tents, up the river not even five miles lay the Army of Northern Virginia. Some daring privates even sailed newspaper boats up the river, asking for tobacco, coffee, and other supplies.

"I am excited about having General Hooker command us." I started stacking the pieces of split fence. "He seems to be an excellent administrative leader, so far."

The sun dipped lower. We worked side by side for another hour until long charcoal shadows cast across our bodies. A spring breeze joined us and brought breaths of fresh earth, newly thawed streams, an awakening around us. Winter had brought too many changes, too much sorrow. I eagerly looked forward to a new season, a new year.

A bugle whined from the tented camp. The axe stopped, and we were finished for the night. Andrew and I each took up armloads of firewood, and loaded it onto a small wagon. We each grabbed one of the jutting rails and hauled our catch back towards the tents. I hadn't realized before how the army had completely engulfed the nearby forest. The vast majority of trees had been felled, so many that the remaining stumps were like the fallen corpses on a battlefield.

We skirted the edge of camp, passing by small cookfires and men seated on hardtack boxes and old blankets. Several songs drifted from tinny harmonicas and mumbling banjos. Andrew recognized a tune and started whistling. The men were grateful for our endeavor and many thanked us.

After our errand, I retired to my cabin and didn't see Andrew until late the following afternoon, as we both stood in line to receive our pay.

The money wasn't much, but I treated myself to new socks and ink at the sutler's tent. It felt heavenly to slip my feet into the newly stitched wool. I was rolling up my old socks and stuffing them in my haversack when Andrew again caught up with me. He was smiling, the kind of smile I hadn't seen since before the mud march.

"Wanna know what I got!" he taunted.

"A dead fish tale to tell me?" I said. His face screwed into a question mark, but it didn't take long for the joke to register. A boisterous laugh, a slap on my back. He wept yesterday, and today he was jovial. I'd never understand my friend.

"No, rich boy." I'd forgotten he used to call me that, long ago in our Harvard freshman days when he learned I lived on Beacon Hill. "And it ain't for you, either."

"Let's see it, then."

Like a child showing off his new Christmas toy, he proudly held out his hands. A pair of wire-rimmed gold spectacles glimmered in the spring sunlight.

"For Matty," he announced, as if I didn't already know.

"He'll be more pleased than when I passed that *Paradise Lost* examination, I wager."

He laughed, then walked alongside me for a bit. When he spoke again, his voice was lower, quieter.

"I know you'll never say this to him, but I never shoulda dragged Matty from school. I mean, it was all me and my reasons for . . . coming here."

"He would go wherever you went." I gave a half-smile, thinking of all the times Matthew had stopped Andrew from doing something stupid. "He looked out for you, like an older brother does."

"Well, now I have lives I look out for. I have responsibilities no professor at Harvard would give me. Did you know Matty got me into that damn school? I would have run out West or gotten killed on the high seas if it weren't for him."

I nodded. "I, too, wanted to go out West. Did you know that I almost left Harvard our first semester? Mother was outraged when I confessed I had thoughts of leaving."

"You see, Daniel, you don't seem like you have anything behind that pretty face, but you do. You always did."

In his own way, he was complimenting me. I nodded and mumbled my gratitude, glad that he'd at last procured a new pair of spectacles for Matthew. We were both relieved. Andrew coughed, then cleared his throat.

"I'm going to take these right over –"

"Not today, you're not." Sergeant Falls walked right up to Andrew. "I need you to drill those new fish. Private Stuart can visit Private Pierce in the hospital."

My friend was less than pleased, but it was an order from an officer. He reluctantly handed the spectacles over to me, his mouth twisted into a grimace.

"Don't you break 'em between here and there, you hear?" he muttered, then stomped off to help Falls.

The hospital was busier than in recent weeks. Recent cases of dysentery and catarrh plagued the camps and there were many new faces. Nurses rolled bandages and carried buckets of bloody water, doctors pulled medicine bottles from their kits. Mary was on her knees near Matthew's bed, scrubbing the floor. She wiped her hands on her apron and sat back. I peered over at the sleeping soldier in the bed. His face was turned away from me, his bandage absent. He looked to be resting peacefully.

"Did Matthew's head heal?"

She didn't turn around. "Yer friend was moved this morn, Daniel."

My stomach slid towards my knees as I helped her to her feet.

"Where is he?"

"Come on."

Afraid to know, I followed her amidst the maze of beds, hurrying people, limping and ill soldiers. Andrew's hand held before his eyes so I could not see him weep. You'll know. You'll see him.

She led me to the back of the hospital, near the amputation quarters. The operating table was empty, the surgeons gone. It was a quiet place of darkness and smoky lamps. Encased in the gloom, pushed against one stained wall, was a small cot. Tears stung my eyes. I had never seen Matthew like this, shrunken and sickly. I moved closer, ducking beneath the low lamps. His skin was yellow and gaunt, his head turned away from me. The bandage was gone, and most of his hair had been cut away.

Mary reached for my hand, her warm fingers a tiny comfort. "I did me best for him, ye know."

I nodded. Matthew stirred, his head turning towards me. I still had the pair of spectacles in my hand. I opened my palm. Mary smiled and gave me a final squeeze of my hand.

"I'll be outside."

When she had gone, I crept over to the side of Matthew's bed. There was no stool to sit and the floorboards were dark with dried blood. I reached down and gently moved his legs aside. He started to turn over, but I touched his shoulder.

"Matthew, it's all right. It's Daniel."

He relaxed when I settled beside him, easing onto the cot. I steadied my balance. He was still breathing, shallow and labored.

"Where is Andrew?"

"We have new recruits, and they needed extra drilling. But I can fetch him, if you wish."

"No," Matthew whispered. "It hurts him to see me, but he comes."

He reached to his side, and drew out a folded piece of paper from beneath the blanket. He held it out to me, and when I opened it there appeared line drawings, pencil sketches, and small labels. It was his map. I traced the outline of the Rappahannock River, Alexandria, the small square marked Fort Ellsworth, the snaky squiggle of the railroad tracks, crossed lines for Fredericksburg's streets. Landmarks, rivers, every place I had been with the army. With my friends.

"Now you can mark where you fight," Matthew murmured.

"Thank you. I have something for you as well."

I took his hand. His fingers were cold, his hand stiff. I gave him the spectacles, still warm from my palm. His blank eyes widened. A smile slowly eased onto his lips.

"Andrew bought them," I said. "I hope you can see again."

He put the eyeglasses on, and his sickly face assumed a shadow of his former self, like a faded bouquet. The contemplative thinker, the studious scholar. His brow furrowed as he struggled with his absent vision. He closed his eyes.

"I am not afraid. Both Homer and Milton were blind."

His courage caused me to smile. "Then you shall be the next epic poet. I believe Milton would be proud."

A small chuckle. "I believe Milton would understand. We were tempted to leave Paradise and enter Satan's land of war."

"Then we are all guilty," I said. "We all ate of that fruit. But I have lost my home and my garden. We have both lost a friend. A price has been paid for our temptation."

He gripped my arm. "You can make it right again, Daniel. You can make it right by fighting for the right reason."

Deep within me, I felt peace. When I stood in the ranks, when I wept by my friend's side, when I helped the wounded, when I believed, when I followed, when I tried. It was for the right reason.

"I fight for David. I fight for Andrew, and I fight for you."

"That is a good reason." He settled back. "Look after Andrew for me. He is a regular oaf ... at times."

"I will."

Matthew's hand slipped from mine as his smile slowly faded. The blank eyes closed, and his cheek tucked into the pillow like a bird's wing. He slept.

Slept and woke no more.

· 32 ·

I reached in my haversack for David's Bible, stained with his blood. I opened the tender leather cover to the gospel of Matthew. A larger story. I needed, on this warm March day, to hear a larger story.

"Please read from here."

The chaplain nodded, his black eyes soothing and deep. I stepped back and stood beside the soft earthen mound. Andrew held his cap in his hands, his shoulders straight, his head bent. Mary gave me a soft smile and I held her little hand in my own. A simple wooden board had been placed at the head of my friend's grave.

Matthew Pierce, USA
1863

"I will now read from the gospel of Matthew," the chaplain began. "Chapter sixteen, verse twenty-five.

'For whosoever will save his life shall lose it; and whosoever will lose his life for my sake shall find it. For what is a man profited, if he shall gain the whole world, and lose his own soul? Or what shall a man give in exchange for his soul? For the Son of man shall come in the glory of his Father with his angels.' Amen."

Sergeant Falls approached the grave, followed by four new young privates. I recognized the youths from my own cabin. They stood shoulder to shoulder beside Matthew's grave, rifles cocked. The chaplain closed the Bible, and laid his hand upon it.

"Private Matthew Pierce was an honorable soldier, a loyal brother, and a good friend. He will be missed, and his soul is at last at peace. He gave this torn land his life, in the hope it shall be reunited again."

I looked across at the young soldiers. Sergeant Falls gave the command and they raised their long iron muzzles to the sky. The crack resounded through the low valley, and somewhere in the nearby trees a bird twittered. Again they fired, and again. A four gun salute to my fallen friend.

A drum and fife duet began, the sweetness of the wooden flute's notes like the poetry of spring. The drum beat within me, reverberating and stirring my blood. I straightened, and my hand went to my brow.

"I fight for you," I said.

Andrew turned his head towards me, his eyes flickering. No matter what price, we are still here. We remain. We fight. He slowly placed his cap on his head, set his shoulders back, and saluted his fallen brother. His voice was strong and clear.

"I fight for you. Your soldier is your brother."

Sergeant Falls halted the firing. His hand went to his brow, and the four young privates joined him in their salute.

"I fight for you," Falls said. "Your soldier is your brother."

When the music ended, Andrew walked over to the small wooden headstone. He laid a hand on it, and knelt in the grass. I remembered the day on the hill overlooking Antietam, when David brought them both to their knees. He was not forced this spring morning. He knelt willingly.

I reached for Mary's hand and kissed it. She moved closer , and I breathed in the warmth of her body as she leaned against my chest. I placed my arms around her shoulders, her skin soft beneath her wool shawl and cotton gown.

"I'm sorry, boyo," she whispered.

She smelled sweetly. A woodland breeze played with her hair, scent of fresh earth and mossy clover. The stream trickled nearby, and a bird chirped. The world was waking.

"You are a good nurse. I have pledged my life to the army. But I do not fight for it. I fight for David, for his faith. I fight for Matthew, for his knowledge. I fight for Andrew, for his courage. I do what's right for these men."

I would fight until there were no more stars in the sky. Her eyes were wet, her lip trembling.

"And to you, Mary." I smiled. "I do what's right so I can be with you."

She looked beyond me, to the valley and the army. Spring was here. The troops were stirring. We'd march soon.

"Come see me before ye leave."

I watched her walk down the hill, back towards the hospital. If freedom was worth dying for, then love was worth living for.

At last I understood what David meant.

· 33 ·

I sat on a hardtack box in front of the fire and reached inside my coat. I took out the little garden key, dangling by a cord. It shone in the firelight, bright like the brassy yellow mouths of our military band instruments.

Andrew sat down beside me and unscrewed his canteen. "I know what you're thinking, Daniel, but it ain't whiskey."

It was the first time he had spoken to me in weeks. He had been quiet, withdrawn, wandering from drill. I closed my fist over the key.

"Do you have an extra stamp?"

"Another love letter to your nurse, eh?"

I shrugged, tried to smile. "She's thirty feet away, Andrew. The letter would take weeks to go through the ranking officers."

"Ah, but you used Matthew as your own little carrier pigeon once, did you not?"

I stared at him. "You knew about that?"

He took a hearty swallow. "After reading that letter, I knew you needed to be with that camp follower girl. Ease up a bit, will you?"

I didn't know whether to laugh or weep. I should have known better than to trust Matthew with that letter so many months ago, but the fact that Andrew hadn't sabotaged it in some way was such a kind gesture it took me by surprise.

"Now don't you go trusting me again," he said. His voice was calmer, deeper. "I'm liable to save your life from some devil-eyed reb."

"Another grand review before we march out. It seems like the other day it was January and Hooker had taken over command. My, how the tables turn fast here. It would make a gambler's head spin."

"Too true," Andrew nodded. "But we ain't gamblin' on pay coins here. No, we gamble with a godly hand."

He dropped the canteen, let it lie in the grass beneath him. He took a deep breath and blew a sigh that disrupted the fire's smoke. His face was orange, shiny, in the light.

"I need the stamp to write to Erik before we leave."

"Not gonna let the old boy rot in prison, then."

"He's actually out now," I said. "He's with my mother and Mr. Gage. They were married this past winter and share small but livable quarters on Washington Street."

"Your home has truly been usurped, Daniel?"

I pushed the stick into the embers, tiny sparks flitting into the cool night like yellow butterflies. I bit my lip, tasting smoky residue.

"Mary told me not to live for loss. She says we must keep dancing. I cannot even tell you how many times I've thought of that night at the Bull and Boar. Mother reprimanded me for coming home so late, but I'll never regret it. I think it was one of the happiest nights of my life."

A long, crackling silence. Andrew reached into his haversack and took out a small leather pouch. He started counting his stamps, then shrugged and left a handful in my palm. He gave me a smile, and then he was gone, back to his own winter quarters.

I sat and stared into the fire pit for a long time. Little petals of flame separated from the main body of fire and tiny curled embers, like charcoal leaves, drifted about.

20th April, 1863

Dear Erik,

I am not leaving the Army of the Potomac. You may or may not forgive me, but I shall not judge you. I remember our home with great fondness, but I know my garden is gone. The earth blooms here in Virginia. If Milton lamented that we should lose Paradise because of our sins, then perhaps we can regain it when we do the right thing.

Give my love to Mother. I wish you the greatest fortune in your business endeavors. My only wish is that you find joy in living as a free man. It is the reason I fight.

We go into battle soon. Farewell, dear brother. May we meet again in a lighter time.

Daniel

General Hooker lined us up and we were issued something new. Corps badges. We donned our white diamonds and my blood turned when our army crept from its winter quarters to line and stand beneath Hooker. He sat astride his white house, ruddy skin glowing, blond hair shining beneath a new sun.

My Massachusetts regiment was positioned near the Irish brigade. I smiled at the familiar lilt in their voices when they chatted. It was Mary's voice, her people. I looked over at them, at the sprigs of new grass they put on their caps, at the freckled faces, the companionable jockeying.

"Good morning, Private Stuart." Andrew saluted and I returned the gesture. "A pretty day, ain't it?"

"Announcing General Hooker!"

Andrew hastened to my side and we stood in rapt attention when the man of the hour rode by on his sleek stallion. We boasted new corps badges, a cleaned-up appearance, polished buttons and shoes, mended jackets, new stripes for those who earned them. Many were gone and there were holes. But Andrew and I were ready. A warm breeze pulled at me with soft hands. Yes, even the earth was ready.

"Parade rest!"

I crossed my hands and leaned them against my thigh, resting my weight on my back leg. My rifle felt like a second skin, soothing with its solid heft against my knee. The metal tip was cold, the long smooth snout warm from my hands and the sun.

"Attention Corps officers! This army is to be made ready by the end of the week! We march to meet the foe when we are ready! Do your duty and remember the great cause you fight for!"

General, if you believed I fought for any other reason than the man standing beside me, then you were gravely mistaken.

"This army is dismissed!"

General Hooker rode off, followed by his flock of aides like a bird at the head of a flying V. I steadied my rifle against my shoulder and followed Andrew back to camp. After I dropped off my letter to Erik at the post wagon, the regiment commenced with some easy drilling. My feet and my body knew what to do. I slid into the maneuvers like the click of a watch. I marched, and, in so doing, marched as one.

Rations were issued. Forty rounds of ammunition. I tucked the eight days' worth of food into my haversack. I counted and re-counted the cartridges. As I laid the papered bullets on my bunk, I paused. David's Bible, Matthew's map, my father's copy of *Paradise Lost*. Three dime novels, torn and rubbed from reading so many times. Half a bar of soap – God, I'd forgotten what it felt like to have a clean scalp. The handkerchiefs were long gone, shredded to pieces after Fredericksburg and the mud march. My family's daguerreotype was smoky, faded, wet from the Rappahannock River. Our faces looked like ghosts, pale outlines against a darker charcoal. I could still see Erik's half-smile.

Yet, I still had the garden key. It hung around my neck on shoelace cord. Turn the lock, the satisfying click, and slowly close the world away. Smell the summer blooms, soft velvety leaves brushing against my trousers, the jewel of a June strawberry in my mouth. Easing onto the silvery garden bench, the wood smooth and welcoming. Blossoms nodding their sleepy heads, a new rosebud tightly curled.

I stood before the hospital, nauseous and tired. Wagons were hitched, saddles polished, and barracks were burning. The camp smelled of acrid smoke. The army was preparing to leave. One hundred and thirty thousand men strong.

I waited for her until she was ready. Many beds were empty and fresh supplies were prepared for the coming wounded. She spoke quietly to another nurse. Someone had put lily of the valley flowers into a vase on the windowsill beside Matthew's old bed. Tiny white bells.

"I came to say good-bye."

Her face was teared, aching. I breathed slowly. In a summer past, I saw a face watching me in the garden, so I plucked a rose and gave it to the pretty maid. She called my name and held out her hands and I looked down at her and I saw petals and I saw dark eyes beneath a candle. I had no words for that moment, as I had no words now.

"Daniel?"

Here. Now. Two lovers parted and a curtain fell. I knew, perhaps like all men knew when it was time, that I had never felt the fullness of nothing like I felt now. It was so present, like loyalty was so present. Like the loss of my garden was so present. Things that were heaviest had no weight, and silence burst with its own tormented music. Notes of nothing.

A smile. Quietly illuminating her face.

"Ye can be so daft, boyo. Ye must know I love ye."

My words died inside my smile and I could not speak anymore. I was weaponless, vulnerable, laid bare like an unshaded flame. I was complete, in and of myself and her.

"You save me, Mary. You care for me and you save me. How can I . . . ?"

The emptiness in my palm she filled with hers, skin to skin. Circled her arm about me, her cotton sleeve against my neck. So slight she was, so sweetly she pressed upon me and lowered me. We pressed lips, like roses nodding against one another. I tasted fruits of other times, salt from her dew. We wept alike, my Mary and I. And we ached alike, aching ourselves not to part.

I broke away, reeling from her like my feet were on a shoreless floor. I must leave. I would love her until I was drained by the fullness of it. A fullness of nothing.

"I'll come back to you, Mary."

We pressed our hands together, skin to skin. I kissed her hands and she kissed mine. I kissed her mouth and she kissed mine. No answers in a poem, no questions in a war. Love and love only. It was all that remained before the killing began.

I did not look back when we marched away. I tasted battle in the air, tasted the dust of the march. I'd come back to her. I pressed my hands together, and felt her kiss. The weight of my name on her lips.

It was the fullness of the nothing that I needed.

· 34 ·

Rat-a-tat-tat. Rat-a-tat-tat. Striking drumbeats and cooing fifes lilted notes above the breeze. The brigades paraded past our regiment. Row after row after row of blue and silver. Rat-a-tat-tat. Rat-a-tat-tat. Regimental bands struck up the tunes as Hooker's long blue arms began their journey from the winter camps at Falmouth. Tomorrow was the first of May. We were due to march southwest, back towards the Rappahannock River. The men were singing.

The Union forever! Hurrah, boys, hurrah!
Down with the traitors! Up with the stars!

Yes, I was among stars. The great constellations, scattered like flour grains upon the black marble of the night sky. Down with the traitors ... and up with the stars!

I shifted my haversack from one shoulder to the next. My days of rations – salt pork, hard bread, salt, sugar, coffee – clanked and bumped against each other in the coarse linen belly of the knapsack. My cartridge box was full, the little papers rustling against the walls of the leather pouch. Tin cup dangled from the strap, clinking against the buttons.

General Hooker was at our helm. He rode by, followed by his aides and adjutants. Andrew marched beside me, his arms pumping, his legs jerky in their blocky brogans. His uniform was too tight, too small. A patch wore across his knee, where his trousers tore during Fredericksburg. His hands were scarred from the slicing rope during the mud march. We were veterans now. We carried the war with us, on our bodies.

Andrew scratched the back of his neck. "Didn't miss the God damn flies."

I laughed. His cap was jauntily stuck on his head, his brow already dappled with sweat from morning sun warmth. His drinking and his fighting and his cursing and his temper. But he was a soldier, true to the heart. He loved his brother as I loved mine. I fought for no cause and he fought for no man.

"You and me now, Sergeant Pierce," I said.

"Well, well, Private Stuart," grumbled a familiar voice. "You talking in the ranks again?"

I saluted Sergeant Falls with a smile. My legs were loosening, the morning coffee warmed my belly, and the sun was high in the sky. It was a beautiful day for a march out.

We marched along the same roads. No rains fell, but I could clearly picture those deep ruts where the cannon moaned and the horses strained. A soft, Irish rain gave way to a New England fog. Like home. It was nearly impossible to see my comrades, outlined like gray ghosts in the mist. It was still quiet and I was grateful. Andrew was also silent and I hoped he would remain as cheery as he'd been the past several days. But I did not have much time to linger, for then Colonel Blaisdell advanced to the front of the blue lines and read a message from General Hooker to us. Immediately the serenity was abandoned for wild cheers to "Get the Rebs!"

"So he thinks this kind of talk will win us one, eh?" Andrew sought the horizon. "Where's that damn balloon?"

Our general was fond of Professor Lowe's hot-air balloon and used it on several occasions. It rose in the southwest, away from the camp, appearing to be behind the dreaded heights of Fredericksburg. More cheers erupted from the Federals for the aerial wonder. Would any of Hooker's boasting align with a victory?

At noon, most of the Third Corps under General Sickles advanced towards a little church. This march, conducted through valleys and over sloping ground, carried a fresh share of burdens with the extra rations and warm weather. A tall white church steeple rose out of the pastoral hillside. Andrew took a drink of water from his canteen, and pointed at the church. The men curved around the quaint white building. The iron bell was silenced for the night. No figures moved in the church. Maybe it would still be standing at the end of the war, neither shelled nor riddled with bullet holes. Orders came to clear the space, feed the tired horses and mules, and gather water and wood for the evening's meal.

After coffee drained from tin cups and bacon disappeared from tin plates, I sat in the grass. The church was outlined against the vague blackness beneath the stars, its surrounding grassy earth devoid of snow. I curled upon my blanket beside Andrew. We both cast our winter overcoats along the way to the church, leaving them beside so many others discarded in the road.

A pretty dawn illuminated the stark architecture of Hartwood Church. I paused before stirring, before the men rose and resumed their march. Pink sunrays spread from the trees and engulfed the misty clouds. It looked a little like the Old North Church, the same quaint New England design. It was the first time I truly smiled when I remembered David.

Andrew was more congenial than usual, chatting amiably with the new recruits from my old winter cabin. He took a liking to the youngest boy, and I heard him laugh like he used to.

Though Andrew's knowledge of the army's movements could never match Matthew's, his ability to let loose scourges of rumors and funny stories of generals kept us entertained and enlightened. I laughed at the jokes, lightness coursing through me, the humor lightening the mood.

This was ground we traversed before. I fancied I could see my own footprints when we resumed the road. I remembered it vividly, in the rains of a distant January. And here . . . here was the place where an unruly pontoon boat struck Matthew's head and where we tried in vain to keep the pontoon bridge together. Here was where we all met the waters of the Rappahannock.

The regiment reached the shores of the United States Ford. Andrew tightened his hands on his knapsack straps. His huge hands, lashing the ropes together. Catching, holding, trying. If he was remorseful, his face did not reveal it. Blocked and chiseled like ice, his green eyes glittering.

The pontoon bridge was built quietly, without Andrew's help. The strange wooden boats rocked back and forth on the still glassy waters, like a long pirate gangplank bobbing on the waves. I stared down at the waters beneath when we crossed the river. Sunlight dashed off the polished mirror of the quiet currents. The plank wood thumped against my old brogans. When we reached the opposite bank, I could not help but turn back. I wanted to see Matthew, I wanted to see him running to catch up with us, pushing up his glasses and laden with his maps.

There was a slight commotion up ahead. Andrew looked at me, rolling his eyes. The steady clinking, the plodding feet, the downcast eyes, the faded scant gray uniforms. A prisoner line, must be nearly a hundred in all. A prisoner line so much larger than the one we'd escorted in Washington. I tried to see if I could recognize a face, but to no avail.

"You're gonna need three years' rations afore you git Richmond!" shouted one cheeky fellow.

A Federal, one of our own, stuck out his foot and tripped the loudmouth. Andrew located the offender and pulled him aside for a scolding.

The prisoners passed soon enough and Andrew returned to his place. An old Confederate camp was our temporary dwelling after our river cross, and we spread blankets upon the smoothed ground.

The next morning, a distant rumble stirred old feelings in my breast. I hadn't heard the sound in so long. Their muzzles silent for months. Guns were in position and firing. Their terrible spit of shot and shell exploded into Virginia soil. Cannonading increased in intensity. My ears rang with the noise, the pounding pounding pounding. Sloshing like fierce tides. I was in the midst of the terrible crashing of grape shot and minie balls.

"Double-quick to the front!"

I tore a fresh cartridge and poured the smooth black powder down the hungry rifle barrel, grabbed up the muzzle and double-quicked over the road. The rest of the Union army swarmed around a large brick building in a nearby clearing. I pulled out my ramrod and forced the bullet into the gun.

I gasped in surprise at the sight of the huge square brick building and stood, rooted to the spot and frozen with horror.

"Come on, Private!" Andrew yelled.

"What is this place?" I shouted.

"The Chancellor House!"

It so greatly resembled my lost home in Beacon Hill I expected Erik to drive up and Mother waiting beneath the portico for us. Flaming sunlight illuminated the huge front columns.

God, I never thought I would see it again! The promise I made to myself so long ago had been fulfilled. I saw my home!

But then the real horror overcame me. I was not home in Boston. I was in front of a Southern plantation on Southern soil in a Northern uniform clutching a loaded musket, ready for the onslaught.

We rejoined the main portion of the army. The familiar glint of the fight in Andrew's eyes, a look absent since August. This large mansion was not alone in the clearing, but surrounded by smaller buildings for slaves.

We circled the house to find the ground we were ordered to occupy. The men looked livelier than months past. Carrying regimental flags high, their muskets tautly balanced upon their chests. This General Hooker, brash though he may be, accelerated the army's vigor.

I gazed at the Chancellor House and my heart stopped. For there, tucked beside the southern wall, was a small garden.

Scrub brush clamored against the faded brick. When we came closer, I could also see within this garden's fenced walls a small private cemetery. Several graves stuck haphazardly into the ground like stone playing cards. The dead in the garden.

Yours is a decision of mortality!

Why do you grieve this way?

You'll get home, Daniel.

You must fight for the right reasons.

Erik, I loved you. You were my brother. I had to come here, had to fight for something I could be proud of. Something I could wrap into myself so that I could claim it as my own. I called these dead my own. Dead dreams, dead soldiers, dead friends. Are you not dead, Erik? Then why have I nothing but memories?

Nothing to claim as real, as alive, as pulsing with the blind hot white lights I saw here. When the trumpets ceased their mournful song, when the last drum fell silent upon the field, caught within the dead leaves. I would still reach for beauty. I would still stand in the doorway and wait for my friends to fall beneath the hours.

Oh, Mary.

I crossed the clearing and went over to the little fence, picking my way past the weeds. Men and horses milled nearby, some pawing the earth. I walked past them and grabbed the fence. I felt its splintery skin beneath me, curling tendrils. Small pink flowers, some yellow. A sheaf of lily of the valley tucked by the shadow of the house. Tiny white bells. The gravestones, the mossy tomb markers.

"Come on, Daniel."

Andrew held his gun, standing quietly, his grizzled face alighted by the sun. I gazed across the little scene once more, then slowly walked away from it. I saw my home again. And I saw what had become of it. My garden, a cemetery. My flowers, still in bloom after all these months.

"Did you see it, Andrew? Graves. In a garden."

"We have seen hell here, haven't we?"

Yes. Too much. I straightened my shoulders, pulled upon the straps of my knapsack. I took off my forage cap and dusted it off. Shiny white diamond. I smoothed down my jacket.

"Well, Sergeant Pierce? Do you think me battle-worthy?"

He looked at me, the look of a proud father. His green eyes shone clear with the light, the immense light I needed.

"Yes, Private Stuart. I am honored to serve beside you today."

I smiled. "I do my duty, sergeant."

Sergeant Falls stepped around to the front of the regiment, unsheathed his sword and pointed towards a clearing.

"Forward, march!"

We stepped beyond the boundaries of the Chancellor House plantation and into the surrounding Virginia wilderness. A short distance from the mansion, we bivouaced among the stunted oaks and stubby bushes. The stocky brick house was through the trees. It was as if it had been plucked from the streets of Beacon Hill and brought here to rest amongst the quietness of the forest.

Andrew dropped his knapsack in the grass and we rested against a fallen log. The scents of the forest, musty pine needles, growing things, the lush dampness of moss and soil, rose up around us. Andrew picked up a stick and drew circles and swirls in the sand. It was too dark to read, so I lay back and looked up through the trees.

A carpet-web of stars spread out above us, some scattered and others clustered. Down with the traitors and up with the stars.

"The stars, Andrew. The stars give us the answer, don't they?"

He wiped the sand of his drawings. "What answer?"

"How to end this war."

He glanced up. "They don't say a damn thing."

"You do not think Matthew watches us? That David is up there, too?"

"I ain't betting on it, if that's what you mean."

"I am not, either. I know it to be true."

He tossed the stick. "You think that, if it brings you comfort. But you were the most stupid when it comes to real things."

"Oh, real things like death? My father is dead and my home is gone. My friends are dead. I saw the dead in that garden. That is real, right?"

"War is simple. I don't care what those damn rebs have to say to me. I don't wanna sit down and drink tea and talk about we all getting together and being all like a family. They took my family, Daniel. There ain't nothing I want but them dead, too."

I sighed. "The stars do have the answer, Andrew. The myths live on, become a part of our story."

"I didn't read those stories like you."

"Matthew did. During the Trojan War, there was a mighty hero named Achilles. Son of a goddess. He lost a man of his family, a cousin. Slain by the greatest of the enemy warriors. So Achilles challenged him to a duel and it was the mightiest fight of the ages."

"Achilles got whupped, I imagine."

"No. But he died in that war, too."

"Look, I ain't smart like you. I don't give a cursed thought to any of your stories. Let's fight this God-damn battle tomorrow and let's win one sweet victory. That's all I want. I want to triumph over these ignorant, heathen animals."

He folded his haversack and rest upon it in the grass. "And you know what, Daniel Stuart? I want it at any cost."

"You think Matthew's death is that cost?"

"He knew me better than anyone. He'd agree with that."

I bedded down in the moss, inhaling the scents of the forest. The stars did have the answer. I stood with my brother beneath the portico on my last night at home, looking up at the stars. Watch over us. Watch over us when we fight.

For you are the larger story.

· 35 ·

"Daniel, wake up!"

I rolled over, blurred colors. Greens, blues, browns, bright yellow. I rubbed my eyes and sat up. Andrew rested by a tree, one leg tucked under him like a bird, foot planted on the trunk.

Pop. Pop.

Musketry, skirmishing nearby. I scrambled to my feet, blood seeping from my head. I grasped onto a fallen log for balance, steadying myself. Andrew cocked his head at me and laughed.

"Easy there, rich boy." I forgot he used to call me that. "It's a hundred yards away."

He quietly loaded his rifle, long slick ramrod pushing the bullet down. The sky was bright, spring-splash bright. I squinted, rubbed my eyes, steadied my balance. God, I was hungry. I searched in my pockets, found some crumbly bits of pork and floured biscuits stuck together.

"Anybody make coffee?"

Birds twittered in the trees above us. A squirrel skittered down a tree trunk, then raced back up again. The rest of the regiment was also stirring. Some eating, others ducking behind trees to relieve themselves. Nobody built a fire, nobody made coffee. Damn. I had a headache.

More shots fired, closer this time. A bullet whizzed by and splintered a sapling. Several men ducked, holding knapsacks, blanket rolls, anything above their heads. So it would be that kind of day. It was like a game from childhood, the fox chasing the geese, picking off their fat young bodies until only a few were left.

It was beautiful here. Shafts of sunlight, long skinny bars trickling through trees, prisms of a chandelier. The beauty of the land, the clearing and the trees, washed like a wet brush on canvas. Blue above, as blue as could be.

"Wake up, boys!" Sergeant Falls stomped through our sleepy clusters. "We're moving out! Fall in!"

Andrew hoisted his rifle and organized us. I joined the others and we started into the underbrush, away from our clearing. The grass had been trampled, bits of paper from torn cartridges like fallen butterflies. My box was full, all lined up like neat white soldiers. The skirmishers were out in force, tossing bullets back and forth like clucking chickens. A strangled cry. Then a crackling underfoot and a soft thud when a soldier fell. I was surprised how casual I felt about it. As if we strolled about the Common on a summer afternoon.

Several privates broke from the line and helped Sergeant Falls and the captains clear out the brush. We were mired in its tangled, wiry currents, fighting against it like the rushing river. Then there was a break in the trees and we found ourselves in fields, rows of tiny vegetables and plants. The outskirts of the Chancellor House plantation. From behind, its massive square brick face sat shadowed in the trees. Great wide columns like ships' masts, thrusting high above us as we trudged beneath. Open ground near the house was occupied by other Union regiments, swarming around the house like ants near a colony.

We halted near the edge of this open field. A small guard separated from the main line and we were ordered to shed our belongings. The soldiers stood about and dumped their blankets, haversacks, tin cups, knapsacks, books, and daguerrotypes into the main pile. I pulled on the straps, feeling my own things slide from my shoulders. The pile reminded me of the amputation room at the hospital, legs and arms and hands and feet tossed into a grisly conglomeration of blood and flesh and flies.

Andrew carried nothing but a rifle and a cartridge box.

"Hurry it up, Private Stuart."

I chose a mossy spot near the pile and lay down my burdens. In the same clearing, within the sight of the Chancellor House, I shed my things. I didn't want to and I was the last to rejoin the group. I still had the garden key about my neck. It was all that was left.

Hooker's plan to rejuvenate the army had worked. A surprising number of men were present for duty today. Any stragglers caught were right up in the front, placed by the provost-guard who had arrested them.

We marched over to the open ground, our backs turned away from the woods. A battery of artillery cannon, snouts pointed out beyond the Chancellor House, lay scattered around the house. We skirted the grassy edge of the house and onto a wide road made entirely of flat boards. It was like walking on a stable pontoon bridge. We clumped noisily across the boards in our nailed sole brogans. An order trickled down the ranks that we were to support the artillery. I glimpsed graying coats beyond, the shiny silver of enemy bayonets.

Great shouts rose up behind me. The artillery officers cheered us forward. Sergeant Falls unsheathed his sword and waved it at our advancing line. I realized with a start I hadn't been part of this line, this steady advancing line, since the dusty streets of Fredericksburg. I didn't know if I could fight again. But I would try.

I smelled something beyond burnt powder, earthy sweat, spring moss. Something familiar. The first line of the men rested behind a strong breastwork, the soldiers roasting coffee upon open fires. Coffee? In the midst of battle? We were fighting! Why did they not join us? The degree of nonchalance was more than I could bear.

Not another second elapsed before we were caught in the smoky embrace of battle again. Confederate forces miraculously gained a hundred yards of ground and lined up before us like the wall of a castle. Their metal ramrods slid in and out of their rifle barrels. I could hear them before I caught sight of them through the smoke.

"Shoulder arms!" Andrew shouted. "Load!"

I poured the powder before my mind registered what was happening.

I shoved the ramrod down the gun and cocked it.

"Ready, aim! Fire down the line!"

Pop. Pop. Down we fired, the bullets fast and accurate. Tiny flames leapt from the rifle mouths. We were seasoned and sure, cutting our teeth at Fredericksburg and Second Bull Run. Volleys pelted down the clearing, smoke acrid and hot. I tore another cartridge, poured another bullet. Drum rolls cut through the orders. It was too loud to hear Andrew, too smoky to see anybody. A navy blur in the corner of my eye.

"Fire down the line!"

The heat of the gun felt good, the sturdy weight of it in my palms. Long snouty muzzle spitting into the enemy lines. Some toppled, others wavered. Some screamed, some groaned and clutched a leg or a knee. Trees peeked through the lines as the men fell, bodies sprawled, peppered with white cartridges, blood spatters.

Cannon allied with us, bass rumbles shaking the earth and alighting the woods. Striking shot and shell exploded their lines. By the time I'd loaded a third cartridge, the enemy brigade lost half its number. I could hear their captains shouting to fall back. Their flags wavered, disappearing into the chaotic melee.

"Re-load, boys! Fire!" Sergeant Falls screamed.

I raised the rifle to my shoulders and fired into the trees. My body hummed with the backlash from the shot, my fingertips tingling. I reached in my cartridge box, grabbed another round, loaded again. Tiny bits of leaves fluttered about my shoes, balanced slightly backwards to offset the weight of the gun. Andrew screamed orders behind me, and once I caught him smiling as he picked off a particularly large Confederate struggling to load his rifle. He was enjoying himself.

"Company! Fall back!"

Falls whipped his sword like a Western lasso, urging us away from the fight. Andrew rolled his eyes, but lowered his rifle. Damn it all.

"Company! Reform the lines!"

Ah, so we were not being called from battle after all. I managed to nudge Andrew with my elbow and we shared a smile. Today we would not run from the field. We would not cower and turn like dogs.

The clearing began to fill with reinforcements, new troops with fresh rounds and pristine uniforms. I nodded to some of them. They'd continue to fight the assault. Meanwhile, somebody higher ranked had different plans for us.

We left the clearing, and headed towards a deep rutted road, five companies deployed from our regiment as skirmishers. We advanced on both sides of the plank road in the form of an inverted V, with the apex in the center. A new brigade of the Confederate army happily greeted us, their columns marching from the opposite direction. All of a sudden we were engaged again. I braced myself against a split board.

"Pour it in!" Falls screamed. "Let 'em have it, boys!"

Shots thundered into the advancing enemy lines. Horses shrieked and threw their wounded riders, dragging half-slain corpses away from the front. I loaded and fired again and again. Down the slick black line of my rifle barrel I watched my enemies perish by my hand. Hands were thrown in the air, as their bodies tumbled backward against the plank road. I caught one soldier on the side of his neck, and his scream drowned in a bubble of blood. I reached in my cartridge box again. Andrew fired his pistol with the speed of Mercury. Three men tumbled for one of mine.

They fell back. The road emptied and became so quiet I could hear a breeze ruffle the tops of the trees. We were victorious for the moment. I licked my lips, replaced the ramrod, put the cap on, and raised the rifle to my shoulders.

"AIYEEEEE!"

My breath caught. What the hell was that sound? Andrew lowered the pistol, his eyes darting along the forest and the plank road.

"They're coming again, boys!" Sergeant Falls frantically reloaded. "Keep your eyes on the road!"

All of a sudden, a terrific explosion rocked the ground directly behind us. I cowered in the road, my rifle above my head. Enemy cannon found us! Shot and shell burst from the forest in front of us, igniting the forest all around me. I coughed as the shrubs and trees began to catch fire. It smelled like a bonfire as more and more trees caught fire.

"Here they come!" shouted Falls.

Confederate troops launched up the road, shrieking like the Furies of hell. I immediately straightened, swung the gun back up to my shoulder, and picked off an enemy. The reb floundered backwards, dragging a comrade onto the road with a thud. A lump lodged in my throat as I remembered Fredericksburg. David, dear David.

"Watch out!" cried Andrew.

I ducked as a flaming sapling tipped and bent over. Like a fiery whip, it blazed a path on its way to the ground. Screams of pain and anguish as members of my own regiment were burned. I shoved dirt and loamy leaves onto the fiery wood.

Bullets zipped between us. A Federal soldier I helped coughed up blood as he fell, half of his face burned by the falling sapling. Shots thudded into the flaming trees, and pinged off broken shell fragments. I ducked beneath a rotting log by the side of the road to reload my gun.

Peeking through the mossy branches, I realized the Confederates were falling back. They didn't have the strength we did, the sheer numbers. I felt a surge of joy as I shoved the cap on the gun and cocked it.

Andrew stepped aside to reload, and I hurried back into the line between exploding enemy cannon shell, bits of bark and twigs raining down from the ripped forest, heavy smoke. Sergeant Falls shouted behind me, and I raised the rifle and fired into the gray lines.

"Pour it into them! Fire! Reload!"

I grabbed a cartridge, reloaded the gun, and fired again. I fired again and again. Yes! They were falling back! We were gaining ground!

"Reform the lines!" Falls shouted. "Forward!"

Greedy for the ground, ready for the push. Our line moved forward, a solid wall of armed blue. Muscles taut, limbs stretched like a banjo string. Ready to assume our ground.

"AIYEEEEE!"

The hairs on the back of my neck stood up. What an animalist sound, like a blaring lamb. I shrugged my shoulders. Let them yell. We were the ones advancing. I stepped between sprawled horses, broken wheels, enemy bodies. My shoe squished a dead hand, and I gulped back the horror. Keep moving. Crashing shook the trees behind us, horses whinnying. I could hear shouts nearby, muffled orders.

"It's our artillery," Andrew said gleefully. His green eyes shone like dappled leaves. "Now we have the advantage in this game."

I couldn't help a slight chuckle. To Andrew, it was a game. A mighty and fierce game, but a game nonetheless. A game.

BOOM! BOOM!

Cannon were awake once more. Screaming blasts soared above and plummeted into the advancing thicket. Fattened clouds of smoke enveloped us, gorged by the artillery. Hot wind blew in my face, and I blinked as my eyes watered.

The road widened until we were in a clearing. Gray troops were firing into other Federal regiments, entangling with them in a chaotic snarl. An enormous group of reserve companies gathered towards us. Strengthening our lines, filling in the empty gaps where blue-clad comrades once screamed. Sergeant Falls halted us, pointing at the enemy lines.

"Massachusetts! Rank and file!"

Shoulder to shoulder, I stood beside my comrades. On my left I recognized one of the new recruits, the youth who lived in my cabin. Regimental colors stepped out in front of us. Spring breezes tickled the flags, dappled red and white stripes dancing like buoys. Down with the traitors and up with the stars!

"On my command!" Falls shouted. "Ready! CHARGE!"

I smacked the gun into my palms, stinging metal against stinging flesh. We swarmed from the trees, engaged in a massive footrace across the flattened May grass. I took off across the open ground, Andrew at my side. He snorted like a fiery bull. My feet alighted with the freedom of the wind. The earth spongy and yielding, breeze magnified in my ears, my fingers gripping the rifle, lover-tight.

Union troops tore out of the woods and into the rebel lines. Sudden solid warmth when I slammed into the enemy, fists of gray and yellowed wool in my hands, smoke blurring my eyes, blurring the bearded faces. I grappled with them, slicing my bayonet into their flesh. One dared to pluck his bloody bayonet from a screaming Federal and advance upon me. I hiked up my rifle to my shoulder and shot him in the face. A red bud bloomed on his forehead. He burst into petals and fell. I would end this one man at a time. I would pull the weeds and purge this garden.

I shot another. I loaded and Andrew shot another. He loaded and I shot another. We worked like two gears in a machine. We sliced and fought and slammed and shot.

They were weakening. I could feel them press back. One more step in the ground, one more knee into a groin. I could feel their heavy weights tumble onto me. I was splashed with their blood, red like rain. A wave of weariness gripped me and the rifle gained a hundred pounds. The firing dwindled, the machine slowing. The gears and wheels ground to a lazy halt and our work was done. Smoky, hazy, dim light over the clearing.

Andrew tugged his bayonet from a slumped Confederate and we stared at one another over the bodies. I reached out and gripped Andrew's hand. His green eyes were like clover, dancing in the smoky light.

Cheering roars erupted from our lines. There were few dead and many well enough to smile. Lee's gray arms retreated, pulling back into the main body. But like Death, the general had not finished his day's gruesome work. Treetop sentinels reported the enemy battle lines reformed on the left. Three companies were supported by small details from several regiments in General Hancock's division of the Second Corps. On the right, at the same time, another rebel force menaced those troops. The Second Corps body of troops occupied a rifle pit, straddling the width of the plank road like a man astride a horse. Two battle lines met at a right angle, forming a slanted V. Confederate bullets in the front would rake across them, but nature supplied several large oaks and a slight rise for protection from this murderous set-up.

My mouth tasted of metal and dry cotton. An officer in gray brought men into place. They were close tonight! I could even hear him shouting orders. The sliding of their ramrods, the slight cough and occasional mutter.

"What are they doing?" I asked.

"Reforming, regrouping." Andrew began loading again. "What does it sound like? They used Hardee's Tactics Manual same as us."

I continued watching the rebel troops. I already killed many today. Yet I stood by as a spectator, helpless as a babe. I watched my enemy prepare to fight and my resolve slipped.

Evening approached, coolness slowly painting over the heat. The forest was eerily quiet. A howling scream, like a wounded animal's cry, erupted from the darkened woods. A force was still engaged on the left. Dejected Confederate soldiers tried to reinforce the troops that hit upon the blue lines. Then the Federals retaliated, lining shoulder to shoulder like wool-clad statues and firing a volley upon them. The smoke and the gray mixed into a deadly concoction. Twigs snapped and men fell. The woods shook as the rebels retreated.

"Union ammunition is low," Andrew commented. "Scariest thing to happen in a fight."

I agreed. It was like a hammer and no nails. Pounding bluntly and uselessly. We all reached into our cartridge boxes and five of my own papers were added to the collection. I wondered if all five would find their mark.

"Attention company!" Sergeant Falls strutted out in front, his face crimson in the last moments of sunset. "Double-quick to the pit!"

We moved into position behind the breastworks, and I came face to face with a solid mound of earth and wood. The smell of the soil, loamy and spicy, hit me and I nearly fell face-first into it. Digging, planting, seeds in a soft bed.

The light disappeared and night was upon us. I was hungry, but had been a soldier long enough to learn how to ignore it. Andrew and I curled against the breastworks and watched the rifle sparks of the men fighting in the darkness. I appreciated Morpheus's black cape, comforting and concealing. The plank road glittered silver in the moonlight, pings striking its wooden boards when bullets struck. Several hours after dusk, the musketry fire faded.

"I think the rebels retreated," yawned Andrew.

I heard a groan and sat up. I did not realize the wounded were so close. They were faintly outlined in the dark, writhing like Hades demons. The tear of buttons as someone ripped off his coat. I hated that sound. It was like when David lay dying in the streets of Fredericksburg. I brought up my knees and balanced my rifle on my lap.

"Don't move," Andrew hissed. "They may still be in the trees."

A whippoorwill's hooting call whistled through the forest. Another, nearer, answered it. Confederates were signaling. They continued back and forth for several minutes.

But the whistling was drowned out by the sudden distant yell of a nearby force of men. It carried over the May breeze, a screaming taunt containing all the passion of the earlier fight.

An order whispered down the line. Our company rose from the breastworks and traveled back towards the plank road, following it until we reached the Chancellor mansion once again. It looked eerie and ghostly in the night, a silvered moon coating the brick with frosty light. There were no candles in the windows and the rooms were dark. I felt a twinge of sadness, but it passed like a quiet tide. This was not my home.

Our haversacks waited at the edge of the clearing. I groped in the dark, gnawing at hardened bread and crackers as if it was my last meal. Fresh water from the canteen soothed my dusty lips. Someone lit a tiny fire of twigs, and Andrew soon joined me with fresh coffee and strips of hot bacon. We enjoyed a midnight feast.

"Eighteen hours," Andrew muttered between mouthfuls. "How long did they think we could go without eating? Stupid bastards."

Sometimes it was nice to know my friend hadn't changed.

A small section of wide-eyed men from another regiment rushed through the forest. I sat up. Distant yelling and screaming came from the direction these new men fled. Our colonel strode out in front and stopped the men.

They were involved in the most serious hand-to-hand combat against an enormous force of oncoming Confederates. Sergeant Falls was no fool. He poked at their cartridge boxes and found full rounds. Not a speck of dirt sullied their uniforms. Scolding them for cowardice, he dismissed them and threatened to shoot and court-martial them for lack of fortitude.

These cowardly men came from a German regiment in the Eleventh Corps. What were they doing on the far flank of our army? What happened in that inlet of men? They represented no more than a tide pool of our mighty ocean, but I saw real fear in their eyes when they shrugged off the sergeant's threats and continued pell-mell across the Chancellor House clearing.

"I think they did see the enemy, Andrew," I remarked as we settled down once more. "Though it's plain they weren't fighting."

"Ah, who cares?" Andrew said. "An owl hooted and they thought it was a ghost."

"Do you think Lee sent a section of his army around behind us, like at Bull Run?"

"Maybe, the old fox. We've done our share for the day. Let it go, private. There will be more killing in the morning."

My friend was no fool, but there was naught to do but rest and replete my energy. He was right about more fighting. Though we repulsed a great number of Lee's regiments, the battle at the Chancellor House was not yet over. I glimpsed the silvery wood of the garden fence, shadowed gravestones through the swaying trees.

Sergeant Falls stepped by, nudging my leg. His order was for all of us: "Company C!"

Oh, no. I struggled from the edge of sleep. What did the man want now?

"Come on, it will be fun," Andrew was saying. "Give you men some muscle!"

I hadn't the foggiest idea what he was speaking of, until someone came up to me in the darkness and forced a shovel into my hands. So, we were to dig. I stepped over to the moonlit clearing between the sleepy youths from my winter cabin and hacked into the soft earth. A musketry pop here and there prickled the hairs on my arms, but we were not assaulted by another Confederate force.

Shoulders aching with the renewed pain from my hospital episode, I threw down the shovel and curled up next to the fresh loamy trench. I would appreciate our new stronghold in the morning, but I dropped quickly to sleep, as only a soldier could when he was that exhausted.

· 36 ·

I awakened to war.

Andrew stopped shaking my shoulder. I started against the side of the trench, locking my fingers around the muzzle of my rifle. Bullets whizzed over us and thunked into the trees. I slipped beneath the top of the trench, crouching low. Andrew reached into his cartridge box and steadily loaded. There were few bits of bread left, and I devoured them. My fingernails were black from the night's work of digging. My shoulder ached, too. I thought of Mary and her salve, sweet lavender pillow. I missed her.

"What's the time?"

Andrew cocked his pistol. "About six o'clock, I imagine. Stay low. They'll be coming towards us in a minute."

"From where?"

He pointed beyond the trench. "Across the clearing. Stay low, damn you."

I resisted the urge to peek. My back lay against the trench, facing opposite the clearing. The rest of our regiment was awake and readying itself. We would receive an order soon, or maybe we already had. I didn't like not knowing. Would we defend the trench or leap out over it, fighting on our feet? A sudden bloody memory of the trench at Antietam flew across my mind. Oh God, those soldiers were trapped!

I struggled in the dirt and managed to flip onto my stomach. Soil crawled up my nose, gritty dirt on my tongue. When the first broad peek of sunlight bathed the field, I peered over the edge of the trench. The Confederates amassed one brigade thirty yards directly in front of us. The shadow of the Chancellor Mansion loomed down upon the field. An enormous square block of shade. Not one shot was fired.

The devastating fire from the artillery shattered the peaceful scene. Holes burned through the trees and shell exploded over our heads. I dropped into the trench again, cowering with the rest of the regiment. Even Andrew neglected his usual cockiness and lifted his arms above his head.

Rebels screamed like devils when they smashed into the lines defending the plank road. The far Federal line reformed again, trying again for the position. They pulled back through the forest, but not without losing many generals and suffering under the incompetent commands of those who lived. I whispered silent gratitude that we abandoned our position along the plank road.

Sergeant Falls urged us out of the trench. I crept from its comforting mouth and hurried into the forming line. The open field near the Chancellor house was our ground of play for today. The landscape belonged to us, to frolic beneath the windowed eyes of the house. Shoulder to shoulder, I formed in the lines. Andrew ducked behind me.

"Look out!"

A terrific blast burst a hole through the Chancellor house and brick fragments rained down upon us. No, not my home! You cannot shell it! But I could do nothing. I peered from beneath my elbow, my eyes tearing as the witness to the destruction of the mansion. The Confederate artillery, the dreaded batteries with their mouths of fire and flame. They were destroying it!

Brick by brick, down it tumbled. The shells ignited the fabrics within and a blaze struck up. I stared up at my home. My home being burnt before me.

"No!" I shouted into the morning. "Leave it alone!"

"Daniel!"

Andrew reached through the smoke. The lines were reforming again. I didn't want to fight. I couldn't anymore. I tried and I failed. I couldn't save anything. I couldn't do anything.

Screams pushed through the smoke. There were people trapped inside! Oh, God! Erik, get out of there! I will save you. I can!

I freed myself from Andrew's grip and began running toward the house. The shells kept coming, the smoke kept rising, the cannonading fierce and the shells struck like serpent bites. Eating my home, consuming it with a hunger that terrified me to my soul.

"Daniel!" Andrew came puffing up behind me. "Get away from there! Are you mad?"

It was all smoke and fire. It was flames and burning red. Squirrels fled from the shelled home. Nearby trees caught fire and the entire clearing was a bloodbath of fire. Smoke stung my eyes, and I dropped to my knees.

"I want to go home. I want to go home."

Hell enveloped me and I closed my eyes. Let it come down. Let it all come down upon me. I fought the war no longer. The enemy won. We were divided. My family was gone. My home was gone. My garden burned.

I knelt in the grass. The garden fence, rails of licking flame. Fire consumed. It spread over the flowers, singing their white petals. It roared over the gravestones. It washed the growth and the dreams and the hope and the love. It blazed with the heated hooves of Apollo's fiery steeds, a living sun descended from the heavens.

I coughed, sputtering. I reached out for the fence. I tried to touch it. I wanted to go in! Let me past the gate, let me inside. I had the garden key. I could be safe inside. I could have peace at last.

"What the hell are you doing!!" Andrew spun me around like a doll. "Let's get out of here!!"

I was yanked to my feet. Andrew pulled me away from the house, dragging me through the smoldering grass. I coughed and coughed. Smoke danced in my lungs, played on my breath. Shells bombarded the house. It was nothing now, nothing but a half-remembered brick shell.

All of a sudden I saw something. Something by the house. A small hill, its outline shining through the smoke. It was our trench on fire. I looked down, grabbed at my waist. My haversack!!

"No, let me go!" I tried to free myself from Andrew's grip. But the vise of his hand was pulling me. "Andrew, I left my things! Andrew!"

"What??" He dragged me away from the house and threw me on the ground.

I point to the house. "My haversack. I left it! It's all gone, Andrew! It's all gone!"

"Daniel, stop!"

"David's Bible, Matthew's map," I was sobbing, my face burning with hot tears. I tasted smoke, coughed again. "It's gone!"

He knelt in the grass, his face scorched black. "I don't care, Daniel."

"*Paradise Lost!*"

"You think that is all that matters!!" He reached back and hit me across the face. "Get to your feet, soldier!"

He grabbed my shoulders with both hands and heaved me back onto my feet. I was vaulted upright. My face stung from the force of his palm. A volley of musketry sounded from the line of Confederates. They were shooting into our lines! They were killing our regiment!

I ran past Andrew and into the line of Federals. I grabbed up a rifle from a fallen comrade and I ran into an open hole and I fired into the Confederates. Sergeant Falls was gripping his shoulder, blood streaming candy red down his arm.

"Load, boys! Re-load!"

I tore the cartridge and rammed the ball down the barrel of the gun. I never loaded so fast in my life. I put on the cap and fired. I shot into the smoke. My enemy died by my hand, embraced by the smoke. I tore another cartridge. I poured another ball. I swung the gun to my shoulder and fired again.

Andrew fired into the enemy, his green eyes dancing like summer leaves on wind. We fought together, my brother and I. We fought for each other. I would never let anyone keep my brother apart from me again.

Andrew shouted: "Fire! Fire!"

He turned and he fired and he stumbled. God, my brother. Get to your feet, soldier! Come on, soldier! Daniel, wake up! Daniel, it's time to go.

I stood in the full sunlight of the morning. There was no shade. My home was a bricked mass of ruins. The trees were on fire. The spring woods erupted into a blazing tapestry of crimson and ochre.

"REGIMENT!"

"Daniel, they're coming!" Andrew shouted.

Gray troops amassed. I stood in the middle of the fire and I screamed, let them come! I was ready for them! I signed my name and I was a soldier in the Army of the Potomac. The flag waved high above us, unfurled into red and white flaming stripes. I stood beside my friend.

"CHARGE!"

I reached inside my jacket and gripped the garden key. Mary. I did the right thing so I could be with you.

"Massachusetts! FIRE!"

God spread smoky arms upon me and I tasted flaming air. Screams and screams and screams. In the shadows of a burning home. I longed to be cleansed, to be free. God waited for me in the smoke, and I felt the searing heat in my limbs, in my veins, in my blood, in my soul, for all was smoke and flame. War was paradise, sweetly enveloped in a dewy mist, comforted by home and death and love. I hoisted my rifle high. White smoke blossomed around me, a cloudburst of shooting stars.

The gray troops came out of the flowers. I stood amidst the blooming petals of a summer bounty. In this luxuriant garden, I waited within the flowers. I waited within the flames. I waited for the ghosts to come to me.

I would fight until we all became stars once more.

· 37 ·

Gentle whooshing tide of breath, in and out, in and out. Filling the emptiness, and then vanishing into the air. Whiteness above me. Blurring whiteness, pale ivories and creams. Clear and clean and cool. I licked my lips. Something flickered softly, a lamp. Soft golden glow, illuminating the whiteness. I watched the candle dance in cream and white shadows.

A shadow fell across me, a gray shape against the whiteness. Peace soothed me like a welcoming tide. Haloed by the candlelight was an angel. Her eyes were kindly, her soft voice calming and pure. Warmth trickled into my fingers as she took my hand.

"An angel," I murmured. "You are an angel."

She pressed her soft lips against my hand, then my cheek.

"Ye're safe. The fight is over. Here, Daniel. Drink this now."

Cool water dripped into my mouth, gentle and refreshing. She dabbed my face with a soothing cloth. The world was coming into view. I lay in a hospital bed. Feet shuffled and voices sounded nearby. Someone was weeping. It came from far off, as if through a watery wall. Mary stood by the bed, a silver bowl curved against her hip. I moved my arm towards her, then winced in pain. My chest ached, low, down near my ribs, on the right hand side. I reached down, gingerly touching wet bandages with tender fingers. I groaned and lay my head back upon the pillow.

"Ye're a lucky one," Mary said. "The surgeon got yer bullet out an' ye'll be fine. Most o' the ones in yer regiment didn't make it."

Fire. Orange fire, hungry licking flames. Booming shot and shell bursting my home, bricks and boards raining like petals. A line of gray men marching from the fiery trees. I quietly squeezed her hand.

"My home . . . I saw it burning . . ."

Mary leaned down and kissed my forehead. I did not wish her to leave, not yet. I smiled through my tears.

"I returned to you, Mary. I love you."

Her forehead touched mine, warmth trickling and spreading like the sea. I breathed deeply, my pain washing away. She kissed me, and I felt myself slipping into all that was light and sun. A radiant glow alighted my chest, and I knew then I'd never leave. Wherever Mary was, was home.

"Rest now. I will return. Ye'll soon be up an' dancing again."

She left, and my hand chilled. Not many in my regiment made it. I remembered the fire, but how had I escaped its jaws? My heart suddenly squeezed with a sudden fear. Andrew. Andrew must have saved me. I could still see him, reloading and shooting, his eyes like green sparks. He saved me, but he was gone. I closed my eyes.

"He died for me," I whispered. "He died so I could live."

"Private Stuart?"

I opened my eyes. A man stood by my bed. His arm hung in a sling, curled against his chest like an infant.

"Daniel," Sergeant Falls said gently. "Thank God you're alive. Andrew thought you weren't going to make it."

"Andrew?" I licked dry lips. "Is he here?"

Falls slowly shook his head. "The Confederates overtook us in the clearing. They blew our line apart. You were hit, and Andrew threw down his rifle. He didn't care about fighting any more. He had to get you out of there."

Tears trickled down my face. "He saved me."

"We both did. He couldn't lose you, Private. I owe my life to him, too. The woods were on fire, and we barely escaped. I'll never forget leaving my men to die."

"Good God," I said. "So, Andrew is alive."

"Yes, but the rebs surrounded us. They took him prisoner."

He held something in his hands, charred and black. "The last thing Andrew said was that I was a damn fool. But he knew I was doing it for you."

It was my haversack. I wept as I folded back the scorched flap, tiny charcoal leaves of burnt leather coating my fingers. Inside, nestled in a cradle of miraculous preservation, were a small Bible, a torn and folded map, Milton's poem, and a framed daguerreotype portrait.

Falls saluted me. "It is an honor to serve with a Stuart, sir."

Reaching in my coat, I drew out the little golden garden key. "If Andrew is alive, then I will find him. The only thing worth fighting for is each other."

I will save you, Andrew, as you have saved me. You are my brother, my family.

I added the key to the pile. I knew I did the right thing, for the right reasons. For the love in her kiss, for the brother who fought by my side, for the friends whose stars shone bright in the heavens.

Though I leave my garden, I am never alone.

* * *

Made in the USA
Charleston, SC
28 November 2015